PROLOGUE

Yamashima and Takeda
Five Years Ago

Ayane Yamashima's look was sharp. As she lifted her head, her ears detected the distant screams; they were very faint but broke the night-time stillness of the palace grounds with a creeping terror. She knew at once what was happening. Turning back to her youngest son, the only person in the room with her, she forced a smile across her face. His gaze was upon the door, a frown gathering over his large eyes.

'My love, finish reading the haiku. You have a beautiful tone.' With this, Ayane rose to her feet and shuffled to the door. Her long kimono trailed behind her in ripples of red, gold and green silk and the ivory hair adornments clicked together softly with each gentle movement. Reaching beneath her sleeve, she felt her tanto dagger and, at its touch, relief washed through her. However, dread already had its claws deep in her chest. 'Kenta,' she encouraged, not removing her eyes from the bamboo door.

'On the riverbank,' Kenta spoke measuredly but his eyes kept flickering to the door his mother now stood beside, 'contemplating plum blossom, strangers are like friends.' The matcha tea Ayane had been sipping steamed, catching the red light of the brazier coals. The burgundy zabuton cushion was still dipped where his mother had been sitting. He paused before moving on to the next poem, again reading the way his mother enjoyed. 'The moon's cheeks puff out.'

Ayane slid the door open a crack and lent her ear to the darkness beyond. Nothing, but she had not misheard the sounds before.

'Full and fat and silver-white, casting light upon us all.'

Ayane had known this was going to happen. He had come, as he said he would. From the door stretching far ahead was a Nightingale floor; she would hear the attackers before seeing them. *And they will come.* She wondered if they had already killed her husband, the Emperor. *Not Junpei, please, spare my other child, my eldest son.* The wish would not be granted, but she chose to ignore the fact and wish it regardless. She stared at Kenta again; her precious baby, the good boy, the sweet child, the hidden talent of the Yamashima. 'Kenta, do you have your katana?'

He nodded, his eyes growing stormy. 'Yes, mother.'

She gave a weary smile. 'Give it to me.'

Kenta squinted; he did not understand why his mother was making such a request. 'Mother, I can wield a blade almost as well as Junpei.'

'I know that, my love. You wield it far better, but please give me your blade.'

'Is it the same group of people who murdered Kimi?' Kenta felt anger roil in his stomach. 'Have they come at last?' The face of his elder sister was so easy to recall, as if he had only just seen her placid features.

Ayane sighed, Kenta was no fool. 'Yes, I believe the Senkaku Nin have returned.'

'Then I must go to father.' Kenta stood, his hand on his katana, defiance and fear tussling over his features.

Ayane swallowed and shook her head. 'You are still a boy but so much the man already. It is too late.' She refused the tears which burned her eyes. She would not let the Senkaku Nin have Kenta, no matter the cost. 'Give me your katana, Kenta.'

Reluctantly, he handed his weapon to his mother, placing the hilt in her outstretched hand. He had never felt so uncomfortable, so unsure, so fearful, and he hated it. He would not let his mother see it; he hoped his eyes were not betraying him. She had always said he had honest eyes.

Ayane smiled and the katana. 'Now hide in the samurai closet.'

'I will not hide.' Kenta was shocked. 'Samurai do not hide.'

'Kenta.' His mother's tone was hard yet gentleness remained. 'I do not know what state the palace is in. I do not know if your father and brother are dead. You may, as we speak, be the last child of the Yamashima, the last inheritor of the Divine Right to Rule; the Emperor of Akegata.'

Kenta staggered back. He did not want to be the Emperor, that was his elder brother's responsibility. 'Mother.'

Ayane could see the anguish in Kenta's gaze; he had never been good at hiding the truth. She placed a hand upon his cheek and kissed his forehead even though he was the same height as her. 'You can trust Akio and Shin with your life, they are better brothers to you than Junpei ever was. They will keep you safe. Cherish your friends. Hiroshi and Kannushi Masato are the wisest people, you should always listen to them. Mostly, Kazu Takeda will be your protector and guide. You are perfect, Kenta. Do not ever change. Restore the Yamashima peace and do not doubt that you can.' Ayane's faltering breath betrayed her calm. 'No matter what you hear or see Kenta, you are not to come out. Do you understand?'

Kenta didn't move nor answer. Ayane gripped his arms and shook him slightly. 'Kenta, please promise me.'

Kenta knew that this was the last time he would speak with his mother, the last words she would give him. He understood, he could see it plainly in her expression. He also comprehended that there was nothing to be done. All he could do was grant her this one thing. He embraced her; taking in her smell, how she felt, her warmth, her love which was always so tangible. 'I promise, mother.' He nodded as she shoved him toward the samurai closet. The Nightingale floor sounded, as if hundreds of birds had erupted into flight in the corridor. *They're here.*

Ayane waited until Kenta was concealed and then flung the window open. The screeching on the other side of the door grew louder and louder until it was unbearable. Then suddenly it ceased. She walked back to the centre of the room, faced the door and lifted the katana.

Kenta could see his mother's silhouette behind the papered wall so he shifted his face to peer through the slimmest of cracks with a single eye. She had adopted the stance of the Seishin no Ken style; the imperial technique developed for the royal family by the samurai-spirited Takeda clan. The door to the room was wrenched open and several men entered, all dressed in the deep indigo and black of the Kageyama shinobi. Leading the group was a bald-headed man clad all in white. His head was covered in a striking black tattoo, the ends of which met in a point at the centre of his brow. The last thing Kenta glimpsed before this man moved beyond his vision was a sleeveless kataginu reaching past his knees. Embroidered on its blood-stained surface was a dark moth. Its wings were open in flight, the tips fragmenting off into smaller moths. On his face, the man wore a smile.

Ayane felt her blood chill. 'Sen,' she hissed, staring at the young man in front of her. He held his hands up in greeting, but Ayane continued to grip the katana.

'Now, that is no welcome for an old friend, Ayane.' Sen's expression was arranged in mock upset, but his tone was amused.

'You were never a friend, Sen. You are a murderer. An extremist.'

'Well, I cannot contest you. Why, just now I took your husband's life with these very hands. This is his blood. I wonder if divine blood tastes different?' He touched his stained white kataginu and turned his hands over, staring at them before licking the liquid from his palm. 'Then I watched as my men overwhelmed and killed your son. Junpei fought well, honourably, but we all know that honour is the death of a samurai eventually. He did not seem so divine in the end, either.'

Ayane pressed her lips together, willing her rage to the back of her mind and forcing her tears to the bottom of her stomach. 'Dying with honour is far better than living with none.'

'How simple you are. To think, I used to hold you in the highest of regard. But here I am, honourless and alive.' Sen spat out the words, the disgust clear on his face. 'I am here for Kenta.'

It was Ayane who laughed now. 'You lunatic. You will never have Kenta. He is far beyond your reach now. Spirited away on a divine wind.'

Sen frowned, his eyes flashing to the open window through which snow had begun to flurry. He clicked his tongue in annoyance. 'Find him,' he snapped, and the Kageyama shinobi vanished out of the window silently, leaving Ayane alone with Sen.

'Kazu Takeda will not let you get away with what you have done.'

'Oh?' Sen's voice was almost maniacal. 'And how is that?'

'He will find you and he will kill you for what you have done. He will bring justice for all those you have murdered. He holds the hope of Akegata.' Ayane thought of the young girl, Kazu's daughter; he had kept her secret well.

'Kazu Takeda will not be bothering me.' Sen's words were arcane, but Ayane did not have a moment to speculate on his meaning. He pulled a concealed ninjato short sword from beneath his kataginu as he closed the gap between them. 'But you have already bothered me too much. No one has reached beneath my skin as you have done.' He slashed his weapon down, Ayane raising hers to meet it. The singing of steel on steel was dulled by the rust on Sen's blade as it scraped against hers. She had to use both hands to stifle the strength of his swing. With his free hand Sen thrust his fist into her abdomen.

The blow sent Ayane flying back against the wall, her katana clattering to the floor.

'You never were a fighter. Forever the peace-lover. It's why you married into the Yamashima clan.' Sen advanced, sweeping her weapon from the floor and studying it. 'What were you hoping for? To kill me?' The rage on his face was terrible and he swiped his blade down viciously.

For a moment Ayane thought he had missed, but then an odd warmth began to spread across her chest. She looked down, her kimono was fast becoming soaked with her blood. She touched it and looked at her fingertips, they were a bright scarlet. *A beautiful colour*, she thought.

Sen crouched down, his face close to hers. 'Look into my eyes, Ayane. Look at me. This is the last time I shed a tear for the woman I loved.'

Ayane lifted her gaze. 'You have achieved nothing, Sen. Absolutely nothing.' She struck out, her arm like a snake, and grabbed Sen by the throat. As he moved his arm, she lifted her small tanto dagger and stabbed him through the cheek. He growled, his eyes squinting against the pain. Ayane felt his blood wash over her hands as he thrust Kenta's katana through her chest. His eyes never left hers, and hers never left his.

***

Amaya slipped beneath her mother's outstretched arm, pausing only to wiggle her feet into her bearskin boots, and stumbled out onto the pathway. She heard her younger brother's laugh and her mother shout the usual caution. Leaping across the large slabs of stone which wove between the clusters of bamboo, she hurried on. Snow had only begun to fall the previous evening, but a thick layer had already settled over the city. Despite her footwear, Amaya felt her toes grow numb with each step. The stone path reached the great wooden doors which marked the entrance to her estate. The high, pale wall skirted it both left and right ,but the doors were always open; her father liked it that way.

The thought of her father drew her back to the journey at hand. Every evening she would run to meet him as he made his way home from the palace. Every evening she would try to beat him to the little path which ran along the back of old Mizuki's ramen shop in the city. However, competition wasn't what drove her feet now.

The snow continued its perpetual plummet. Large, fluffy flakes clung to Amaya's hair, skin and clothing, melting until she was damp all over. Her billowing hakama trousers were beginning to absorb the snow she plowed through and her steps became laboured. She pumped her arms, her bony elbows swinging high, her hands clenched into white-knuckled fists. The snowflakes looked like falling stars from the darkness above, but she disregarded both the snow and blackness as she rushed down an empty street and joined another, then another. No footprints disturbed the pale blanket except the ones she left behind, and the chill reached its sharp fingers into her chest as she drew in gulps of winter air. Her heavy cloak flapped as she hopped or skidded around familiar corners, gritting her teeth against the cold, but the further she ran the more her composure began to sink beneath her panic. The dark had never scared her, and she knew the streets of the capital well. However, her father had seemed peculiar that morning. A curious urgency had overcome him before he had marched to the palace muttering under his breath. His easy smile had been absent, his unusually light brown eyes had held only unease. He had even forgotten to kiss her goodbye.

And in the waning light, as she wrenched her feet through thickening undisturbed snow, she could not rid herself of the unsettling sensation that her father's countenance had inspired. She reached the street before old Mizuki's ramen shop; the houses behind their walls were still. The salty sweet smell of Hiyashi broth lingered about the buildings, imbuing the delicate scent of winter with something more tangible. Shouts, borne on the snow, reached her ears. *The palace*, she thought. With an icy sensation, which had nothing to do with the weather, she realised that the shouts were screams. *What is happening there?*

Then she saw the broad frame of her father, Kazu Takeda, caught in the light of the large braziers which lined the street. He was not in his usual military attire, but his strength was still present: comforting and terrifying all at once. Kazu was standing at the other end of the row, his shadow thrown meters before him until it almost touched her toes. Her grin was shaky as she continued forward, stepping into her father's shadow. He had stopped, his attention taken by the same screams Amaya had heard.

'Father.' She ran, half tripping over her feet, which the snow tried to suck down. He faced her now, hearing her voice. She raised her arms ready for his strong embrace, her legs coiling in preparation to jump into him, but before she could call out, he lifted his hand; a small gesture, but Amaya knew to stop at once. Then his eyes found hers in the darkness and she smiled. His irises glimmered a deep bronze and the corners of his eyelids folded into slender lines with his grin, but the smile was tainted, worry lurked beneath.

Amaya didn't notice the katana's end until her father looked down. The glistening, scarlet tip protruded from his centre. Dark liquid dripped from it and Amaya stifled a shriek as the realisation of what she was watching collapsed upon her. Her father was still alive as the blade was wrenched free of his body. He didn't flinch but lifted his hand to the wound. Blood, which appeared black in the night, began to stream freely, rippling over his fingers and trickling to the floor. Amaya's voice had been chased away by the sight of her father's blood.

It was the second slice of the katana, the one which took off his head, that killed him. His body fell forward heavily, snow clouds erupting around him, but the white became red, and the red soon grew until he was swimming in it. His head tumbled into shadow, but not before the eyes she had looked upon so often flashed one last time in the flickering light.

    A silhouette still remained; the silhouette to which the katana belonged. Amaya stumbled forward, wanting to look him in the eye. The man wiped his blade clean, as those trained in the Way of the Samurai were taught to do. He looked up and she saw him; his face was familiar, but she could not recall a name. He grimaced at her, disgusted and irritated. Amaya found her feet stuck as he strode effortlessly through the snow toward her, raising his still-bloody blade. She didn't feel fear though, rather hate: an overwhelming hate. He had not reached her when her senses were knocked from her. The ground felt as though it had been pulled away from her as she fought against the black.

CHAPTER ONE

The monk's low dulcet chanting filled the large room, punctuated occasionally by the chime of his bell or the knock of prayer beads. Amaya found herself swaying instinctively to the rhythm but she couldn't have predicted it. Clammy palms pressed against each other as the heat of the summer stifled the air. Amaya's mind was not quite her own, and her thoughts belonged to memories which she rarely permitted to roam. Her eyes fell on the figure of the monk but did not truly see him. His hummed words of the New Faith reached her with an odd clarity however, and she allowed them to lull her away from feelings she wished to shirk. With each rock of her body a memory presented itself: the smell of matcha tea; her father with his katana; sweat that smelled like azuki beans; watching on from the shadows of the dojo door; her father teaching her his technique, the energy, her delight, his enthusiasm; temple bells.

Amaya was pulled from the falling thoughts by a particularly loud ring of the monk's bell. He, Amaya, her younger brother Kyo, and their mother all knelt. They faced the altar which dominated the room they were in. The black lacquer of the wood appeared blacker still against its golden interior, which threw an odd light around the room. It placed the monk in a warm glow and the same light brushed against Amaya and her family, including them in its delicacy. Within the altar's open doors Amaya saw the eggplant cow she had made and Kyo's cucumber horse beside it. Other offerings filled the space, but it was the fire bowl beside the front gate outside which Amaya was most interested in. It was the light her father's spirit would need to find his way home, and Amaya would not permit it to go out. Every year she assumed the responsibility, every year since her father was murdered.

It took Amaya a moment to realise the monk had stopped his swaying and singing. The sounds of outside crept in through the open window and reclaimed the silence left by the monk, and soon Amaya's mother was thanking him loudly, competing with the shrill din of the cicadas outside. They each thanked the holy man and remained bowed until he had left the room, guided by her mother. Turning to the altar, Amaya placed an arm around Kyo's shoulders and gave him a gentle squeeze. He appeared fresh from sleep, but she knew he was exhausted. It was the first day of the Spirit Festival and already Kyo was wilting.

'Here,' Amaya pushed a smile forward. In her hand she held incense. 'It will help father come home. We do not want his spirit to go to the neighbours instead, do we?' Amaya could hear the strain in her own laugh, but she persevered. Kyo looked up, his narrow face taking the laughter greedily and his eyes widened with an effort Amaya was so familiar with.

'Thank you.' He took the incense. 'Amaya?'

'Hmm.'

'Do you think father comes back every year?'

'Oh yes. He would miss us too much if he didn't.' Amaya shoved him forward gently. As she watched Kyo bend down to light the incense, she recalled the day her father had brought him home. Amaya had only been ten when Kazu returned from the Water Province carrying a tiny Kyo atop his shoulders. Still, she had seen in Kyo's countenance that something beyond her understanding had happened to him. Kazu never spoke of it and Kyo's memory had faded to vague images as he grew up, which meant that Amaya never discovered the true horrors Kyo had experienced. However, it was clear for her to see that his spirit was old because of it, his innocence gone before his life had begun.

She was distracted from her thoughts of Kyo by her

mother, who had returned.

'Here.' As Amaya had done with Kyo, she handed her mother incense.

'Thank you.' Megumi smiled at her daughter, and gripped the incense in both hands, her veins showing clearly. As she bent down to light the stick, Amaya could see the ridges of her mother's shoulder blades prominently through the indigo yukata. Megumi's beauty remained, but as a ghost. It was hidden by the same exhaustion that shrouded Kyo, and each day that passed stole a little colour from her face, a little flesh from her bones. Amaya waited in quiet whilst Kyo and their mother lingered beside the altar. She knew that neither truly wanted to continue the day, yet they did not want to be idle.

Kyo gripped their mother's hand and together they left the room, leaving Amaya alone. She was grateful for their continued understanding. Releasing a breath, her short tanto dagger slid the smallest amount in her obi belt. She refilled her lungs slowly. Crouching down she put the end of the last stick of incense into the small flame. A trail of smoke imbued with the scent of cinnamon and cloves rose lazily out of the window, joining the aroma of the honeysuckle and peonies in the garden. She closed her eyes and called forth the names of her ancestors, each of which she hoped would find their way safely home. Ignoring the twinge of guilt, Amaya hurried through the customary prayers. She was impatient to go to the dojo where she believed her father's spirit truly dwelt.

The cicadas' din was incredible. Inside it had been loud but now, as she strode through the verdant garden, the sound was grating. Amaya flinched, the noise tethered her growing emotion, reminding her to maintain composure, and her pace slowed. Still, she was untouched by the junipers with their clustered leaves, so much like green clouds. Nor was she moved by the Koi carp that caught the sun in red and white shimmers within the pond she crossed over. She remained unaffected by the gentle hollow knock of the bamboo water feature, as it filled and decanted with a natural harmony. And she was impervious to the euphony of the bamboo copse as the lethargic wind played with it. Amaya shuffled on, and soon the teahouse appeared: simple, refined. Its interior was dark, and Amaya could not recall the last time her mother had hosted a tea ceremony there. However, for her the tea house had always served as a mask. When her father had trained her out of doors, he had done so beyond the wooden construct where none could see. For a woman to wield a katana was unheard of. In the eyes of the public she practiced arts befitting a woman, but she was thankful every day for her father's holistic education. It had served her well in the years since his death.

    Leaving the tea house in her wake she pushed on. Abandoning the path which would have led her through the moss garden, she entered the small bamboo grove, weaving her way through the dense foliage. She saw the dojo before she left the copse; its wooden walls were in shadow, the sun directly above it. The ends of the black tiled roof curved up towards the sky in the shape of dragons, their mouths agape in silent growls. Breaking free of the tree line she walked directly to the entrance and slid the door open revealing the polished, wooden floor. Slipping her feet out of her geta sandals she placed one foot followed by the other upon the gleaming surface. Enjoying the cool sensation on the soles of her feet, she remained still for a moment. The light was softened by the papered windows and fell in indistinct pools upon the floor. Across the space, affixed to the opposite wall, were the weapons. All were bokken training swords.

    Amaya strode forward and not a single floorboard creaked beneath her. She stopped when she reached the weaponry but did not touch any of them. Her eyes were focused upon the empty space at the top of the stand, the space where her father's katana, Meiyo, had once been. She had not seen it since he had died, and to this day she had no inkling as to its whereabouts. She recalled its every detail though; the sheath was dark blue, a blue that at first appeared black like the night sky. Nearer the hilt was engraved in gold the Takeda clan's mon; four diamonds, united together to form a larger one: a simple yet distinct crest. The same crest was engraved upon the steel itself. As the unspoken Assistant Master of the Seishin no Ken style, Amaya longed to wield it. It was the extension of her father's soul, his samurai spirit. It was a piece of him.

Amaya's eyes burned with the light of the flames as she gazed into them. She didn't want to look away even though light scars were beginning to blind her. In her periphery she could see the flicker of her distant neighbours' fires along the street, guiding their ancestors. She had seen the Spirit Festival at the palace in previous years; it was elaborate, the fires huge. At night they consumed the dark, their glow seeping into the streets of the capital, Chuto. Amaya remembered a little over five years ago how the screams from the palace had filtered through the streets of the capital. Then she hadn't spared a thought to them, the murder of her father had eclipsed all else. Later she had learned from Akio Izumi that almost the entire Imperial family had been murdered during the attack, all accept the youngest son, Kenta Yamashima. *He's the only one left to guide them home*, she pondered sadly, envisioning herself in that solitary state.

'Amaya.' It was her mother, Megumi.

Distracted from her wandering thoughts she looked up from the fire. 'Mother. How are you?' She reached out and found her mother's hands. They were cold even though the nights were as warm as the days.

Her mother smiled. 'I am alright. Kyo is in bed.'

Amaya sighed. 'He is drained.'

'We all are.' Megumi leant her head against her daughter's.

'His strength is greater than mine. I cannot wait for him to come of age and lead the Takeda clan. I am certain he will restore its honour.'

Megumi laughed. 'He has many qualities desirable in a

leader, but his heart is kind, very kind. He does not possess the samurai spirit which the Takeda are famous for. I fear that he will not weather the corruption in the court as well as you might.'

Amaya felt the old frustration emerge. 'I wish I were able to lead the clan, but it is not my place as a woman. I will be Kyo's support for as long as he needs it.' Amaya was able to soothe the annoyance she harboured with the knowledge that Kyo would replace her father someday.

'Uncle Jiro will arrive tomorrow,' Megumi said.

Amaya felt her shoulders lighten a little. 'I am so glad. He will be a welcome comfort.'

Jiro reminded Amaya of her father. As Kazu's younger brother, he shared some of the same features, his temperament was similar too. However, Amaya felt guilty. She loved her uncle dearly, but in the deepest recesses of her heart, she knew that she sought her father in Jiro's strong face and knowing eyes. She never found Kazu in there though, and it left her a little emptier than before, stoking the anger she longed to let go of.

'Are you alright?' Megumi echoed her daughter's question.

Amaya nodded slowly. 'Yes, I am. These three days are the most difficult of the year.'

'Do not forget the Spirit Festival is a celebration. We must celebrate all our ancestors, as well as Kazu. All spirits must be guided to their home at this time.'

Amaya nodded again. As a child, she loved the Spirit Festival, the idea of celebrating an ancestor's life and accepting them back for a little while to have them around you. Her father had told her stories of her various relatives who had achieved great things and were the foundations of the Takeda Clan. Kazu was the greatest samurai of the Takeda however taking that reputation from his great grandfather, Kazuhiro Takeda. However, when she considered the nature of her father's demise, mustering the energy to celebrate the

Spirit Festival became a near impossible feat. Every year she persisted. 'Would you like me to ready uncle Jiro's room, mother?'

'I will help you. I do not think that fire will ever go out. You have done well.' Megumi indicated to the burning bowl with a grin, and then gestured Amaya to follow her.

They readied the room in silence and, as they placed the futon upon the tatami floor, Amaya forced the enmity from her body with a great effort. She placed her hands upon her hips, her mother doing the same.

'Jiro will most likely want to spar with you,' her mother said.

Amaya smiled. 'I would like that very much. I usually have to train alone as Kyo trains in the city with the men.'

'It can focus your mind when you practice alone, help you truly comprehend the Way of the Samurai. Your father's technique is more a way of life than purely a way of combat,' Megumi said, nudging the futon into place with her foot.

'And that is the reason it is the technique employed by the Imperial army.' Amaya felt pride as she spoke the fact. Her father's philosophy was evident in the katana technique he was the Master of, the Seishin no Ken style. 'Blade of the Spirit,' Amaya said, aloud.

The two left the room, the veranda their unspoken destination.

'The General and the Master of the Sky Province is the same man? Like father,' Amaya questioned, sliding her feet into her geta sandals. 'That is what Lord Akio Izumi informed me,' Amaya mused, thinking of the letters she had received from the Secretariat over the years.

Her mother nodded. 'I believe Lord Izumi is correct.'

'Have you met the man?'

'No, I never did. I have been told he is young to be the General, only seven years your senior.'

'He has never seen war then,' Amaya stated. 'Yet, he must be deserving and capable of both titles if father bestowed them on him when he was only twenty summers old.'

'Perhaps you will meet him one day.'

'I do not even know his name,' Amaya replied. 'I have only ever known him as the General, or sometimes The Stag. However, I do know the man who took over father's role in the Court even though I have never met him in person,' Amaya continued, thinking of Akio Izumi. Her father had often spoken of him; his intelligence and bravery. Amaya felt as though she had met the man many times although she had only received letters and sent them in return. Now she wished she had put aside her pride and visited Akio. She longed to put a face to the man her father entrusted his third and final role to. From his letters she imagined him to be an assiduous fellow, with fingers smudged with ink and skin which smelt of gampi paper. In her mind, she saw him as a little hunched but possessing a kindly and wise demeanour.

'It is my understanding that Kazu recommended Lord Izumi to become the General first.' Megumi raised her eyebrows. 'He declined, and so the position went to another while Akio Izumi assumed the sole role of Secretariat in Court.'

'I did not know. Why would he decline such a position?' Amaya asked, shocked. To be the General was to be equal to the Chancellor, who is second only to the Emperor himself.

Megumi gave a small shake of the head. 'Kazu never told me the reason the genius gave, but it was clear from your father's countenance that the matter was closed. Akio Izumi was not to be persuaded. The very next day Kazu made the request of the man he had bestowed the title of one of the Five Masters upon. That is why the General is also the Master of the Sky Province.'

Amaya and her mother often had the same conversation each year. Simply talking about Kazu's life and the worthiness of the ones who had continued his work never ceased to be interesting. Amaya felt the smile on her face, and it ached.

Jiro's palanquin arrived before noon the following day. Amaya was in the forecourt and heard the convoy before they came into sight. Placing the lavender flowers she had picked upon a large, round stone, she straightened her navy yukata and went to greet him.

'Uncle!' Amaya said with laughter in her voice. 'Mother, Kyo, uncle Jiro has arrived!' she called behind her, hoping they would hear her shout through the open front door.

Jiro stepped out of his palanquin, the black lacquer shining in the sun, heat rippling from its roof. The cicadas were still deafening, but Amaya didn't mind.

'Amaya, my child.' Jiro's face was flushed, his shaved head beading with sweat. He bowed low.

Amaya bowed also, and on rising noticed a change in his appearance. 'You have grown a beard!'

Jiro raised his hand and stroked the small, pointed patch of hair which covered his chin. 'Gives me a more intelligent air, don't you think?' He laughed.

'Oh, you have always been intelligent uncle, beard or no,' Amaya replied, allowing Jiro to place a hand upon her head.

He waved away her compliment. 'You've grown, again. You are a young woman now, Amaya.'

'It has been over a year, uncle.'

'Has it really!?' He shook his head. 'With the number of letters we exchange, the time goes so quickly.'

'How was your journey? The Air Province is so far and travelling in this heat is taxing.' The worry lingered in her question.

'Well, it was not easy, but there are many places which welcome a priest, and that breaks the journey into a manageable thing. There are many stone statues of Jizo dotted along all roads. I am sure the New Faith's Guardian of Travellers and Pilgrims aided me.' He smiled, pleasantly.

Amaya sighed in relief. Her uncle had been ordained in

the New Faith when he was only eighteen, her age now, deciding to pursue his beliefs rather than the Way of the Samurai. Kazu was to inherit the clan and the Takeda samurai spirit. Still, Amaya wished Jiro was able to act as steward for the Takeda family. He was respected in his circle, but he lived in the northernmost province, too far away to lead. He was also a monk, and therefore unable to assume leadership. Amaya had never voiced her thoughts on the subject; she didn't want to upset him or to incite frustration. However, she marvelled at the way her uncle embraced both the Old and New Faith.

'Jiro.' Megumi had emerged from inside. 'Jiro, it is so good to see you. Thank you for travelling so far.' She bowed, Jiro doing the same.

'My dear Megumi, still so beautiful.'

Megumi raised an eyebrow, amused. 'Your words are kind, but I fear that is all. I am older.'

'As we are every day of our lives, which is why they must be lived.' He looked pointedly at Amaya. 'I hope you have been enjoying your youth, Amaya.'

She felt suddenly under scrutiny. Her uncle had an ability to read others, and Amaya knew that he understood her secrets. Perhaps all priests and monks possessed the same skill. 'Of course, uncle. I train every day and I try to further develop the Seishin no Ken style. I read the books father left to me. I am teaching Kyo calligraphy too.'

'Yes, but do you venture into the town? Have you met any suitors? Have you had fun?'

Amaya felt startled but was saved having to answer.

'Uncle!' Kyo came running around the corner of the house, calligraphy brush still in hand. He bowed at the waist.

'Hello, Kyo,' Jiro laughed. 'I see you have gotten bigger too. How are you?'

'Well, uncle. And you?'

'Shall we go inside? I will tell you about the trip, perhaps I could inspire your next haiku. I passed a band of travelling Komuso Monks. Who knows, they could have been undesirables in disguise?' he whispered dramatically.

The last day of the Spirit Festival came quicker than the year before, Amaya thought. The day was getting late and as she watched the sun, she willed it to pause. It did not oblige.

Kyo's stomach rumbled loudly, interrupting Megumi and Jiro's discussion. Everyone laughed, and Amaya found her own chuckle join the others'.

'You are hungry. We're probably all hungry. Shall we venture into the city? It is the last day of the Spirit Festival. We can eat before we release the lanterns,' Jiro suggested, rubbing his stomach as Kyo had done.

'Let us visit Jiji,' Amaya replied, thinking of the elderly man she had known all her life. 'His restaurant is very popular.'

'Jiji!' Jiro said, loudly. 'He's still alive?'

'Uncle!' Amaya said, in sharp amusement.

He shrugged a little. 'Well, I remember him from when I was young.'

Megumi and Kyo were equally as enthusiastic, and soon they left the house. Amaya glanced back at the fire, certain her father had joined them. He had always loved Jiji's.

Chuto was busy, but the pace was slow. The day's heat was lingering in the dust about peoples' feet, in their movement and in their speech. As Amaya observed each passerby, she imagined the phantoms of their ancestors following behind them like welcome ghosts. An entire spirit world drifting through the crowd, unseen but not unfelt she hoped. Amaya glanced behind her with a question, *are you here*?

Beating fans were everywhere, every hand gripped one but the heat was cloying. Amaya's fan was a burnt pink, with insubstantial cherry blossom falling across its large surface. The Face of Spring had been and gone, but it was Amaya's favourite season and her fan was a gift from her father; it seemed fitting that she use it. She and her family paused at numerous stands, which all displayed goods traditionally for the Spirit

Festival. Amaya was offered several slices of watermelon, which she gratefully accepted but gave to Kyo. They were devoured in a moment.

The booming of the taiko drums was quickly becoming louder and the crowds were thickening as they drew nearer to the palace. The clamour of shouts interspersed by the happy clanging of bells surrounded Amaya and soon she could see the tops of the decorative floats. The vivid colours seemed aglow in the early evening, throwing shadows of the inked dragons and phoenix designs onto the ground and milling folk alike. Lanterns were being lit along the streets in lines which seemed to stretch forever like so many stars, and soon the road and people filling it were bathed in brightness. The pale yellow of young girls' yukata seemed orange, whereas blues became purple, pinks became magenta, white became a rainbow. As women strolled along the street and children ran around legs, hair adornments caught the light in kaleidoscopic patterns, and Amaya felt that the whole scene had been spirited away, plunged into a different world.

She and her small group drew closer to the huge yagura scaffold. It was in the centre of a web of coloured lanterns and many moving bodies which swayed beneath the lights. They danced the slow Spirit Festival dance in the hopes of welcoming the spirits of the deceased. Their claps and steps were synchronised, their movements telling the ancient story of a priest who retrieved his mother's spirit from the Realm of Hungry Ghosts many aeons past.

At the apex of the massive structure were four taiko drummers, their bronzed chests and backs slick with sweat and their muscles thrown into relief in the shifting light. Beneath the drummers were the flautists; six women, dressed in different coloured yukata, pressed shakuhachi flutes to their lips. Their hair adornments shivered iridescently in the light of the yagura lanterns. The shrill treble of the flutes was accompanied by the warbling voices of the singers below them, men and women both.

A voice reached Amaya's ears through the oddly enchanting music.

'Proof has finally surfaced. It was indeed the Shinobi who murdered Emperor Yamashima. That is why the guards were too late to raise the alarm. It was inevitable really.'

The mention of shinobi startled Amaya; they were never usually discussed so openly. She glanced without turning her head. The men speaking were dressed in the white and blue kimono of the court, they were officials.

'How can we be certain it was a shinobi?' The second, shorter man replied, and there was trepidation in his tone. 'The late Emperor's spirit has spoken to you has it?'

'Who else could scale a wall like the one which the palace sits on?' He gestured behind him, along the main street. Amaya briefly followed his outstretched hand. Encircled by a wide, deep moat, rested the palace atop a high stone base. Its white walls were in stark contrast to the black roofs, which curled up at the corners into far more elaborate carvings than the ones on Amaya's own house. The sprawling splendour was famous throughout Akegata, and it was rumoured that many of the previous emperors never left its confines. Amaya hadn't been inside the palace grounds since she was a newborn, but her father used to comment on the gardens and the pagodas dotted around the land... 'It is a world all of its own, Amaya. Very beautiful.' Kazu's words played in her mind and suddenly she wanted to go, to see the place her father had worked in. The men conversing close by pulled her back to the Spirit Festival and the music.

'I do not believe it is that simple. The defences within the palace are formidable. How could anyone pass through undetected? There are several nightingale floors in the palace crafted by the best carpenters in Akegata.'

'That is why the investigation was so thorough. Whispers in the court spoke of a traitor. Someone who knew every hidden compartment, every trick floor and every samurai's cabinet. I heard mention of the Senkaku Nin.' The man's face paled despite the warming patterns of light.

Amaya, whose attention was now entirely on the two men, felt her breath quicken. *The Senkaku Nin?* She hissed inwardly in disbelief. 'Excuse me?' Amaya said, with false politeness. Both men turned, surprised. 'The Senkaku Nin murdered the Emperor and his household?' She could see their shock but she did not care that her question was direct.

'That is sensitive information, young lady,' the shortest man replied, finally.

'Yet you are discussing it in public during the Spirit Festival. You should be careful who hears you speak of the Senkaku Nin.' Amaya arched an eyebrow, her voice low.

The tall man, whose eyes were a little too far apart, frowned. 'I do not understand your interest.'

'The Emperor would not have been assassinated had my father been with him. I was merely intrigued as to how such a thing occurred. Incompetence should not be tolerated. I hope the retainers redeemed themselves?'

'No need for suicide. They too were slain in the attack,' the second man said, his voice cold.

'At least it was an honourable end, dying to protect their master.' Amaya felt discomfort at her own rudeness, yet she could not stem it.

'You mentioned your father?' The tall man queried. 'What is your name?'

'I am Amaya Takeda.'

Both men shrank back a little. They hoped for nonchalance, but Amaya could see their disdain clearly.

'You are Lord Takeda's child. He was a great man, such a loss.' The short man bowed his head, the tall man following.

Amaya nodded curtly. 'Yes, he was.' She willed them to misstep, to show disrespect.

'Please excuse us, Lady Takeda.' The tall man's apathetic stare lingered just a little too long before they walked away.

Amaya watched the two court officials until they were

swallowed by the throng, leaving her smothered by her own impotent anger.

'Amaya?' It was Kyo who spoke, tapping her arm.

She jolted. 'Kyo! I'm sorry. I was daydreaming.'

Kyo didn't look fooled. 'Here.'

Amaya accepted the gift. She looked down; draped across her palms was a paper lantern. As she opened it up, two characters were revealed. Amaya recognised Kyo's elegant hand in the brush work. 'Meiyo,' Amaya read aloud. 'Kyo, thank you.' Her toes curled with the gratitude, but she battled with tears behind her smile.

'The name of father's katana. I thought it would be a nice lantern for his spirit. I know it's not traditional,' he said, suddenly doubtful.

'It is wonderful, Kyo, wonderful. Are you sure you do not want to be the one to release it later?' Amaya said, placing a kiss on her brother's forehead.

'His katana is now yours, Amaya. You are the Assistant Master of the Seishin no Ken style. You should do it.'

'We will do it together then,' Amaya grinned.

Kyo nodded fervently, his own grin momentarily freeing his eyes of grief.

Her mother and uncle were conversing, their tone light. Megumi's face was animated, more than it had been in a long while, and Amaya's fondness for her uncle grew more so. Kyo was looking in every direction, evidently led by his nose because his head turned whenever they passed by a food stand or shop. Amaya felt her own mouth water as she detected the sweet smell of yakitori, the rich scent of roasting eel and the sharper tang of rice vinegar.

'Jiji!' Jiro said, loudly. 'Jiji, it has been a long time. How have you been?'

Jiji straightened up and turned to face them. He was shorter than Kyo, his face like an old monkey's. 'Who are you?' he whistled through his teeth.

'Jiji. It is me!' Jiro held his hands up as if presenting himself. 'Jiro. Jiro Takeda.'

Jiji squinted, hobbling a little closer on bowed legs. His wispy, white beard, which had been twisted into an string-like braid, caught the light of the fire bowl beside his open door. 'No. I do not know you,' he said.

Jiro shook his head. 'I cannot deny this saddens me, Jiji.' He placed a hand over his heart and made to turn about.

Amaya heard the wheezy chuckle easily above the music of the street. She looked back at Jiji. He had a toothless grin upon his puckered face. 'Get back here. Of course I remember you, boy. Did you think I had become that senile?'

Jiro bowed low. 'The thought never crossed my mind, Jiji.'

'Come in, come in. I haven't seen you for a long time either, Lady Amaya,' Jiji said, as Amaya passed him.

'And for that I apologise, Jiji. Please forgive me.'

He waved her apology away. 'Kyo visits me every week. You should leave that estate of yours more often.'

'But I do, Jiji,' Amaya protested.

Jiji didn't reply, but merely made an incredulous noise. Amaya chastised herself, she knew the old man was right.

When the time came to leave, Amaya's face ached from smiling. Smiles that weren't pretenses but smiles that steadily reached into her chest and assuaged her heart.

'Shall we release the lanterns? I am sure Kazu has better things to do than listen to us prattle on about him.' Jiro slapped his hands against his bent knees.

'You are quite right,' Megumi replied, poking a sleepy Kyo.

Amaya stood first and held out a hand for her mother. Kyo stayed beside his uncle. They each bowed to Jiji, who saw them off with a large helping of dango.

'Where shall we release the lanterns? Near the palace with everybody else?' Kyo asked.

'No, I think this year I want to release it in our garden, next to the dojo,' Amaya replied.

'That's a fitting place,' Megumi said, linking her arm through her daughter's. Jiro nodded his agreement and the group turned about and walked in the direction of the Takeda estate.

The dojo rose before them but did not cover the moon. The pale light, so delicate compared to the lights in the city, soothed Amaya. Now, away from the noise and bustle, she felt restful. They each held a lantern and Megumi held the lit kindling She went around and ignited each wick. She approached Amaya last and carefully lit her lantern. The white of the paper turned a soft orange, and the characters stood out clearly. Amaya marvelled at Kyo's talent for a moment, then turned to him and reached for his hand, placing his fingers upon the lantern, hers over his.

'Shall we?' Jiro said, looking around. They each nodded and lifted their hands. The next moment, they released the lanterns.

Amaya watched them rise steadily into the night, carried by the heat of the small flame which rested in their hearts. As she gazed at the three flickering lights, she envisioned her father departing with them, his face content. All at once, she felt ashamed of herself. *I am sorry father. I'm sorry. I'm sorry.* Amaya gripped her fan. *I have wallowed too long. I have been wasting the strength you have given me. I will restore the Takeda honour. I will correct my mistakes. I will bring about change. I will avenge you.* She wondered if her words had been too far-reaching, but she pushed panic aside. They all remained, watching until the lanterns had become indistinct blemishes amongst the stars.

'Mother, I need to prepare my summer kimono,' Amaya said.

'What for?' Megumi replied. Jiro turned, looking intrigued.

'Tomorrow I am going to the palace. I intend to speak with the Secretariat, Lord Akio Izumi.'

CHAPTER TWO

As Amaya stared at the huge palace gate beyond the moat, she was glad that her uncle was beside her. They walked on and passed through the ornate pillars which seemed as thick and colossal as a sugi tree. The smell of the deep mountain forest still lingered in the wood and Amaya drew in the scent hungrily. However, the monstrous sculptures which filled each pillar bore ghastly and terrifying expressions. Amaya thought were she a demon or an enemy of the state, she would feel compelled to run under the gaze of the hideous twins. As she and her uncle stepped out of the gate's shadow, Amaya saw, for the first time, the palace grounds; symmetrical pathways and flowerbeds framed the long walk toward the palace steps. She could see many people going about their business: Court Officials, samurai, monks, warrior monks, all crossing the main path at intervals, their heads either buried in open scrolls or held high and proud. Some strutted, others seemed to glide and, out of sight, Amaya thought she could hear the distant plucked tune of a shamisen. She had only ever seen the palace from afar but now it demanded attention. The high round stone wall acted as a platform supporting the palace and offering near-impassable protection. The white painted stone reflected the sun and the many sloped black roofs shone like black lacquer. The smell of cinnamon incense still permeated the air about the palace, spicy and sweet.

Red pagodas, which were strewn throughout the estate, rose above the canopy in silent salute. Each eave was a wooden masterpiece, their spires piercing the cloudless sky. Amaya squinted as the gleam from the scarlet shrine roof caught her eye but it soon disappeared from sight behind the verdant trees as she continued to walk behind her uncle. Her attention was taken by the verandas of the outbuildings. They spread out like gleaming rivers leading to and connecting the rest of the palace estate. Amaya suddenly felt small and lost for a moment in the labyrinth of splendour; an unfriendly, beautiful island. They approached the thick stone steps which rose to the main palace building and the Six Ministries.

'Thank you for helping me arrange an audience with Lord Izumi. I know the Secretariat is a busy man.' Amaya glanced at her uncle. He had initially opposed her desire. After her plea and Megumi's persuasion, he had agreed to accompany her but only if the Secretariat agreed. He had.

'I still believe this a risky move, Amaya. You have not been forgotten by the Chancellor.'

Amaya drew in a breath, unprepared for the mention of the man who she had seen murder her father. 'My accusation was legitimate. I saw Rai Kimura kill my father.'

Jiro's reply was hushed. 'Yes, Amaya, you may have done but a child's word against the Chancellor's is worth almost nothing. It was the Takeda name that saved the family from honour suicide. To all in Akegata, and to the law, it was the Senkaku Nin and Kageyama shinobi followers who killed your father as they did the Imperial family. Do not forget what your accusation of the Chancellor cost the Takeda clan.'

Amaya's throat constricted with her anger. She recalled the humiliation distinctly. 'I apologised, uncle. I have never set foot in the palace since. I have kept myself quiet and distant.'

'I know, I know. I was merely glad you did not have to take your own life as payment, although Rai implied that was his wish. I never understood why he did not kill you that night also. He would have saved himself from many troubles.'

Amaya squeezed her lips together as the old frustration emerged. 'I have never been able to remember, uncle. I see father murdered. I see Rai Kimura in the snow.'

'You awoke at home,' Jiro whispered gently. 'How can you not remember that journey?'

'It is all that has been on my mind since that day. Did I faint? Did someone carry me? Did Rai Kimura-' Amaya shook her head. 'Did that man spare me?'

'I understand your desire to avenge Kazu. Do you think it has not been on my mind also? He was my brother. Yet we must live in accordance with the decree and ensure that the Takeda clan is not forgotten.'

Amaya nodded, but her uncle had not seen Kazu impaled upon Rai's katana, he had not seen Kazu's head rolling across the snowy ground with staring, empty eyes. For an entire year, Amaya had been terrified that her father's spirit would be stuck in the Realm of Hungry Ghosts, like the old monk's mother in the tale. However, the first Spirit Festival after Kazu's death had shown her that her father had risen above after all; she could sense it somehow. He was not tormented but he could not wholly rest either. His death had been so violent. 'I am sorry, uncle. I know you also want justice. My visit today is to rectify my past mistakes. I cannot let the Takeda Clan be forgotten. We were once so great. We were leading change in the Court and country. The militia still employ my family's sword technique. We can still be of use to Akegata.'

'Very well. You will see Lord Akio Izumi alone as you and he are acquainted albeit via correspondence. I must attend to other business whilst I am here, as I must away soon.'

Amaya swallowed. 'I understand.'

Jiro accompanied Amaya as far as the Archives where he explained the Secretariat worked. The large double doors were open, revealing numerous tatami mats which stretched far ahead to the opposite side of the large room. The smell of fresh reeds reminded Amaya of spring and autumn all at once. Spanning left and right were tall shelves housing scrolls, and a desire to read them sprang forth at once. Her imagination permitted an image of her father working tirelessly, drafting decrees, passing laws, surrounded by philosophy and knowledge, dressed in his battle garb, the most revolutionary samurai in Akegata. She wanted to touch everything he may have touched.

At the far end, Amaya detected a desk and, behind the desk, a person. Their figure was in silhouette against the papered window they sat in front of. *Akio Izumi*, Amaya thought to herself, suddenly eager to meet the man she felt she knew so well; the man her father regarded above all others.

'Come, Lady Takeda,' Akio spoke from his seat.

Amaya obeyed, bowing low. Her eyes stared greedily at the stacked scrolls as she passed them. Some were crisp and newly rolled, others were yellow with age and ragged. The closer she came to the desk, the stronger the scent of burnt pine knots and the ocean became. Amaya recognised the smell of ink; Kyo had many different kinds. She reached the desk and bowed low again. 'Lord Izumi, thank you for granting me an audience with you.' She didn't rise but waited for him to speak.

'I am glad to finally meet you in person, Lady Takeda. I have long wanted to meet the daughter of my mentor, the woman who penned the interesting letters which kept certain monotonies of palace life at bay.'

Amaya smiled at the floor. 'My father told me much about you, Lord Izumi. Your letters have been a great comfort. Without them, I would not know a thing about my father's life here in the Court.'

Akio laughed, the sound was natural and unhindered. 'Please, lift your head, Lady Takeda. I have something I have wished to give you for some time but only in person.'

Amaya obeyed feeling suddenly uncertain. She lifted her head to face the Secretariat and blinked stupidly. Akio was nothing like her imagination had led her to envisage He was far younger than she had expected. Perhaps no more than a few years older than herself, yet he was the Secretariat. She recalled the compliments her father had given Akio and found her curiosity piqued. He was not short, nor did he appear weak but she sensed he was not a military man because of the gentle eyes beneath his flyaway fringe. His hair was also not in the style of a samurai; it was loose and tousled, falling just above his shoulders in dishevelled layers. However, like a samurai, he still carried a katana and wakazashi blade. Confusion appeared as a frown upon Amaya's brow and then a jagged scar caught her eye. White and pink twisted into each other, marbling his skin and reaching up Akio's neck from beneath his clothing, stopping at his left ear. Aware that she was staring, and that neither had spoken, she bowed again.

'You have something to give me?' Amaya repeated his words, intrigued.

Akio turned to the ornate cupboard behind him. It was a dark wood and looked foreign to Amaya's eyes. *From across the sea, from the mainland,* she pondered. She watched as Akio opened the draw with deep engravings on to reveal a narrow space. From its depths, he withdrew a long and narrow package, wrapped in a striking silk of blue and silver. She recognised it at once, but she could not speak; her eyes were filling with unbidden tears.

'This is yours, I believe. It has been since your father passed away.' He held the package with a certain reverence, his eyes filled with awe and nostalgia. 'This is no place for such a weapon.'

Amaya reached out and took her father's katana, Meiyo. This was the cloth he always wrapped it in when he was not using it. Unthinking, she pressed the loose end of fabric to her nose hoping for even a phantom scent to remain. 'You have had it all this time?'

'I have been caring for it. I have wanted to return it to you many times, Lady Takeda, but never once has the opportunity arisen. I wanted to return it to you in person. It is yours now and should be used. The weapon of the Takeda clan should not be wrapped in silk forever.'

Amaya nodded, clutching the weapon to her chest.

'How do you come to have it?'

Akio replied sombrely, 'it was brought to me after he had passed away.'

She understood his meaning, but her gratitude was swelling over everything. 'Thank you, Lord Izumi. I cannot express what it means to have my father's katana back.'

'Am I right in thinking you have something important to discuss with me?' Akio continued, pretending not to notice her tear-filled eyes.

'Yes, Lord Izumi. It is a request of sorts. An unusual request.'

'Unusual?' Akio said. 'I am intrigued.'

'As the Secretariat and protege of my father, you must be aware of the current state of the Takeda clan.'

Akio nodded, but did not interrupt.

'My younger brother is to assume leadership but only when he comes of age. I am fearful that the clan will be unsalvageable by that time. The Takeda's absence has wrought as much damage to my clan as the shame has done. Yet I fear our absence has inflicted harm upon the Court and the Emperor himself. The Takeda have long stood at the side of the Emperor. My request,' Amaya's mouth was dry, 'my request is that I be permitted to assume leadership of the Takeda clan myself, not merely act as steward.' She bowed again, her hands clutching each other against her thighs. Her determination had flared, her resolve to rectify past mistakes and bring to justice those who had gone unpunished for so long stirred undeniably.

The laugh she expected did not come. She chanced a glance; Akio was looking at her, his expression odd. 'That is an unusual request, Lady Takeda.' He drew in a steady breath.

'I understand that a woman has never led her clan before,' Amaya added.

Akio bit his bottom lip, thoughtfully. 'The Takeda clan is a valuable one, especially to the Emperor. It is the clan known for embodying the samurai spirit. The Emperor needs loyal supporters and, if the power of the Takeda could be revived, it would bring about more stability. Still,' Akio's light expression turned serious, 'even I, the Secretariat, could not bring about such a change so quickly. It would never pass through the Court. The Chancellor would never agree to it.' Akio's tone seemed irritated, but Amaya's thoughts had immediately flown to Rai Kimura and the night he had murdered her father.

'But you agree?' She ventured, trying to push away the echoes of the humiliation she had brought upon her clan.

Akio nodded, slowly. 'I do. Times need change. Evolution and survival go hand-in-hand.'

Amaya felt taken aback, he sounded exactly like her father. 'Then what do you suggest? How can I bring about such a change?'

Akio gave a derisive laugh. 'Magic?'

Amaya felt her hope quiver nastily. 'It seems so.'

'Joking aside, I believe there may be a way you can help, a way to assume leadership over your clan. You will have to prove yourself capable in the eyes of the Court, and in the eyes of Emperor Kenta Yamashima.'

Amaya bit her cheek and tasted blood. The words she had spoken to her father's spirit rang loud in her mind. 'I will do what I must.'

'I thought you would say that.' Akio nodded. 'It will not be easy, Lady Takeda but you have my support, and I am sure the Emperor will be receptive.'

Amaya bowed. For the first time since her father died, she felt that she had been granted a modicum of luck. 'Lord Izumi, you have given me more confidence. I did not expect to find such openness in the palace or Court.'

'Your father worked within the court.' Akio's reply was quiet in its poignancy.

'And I am glad to see his teachings were bestowed onto another beside myself.'

'I will be utilising your intelligence, but I warn you,

you may find that some are not comfortable with a smart woman, especially one who is proficient with a katana and houses the samurai spirit.' Akio raised his eyebrows knowingly.

Amaya looked at him. 'They need not know everything about me. I have been playing the good woman my entire life.'

Amaya wandered through Chuto in the direction of her home. The city seemed to have a different colour to it than the previous day; warmer, calmer. She didn't challenge the change, she enjoyed it. Her thoughts kept meandering back to Akio, surrounded by the scrolls of history and learning. She touched her face and found that a small grin had appeared. Subduing the momentary desire to skip, she turned onto the road which led to her estate. *I am glad I have met him,* she thought to herself. *It was a meeting long overdue.*

'Mother!' Amaya called out as soon as she stepped into the forecourt. The clusters of bamboo, which the path wove around, were incredibly green, but Amaya knew their small leaves would soon be turning a blood red as the Face of Autumn arrived.

'Here.' Megumi's voice issued from the left of the house. Amaya hurried through the small moss garden, until her mother came into sight. She was sitting upon the wooden causeway which jutted out across the pond. The gentle trickle of water was constant and soothing in the waning summer fug. Her mother was sitting at the water's edge, the Collection of Ten Thousand Leaves in her lap. She waved at Amaya.

'Mother, I have good news.' She joined Megumi, taking a zabuton cushion for herself. 'Akio Izumi is a great man. It is clear to see why father chose him.'

'What was discussed?' Megumi leant forward, her eager expression illuminating her features.

'I requested that I become the head of the clan.'

'Tread carefully, Amaya. I want nothing more than for you to lead us but there are those who do not wish to see the

Takeda rise back to power.'

'I am aware, but Lord Izumi wishes to help. Mother,' Amaya clenched her hands, 'he sounds like father. I mean, he shares the same ideals.'

'Lord Izumi has always been able to open his mind; that is what makes him the genius he is. People have been forced to acknowledge that young man, even if they disagree with some of his ideas or his experiences.'

Amaya thought about her mother's words. 'How well did you know Lord Izumi? I recall father speaking of him often and Lord Izumi and I have been in correspondence over the years, but I had not met him in person until today.'

'I met him only once, but it was easy to see his potential. I met him at his induction ceremony, which I attended with your father.'

'But how can that be?' Amaya did not understand.

'Akio Izumi was made a Court Official when he was just thirteen. Your father was still alive and oversaw the whole ceremony.'

Amaya's back straightened. 'I didn't know that. I heard father mention him, but I had no idea the extent of his intelligence. Or the extent that father acknowledged him.'

'Lord Akio is quite accomplished in all regards, but he is also innately benevolent. That is why Kazu chose him to continue his work once he had retired, both as the Secretariat and the General. He accepted the former and, as you know, refused the latter.'

'I am glad that he upholds father's philosophies.'

'You too have inherited your father's will, Amaya.'

'Yet, I was born a woman; powerless to use those ideals.'

'Never wish you were anything different. Powerful men rule. Women are powerful too in a far more subtle and enduring way. We are the pillars and foundation that support that power. Where would they be without us? Where would we be without them? It is the balance between us that everyone seems to forget, or neglect.'

Amaya stared at her mother. 'I had never considered that.'

'I have not lost my wits yet, Amaya. Change will occur, eventually. You need more patience. I gave that to your father, created his balance. And he gave me so much more.'

'I can see why father loved you so much.'

Megumi's eyes brimmed and she looked towards the dojo. 'Yes, well, he loved us all, which is why I believe you are on the correct path, but please remember patience. Do not let your anger or vengeance overshadow the reticent sense you carry. That will only lead you down a road you will find difficult to return from.'

Amaya let out a breath, realising there was something more to her mother's meaning. 'I will try, mother.'

'What did Lord Izumi say you must do?'

'I have to work at the palace, within the Court. Use the education father gave me to prove myself capable of leading the Takeda.'

'You know it will be difficult. Are you prepared for the disdain and prejudice you will receive?'

Amaya gave genuine thought to her mother's question. 'Yes.'

Megumi nodded. 'Good. Then you have my support. Jiro will be here soon, he will be excited by this I am certain, Kyo too. You know how much he wants you to become our leader.'

CHAPTER THREE

Amaya scoured the Archives, but she could not see Akio. She turned, thinking she would await his return outside in the stillness of late morning. On opening the door, she was immediately knocked back inside.

'Apologies, my Lady,' a quiet, deep voice rumbled.

Amaya rubbed her nose as she righted herself. 'No, no. I am sorry. I was not concentrating.'

A large hand presented itself. 'Let me help you.'

Amaya accepted and felt weightless as the man pulled her upright. She could feel concern in his touch; a warmth with an ebb and flow to it. There was the smell of earth and something metallic about him. As she stood, her eyes fell upon his attire: bronze gilt peppered the black lamella armour and each hardened leather scale was sewn to the next with precision and refined detail. The gloves and leg protectors were also scaled, reaching up to his elbows and knees atop dark cloth undergarments. Amaya's gaze finally reached his face. She stepped back a little under his stare, it was full of unbridled pain. Amaya wanted to look away but found herself unable to. Wisps of black hair fell from his high ponytail, trailing across his face and striping his eyes. His jaw was as strong as his glare, and his skin was darker than most but his mouth indicated nothing of his character; it was static.

'Thank you...' she began, waiting for his name.

'I am General Shun Kimura.'

Amaya faltered, discerning who she was conversing with and bemusement fluttered nastily. 'Thank you, General Kimura.' She bowed, rediscovering her manners.

'Again, I must apologise,' his sentence hovered, as hers had done.

'I am Amaya Takeda.'

Unlike Amaya, Shun did not flinch. Instead, he nodded politely. 'I believe Akio Izumi is in the moss garden, near the palace shrine. You have to walk through the copse just there.' Shun pointed toward the largest red pagoda, which was partly concealed by the trees.

'Thank you,' Amaya replied.

The instant he was out of sight Amaya steadied herself against the wall, her shock paramount. Shun looked nothing like his father, he didn't even possess the same air. Rai Kimura's son was the man her father had made General of the Imperial army and the Master of the Sky Province. *The man who murdered you,* she spoke inwardly to her father's spirit, *you raised his son up.* Amaya now understood that the metallic smell she had detected was that of steel. Or was it blood?

Amaya was unable to shake the residual discomfort left by her meeting with Shun, but as she approached the small woodland, it shrank a little. Amaya paused, the trees were much taller than she had expected. The many slender trunks streaked her surroundings, only split by the path which stretched before her. The walkway was wide and flat, interrupted only occasionally and sporadically by shallow steps which grew in number further along. The stones which comprised the paving were like broken pieces of glass, each somehow fitting alongside their neighbour. In the distance, about to go out of sight, were six monks of the New Faith walking towards the unseen temple. They stood apart in their orange kesa robes; a bright blot on the otherwise viridian woodland. The sun was creating a veil which coloured everything green. Even the smell was green. Amaya looked at the skin of her hands, her yellow yukata, her white split-toed socks, each was tinted a startling emerald. Occasionally, sunlight managed to find its way through the many leaves, in shards of white, to the ground beneath. The wind teased the treetops, and the light danced with each gust. She proceeded along the path until completely consumed by the copse.

'Lady Takeda?'

Amaya jumped. 'Lord Izumi.'

'I am sorry to startle you,' he grinned.

'Oh, I was distracted by this woodland. I had no idea it could be this beautiful. From the Archives it looks like a simple cluster of trees.'

Akio took a moment to gaze around. 'There is something enchanting about it, isn't there? It is my favourite part of the estate. The flower gardens are wonderful, but I prefer this simplicity. It is less inhibited by design.'

Amaya smiled. 'My thoughts exactly.'

'Were you looking for me?' Akio continued.

'Yes, I was hoping to discuss my duties with you. I would like to begin as soon as possible.' She bowed with her request. 'That is if you have the time to spare?'

'Of course, Lady Takeda. Would you care to venture from the path? There is no need to be within the Archives for our discussion. It is far more copacetic here.' Akio gestured around them.

'I would like it very much.'

He led her from the path and into the woodland. It was uneven underfoot and her geta sandals wobbled. Akio slowed his pace.

'Will I be working in the Archives?' Amaya continued.

'Yes, as well as other places. At first, I will need your skills in calligraphy. Recently, there have been more decrees made and my hand can only work so fast through the legislation.' He wiggled his fingers.

'My knowledge of writing decrees is lacking.'

'I will dictate at the beginning. I am certain you will pick it up very quickly once you have penned a few documents. After, I will give you only notes to work from, and you can write freely.'

Amaya felt daunted; she knew the importance of the

work but was eager to start. 'Thank you for this responsibility, Lord Izumi.'

'We will meet with His Majesty also.'

'When?' Amaya asked, sharp with anxiety.

'Today, this afternoon.'

Amaya stumbled in surprise, her ankle twisting.

Akio gripped her hand and steadied her. 'He is not that frightening, Lady Takeda.'

Amaya could see his cheeks flush a little, even in the green glow of the copse, as he released her.

'I was merely unprepared. I did not think I would meet the Emperor at all.'

Akio nodded. 'Oh, but he very much wants to meet you, the daughter of Kazu Takeda. I think you both would find a great deal of common ground.'

'Then I would be honoured to meet with His Majesty.' Amaya doubted there could be another to share as much common ground with her than the man walking by her side.

Once Akio had described the palace layout and shown her the places she would be frequenting, the time came to meet the Emperor. They reached the top of the large stone steps and proceeded to the Archives.

'I would have taken you to him sooner but he has been with the Six Ministers all morning.'

'I hope it is no trouble for him to meet with me today. I am honoured he wishes to hold an audience at all.'

'Do not fret, Lady Takeda. You do that often, don't you? Worry.'

'Not at all,' Amaya said, a little louder than she had meant, but Akio's faint smile told her that he did not believe her. 'Do I need to change my attire?'

'Your yukata is ideal. His Majesty dislikes frivolities and enjoys the simple things in life. He does not get to enjoy them as much as he would like. You will find him less than traditional. There are some select documents I must bring to our meeting. Would you mind waiting for a moment whilst I retrieve them?' Akio indicated to the Archives.

'Please, go ahead.'

He slipped inside and out of sight and Amaya turned to face the palace grounds. The copse appeared small again, as she looked at it from the Archives. She hadn't made it to the red pagoda or to the shrine of the Old Faith. She promised herself she would make time to visit and pray there.

'Are you lost?' A voice issued from her left.

Amaya jolted and spun about, surprised for the second time that day. 'No, I am not, thank you. I am waiting for Lord Izumi.' She bowed low. The man before her had a casual elegance, both in his posture and expression. His tapered face housed a slender nose and an equally slender mouth, which didn't look as though it smiled easily, but would like to. She could see that his eyes were clever yet benevolent as he gazed at her with curiosity. His long hair was tied in a low ponytail with a thin cord, which had a small brass bell at each end. The black locks trailed over his shoulder and down his chest. It was then she noticed his kimono; the fabric and embroidered detail were unparallelled but uncomplicated. Purple silk rested atop white in a relaxed manner, and golden chrysanthemums flourished across the fabric. The obi belt was unusually thin and tied in a simple bow to the side. *An odd style*, Amaya thought.

'Ah, yes, the Secretariat. How do you find Akio?' He questioned, dropping proprieties.

'Most agreeable.'

To Amaya's surprise, the man laughed, and his face transformed because of it. His prominent cheekbones partially hid his eyes for a moment. 'Yes, I suppose he is.'

'You know him well?' Amaya continued, unsure of what to say.

'Oh, yes. I have known Akio since I was a child. You could say he is a brother to me, a guardian of sorts.'

Amaya noted the casual address the man used but felt cheered to meet someone from Akio's adolescence. 'I cannot imagine Lord Izumi as a child.'

'Nor would you want to. You would not think it now, but he was quite mischievous. That's what happens when you are so smart I suppose. He was easily bored. Only the Way of the Samurai could keep him occupied for any length of time. Quite the talent with a katana and a bow is our Secretariat, but do not tell him I told you. Underneath his amity must be a starved ego somewhere, though I have yet to discover it.'

Amaya shook her head, a laugh chasing away her earlier surprise. 'I cannot believe he was mischievous.'

The Archive door slid open. 'I thought I heard your dulcet tones, Kenta.'

Kenta, Amaya pondered. 'Kenta Yamashima?' Amaya felt struck, horrified. She prostrated herself, falling to her knees, her forehead touching the floor. 'Your Majesty, please forgive me! I did not know it was you to whom I spoke. I did not expect to see you alone outside the main building.'

The two men were silent for a moment.

'Please, get up,' Kenta said, quietly. As Amaya rose to her feet, she saw awkwardness crowd his features dispelling his earlier happiness.

'This is Lady Takeda, Kenta. Kazu Takeda's daughter.' Akio's tone was bright.

'Lord Kazu and Akio spoke of you often, Lady Takeda. I am very happy to finally meet you.'

Amaya felt her chest grow tight as her words flurried together. She did not expect the Emperor to be so forthcoming. 'And I you, your Majesty. I am certain my father exaggerated greatly, but it is kind of you to say.'

'Please, call me Kenta.' His eyes turned solemn.

'Is that permitted?' Amaya was torn, and unable to say another word she bowed again, berating herself for becoming unnecessarily flustered.

'Kenta, you know she must call you by your title, in public at least.'

'I know. Still, *His Majesty*,' Kenta replied with the tone

of someone who had just eaten something unpleasant. Amaya studied him as he spoke to his friend. His grace was not enough to cover the discomfort that was plain in his dark eyes. Amaya found him intriguing, and not at all how she imagined the Emperor to be. She had never met Kenta's father, but she had overheard her own describing him to her mother before he had been assassinated; irascible, unpredictable, misguided. Realising she was staring, she averted her eyes.

'Well, shall we sit?' Kenta said, looking from Akio to Amaya. 'I think the garden.'

'Kenta, you are the Emperor,' Akio reminded him, gently.

Kenta sighed, closing his eyes. 'Yes, so I am. Inside it is.'

Amaya looked to Akio, who shook his head a minuscule amount as if requesting her patience.

The room which they occupied was large and the entire floor was covered in fresh tatami mats. It smelt faintly of grass and reminded Amaya of spring and sakura blossom. Four wall-hangings decorated the room, one for each season. Amaya found her attention taken by the inked autumnal mountain range; her eye drawn to an imaginary distance. The scarlet leaves that swirled about the foreground seemed to move with the brush strokes which had created them.

'My mother selected these,' Kenta said, taking Amaya from her reverie. His face had a closed look upon it, and Amaya caught concern cloud Akio's. 'She loved all the seasons, saying each had a different face, like the tales of the Old Faith.'

'They are very beautiful. I particularly like the autumn illustration,' Amaya replied.

Kenta smiled to himself. 'That is also Akio's favourite.'

'Of course, your name means autumn,' Amaya said.

Akio nodded, before gesturing Amaya to sit upon a large, silk zabuton cushion. She hesitated, waiting for Kenta.

Her shoulders were never far from her ears and her hands gripped each other, as she sat across from the Emperor. Akio was beside her, and between him and Kenta there was never a prolonged silence. Amaya could barely detect the hidden samurai in the walls; the protective shadows that followed the Emperor wherever he went.

'Lady Takeda will be aiding me in the Archives. She has kindly agreed to help draft the decrees and legislation passed by the Six Ministries,' Akio informed Kenta.

'Thank you, Lady Takeda. I have been told that you are able to write the complex characters. I may have to utilise your talents myself.'

Amaya inclined her head. 'I would be honoured, your Majesty.'

Kenta looked at her pointedly, but a soft grin had appeared. 'Whilst you are working at the palace please feel free to enjoy the gardens and, if you like to pray, there are several holy places. We have a temple of the New Faith and a shrine of the Old Faith. Mostly, I would like you to meet Kannushi Masato.'

'Is he the head priest?'

'He is the only priest,' Kenta corrected. 'We have numerous monks for the New Faith, but only one priest of the Old.'

Amaya wanted to question, but Kenta continued. 'Oh, and you may use the dojo to train should you wish, but I understand you have a dojo within your estate.'

Amaya nodded. 'Yes. My father developed and honed the Seishin no Ken technique in that dojo. He trained many samurai of the city within its walls.'

Kenta grinned. 'I can picture Lord Kazu now, training hard. I would often sneak to train with him once my elder brother had finsihed. My mother thought very highly of Kazu.'

'There is plenty of time for Lady Takeda to see the palace, Kenta. I'm sure she will be pleasantly surprised,' Akio interrupted. 'I understand that the Six Ministers wish to hold an even larger meeting, one which all the Governors will be invited to.'

'Word travels fast.' Kenta drew in a breath, releasing

it gradually. 'The Ministers are already hovering, trying to further themselves by making poorly masked requests. The Chancellor is now the Minister of War, a fact which will be announced officially tomorrow.' Kenta's eyes flickered to Amaya.

She swallowed, her hands clasping each other tighter still, and looked at the floor. The last person whom she had overheard speaking of such affairs was her father. As a woman, she did not feel at ease in such conversation. Yet, as she listened, she found natural comprehension forming alongside a delicate gratitude.

'I thought that would happen eventually.' Akio shifted in his seat. Amaya looked at him as an unexpected anger flared momentarily within his genial eyes.

Kenta spoke, 'I am sorry, Akio. There was little I could do to oppose. The Court followed all his decisions and, without good reason to deny him, my hands are tied. In everyone's eyes he is the logical and best choice for the role.'

'I know full well that this is Rai Kimura's doing.'

Amaya comprehended Akio's anger and fear. 'Permission to speak, your Majesty?' Regardless of Kenta's apparent casual demenour, Amaya still felt uncomfortable addressing him as anything less. He was Akegata's ruler by Divine Right; his clan supported by the spirits.

'Please do, Lady Takeda,' Kenta replied, his tone encouraging.

Amaya swallowed. 'That man is slowly eroding your power over the court, and I believe it started with the plot to murder my father.' She bowed her head quickly, surprised at the fear of speaking so openly. Yet as she battled with it, she realised the fear came from herself; it was not inspired by the two men before her. With a sickening jolt, she comprehended that holding her tongue over the past years had not served anyone but Rai Kimura.

'That is our thought. Rai Kimura understood your father's position; Kazu Takeda held sway over the court. However, this all started long before then,' Akio observed Amaya's face.

'There was another person, the one who led the attack on the palace the same night your father was killed,' Kenta whispered. 'A man I have spent many years trying to locate. It is my belief he is the true puppeteer of all this.' He waved his hand at nothing.

Amaya frowned, unable to stem her curiosity. 'And Rai is simply in a partnership with him.'

'This man is as much to blame for your father's death as Rai Kimura. It was this same man who murdered my mother, father and my siblings,' Kenta growled through the anguish which still stung him.

Akio shifted in his seat. 'Kenta.'

Amaya did not speak immediately; the echo of Kenta's words muffled all else. 'His name?'

'Sen Sanjo.' Kenta's frustration with himself was plain for Amaya to see. 'He had a tattooed head and wore a sleeveless, white kataginu with a moth emblazoned on it in black; I have never forgotten. I watched him slay my mother with my own katana, whilst covered in my father's blood.'

Amaya felt a chill the length of her body. She swallowed down the disgust and pity, as she watched Kenta's face close and his kind gaze retreat like a wounded animal. She could understand him, truly understand. He had witnessed the death of a beloved parent, as she had. He had lost that much, and more. The urge to reach out to him swelled with her sympathy, and she found herself pondering if her eyes looked as his did in that moment.

Akio sighed. 'The search for Sen has never ceased, we have a man who travels Akegata in search and I have faith that he will discover Sen. We have another ally, Shin Nakamura, who is posted in the south. At the beginning, I wanted to search for Sen myself, but I was not permitted.'

Amaya looked at Akio. 'Why?'

'I am his first retainer and have been since I was fifteen.

My place is by his side and I would not trust another with this role.'

'You must have faith in this man who is hunting down Sen.'

Kenta cleared his throat. 'We do not speak his name because we do not wish to risk his life. This man, Akio and Shin Nakamura have been loyal to me from the start and are my dearest friends.'

Amaya did not know how to respond. 'Why have you allowed me to be privy to all this, your Majesty?'

Kenta sighed, as if releasing something he had been holding on to. 'Because you are Kazu Takeda's daughter, the Assistant Master of the Seishin no Ken technique and the true successor to the Takeda clan. Your father often spoke of you; and we have spoken of you often since his demise. We have had to keep you at arm's reach to draw Rai's attention from you. My mother was a great friend to your father, and he to her.'

'Your father believed you would be able to aid us in time but we were not to seek you out until the opportune time.' Akio nodded, his look apologetic. 'There are some in the Court you can trust, but most you cannot,' he explained. 'I will be by your side to guide you until you find your feet.'

Amaya felt a twinge of happiness at the thought of Akio as her guide. Happiness and gratitude that he had not assumed to protect her.

'I must speak with Lord Hiroshi,' Kenta continued. 'He is one of those who Akio spoke of, a man you can trust. You will meet with him, Lady Takeda. He has long wanted to meet with you. He was the only person who stood with your father against Rai all those years ago.'

'I am afraid I do not know Hiroshi Katou well,' Amaya admitted.

'He is the Advisor who has served the previous two Emperors,' Akio replied.

'But my father proved rather difficult to advise in the end,' Kenta said, with a derisive laugh. 'Hiroshi was also our scholastic teacher,' he finished.

'I look forward to meeting him.' Amaya inclined her head.

The group conversed into the late afternoon, and Amaya found herself struggling against exhaustion. Her involvement still felt odd, but she comprehended that outside of the few friends she had made, she was still regarded as an outsider; the girl who had had the audacity to accuse the Chancellor of murder, and now she was back within his gaze. *I must be careful,* she told herself.

'He still does not think of himself as Emperor yet,' Akio said quietly, as they left Kenta.

Amaya turned, the late afternoon sun falling shy of the pathway they were upon. 'He is not what I expected.'

'He does not behave like an emperor yet, either,' Akio continued. To Amaya's surprise Akio's face fell. 'He will have to learn, and I hope it is not a hard lesson.'

'What is your meaning?' Amaya replied, not sure she should venture into such a topic.

'He was not supposed to be the Emperor. Kenta is the third and youngest child of Kado Yamashima, only thirteen when prematurely placed on the throne.'

'Still, he has been raised in an imperial household.'

'And largely neglected, save by his mother and elder sister. It was never thought that Junpei would not succeed his father. Your father anticipated the attack, but his worries were dismissed after no empirical evidence was found. Lord Kazu was getting closer to discovering the truth, and the evidence he required to expose Rai and his plots, but we know what happened first; Sen's involvement and partnership with Rai. Kenta does not have confidence in himself, and an emperor with no confidence is vulnerable.'

Amaya felt her eyes widen. 'Lord Izumi, are you truly this concerned? Kenta seemed troubled, yes, but he is not a fool. He has had to grow through his most formative years as the Emperor. Knowing he was meant to die, knowing that there are still those who seek his death. I think it truly awe-inspiring that he still smiles for he must feel acutely lonely. However, with his close friends near, the waters around him will settle.'

'I do not trust those waters,' Akio responded. 'Which is another reason I believe you can help. He needs guidance he can trust, aside from just myself, Hiroshi and Shin. I know you will not pander to Rai like so many do. You live in the city, so you are able to see the effects this corruption is having.' Akio shook his head.

Amaya stopped and held up her hands. 'Lord Izumi, I am sure I do not have anything special to offer His Majesty, or at least, not what you are hoping for. I am simply the daughter of Kazu Takeda. I cannot even bring the Takeda clan under my guidance, let alone the Emperor.'

'Perhaps you can't, but perhaps your father's faith in you will prove sound after all. He was always an excellent judge of character,' Akio retorted, facing her.

CHAPTER FOUR

'Amaya? Are you listening?'

'I am sorry, Kyo. What is it?' Amaya said, straightening up immediately.

Kyo rolled his eyes. 'Wake up, Amaya! You have been daydreaming constantly since you started at the palace. I want to practice calligraphy with you.'

'I have not been daydreaming,' Amaya replied. She stuck her tongue out at her younger brother.

Taken aback, Kyo leant forward and shoved her gently. She returned the action wholeheartedly, and soon laughter travelled through the open door into the garden where Megumi rested Amaya caught her smile.

'How many characters have you managed to remember from our last lesson?'

'All of them,' Kyo stated. 'That is why I want you to teach me more!'

'You are much quicker at learning them than I was,' Amaya praised.

'Yes, but your handwriting is more refined.' Kyo screwed his mouth to the side. 'Father always said a great calligrapher made a great samurai.'

Megumi stepped up onto the veranda. 'Kyo, you should appreciate how wild your flourishes are. They are very distinctive, not at all ugly.' She ruffled his hair. 'It is the artist in you.'

Content with the encouragement, Kyo resumed his practice as Amaya laid out the new characters for him to learn.

'Kyo is correct, Amaya, you have been a lot more distracted since you began working at the palace. Is anything amiss?' Megumi continued.

Amaya leant back reflecting on the month which had passed since her first meeting with Kenta and Akio. 'I still do not understand all there is to know. The politics are far more convoluted than I imagined. His Majesty is trying very hard to right his father's wrongs.'

'He made many it seems,' Megumi said, glancing in the direction of the palace.

'Kenta is still uncertain of his ability to rule.'

'Kenta?' Her mother asked with raised eyebrows.

'He requested I call him such,' Amaya said, a little guarded, uncertain when she had grown so comfortable with the informality.

Megumi shrugged. 'Do not exhaust yourself, Amaya. Your uncle has written and he is concerned for your health.'

'He needn't be. I shall write to him and explain. I am glad he is in the Air Province. His help is greatly needed in the north.'

'I worry for him. The rebel army are in the north. They continue to grow as the Capital's power shrinks.'

'They have yet to make a serious move but they will, and Kenta and Akio know this.'

'Oh,' Megumi said in surprise as the chimes sounded from the entrance. Both women stood and approached the sliding doors, which led out onto the forecourt.

'Lady Amaya Takeda.' It was a palace courier who spoke, his body bent at right angles in a bow.

'Yes.'

He handed her a scroll and bowed again before leaving. Amaya watched him until he vanished out of the main gate. She studied the wax seal, it bore the Heron of the noble Izumi clan, Akio's family. Breaking it open she unravelled the letter, immediately recognising the Secretariat's hand.

Lady Takeda,

Your assistance has been requested to help with the hanabi festival this coming month. It is Rai Kimura's wish for you to work on the preparations. I volunteered to write you this letter. Do not fear; you will not be working directly with Rai. I have ensured that your position does not require it.

If possible, could you come to the palace tomorrow morning? I think it best you stay here until the festival has ended.

Akio Izumi, The Secretariat.

Amaya frowned passing the letter to her mother. She waited in silence until her mother had finished.

'What are Rai's intentions?'

'I mean to find out,' Amaya replied.

'Be careful,' Megumi said, her face marred by worry. 'This request may be a veiled attempt at lowering your station and painting you as an inexperienced woman in the Court.'

Amaya folded the letter carefully. 'I have no doubt of Rai's intentions here, mother. However, it is his choice to underestimate me. I choose to see this as an opportunity.'

Amaya found Akio in the Archives, his head resting against his hand, his black, untidy hair obscuring his eyes, as he leant pouring over the numerous parchments. Amaya announced herself and bowed low.

'Lady Takeda, thank you for coming. I am sorry such a request was made.' He got immediately to the heart of her visit.

'Not at all, I knew one would come. I am surprised it was not sooner. Still, I am determined to use this to my advantage.'

Akio's smile was sympathetic. 'And I am sure you will excel, my Lady. The Minister of Personnel, Makoto Ka, has compiled a transcript of your duties. I have it here.' Akio rifled through a few pieces of parchment and held one out. Amaya accepted it.

'Makoto Ka? The Court Official Rai recently promoted?'

Akio nodded ruefully. 'Not quite. The Chancellor promoted Makoto's son, Riku, who now sits in Court as the Minister for Justice. Makoto Ka is the Minister of Personnel.'

'Oh, I see. How convenient for them all,' Amaya said no more.

'I believe your main duty will be to arrange the fireworks.'

Amaya was already reading the details. 'That is not as dire as I thought. I assumed I would be working alongside the servants.'

Akio shook his head. 'Rai's original order was just that. Kenta and I quickly quashed the blatant disrespect but be prepared for such requests to be made of you regardless.'

Amaya bowed again. 'Thank you, Lord Izumi. Thank you.'

Amaya left Akio to continue with his work. He had told her that the fireworks were being stored in the red pagoda near the shrine and that Kannushi Masato would be aiding her. Amaya felt her pace quicken; she was anxious to meet the singular priest.

The copse was not green like the previous time she had walked through it. Instead, a red light filled the area. Autumn had crept down the mountains during the course of the two months, and now the whole of Chuto was a deep scarlet. The Change was almost complete and soon Amaya would have to begin wearing a thicker kimono for the air was cooling with each passing day. The pagoda grew as she approached, and it was immense. Before her, Amaya could see the many stone steps which led up to the temple, shrine and pagoda. Numerous red torii gates arched over the stairway. She walked under the first gate and onto the first stone step. The passing from common land to holy was corporeally comforting.

Eventually, she reached the summit, her breath coming short. The approach to the shrine and temple stretched out before her, lit by decorative stone lanterns. Amaya paused for a moment beside the Temizuya basin. Numerous long-handled ladles lined the sides, resting beside the spring water which shimmered as the light gleaned from its black surface. Amaya could feel the warmth of the natural spring before she touched it. She gripped the nearest ladle and washed first her left hand and then her right. Cupping her hand, she sipped some of the water and washed her mouth. Finally, she turned the ladle upside down so that the handle itself was cleansed of any impurities.

She stared at the New Faith's place of worship: the temple. It had been erected after the scarlet shrine of the Old Faith, but she could see parallels in their designs. Both had dark, sloped roofs with corners that curved skyward as if reaching out to the spirits above. However, where the temple was white or black walled, the shrine was an alarming, passionate red. It was no wonder, Amaya mused, that the Old Faith dealt with matters of life, and the New Faith matters of death.

Dotted about the large, open space before the shrine where the worshippers could gather, she saw hundreds of Ema hanging upon little hooks. They lined walls, dangled from trees, or found a home in the beams of surrounding outbuildings. The small wooden plaques had prayers and wishes inscribed on them and Amaya began to think up her own wish. The wind scurried about the entrance, causing all the Ema to bump against their neighbours. The area was momentarily filled with wooden clatters, as if the wishes had a voice. Beyond the space lay the oratory, where she could make her offerings and pray. Beyond the oratory, Amaya knew, lay the honden, where the Spirits were enshrined. Only the priest could enter that sacred space. She had only ever seen a shrine's honden once. Her uncle had taken her into Shiroshi's honden when she was just five years old. She couldn't recall the interior now, all she remembered from the visit there was the cold which blasted across the land from the Ice Planes of the Air Province.

Amaya walked past the large bells either side of the entrance which rested in their own wooden homes. She always heard the shrine bells near her home when they tolled. The streets were filled with their bucket-like clangs at the turn of every New Year. Removing her sandals, she entered the large oratory. It differed greatly from the humble shrine she visited with her family. Where hers was simple, this one was grand. Where hers was pleasantly frayed around the edges, this one seemed as glorious as the day it had been built. She found, however, that the atmosphere was the same. Spirits dwelt in all things, in all people, and the shrine seemed to place a calm arm around her shoulders. She turned, bowed and quietly clapped her hands together twice.

Feeling lighter, she stepped away from the shrine.

'You must be Lady Takeda.' The voice was a croak, and the man it belonged to resembled a toad. The sweeping sleeves of his grey gown touched the floor as he bowed. The tall, black hat lengthened his small, incredibly wrinkled face, and as a beam broke across it, his wide-set eyes were lost for a moment in the folds of skin.

'And you are Kannushi Masato,' Amaya responded, returning the bow.

The old priest nodded, his hat wobbling with the movement. 'Yes, I am he. You are here for the fireworks? Akio has already spoken to me. You look just like your father,' he hummed, agreeing with his own observation.

'Really? People say that I look like my mother.'

Kannushi Masato shook his head, his hat wobbling again. 'Perhaps a little, but I see more of Kazu in you. Yes, especially your eyes. Very much like Kazu's.'

Amaya felt a smile awaken her cheeks. 'I am glad I have met another who knew my father.'

'He is missed.'

'Yes,' Amaya replied, her grin fading. 'Lord Izumi informed me that the fireworks are kept in the pagoda here.'

'They are. I will take you there.' Kannushi Masato

chuckled and clasped his hands behind his back, the long sleeves oscillating.

As they walked through the shrine's ground toward the towering pagoda, Amaya spoke reluctantly. 'I have to confess that I have never done anything like this. I do not know the first thing about fireworks, except how to enjoy them.'

Kannushi Masato waved a hand. 'That is why Lord Izumi asked me to aid you. I am usually the one who prepares this festival, but if I am honest, I could do with the assistance. I am quite old you see,' he chortled. 'Next year, I suspect I shall be in need of a holy staff. To lean on, I mean.' He tottered on still chuckling, and Amaya followed. 'Only the Spirits know my age. Even I have lost count.'

Amaya laughed at the arcane words. 'Surely not, with the wit you still have.'

'Wit? That is something your father had no small measure of.'

Amaya didn't mind Kannushi Masato talking about her father. 'He did.'

She stopped at the pagoda's entrance. The inside had been gutted of all spiritual artifacts, replaced by boxes of fireworks. The octagonal space was light, despite the lack of windows. Amaya realised that the walls were lined with gold; gold taking the form of lotus blossoms and phoenixes. Ahead, she could see a gold relief of Amaterasu, the Sun Goddess, as she was portrayed in the Lotus Scroll: Amaterasu emerging from a cave, bringing with her the light of the sun. The beams fell upon all before her, illuminating them. Her radiance fell over the mountains, the forests, the rivers and waterfalls. It touched every face and reflected from every upturned eye. Even the seasons were aglow. Even the Face of Winter, with its frozen tears and knowing stare.

'Why is the pagoda no longer used? It is so beautiful.'

'There are no priests here to use it, aside from myself. There were many here, of the Old Faith and the New. Different priests from across Akegata,' Kannushi Masato said. 'Emperor

Kado Yamashima began using it as storage after the massacre.'

'Excuse me, the massacre?'

'It was kept very quiet, very few know what truly happened.'

Amaya wanted to probe, to question, but she was saved having to. Kannushi Masato continued. 'The massacre is the reason that I am the only priest here. All the others were slaughtered.'

Amaya gasped, her hand going to her mouth as she looked about her. 'In here?'

'They were killed throughout the shrine and the temple. In here as well.' He waved a crooked hand about the pagoda. 'I thought the blood would never be cleaned.'

'Was it a shinobi attack?' Amaya asked, her voice quiet.

'It was the work of just one man.'

'One?' Amaya said, her voice rising at once. 'One man killed a shrine full of priests.'

'Yes. Only myself and one other survived.'

'And what of the one who committed the murders? He was put to death I hope?' Amaya felt sickened at such desecration. Her mind spiralled; she found herself envisioning bodies scattered throughout the holy place, littering the floors of the worship halls, their blood dirtying the spring water of the Temizuya basin and white paving. Crimson-stained wood and stone.

Kannushi Masato shook his head. 'He escaped with his life.'

Amaya frowned. 'What of the other survivor?'

'He was banished, never to return to Chuto again. I have seen him only once in the sixteen years that have passed since the incident.'

Amaya frowned. 'I do not understand.'

'The man who was banished was named Kin Sanjo.'

A faint trickle of recognition seeped into Amaya's mind. 'Sanjo. I know this name.'

'Yes, you would, but it is not Kin who you have heard of.

It is his brother, the man who massacred the priests here, that you know. His name is Sen Sanjo.'

Amaya felt her mouth open and her back stiffen with understanding and remembrance. 'You mean Sen Sanjo, the leader of the Senkaku Nin? The man who murdered Kenta's family.' Unbidden fear swept all else from her mind.

'Not simply the leader, he is the founder of that organisation.' Kannushi Masato shook his head, his wrinkles collapsing in weariness. 'He was once my student.'

Amaya swallowed the words that fought each other to be heard. 'Sen Sanjo founded the Senkaku Nin?'

'Yes, he has become quite the monster, as are those who are members of his group.'

'I feel as though they are just stories but that is simply the wishful thinking of the child in me. He was your student?'

'Yes. He ventured down a path I could not help him come back from. We all tried to help him but our efforts were in vain.' Kannushi Masato sighed and was silent. Amaya could see that he was consumed by memories.

'Why was his brother banished? Did he help Sen?'

Kannushi Masato made a strange noise that was neither a laugh nor a sigh. 'Kin? No, no. Kin is a kind man, a very wise man. Unjustly exiled.' Kannushi Masato tone was curt.

'These are the fireworks?' Amaya spoke quickly, indicating the stacked boxes, which filled the space in front of them.

'Yes! Some of the best in Akegata,' Kannushi Masato replied, rubbing his hands together and tottering forward. 'Now, let me show you how I usually arrange these spectacular flowers of fire.'

Amaya left the shrine late, after she had prayed for her father. Kannushi Masato had retired into the sacred confines of the hondan, letting her have privacy. After some time and once her knees began to protest, she rose to her feet, collected a plain paper lantern from the entrance and began the walk back to the palace. The braziers lining the wide path before the stone steps were all aglow. The light kept the dense blackness at bay; the pathway a single illuminated stretch. She left the light of the shrine behind and descended the steps slowly.

She paused as she approached the woodland. The trees were barely distinguishable against the night, and she could only make out the closest ones; tall, skinny shadows which towered above and out of the light of her lantern. A few braziers dotted the walkway, but there were gaping pools of darkness between each. Proceeding, she thought back to the massacre that Kannushi Masato had spoken of. No word had reached the city folk but, she thought, she had been very young when the incident had occurred. Perhaps she simply did not remember.

Amaya's ears twitched. 'Hello?' She spoke clearly into the black, unafraid. The whispering trees were the only reply to be heard. Laughing to herself, relieved, she continued on her way.

It was as she passed through the heart of the copse that a tall figure stepped out onto the path, just beyond the light of her lantern. Amaya halted abruptly. The wind whipped all sound away as she called out, demanding a name. His hand went to his side and he drew his katana without a word. An unwelcome terror snared Amaya's legs to the ground but only for a moment.

The man moved fluidly, devouring the distance between them. His face was mostly covered by a tight black mask and his eyes rested in the shadow of his fringe. She slid to the side as he brought his blade down, her body moving the way her father had taught her. Her mind had yet to catch up and she stumbled on the hem of her kimono. She grunted in frustration as he spun about and brought his blade up again. Whirling the lantern around she smashed it upon his head, but it did little to hinder him, and he assumed the offensive once again.

The blade slashed her shoulder and the fabric of her

sleeve tore open. The silk flapped about, and she could feel the blood rolling down her arm and dripping from her fingertips but she refused to cower. She adopted the stance of the Seishin no Ken technique and took a deep breath. Sliding the hairpins from her hair, she observed the man's movements. He turned to face her once again. Still not muttering a word, he slid forward. She gripped the hairpins between her thumb and rigid fingers. Lifting her arm in his direction, she flicked her wrist and sent the hairpin flying, but the man merely side-stepped and ran forward.

She clenched the remaining hairpin in her hand as he lunged, Amaya pirouetting around him. The movement caused her long kimono sleeves to billow like a bird's wings. She sank into the memories of her training with her father, and moved quickly, sweeping the ground with her feet until she felt her ankle collide with the man's. She watched him stagger. Grasping the hairpin, she turned and fled, but her kimono restricted her movement. The man was behind her.

'Help me!' Amaya yelled out.

A moment later, he grabbed her loose hair and yanked her back violently. Using her free hand, she struck him between the ribs, but he did not relinquish his grip. He raised his katana. Amaya grabbed hold of him, wrapping one of her arms around his waist and pulling herself close, hoping that the action would make striking her more difficult. She screamed as he pressed his thumb into the wound on her shoulder. With a swift movement, she took the opportunity and stabbed the last hairpin through his forearm. She felt blood gush around her own hand. He growled in pain and threw her to the floor. Cracking her head hard against the dirt, Amaya tried to crawl back towards the shrine. Her eyes were filling with warm blood and her head throbbed. The man loomed over her, breathing heavily, his katana raised. She held out an arm to protect herself, but he whipped his head around and fled into the woods.

'Lady Takeda?'

Amaya squinted, struggling to sit up. A shadow was hurrying in her direction. She lifted her hands defensively. He soon reached her, and Amaya shrank back. It was Shun Kimura, the General. He skidded to his knees beside her, shifting his katana aside as he did so, and placed his arms around her shoulder. Amaya shrieked in pain and saw Shun look down at his bloodied hands.

'We need to get you to the palace, Lady Takeda. Can you stand?' His voice was fearful. Blood still flowed from the cut on her hairline as well as from the laceration on her shoulder. Shun snatched the material from Amaya's ripped sleeve and pressed it to the injury. 'Hello?' Shun yelled out apprehensively, his hand immediately brushing the hilt of his katana. Amaya hadn't heard what he had. He squinted at the bobbing bright lantern. 'Kannushi Masato,' Shun sighed, relieved. 'Lady Takeda has just been attacked.'

'Kannushi Masato,' Amaya muttered, as Shun helped her to stand.

'Amaya, I will take you to the temple, it is closer. Dear boy, please can you go to the palace and call for a doctor. Then please inform Lord Akio Izumi and Lord Hiroshi Katou. No one else. Do you understand?'

Shun nodded, his dark expression unchanging, and ran toward the palace as Kannushi Masato accompanied Amaya.

The old priest steered her into the oratory. Once inside Amaya sat down and held a piece of material to her head. The adrenaline had left her body weakened and her stomach coated in a persistent fear. She shook herself inwardly, hating the sensation. 'I am only shaken. The wounds are not deep. If I could just have some water?'

Kannushi Masato nodded but looked unconvinced. The instant she was alone, Amaya tried to fathom the reason behind the attack, and who the man could have been, why they hadn't killed her.

When Kannushi Masato returned with a large jug of water, his face seemed more wrinkled, darker. 'I should have warned you directly. We all should have been more careful. Especially since visiting me here.'

Amaya blinked, trying to ignore the swelling pain in her shoulder and head. 'I am sorry?'

'Your father left me with very few words regarding you the night he died. He was adamant that you should be protected, kept at a safe distance from the palace until you had come of age. Well, that time passed over a year ago and we still did not send for you. Call it caution, kindness, cowardice...'

Amaya was now fully facing the aged priest. She could make no sense of his words.

'I am sorry you have been attacked.'

'It is not your fault, Kannushi Masato.' Amaya said concerned. 'You did not weild a blade against me.'

'I will tell you all your father told me and then you will see why I am sorry for my inaction.' He held out the water.

Amaya accepted the drink but did not remove her eyes from the priest. A thirst had fluttered within her, not born from the need to drink, but from the knowledge that some of her unanswered questions would, finally, be resolved. She knew her father had withheld information; she knew there had to have been more behind his murder than simple clan rivalry.

'Ueten and Gekai. You have heard these names?'

'Ueten and Gekai?' She repeated but could not think from where she knew them.

'Have you heard of this history of the Old Faith?'

Amaya's eyes travelled upward in thought. 'They are spirits, are they not? Ueten is the light spirit from Amaterasu the Sun Goddess and Gekai is the spirit of the shadow created by that light.'

'Yes, they are two renowned spirits of the Old Faith, thought to, on occasion, inhabit the mortal world. The accepted interpretation of that ancient text is that one's character reflects the qualities of either Ueten or Gekai. That it, somehow, saturates the very blood and spirit of the Prophet.

This affinity bestows a very real gift; in essence, that person's blood is special, celestial, a gift from Amaterasu herself. This was a firm belief for many centuries and still followed in a fashion to this day. Those with this affinity were thought to have the ability to produce Divine Children, Divine Heirs, worthy of ruling Akegata; or perhaps be Divine Heirs themselves. The Ancient Scriptures are extremely rare and often incomplete. You can imagine much was left to scholars' translations.' Kannushi Masato was clearly drawing verve from the imaginings of the old creation story.

He shook his head and controlled his meandering thoughts. 'In order to prove themselves touched by Ueten, by Amaterasu, a Prophet would embark on a pilgrimage of sorts; the exact reason behind such a pilgrimage has remained unclear. All but one detail: the Prophet would seek out those which most powerfully reflect and support Ueten's gifts, the Elementals.' Kannushi Masato held up four fingers. 'Four Elementals were always by the Prophet's side.'

Amaya held her eyes shut to allow the drawings from her local temple to stream into her forethought. 'Many temples of the Old Faith display images of Amaterasu and the light she bestows upon Akegata. It is said our rulers are descended from her. Is this more than a simple tale of purity?'

Kannushi Masato wagged his finger in appreciation. 'Kazu was exceedingly shrewd. He has ensured you hold the information but has not told of the golden thread which connects all aspects; this is what I can help you comprehend. At the dawn of the first dynasty, Swordmaster Kuroshima, famously wed a fisherman's daughter, known only as Keiko of the Sea. I say *famously* wed because it was believed she had such an affinity to Ueten and her light; she was a Prophet, touched by Ueten and bestowed gifts from Amaterasu. Swordmaster Kuroshima supported her through her pilgrimage, ensuring her success and safety. It was written in the Ancient Scriptures that their child held gifts of healing and purity as well as a mind as sharp as a katana. This child was the first True Divine

Heir and became the first official Empress to rule over Akegata. From that momentous time, a long line of Emperor's and Empresses ascended the throne with the Divine Right to Rule; a lineage bestowed by Amaterasu through her light, Ueten. Prophets were revered and beloved; all believing they would renew the touch of Ueten and the blessing from Amaterasu.'

'Yet, such a Prophet is forgotten. It is not in the teachings of any shrine or temple I have encountered,' Amaya pondered.

'That does not necessarily mean they do not exist. A thousand years ago, when beautiful Empress Mimiko fell in love with and married Lord Genichiro Minamori, a catastrophic war devastated Akegata. And so began the First Warring States Era. It was believed that Lord Minamori's affinity was not to Ueten but to that of Gekai and the shadow. It was deemed trickery and deception from him. That bloody stretch of time lasted for five hundred years until the Yamashima clan ascended through the last known True Divine Heir: Lord Kazu Yamashima, your father's name sake, and have ruled for nearly twenty generations. Akegata suffered under Lord Minamori and a growing radical faction sought to seek out and destroy any proclaimed Prophets so that such violence would never ravage Akegata again. A small fellowship, protectors of the Ancient Scriptures, believed that it was jealousy and greed which spurred the non-believers and haters forward. Still, Akegata lost Ueten's light.' Kannushi Masato bowed his head. 'Since then, Ueten and Gekai have been lost to time and recordings dwindled to nothing. Any supposed Prophets were hidden and never revealed; many of them had no knowledge themselves and remain undetected. There were connections made between samurai and the legend, but it is not even taught to monks and priests any longer. It is a once-influential, now forgotten history.' Kannushi Masato had rested back upon his heels.

The autumn air was strangely still, save for the tendrils of incense which encircled the two.

'There are many tales in this world,' Amaya mused.

'Your father believed you were proof that these spirits still thrive. His Way of the Samurai is evidence of your family's connection to this tale.'

'What exactly did my father believe?'

'I shall lend you a scroll which your father referenced. Once you have read it, you will understand what your father, the Takeda clan, believed. What he was trying to determine and unravel in the old scriptures.' Kannushi Masato bumbled away, returning shortly with the scroll. Placing it in her lap, he continued to clean her wound. 'Your temperament, your essence and character, your looks. All imply that you have the affinity towards Ueten. Your father believed your blood is that of a Prophet. I was the first he approached and, together, we researched the Ancient Scriptures in secret.'

Amaya nodded, and then the weight of the priest's words settled. She started, 'I am not some Prophet of the Old Faith.' Laughter escaped without her intending it to. 'It is fanciful.'

'Tell me, do you have a birthmark, or a blemish or scar?'

Amaya scrutinised him. 'I do.'

The priest mumbled to himself further but did not elaborate as he fussed over her injury. 'You are extremely lucky, Lady Amaya. Your bone remains intact, as does your muscle. You will have to rest your arm for a week at least, allow the wound to knit.'

'It was not luck, Kannushi Masato. It was that man's moment of mercy. He had the opportune moment and he did not take it.'

The priest's weathered skin sagged a little. 'Peculiar.'

Amaya knew more thoughts were bombarding the small man, yet he did not voice any of them.

'The man who attacked me was left-handed.'

Kannushi Masato's eyes widened. 'How can you be certain, Lady Takeda?'

'Because I am also left-handed.'

The old priest's expression seemed convinced. 'It is as expected. Then he should be easy to find.'

'I fear not. My Father encouraged me to train my right hand because of the stigma that follows left-handed people. I believe my attacker underwent similar training. To an unknowing samurai, he would appear right-handed.'

She couldn't' dwell on the thought because Shun Kimura and the doctor had entered the shrine. The physician began his work at once; his touch soft but purposeful.

'Lady Takeda, you are lucky that none of your wounds are a threat to your life. Poison was not used it seems. However, we must sterilize them at once. Kannushi Masato can you boil me some fresh water and bring clean linens and silk for a suture.'

Kannushi Masato departed and returned not long after with the necessary equipment. The physician cleansed her wound. The sting was horrible.

'Should we not take her to the Healers' Hall?' Shun questioned.

'Here will suffice. I would like to close this wound as soon as possible. Lady Takeda, I will need to stitch your injury Only a few stitches, but it will hurt.'

Amaya looked at the physician, and then to his hand. In it she could see the long needle and thread with finest silk from the Fire Province. She gave a stiff nod. 'I will not struggle, just be quick, please.' She looked up seeking a distraction. 'Thank you, Lord Kimura.'

The look in Shun's eyes was indecipherable, but the ingrained pain still lingered there, beneath his calm. 'Lady Takeda, did you see your attacker?' He asked.

'No.' She grit her teeth as the first suture was pulled into place. 'He was masked, but most of this blood on my hands is his,' she finished determinedly.

Shun looked confused and Amaya continued to explain; talking seemed to dull the pain. 'I was able to use my hairpins to injure his forearm, but he fled when you appeared,

Lord Kimura. I remember that he was left-handed, although well-trained in the right since childhood.'

Shun's black eyes grew large, his look darkening. 'I am sure this person will be caught. Do not worry yourself further, you need to rest. I will accompany you back to your quarters.'

'Thank you, Lord Kimura. I do not wish to cause you any inconvenience.' Amaya felt a twinge of guilt, but she did not wish to be beside Rai Kimura's son; a feeling she knew was irrational in light of his kindness.

'I am walking back to the palace myself, Lady Takeda. It is no trouble.' Shun bowed his head slightly. 'I would feel more at ease escorting you. The attacker is still at large.'

'Then I thank you,' Amaya responded, giving a resigned bow.

Amaya lingered as Shun neared the door. 'I will read this scroll, and then return to speak with you,' she whispered to Kannushi Masato.

'You will understand once you have read the content of this scroll,' Kannushi Masato spoke quietly. 'You may not believe it though, but I implore you to take a moment and consider it. Keep your mind open as your father did.'

Shun did not speak as they walked to the palace. Amaya snatched glances at his strong face, and she could see that his jaw was clenched. She closed her eyes. 'Lord Kimura, will you be attending the hanabi festival?'

'I will. I understand that you are the one organising it this year. I am surprised, usually Kannushi Masato oversees the planning.'

'So he told me. I am happy to do it though. I am keen to do well.'

'I have faith that you will. I am excited to see your firework arrangement. I am certain it will be unique.'

Amaya didn't think that Shun sounded excited at all, but his discomfort contested her thoughts. 'Thank you, General. I hope I do not disappoint His Majesty.'

Silence carried them the remainder of the way and

Shun bid Amaya goodnight at the door to her chambers. He hesitated, seemingly on the verge of speech. His face still bore a troubled expression, but Amaya was too weary to ask, so instead she thanked him again and slid the door closed.

Once she was alone, she stared at the scroll Kannushi Masato had given her, almost forgetting she had been carrying it. She stood for a moment, unmoving, the sounds of the garden leaking in through the window. The cicadas had hummed for the last time over a week ago, and the grounds were strangely quiet, as if mourning the loss of their most raucous inhabitants. Shaking herself, she strode across the room. The scroll was half-unravelled, revealing the top of an inked illustration when someone knocked at her door.

'Come in,' she said, slowly, placing the scroll out of sight. The door opened with a purposeful *swish* and Akio entered looking distraught.

He bowed politely. 'Lady Takeda, I heard what happened.' His eyes found the tattered sleeve of her kimono and the fresh bandage, which was already spotted with blood. He walked up to her and looked at the wound on her arm and forehead. Lowering his gaze to the floor, anger made itself apparent in his expression. 'I will stand guard outside your room this evening.'

Startled, Amaya refused. 'Lord Izumi you cannot. It is not appropriate for the Secretariat to do such a thing.'

'Kenta agrees with me,' Akio continued, ignoring Amaya's protest, his expression unusually fierce. 'He is angry that he cannot come himself to see how you are. He believes that his growing friendship with you may be partly to blame.'

Amaya was taken aback at Akio's words. She shook her head in disbelief. 'Surely not.'

'I am afraid it is not uncommon.'

'It is a ridiculous reason to attack a person. No justification warrant could be issued for such a thing.'

'There are many ridiculous people. Amaya, do not forget who your father was. Think of who you are to the Takeda

Clan.'

Amaya stepped back, understanding following her disbelief. 'I see.'

'I cannot allow you to be alone after such an incident has occurred. Not until I believe it safe. I did not think this would occur so soon.' Akio muttered the last sentence, his face unmoving. He placed a hand gently on Amaya's unhurt arm and stared at her, his light brown eyes pleading. 'Amaya, I will not rest easy tonight if you are alone.'

Amaya nodded knowing that she would not be able to sway Akio's resolve. 'Well, at least have some tea with me on the veranda, Lord Izumi.'

Amaya prepared the tea, but Akio carried the black lacquered tray. The two wandered outside towards the small table and zabuton cushions at the end of the wooden walkway. By the light of the moon, Amaya could see how Akio was extremely disturbed by what had occurred.

'Honestly, I am well. It is not fatal, not even painful anymore. However, I am happy for your company, but only if you desist with this melancholy.'

Akio poured tea for them both and knelt on the opposite side of the small table. In the lantern light, the scar which stretched up his neck was thrown into greater relief. Even though it was a grisly defect, Amaya was unperturbed by it. She knew many of the servants avoided staring at it if they could, she had seen them. It hadn't disfigured his face, but at times the pink finger-like tendrils would pull his skin tight when he turned his head a certain way. Amaya thought it added character to Akio's otherwise comely appearance. Scars told stories, the history of the person who wore them.

She broke out of her musing. 'How is Kenta?' She questioned.

'Furious. I was with the Emperor when General Kimura reported to me. Kenta immediately requested that all injured samurai make an appearance in the court to be examined in the Hall of Healers.'

Amaya opened her eyes wide in surprise. 'He should be more careful. What if I am not the only target here?'

Akio looked at Amaya in silent agreement. 'He has his Censorate members stationed with him at all times. The samurai who guard him are not with the Imperial army or the Ministry of Justice. They are Kenta's own personal retainers, handpicked by Hiroshi Katou and myself.' Akio sipped his tea absentmindedly. 'Kenta is well-guarded. I wish I could say the same for you.'

'I am not without skill, Lord Izumi. Although, I ashamed that I was not able to detain my attacker.'

'Detain? I am simply glad you were not more grievously injured.' Akio inhaled, his eyes searching. 'I do not enjoy violence, not since I was young and in training, but I would gladly put aside that aversion to aid you, Lady Amaya. I know you are skilled but attempting everything in solitude is damaging in its own way; something Kenta can attest to.'

'Lord Izumi, Kenta is young for an Emperor, but he seems beyond his years in thoughts and ideas. Still, he does not think himself ready or suitable to carry the burden of his title. What was his father, the previous Emperor, truly like?'

Akio smiled and refilled Amaya's cup. 'It is easy to forget but at the beginning, he was wonderful. Very similar to Lord Kenta. His decline was a gradual one. He became ill-tempered; the decrees he put through Court became harsh and misdirected. Your father tried to reason with him but, with Chancellor Kimura agreeing with these decrees, there was little your father could do openly. Kenta was sensitive to his father's change and I believe he lost faith in him. Even when Ayane, Kenta's mother, tried to advise her husband he rejected her with the back of his hand across her face, something he had never done before. It was then that an assassination attempt was made against Kado. However, rather than the Emperor's death, it resulted in the death of his daughter, Kenta's elder sister, Princess Kimi.' Akio's voice faltered.

'I am sorry, Lord Izumi. I have asked too much. If it

troubles you, do not continue,' Amaya said, leaning forward. She had heard of the Princess's death; the entire city had mourned for Princess Kimi and the tragedy which befell her.

Akio shook his head. 'Kimi was an exuberant and peaceful young woman with a fondness for animals. We were of the same age and spent much of our time together. I believe she was her father's favourite child. When she was murdered, Emperor Kado Yamashima became fearful and rarely left the palace. That is when the Court fell completely under the control of Chancellor Kimura.' Akio laughed unhappily. 'Kenta, Shin Nakamura, Kimi, the unnamed man traveling Akegata; we five were close friends. We would study together, play together, dine together. When we reached adulthood, Kimi and I were engaged to be married.'

Amaya felt struck. Her hand twitched in Akio's direction but instead she curled her fingers into a fist. She did not know how to comfort him.

Akio's countenance was grim. 'Kimi and I were not in love in that sense. Arranged marriages are expected for all nobles and so it was unsurprising to us both that we were matched. I regarded and loved her as a friend and sister, but I knew she loved another. She confided in me as much. You understand the intricacies of marriage and the influence status exerts on choice. She was devoted to this other man, so much so she did not tell me his name. However, once she died, Kenta lost interest in many things. His elder brother Junpei became even more ferocious, even more overbearing, and Kenta bore the brunt of his elder brother's moods. Kimi had been, unbeknownst to us all, the anchor for all those in her life. Junpei had pressures unlike most children; it was not his fault he was so tempestuous. Kenta lost respect for his father, his brother and lost faith in the Court. The second attempt on his father's life was successful as you know. Unfortunately, Emperor Kado was not the only victim.' Akio raised his cup to his mouth and paused. 'That was the last time I used my blade in combat.'

Amaya waited patiently as thoughts passed over Akio's brow, his keen eyes viewing memories that she could not see.

With a deep breath, Akio looked up and continued. 'Junpei was murdered. He fought very hard, he was a talented swordsman, but was overwhelmed by the number of assailants, which had snuck into his bedchambers. It was a blatant attempt to end the succession of the Yamashima clan. Their extinction was the goal. Ayane was also murdered and the nature of her death still haunts Kenta because he witnessed it. Kenta then withdrew into himself. His introvert nature wholly consumed him in a matter of weeks. His sleep is still disturbed by horrors he will not disclose.' Akio sipped his tea again.

Amaya looked into her teacup, trying to fathom what it must have been like to be present the night the Imperial family were attacked: the screaming; the pounding of disparate feet; hurried breath as you scout the long hallways and corridors, your katana in your sweating hand. 'Yet Lord Kenta works on, despite his feelings regarding the Court,' Amaya said, shaking her head.

'You are young, Amaya, but you are wise beyond your years, very like Lord Kenta. I believe he recognises that in you and it has given him something else to dwell on. He feels he can help you where he could not help himself, or his mother and sister.'

'I am not particularly wise, nor particularly helpless, but Kenta is really trying isn't he.' Amaya felt shamed, she had allowed so much time to pass her by. Kenta had not had that indulgence. 'He wants to stop Akegata collapsing from under his feet. He wants to protect those innocents from the horrors he suffered.'

'Yes, he wants to uproot all the disloyal and corrupt Court Officials before they do more damage, but it will be difficult. The Emperor's power, the Court's power and the military's power have become very intertwined and that is because of Emperor Kado and Chancellor Kimura, who reduced the title of Emperor to a mere puppet,' Akio said, ruefully.

'They do hide their true colours well,' Amaya said, thinking of those in the Court.

'That is why they are Court Officials.'

CHAPTER FIVE

Amaya stretched, forgetting her injury, and recoiled, clutching at her shoulder and groaning. The sun had only just risen, and she wanted to visit her mother and Kyo before her day's work began. She dressed hurriedly.

The maid announced herself beyond the closed sliding door.

'Enter,' Amaya called, over her shoulder as she opened the window. She shivered a little, the Face of Winter was already beginning to overshadow Autumn. 'Winter may come early this year don't you think, Takako?' she commented to the girl who had shuffled in.

'Perhaps, Lady Amaya. Do not forget, it is only just dawn, and Autmun has only been looking on Akegata a little under two moons.'

'Still,' Amaya looked out at the scarlet garden.

'You will be preparing the fireworks, Lord Izumi tells me,' Takako chirped as she made about collecting silks and linens, replacing them with fresh. Amaya smiled. Takako seemed a little unused to palace decorum, but Amaya hadn't the heart to tell her she must wait until the chamber is empty before assuming her duties. She secretly enjoyed her maid's company and unencumbered nature.

'Yes,' Amaya replied happily, turning from the vista. 'I am excited to begin.'

'Everyone loves the hanabi festival. The townsfolk can enjoy it too. My mother, father and little sister all watch it from across the moat. I feel it brings the city together; appreciating mutual beauty. You can be wealthy, devout, poor - all can appreciate the hanabi as one.' She fussed over Amaya's kimono, wrapping with surprising perfection, the folds exact.

'My sentiments also, Takako. I used to watch it from the city too.' Amaya grinned, recalling how her father had hoisted her onto his shoulders, and later when she was too big for that, how he had held her hand. 'I will make sure the festival is one to remember.'

'My lady, is this yours?' Takako straightened, an old scroll in her hands.

'Oh,' Amaya said, recognising the parchment Kannushi Masato had given her. 'Yes, it is. Thank you.' She accepted it from Takako. 'I plan to visit my family before I begin today. Please, excuse me.' Amaya inclined her head, and Takako bowed low. 'Thank you, Takako.'

The maid always reddened when Amaya thanked her. It irked her to think that she received such little thanks.

The palace grounds were devoid of Court Officials and the only people hurrying about in the pale light were the servants. Their rushed pace seemed to inject a little speed into her own footsteps, and she soon found herself passing under the large gate and crossing the bridge. The moat was placid, its murky green apparently murkier in the dawn. The shadow of the castle stretched along the bridge, a fragile blanket. Amaya crossed it at a steady pace, the scroll gripped in her hands. She would tell her mother and Kyo about Kannushi Masato's comments. She wanted to hear their thoughts, for them to concur with her doubt.

However, when Amaya arrived, divulged all Kannushi Masato had said and unraveled the scroll, she was shocked to see a drawing in the exact image of her birthmark illustrated upon the ageing parchment. Her mother and Kyo were sitting at the low table, gazing at the parchment too. Kyo's eyes were wide, but Megumi's were narrowed in resignation.

'Your father used to tell you this story years ago when you were a child,' Megumi said, quietly.

Amaya looked at her mother, finally understanding

why she had heard of the spirit Ueten.

'This is real?' Kyo spoke up.

Megumi leant forward. 'Kazu told me this.'

Amaya sat back on her heels, not wanting to relinquish her doubt. 'It is just a story. A forgotten story for royal ascension. A custom barely alive today; a formality.' Her hands curled in her lap. 'Ueten, Gekai, both part of a story from the Old Faith.'

Megumi looked at her cautiously. 'If that is what you believe. However, let me tell you what your father once told me: Amaya's nature is wholly aligned with Ueten. Her birthmark all but confirms my thoughts; that she has been touched by Amaterasu's light, by Ueten. The Takeda have believed this for centuries.'

Amaya took a deep breath. 'Father believed this. Why?'

'The Takeda are descended from the Minamori clan.' Megumi's voice was quiet.

Amaya's back straightened in horror. 'The man who brought about the First Warring States Era? The man responsible for the Prophets being hounded and wiped out? Forced into hiding.'

'The history is fragmented and scattered across Akegata. Most has been reclaimed and returned to the palace Archives but there are still fragments of this history tucked away in unassuming corners of Akegata. Your father and Akio Izumi have worked on restoring much of this lost history. The palace Archives; the Ancient Scriptures, what remains of them, reside there. Within these Ancient Scriptures, your father discovered that Lord Genichiro Minamori had a blind sister. She was a worthy fighter despite the affliction, and admired for her courage. She eventually sought to unseat her brother. Perhaps she could sense his evil intent or perhaps she could not forgive him for the bringing about of the Warring States Era. Regardless, her efforts were not in vain. She vanquished her own brother.'

'But the First Warring States Era lasted for five hundred

years.' Amaya could not understand. 'She failed.'

Megumi chuckled. 'No, she did not. According to the scriptures, Lord Minamori was aligned with Gekai. Yes, he unleashed a bloody expanse of time upon this country, but it could have been much worse if he had lived.'

'What happened to her? To his sister?' Kyo asked in a rapt whisper, his chin in his palms.

'She was killed by her brother. They died at the ends of each other's swords.' Megumi thumbed through the scroll which stretched out before them. 'Look here, near the bottom.'

Amaya and Kyo bent low over the script. It was an old language, but Amaya had been taught to read scripts from history by her father; she now understood why. 'Takeda. Why is our name here?'

'The sister's name was not known in the earlier years. Women do not dominate the pages of history. It was unknown until she married and became Lady Takeda.'

Kyo spun on his behind to face Amaya directly. 'This is why father never took you, or us, to the palace. He wanted to protect your identity. People may seek to use you against your will.'

'Or destroy you out of fear,' Megumi whispered. 'The faction that spawned after Lord Minamori perished, were not friendly towards those who were believed to be Prophets. They, wrongly, blamed the Prophet. I believe that fear transformed into jealousy, rage and indignation somewhere along history's convoluted path. They begrudged the possibility of a Divine Heir and used the tyranny of Lord Minamori to gain supporters. The group hunted Prophets and that is what your father feared the most. It is partially why he trained and educated you so thoroughly.'

'It all happened so long ago. This faction cannot exist.' Amaya shook her head.

'Kazu would not risk your life on mere chance, Amaya.' Kyo squeezed his mouth tight in thought. 'Unless he had proof that this faction still operated in some capacity. Did anyone else know of father's thoughts regarding this?'

Amaya glanced at her brother and his sound logic. She thought of the attack she suffered and Kannushi Masato's apology but did not speak up.

Megumi looked up in thought. 'Only five others knew that I am aware of: myself, Akio Izumi, Kenta Yamashima, Hiroshi Katou and Kannushi Masato.'

'Why is the scroll so torn here?' Kyo questioned, stroking the end of the parchment.

'The remaining entries are lost. The destruction of this scroll would have occurred during the reign of Lord Minamori. Your father dedicated much of his life to locating it and others to complete the Ancient Scriptures.'

'He believed it contained more on all this?' Amaya hummed.

'Indeed.'

'Was this why he was murdered?' She shook the parchment a little. Amaya's question was blunt, but she was suddenly angry. 'Was he murdered so that my identity would remain secret? To discover if there were still those who believed and hunted any Prophet which emerged?'

Megumi shuffled closer to her daughter. 'Never think that, Amaya. Never. It was not your hand which wielded the blade.'

'Yet it is most likely true. I always considered how odd it was that father did not attempt to fight his assailant; he was the Master of the Sky Province, the Master of the Seishin no Ken, the General of the Imperial Army. He must have heard the approach, the ring of the steel blade, yet he allowed himself to be impaled. He regarded his knowledge to be too dangerous. He left my secret in the hands of a few trusted people.'

'This could mean another discovered the truth and pursued you,' Kyo offered. 'Amaya, protecting you is an action father would have felt honoured to do.'

'He is still dead, and the Takeda clan are still shamed,'

Amaya snapped. 'Kyo, I am sorry.' Guilt immediately churned in her chest. 'The histories are still so fragmented and what remains is unclear.'

'But you, the Prophet, are alive. This is wonderful, Amaya,' Kyo beamed at her. 'With this, think about what you can achieve. If you are a Prophet of Ueten, your voice in the Court will surely be heard. You have a destiny, Amaya. Father gave everything to uncover this and that is no waste.'

'I must retreat into my thoughts. I have learned a great deal and my ancestry is clearly connected; it seems the Takeda clan is uniquely bonded to this legend. We are all taught that Spirits create balance, there are those that encourage light and those that encourage darkness.' Amaya felt as though her mind was being tossed about as she churned through the years of reading the Reams of the Old Faith. 'Prophets. Gifts. Spirits. It is all beyond the world we live in. I will not be so arrogant to believe I am a Prophet.'

'Arrogance? That is not the message here, Amaya. You pray continuously to your father, to your ancestors. Do you not believe in the spirits you pray to?' Megumi said.

Amaya started. 'No, I believe my prayers are heard. I believe completely.'

'Why believe in some Spirits but not others?' Megumi continued. 'It is not arrogance, it is duty.'

Amaya frowned.

'Hold your judgement until you are certain of your beliefs and understanding,' Megumi interrupted. 'Do not dismiss this, but do not rush yourself either. Half-hearted belief is not belief at all.'

Amaya shook her head. 'I will do as you have suggested. I will also speak with Kannushi Masato in more detail. A priest should help me find an answer to this. They are learned in the Ways of the Spirits, both the Old and the New. Thank you.' Amaya bowed. Her mind was still in upheaval, but she had a direction now, her mother had given her that.

'What else have you been doing in the palace?' Megumi

asked, her eyes studying her daughter, her look lingered on the healing cut upon Amaya's hairline.

Amaya paused, but only for a moment. 'Well, I am to arrange this year's hanabi festival as you know.' Amaya nodded, her eyebrows raised. She had no desire to concern her mother about what had occurred.

Kyo clapped his hands together. 'I cannot wait to see them. I love fireworks.'

The morning went far too quickly. Amaya wanted to stay longer but as soon as Kyo had given her his most recent haiku to read and Megumi had fed her breakfast, Amaya bade them farewell. The return to the palace felt slower. She slid the scroll of the Old Faith beneath one of her long sleeves and continued towards the shrine, where she hoped Kannushi Masato would be. It was still early but a few Court Officials were striding to and from the various outbuildings. Her gait faltered; at the far end of the main path she saw Shun Kimura in conversation with his father. They were too distant for her to either hear them or make out their faces clearly, but she knew it was them. Shun's tall, broad frame was especially difficult to mistake. A tremble slithered up her arm and over her shoulder as she stared. Another younger man joined them, but Amaya veered from the walkway not wanting to look at Rai a moment longer than she had to. She turned her head, the copse of trees before her; the flat, wide path meandering lazily through it.

She hesitated as she approached. The previous evening's events flickered across her vision. The red canopy threw sanguine shadows all about her, and she could see echoes of the attack amidst the slender trunks.

'Stop being such a child,' she muttered to herself, stepping into the woodland.

'You have every right to feel anxious, Lady Takeda.'

Amaya gave a small shout. 'Lord Izumi!'

Akio bowed. 'I am sorry, I surprised you. I thought you had heard me calling your name.'

Amaya held a hand to her chest, returning the bow. 'I'm sorry, no.'

'Thinking too much by the look of that frown.'

'Nothing in particular.' She touched her forehead absentmindedly, rubbing between her eyes.

'I am going to the shrine. Let's walk together.' Akio smiled at her.

Amaya inclined her head politely, grateful for his care.

She hadn't even realised that they had left the copse until they had reached the top of the stone steps. They approached the Temizuya basin.

'Let me help you,' Akio offered.

Amaya's arm was stiff, and handling the ladles was proving a challenge. 'Thank you, Lord Izumi.'

He gently poured warm water over her hands, followed by his own. He rinsed out his own mouth and half-turned in Amaya's direction.

'I can manage, if you just pour a little in here.' She cupped her hands, and Akio filled them with water. She sipped the water from her hand, but a small trickle had found its way down her chin and onto her neck. She patted her sides in search of her hand cloth.

'Here.' Akio untied the sash about his middle and held it out to Amaya. 'I seem to have misplaced my hand cloth too but please use this.' Akio's apologetic grin covered his face. Amaya looked at the sash he offered as a replacement. The black silk seemed almost silver in the morning glow, and the falling autumn leaves were embroidered in golden thread, each dancing with the next in a strange animation that Amaya had not seen on any other garment before.

'That is far too beautiful,' she protested, dabbing her chin and neck with the end of her sleeve. 'Thank you, Lord Izumi.'

'I really would not have minded,' he replied, retying the fabric around his waist. The ends wrapped about each other in the wind that flurried around the shrine.

Amaya bowed. 'I know, and I thank you. Where is it from? I haven't seen needlework quite like it.'

'My mother made it for me when I was born. It has autumn leaves because of my name. She was from the Air Province originally.'

'Of course, the Air Province is known for fine clothing and adornments.'

'Lord Izumi, Lady Amaya.' Kannushi Masato had appeared from the gardens behind the shrine. 'I thought I heard you.' Beside him stood Kenta.

'Quite excellent hearing you have.' Akio laughed. 'Kenta.' He bowed to his best friend.

'Age has not robbed me of my senses yet,' Kannushi Masato retorted, cheerfully.

Kenta strode forward to greet both Amaya and Akio. 'How are you feeling? How is your arm and head?' He asked.

'Still sore, but the doctor treated me very well. I think I will be almost as good as new come the firework festival.'

'Good, good. Now, I know why Lady Amaya is here, but what about you, young man?' Kannushi Masato looked to Akio.

'Ah, yes. Well, I was looking for Kenta. Are you still planning to gather the Six Ministries after the firework festival?'

'Yes, I am here to tell Kannushi Masato of it myself, and to pray of course,' he added.

'Another meeting so soon after the last,' the old priest hummed despondently.

Akio frowned; his handsome face unusually serious. 'News came from the Air Province. The rebel army are increasingly restless. It seems that the Earth Province has been infiltrated. Rikujou is falling slowly under their control.'

Kannushi Masato drew in a breath. 'The last time things were this dire even the Kusamachi Battalion were sent north. Will Shun return to the camp in the Earth Province?'

'I should think so. I do not know why Rai called him

back, but the army needs their General,' Kenta replied.

'And he is a good one,' Kannushi Masato added.

Akio and Kenta nodded in agreement.

'Shun is not much like his father, is he?' Amaya spoke up.

'No, he isn't,' Akio replied with a shake of his head.

'Quite a different specimen. Now, Lady Amaya, you have my scroll do you not?' Kannushi Masato gave a wicked smile.

Amaya paused, her eyes immediately going to Akio and Kenta, both were looking curiously at her. 'Yes, I do.'

'I see you have been thinking about it. I am glad.' He held out his hand. Amaya reluctantly allowed the scroll to slide from her sleeve into her hand.

'That is the scroll of Ueten and Gekai,' Akio said, his eyes widening. 'Our favourite creation story of the Old Faith.' He glanced at Kenta. 'Your mother used to tell it to us.'

'I have not seen that scripture since Kazu was still in the Archives. You've had it all this time, Kannushi Masato?' Kenta commented, brushing his fingers across it.

'Lord Kazu wanted me to keep it until Amaya was ready to read it.'

'The burden has been lifted. It is passed time Amaya was made aware of this history.' Akio's voice seemed to resonate a calm. 'I never knew the extent of it all, but Kazu ensured I knew enough.'

'It is why Kazu made you the Secretariat, Akio. He wished you to investigate and protect the Archives.' Kannushi Masato replied. 'He knew there were no better hands to leave the history of our land in.'

Amaya walked the few steps towards the priest and handed him the rolled parchment. The paper was covered in fine lines from years of use, and it was strangely soft to the touch, like an aged person's skin. She stared at it for a moment.

'And, what are your thoughts, Lady Amaya?'

Again, she glanced back at the two before continuing. 'I

spoke with my mother and brother. They were illuminating. My mother was relieved to discuss this with me.'

Kannushi Masato grinned. 'Your father believed you are the Prophet. I suppose Megumi confirmed that.'

Amaya nodded slowly, the feeling of being in the dark growing with each word that passed the old priest's lips. 'Yes. It seems it has long been believed by the Takeda clan.'

'What is the Takeda's connection exactly?' Akio questioned.

'That Lord Minamori's sister's married name was Takeda.'

'She is your ancestor,' Kenta breathed. 'So much of your father's research and dedication is clear now.'

'What did your mother say to you?' Kannushi Masato spoke over her doubt.

'She asked if I believed in the Spirits I pray to, and those I pray for.'

'Your answer?' Kannushi Masato seemed to already know, however.

'I said yes.'

'Why believe in one spirit and not another?' Kannushi Masato said, unknowingly echoing Amaya's mother.

'You are as unique as your father claimed. Perhaps that is why he showed me the Ancient Scriptures all those years ago.' Akio was marvelling at her.

'Amaya, this is a wondrous thing.' Kenta seemed as happy as Akio.

'My father had entrusted you with this knowledge. Parts of it, at least. You have always believed?' She asked of them both.

'It is as Kannushi Masato said: why believe in one spirit and not another. Lady Takeda, you have been given a truly clear voice. Use it.'

Amaya bit her lip, her eyes flitting between the priest, Kenta and Akio: the man whose opinion she respected above all others'. 'I want to believe it.'

'The moment you find faith in yourself, that belief will come naturally. The rest will follow,' Kannushi Masato said, sagely.

It was the day before the hanabi festival, but Amaya felt numb to the nerves which seemed to be infecting the rest of the servants. She expected her nerves at any moment, and so, when Kenta requested her company, she gratefully accepted the distraction.

'I do not care what people say, I want to sit outside. It is one of the few warmer days remaining. Winter's black stare is making autumn chilly,' Kenta said, stepping from the veranda into the satsuki garden.

Amaya laughed. 'Very well. Where do you propose we do our work?'

'Work? Amaya, it is the day before the hanabi festival. You have been working very hard. I do not intend to work. How about some poetry?'

Amaya looked about. 'Don't you have the meeting to prepare for? I would be happy to help.'

A small grin twitched the corners of his mouth. 'No. I will continue once the hanabi festival has concluded. Here is secluded enough. No scampering Court Officials around.' Kenta pointed to the huge pond. Stretched out across it was a pontoon. The wooden causeway reached the centre of the placid water, a little four-pillared belvedere sat at the end providing shade. Kenta led the way, and Amaya followed glancing behind her as they neared the low chairs beneath the tapered roof. His Censorate retainers were detectable in the shadows of the garden. They all halted at the entrance to the pontoon, barring access. Kenta took a seat, and Amaya could see his tiredness at once, he melted with rest as he reclined into the cushions and blankets.

'Please could you read me some poetry, Amaya?'

Amaya was half-inclined to say that the Emperor didn't need to say please. 'Of course.'

Leaf flutes, reeds and water hum
Together with natures drum.
Beside me a sigh.
A breath far shorter still
Disturbs my transient sleep.

'Your own work?' Kenta murmured, his eyes closed.
'No, not mine. My younger brother, Kyo's.'
'What talent he has.' Kenta's voice was quieter still. 'Please, recite more of his work. I am already a fan.'
Amaya smiled at Kenta's request.

Sakura sweet and plum bright.
As petals tumble
A hawk teases the sun.
Wing and feather bearing my thoughts
As I think of you.

'Quite beautiful.' A quiet voice punctuated the end of the receital.
Amaya looked up but it was not Kenta who had spoken. Her eyes found a skeletal old man standing close by. His hands were clasped behind his back, his eyes shining. 'I have not seen him so rested in many months. You must be very good company for Lord Kenta.'
His face drooped, skin sagged from pointed cheekbones and from his prominent brow. Even his mustache seemed to droop, framing his little smile. Each fold of skin was a page to the book that was his face. Different expressions played across it often, Amaya thought. The wisps of pale grey hair seemed to crown him in a soft cloud. He stood beside Amaya and continued to watch Kenta's sleeping face. Amaya didn't speak for a moment; the man was gazing at Kenta with such tenderness she did not want to disturb him.
He sighed and turned to Amaya. 'You are quite like your mother to look at, but Kazu shines in your eyes, very strongly.

Yes, you are Kazu Takeda's daughter.'

Amaya opened her mouth, then closed it again, unsure of how to respond. Instead, the man's smile became even broader and he let out a short, amused laugh. 'Kazu pulled that same face the day I offered him the position of Secretariat.' He moved closer to Amaya. 'I am Hiroshi Katou, Advisor to the Emperor, I have just this morning returned from my travels.'

Amaya rose to her feet and bowed very low. 'I apologise, Lord Katou. I have not had the pleasure of meeting you in person. Please forgive my rudeness.' Amaya felt ashamed. This man was the longest serving Court Official, Akio had told her that.

'No matter, no matter, Lady Takeda. I am just an old man.' He bounced on the balls of his feet, his hands still clutched behind his back. 'I remember seeing you on several occasions, from a distance of course, and your father often spoke of you. You have grown up considerably, but I knew your face at once.'

Again, Amaya was unsure how to respond.

'You seem to be a soothing companion for His Majesty,' Hiroshi began again. 'I recognised something different in him. You must have instigated the change. I thank you for that, Lady Takeda.'

'Oh, I do not think I am responsible for any change in Kenta.'

Hiroshi smiled slightly at her informality. 'I believe so. He had been a phantom of the Kenta I knew for some time.' A shadow of sadness swept briefly over Hiroshi's face, a genuine sorrow.

'He has been trying so very hard. He is already becoming an innovative and brilliant ruler, as those bestowed with the Divine Right to Rule are. He will help Akegata find its feet again, I am certain of it. I just hope I can aid in any way I can.'

'You already are, Lady Takeda.' Hiroshi paused and looked from Kenta to Amaya. 'I hear your father's suspicions have proven accurate. I never knew the man to be wrong, and you are no exception, I see.'

'You are referring to the Old Faith and the tale of Ueten and Gekai.'

He nodded once. 'The very same. Such an old story passed from one generation to the next for centuries. No one truly knows its origins, but it is one of the pillars of the Old Faith, of the Takeda clan and the Divine Right to Rule.'

'Are you a holy man?' Amaya questioned.

'Aren't we all to some extent? Even those who claim they have renounced the Way of the Spirits, pray to them in times of need. Belief and faith share many similarities. A broken world needs a Prophet of purity.' Lord Hiroshi repeated, giving Amaya a wry smile. 'Even a reluctant one.'

'Would you like some tea, Lord Katou?' Amaya asked.

'Yes, that would be perfect. I can smell that it is Oolong. My favourite tea from across the sea.'

Amaya poured two cups and handed one to the Advisor gently before taking her seat. 'Did my father speak to you often about the Old Faith?'

Lord Hiroshi nodded as he sipped the earthy liquid. 'Yes. His capacity for belief is unparalleled. Well, unparalleled by many. Sen Sanjo is another person who found a certain strength behind his belief.'

Amaya frowned, disliking her father being likened to such a heinous being.

'Do not fret, Lady Takeda. Belief is as varied as the ones who hold it, or the Prophets that manifest from it.'

'Manifest.'

The elderly man tilted his head to one side thoughtfully. 'Belief takes root and events bloom soon after, whether manmade or Sprit-made.'

Amaya wondered if she could be an example of such an occurrence. An affinity for Ueten had bloomed within her, or so her father believed. Could it be as simple as embodying qualities needed at certain times? 'Another cup?' Amaya offered Lord Hiroshi the tea whilst considerations traipsed through her mind.

'No, no. Thank you. However, I do have matters to discuss with Kenta when he wakes. You are perfectly welcome to stay but at present he would not offer the most animated conversation. Perhaps he will develop a talent for catching flies,' Lord Hiroshi said, a humorous glint in his wise eyes. Amaya held her hand to her mouth as she laughed. Kenta stirred and closed his mouth in his sleep as if in protest to Hiroshi's jest.

The old advisor sat beside Amaya, cross-legged. She thought him incredibly agile for someone so old.

He spoke again. 'Please, I am sure you have other matters of your own. The hanabi festival, for one. I will stay with His Majesty and explain your absence.'

Amaya looked at Kenta again. She had no urge to leave him but the thought of Ueten crept into her mind. 'Then I shall take my leave. Please inform His Majesty.'

'That you had much more important things to be doing than watch him sleep.' Hiroshi finished for her cheerfully. 'Will you hear an old man's advice?'

Amaya paused; half-risen from her seat. 'I would be happy to, Lord Katou. You are the advisor after all.'

Hiroshi laughed. 'Quite right. I happen to be quite good at advising or so His Majesty says. I want you to not worry about Kenta; your face is marred with distress. As you have probably begun to see, Kenta is a strong individual. Simply continue to be the way you are with him. With support like you and Lord Akio, well, His Majesty is in very good company. He will not go astray, as his father did.' Hiroshi sighed, more deeply this time. 'I will not fail Kenta, as I did Kado.'

'Please let me offer my own advice, Lord Katou,' Amaya said, softly and without trepidation. 'You did nothing wrong by Kado Yamashima. I will not pretend to know the intricacies, but I do know that it was through no one's fault but his own that Kado Yamashima failed Akegata. It was his own ears that were closed to the help offered him, and it was he himself who put his trust in those he shouldn't have. I pity him. I am happy to have finally met you, Lord Katou.' Amaya bowed low again and looked into Hiroshi's slightly surprised eyes.

He was silent for a moment before giving a convivial grin. 'Yes, you are most certainly Lord Kazu's girl.'

The day of the hanabi festival arrived too soon for Amaya. However, words of comfort and reassurance helped her stay the impending nerves.

'Go and sit somewhere quiet, Lady Amaya. I will see that the final inspections are carried out. Lady Megumi and your brother, Kyo, will arrive shortly. You do not want them to see you so irate,' Akio implored.

'Please, Amaya. I want you to enjoy this event as much as the rest of us.' Kenta spoke, in agreement with Akio, chivying her away.

'Very well.' Amaya grinned and bowed low, but as she stepped onto the large pathway she did not know where to go. An offer Kenta had once made broke through her chaotic thoughts. She hadn't visited the Imperial dojo for the entire two months she had been working in the palace. She had her father's dojo but she supposed that the palace dojo was also her father's. It was where he would have trained the samurai, instructing them in the Seishin no Ken technique. An odd urgency stole over her legs and her pace quickened. The garden she entered was home to a wonderful variety of plants, none of which she had in her own estate. Shallow, wide steps led away to where she knew the dojo nestled. Several small ponds dotted the area, to the left and right, and she could smell the reedy water distinctly. The trees that fringed them stretched out, their branches casting mottled shade along the bank. The twisting trunks were black against the vivid orange of their leaves, a few of which would occasionally fall to the ground, their descent slow and somehow purposeful. Amaya held out her hand, and one settled in her palm. She stared at it for a moment.

Holding the leaf by its stem, she continued on her way,

climbing the steps until they ended, and the dojo appeared. The wood was a deep, rich brown, which seemed almost red in the autumn surroundings. However, as she approached the building, the silence of the woodland was disturbed by the clash of metal. She reached the entrance. The door was slid halfway open, and the sounds of practice were now crisp. She closed her eyes and listened to the sighs of the katana as they cut the air, and the ring as they collided again and again. The song within the dojo was her most favourite. The twang of a Shamisen or a Komuso monk's shakuhachi flute, which sounded like nature itself, could not compete. Even the Uguisu bird, with its mellifluous announcement of spring could not triumph over the melody of two katana.

Amaya peered around the door frame. Two men faced each other, their profiles in shadow and their katana raised. Amaya recognised the stance, it was from the Seishin no Ken style. As the two men moved towards each other, light fell across them. Shun Kimura's face was as serious as ever, but a focus Amaya had yet to perceive filled his eyes. His long hair swished in the wake of his movements but his height and size did not hinder his grace, which saturated each swing and step he made. He swayed to the katana's tune with finesse. Amaya's eyes brimmed, catching her unawares. Shun moved exactly the way her father did, and now she understood her father's choice to make Shun the Master of the Sky Province.

She almost forgot that there was another in the dojo until he entered her vision. She swallowed back her poignant nostalgia and watched; never had she seen a man so handsome. He reminded her of paintings she had seen in some of her parents' novels, or illustrations of the Spirits in the Reams or Lotus Scroll. He wasn't as broad as Shun, but lean, and his hair was a little shorter too, tied back in a low ponytail. His jaw was uncommonly shaded with stubble, giving his grin a roguish glint. His eyes were harder, bird-like. She did not know him. His movements were as different to Shun's as his looks. Where Shun flowed, the other man sprang nimbly, his movements energetic. Where Shun danced with his katana, the second man played with his. The spar was fascinating to behold; two such different methods but both in the same technique. Amaya watched a while longer, until the two men began to bring their session to an end. Slowly, she slipped away, the sound of the katana still in her echoing in her ears.

The noise of the crowd lining the streets beyond the palace gates reached Amaya before she saw the throng. She stared between the gate's columns. 'So many,' she said to Akio, who stood beside her. She wondered if her mother and brother would be able to make their way through the teeming rabble. The evening was already consuming the afternoon. Amaya lifted her gaze. The land beyond the capital's distant wall was peaked with the mountains of the southern Fire Province. On the horizon, pink was bleeding into orange, orange bleeding into blue, blue fading darker and darker.

'Beautiful isn't it?' Akio commented as he stared beyond the city. 'I am originally from the Fire Province. Kasaichi is my father's home city.' His face glowed bronze with the waning sun, his irises a deep amber, the pupils mere dots.

'Do you miss it?' Amaya questioned.

Akio shrugged, his hand resting on the hilt of his katana casually. 'Yes, but I visit often. One of my oldest friends still lives there.'

'I thought Kenta was your oldest friend?'

'He and one other, Shin Nakamura. I have mentioned him before. The three of us spent a lot of time together when we were boys. Then Shin married Emi Shimizu of the Fire Province. She was not the reason he left though; he is the Governor of the Fire Province.'

'That is quite the title. The Fire Province is the second most powerful province in Akegata.'

'That is why Kenta appointed him the Feudal Lord of that province, to maintain an imperial-friendly presence in the south. The army of the Fire Province is also mighty and loyal to the Nakamura clan. It was sense. Parting with Shin was difficult but it was the safest decision.'

'I hope to meet him one day,' Amaya replied.

Akio faced her. 'You are in luck; Shin is attending the festival. His wife is also joining him. I think you and Emi will get along very well.'

Amaya grinned, thinking of the possibility of making a new friend. 'I should like to meet them both. I can discover some things about you as child.'

Akio threw his head back in mock exasperation. 'Kenta has told you enough.'

'I am sure Lord Nakamura will have even more tales.' She raised her eyebrows.

'Yes. Yes, I'm sure he will.' Akio gestured ahead. 'Your guests have arrived.'

Amaya followed Akio's outstretched hand. A palanquin had emerged from the heaving street and the palace guards parted, allowing them through. They turned back to face the crowd, but nobody tried to force their way in, they were all too engrossed with the festivities which lined the streets. She spied Kyo striding alongside the litter, chatting to the men who carried it. Her brother seemed taller; his face more mature. His hair was longer too, and Amaya began to wonder how much she had been preoccupied with her new life. She hadn't stayed in her own estate for the weeks and her time had bbeen consumed by the preparations for the hanabi festival. Walking forward to greet them, Kyo bowed to her, his face filled with affection. Her mother stepped out from the palanquin, her feet light, then she took Amaya's hands in her own.

'We are honoured to be invited into the palace,' Megumi said, looking up at Akio and bowing. 'It has been a long time since I was here, and Kyo has never been before.'

Kyo wasn't listening. His eyes were roving, his hands grasping one another in eagerness.

'Lady Megumi.' Akio bowed. 'I am glad to meet you again.'

'And I you. I hope my daughter has been a help.'

'Lady Amaya has proven invaluable. Her work has not gone unnoticed,' Akio grinned, which caused Amaya's cheeks to warm.

'I have merely followed instructions and attempted to perform to the best of my abilities.'

Megumi raised an eyebrow. 'Then the festival will be spectacular.'

The group moved away from the main gate, Akio leading the way with Kyo by his side.

Megumi linked her arm through Amaya's. 'The palace really is lovely. It brings many fond memories for me. I feel that nothing has changed since I came here last.'

'Nothing?'

'Well, perhaps a few things.' She looked at Akio pointedly before whispering. 'He will be important to Akegata's survival of the civil war.'

Amaya was unsure how to respond. 'Lord Izumi is a genius, and Kenta's best friend. With a pair such as them, Akegata will weather this.'

'They have you by their side also.' Megumi's confidence added a weight to Amaya's thoughts, but it was not an uncomfortable weight, she felt oddly bolstered by it.

'Lady Megumi Takeda?'

The four turned at the voice. 'Lord Hiroshi Katou.' Megumi bowed low, Hiroshi doing the same.

'You have not changed,' Hiroshi commented, joining them. 'This must be your youngest.' He indicated to Kyo. 'The poet.'

Amaya drew in a breath of pride as her younger brother bowed and offered a polite welcome. 'I am honoured to meet the Emperor's advisor.'

'I understand you have a love of poetry. I was lucky enough to hear your sister recite some of your work. Stunning. Would you permit me to recite some of my own? I could do with a discerning ear.'

For the rest of the journey to the main garden, where the fireworks would be viewed from, Kyo did not leave Hiroshi's side. Despite knowing them both, she was still surprised to see her brother take so quickly to another.

'Mother, I am afraid I will have to leave you during the festival. I am to oversee everything.'

Megumi waved the apology away with a swish of her fan, placing an arm about her daughter. 'I knew that you would be busy but do try and take a moment to enjoy it yourself. Come find us when the fireworks have ended. There is so much to see and do.' She looked at the space around them. The many stands displayed fresh foods or Sake from the mountain villages. Bright toys covered other stalls, and the rest had games with prizes ready to be won. Kyo had already commandeered Hiroshi and Akio, and the three were approaching the nearest vendor selling yakitori. Amaya could smell the tangy sauce from where she stood.

She laughed. 'I will find you all, mother. Make sure you enjoy yourselves too.' With gentle bow, she left her mother and Kyo with Akio and Hiroshi.

Kannushi Masato had done as he had promised and set a boundary around the fireworks. Only those lighting them were present, the court officials and visiting governors were safely in the same garden her family were in. Amaya felt excitement despite herself as she paced the rows of fireworks, counting them. It was finally dark enough, and deciding to stand on the veranda, which skirted the main garden, she left the servants with the instruction to follow Kannushi Masato's signal as arranged.

The rouge garden was filled with an amalgamation of taiko drumming, shakuhachi flutes, bells, shamisen, chanting, smells both bitter and sweet, hazy incense, and the rise and fall of happy shouts. Amaya lingered on the edge of the veranda and surveyed the scene. The noble families were all present, and she silently recited each of the names as she saw their kamons embroidered on their varied garments. The Tozen clan of the Air Province, the Ka clan, the powerful Kimura clan, the Izumi of the Fire. Anger stirred deep in her chest as she watched them. The Takeda clan had been chief amongst them once, before Rai Kimura brought them to their knees. She glanced down at herself and rolled her eyes. Her dark green kimono, although elegant in its looseness, was perhaps too simple for such an occasion, but she did not have time to change. She reached up to touch her hair. It, at least, was appropriate in its refinement. She had strategically placed the tiny flowers throughout her combed and pinned hair and had fixed ivory grips to the two buns atop her head.

As she scanned the milling crowd, a new nervousness stole over her, preventing her feet from moving and joining the merriment. She inwardly chastised herself for being so foolish but still her feet would not move. Her fists clenched in annoyance and shifted forward a little, but as she did so Rai Kimura stepped up beside her, accompanied by another man. She almost toppled from the ledge.

'It is a wise idea, Lady Takeda, to remain on the veranda. You can best survey the festivities from here. No need to concern yourself with the noble families. You do not want to make people uncomfortable after all of your hard work.' Rai laughed a little. His guffaw was echoed by the man next to him.

Amaya knew his face. It was not one she would forget; it was the beautiful man she had seen sparring with Shun in the dojo. He returned her stare.

'This is my second son, Daiki Kimura.'

'Lady Takeda,' Daiki said, his voice dripping with false courtesy. 'It really is a pleasure to meet you.' He gave her a wicked smile, his eyes briefly flitting to his father.

Amaya swallowed. Like Shun, Daiki did not resemble Rai. Yet he looked nothing like Shun either. She pondered briefly on what their mother must look like. However, the more she scrutinised Daiki, the more she saw an ingrained resentment. At who, she could not be sure, but it was present.

His eyes had a nonchalance about them that incited immediate dislike, and his tone only served to augment her growing animosity. She was saddened that it had been this man who had performed the Seishin no Ken so uniquely.

'It is a pleasure to meet you too, Lord Daiki. I am afraid your father has never mentioned you.'

Daiki's smile faltered and he straightened up, his eyebrows raised as he gazed at the crowd. His hand rested on the hilt of his katana. Amaya fidgeted uncomfortably, wishing Rai and his son would leave her be. The laughter of her clan's humiliation suddenly clamoured loudly in her ears. She winced with the memory, and her thoughts started to slip gradually to her father and the night she had witnessed Rai Kimura murder him.

Before any of them could speak, three women passed them by, making their way toward the centre of the party. They moved with small light footsteps, as a nobleman's daughter would. Their feet shuffling along almost timidly. However, their eyes never ceased moving as they scoured the people. Occasionally, one would laugh at something the other said, but Amaya knew the conversation was a mask. Each one was wearing a kimono with long sleeves. *Unmarried*, Amaya rolled her eyes in annoyance, not wishing to observe them any longer. Before she could turn away from the new source of irritation, one of them saw Daiki and shamelessly elbowed her fellows. In unison, the girls opened their fans and giggled behind them, scurrying away, the chimes in their hair clinking with each step. Amaya clicked her tongue loudly in disproval, forgetting herself.

Daiki seemed amused by it. 'Will you accompany me around the festival, Lady Takeda?'

Amaya stiffened. 'I would much rather observe from here. Thank you, Lord Daiki.'

'Lady Takeda. You cannot deny my son. It will be good for the Takeda to be seen with the Kimura clan in such a social setting.'

Amaya drew an indignant breath but swallowed the words she desperately wanted to shout at him. 'Very well, Lord Daiki.'

'Daiki will be sufficient,' he said, ostentatiously offering her his arm.

'I can walk perfectly well, Lord Daiki,' she said, ignoring his arm and stepping into the glow of the many paper lanterns.

The smell of Sake grew stronger as the men drank more and more, but it was infused with the scent of steaming nikuman buns, okonomiyaki, skewered fish sizzling over one of the many small fire pits, the sticky smell of dango, and fresh rice cakes covered in azuki bean paste or walnut sauce. Amaya's stomach came alive in a matter of moments.

'Amaya.' Daiki broke her hunger-induced reverie. She flushed at being addressed so casually. Between his thumb and index finger he held a stick of yakitori. The grilled chicken glistened and, despite herself, she took it from him.

'Thank you, Lord Daiki.' Amaya watched as he grabbed two small cups of Sake but took no food for himself. 'Are you not hungry?'

Daiki shook his head and sipped his drink. 'I had a hearty lunch. A pity, all this food looks wonderful.' He turned, his devilish eyes seeking out hers. 'Here.' Daiki placed the second cup of Sake in her hand. She recoiled at his touch.

The two continued along the path for a time, weaving around gossiping women, rowdy, off-duty samurai and the stoic on-duty ones. Excitable children in their tiny kimonos and hakama trousers flittered across the path, their little sandaled feet embuing the air with energy. Several times Amaya spied Imperial guards or Censorate members, and wondered where Kenta, Akio and her family were, but she hadn't seen any familiar faces. She continued to gaze around in the hopes of finding them.

'You are a silent woman, Amaya,' Daiki commented, his grin widening. 'It shows you understand your place.'

Amaya couldn't be sure if Daiki was trying to rile her, or

if he genuinely believed his words.

'And what place would that be, Lord Daiki?'

He considered her for a moment before replying. 'Why, supporting her husband, or father, or elder brother. Whoever is the head of the family. That support should be given silently, demurely and obediently.'

'I have no such person,' Amaya said, without looking away from the jovial crowd.

'So I hear,' Daiki replied quietly, sipping his drink. 'I also hear you are not particularly demure or obedient. That kind of behaviour would ruin the reputation of a respectful clan. Personally, I like a woman with such fire, but I also like a smart woman. A smart woman knows when to be demure and when to be impassioned.' Daiki stepped closer to her.

Amaya slid her feet across the ground, keeping distance between them. The movement brought the two to an abrupt halt. She opened her mouth to argue, but a hand found her elbow and three people stepped up beside her. She blinked at the newcomers.

'Lady Takeda, Lord Daiki. I trust you are enjoying the festivities.'

'Lord Izumi.' Daiki bowed his head. 'Lord and Lady Nakamura.'

Akio smiled. 'I am sorry to call you away from such lovely company, Lord Daiki, but you are needed in the guard house. Your father has requested you. I hope you do not mind my intrusion, Lady Takeda?'

Amaya wanted to sing. 'Not at all, Lord Izumi.'

Bowing low, Daiki took her hand in a showy fashion, causing a few of the nearest girls to titter. 'It has been most enlightening. Thank you for accompanying me, Lady Takeda.' He departed, vanishing into the red light and tipsy crowd.

'Terrible?' Akio asked, studying her face.

Amaya sighed. 'I would expect nothing less from Rai Kimura's son.'

Akio laughed. 'I would have come sooner, but Kenta

and myself were detained. He is sad that he cannot join you himself. He has to enjoy the fireworks from his private balcony.'

'It would be nice if we could all walk together,' Amaya said, watching two children playing with their new kendama. 'Can we not join him? Is he alone?'

Akio shook his head. 'His retainers are with him. Hiroshi too, with Kyo and your mother.'

'Kyo is meeting Kenta!?' Amaya held her hands up to her chest. 'I am so happy.'

'I thought you would be, but now I would like to introduce you to someone.' Akio held his hands up, presenting the two that had arrived with him. 'This is my dear friend Shin Nakamura and his wife Lady Emi. They are the two who keep the south of Akegata safe for Kenta.'

Amaya bowed low, her hands pressed against her thighs. 'It is a pleasure to meet you both.'

'It is our pleasure also, Lady Takeda. We have heard so much about you. From your father and from Akio.' Shin glanced at his friend. The smile he wore made his angular face seem softer. His eyes were carved atop wide reaching cheekbones, and his hair was as angular as his face, the fringe blunt and the ponytail neat and straight, falling between his shoulder blades.

'I have been wanting to meet you for the past two months, Lady Takeda.' It was Emi who spoke now. She stepped forward and took Amaya's hand in an unusual gesture of closeness. Her face was like a droplet of water, and her bobbed hair framed it well. Her eyes were two crescent moons resting upon her plump little cheeks.

'Lord Izumi has told me that we would get on well.' Amaya grinned, returning Emi's affection without shyness. As Emi gripped her hands, Amaya realised that her mother was her only female companion, and had been all her life. The realisation brought with it a peculiar longing, which she hadn't known she'd harboured.

'Lord Izumi? Address him as Akio. He would like that.' Emi shot Akio an amused glance.

Amaya felt her own eyes widen but, rather than embarrassment, a laugh broke free. 'Well, perhaps I will.'

Akio looked to Shin, seeking support from his childhood friend. 'I have missed your wife, Shin.'

Shin nodded. 'Lady Takeda, you will have to exercise patience. Emi has a wicked humour about her.'

'It is why he loves me so,' Emi whispered, loudly. Amaya stared incredulously at the young woman. Her spirit was so potent, contagious.

'I cannot argue with that,' Shin said, in resignation.

Emi and Amaya flinched as the first series of fireworks were set off. Blue chased the red of the festival lights away for a brief moment, bathing the four in a watery glow as the fire flowers burst across the dusk. Emi laughed, pointing at herself and Amaya, her words lost amidst the volley of bangs and crackles. She turned to her husband and stepped near to him. Amaya felt her chest tighten as she watched Shin secretly slip his hand around Emi's.

'It has only just started and it is already wonderful,' Akio commented, his face upturned, a rainbow of lights playing across it.

'Thank you, Akio.' Amaya looked intently at the fireworks, hoping that her embarrassment at using his name was hidden by the flickering sky. Akio moved ever so slightly beside her but did not speak.

The end of the display was approaching, and Amaya could feel the sense of relief within her grasp. She looked about the crowd, but her eyes were quickly drawn toward the city. A thick column of smoke rose like a writhing, grey dragon into the sky. The early moon's light was trapped in the billows, and a fierce orange lit the dark smog from below. *A fire?* Amaya pondered, her eyes shrinking with the effort to see.

'Lady Takeda. I am sorry for the disturbance.' The female servant bowed at right angles, clearly nervous, her eyes flitting between Amaya to Akio. With shaking hands, she conveyed her message.

Amaya's hand flew to her mouth as she struggled to reply. 'Fetch my mother and brother. Please. They are with His Majesty,' she asked of the servant.

Akio opened his mouth to speak but Amaya had already started running. She could hear him behind her as she weaved between the laughing crowd, muttering apologies as she knocked a few to the side. Once on the veranda, Amaya was able to increase her pace. She hurried, cursing her kimono, hitching it up as best she could.

The main steps stretched out left and right and flowed down in ripples of stone to the expansive path. Running down them as fast as she dared, she felt the elaborate hairpins and decorations shift and slip from her hair. She passed Shun, who was walking up towards the palace. He opened his mouth in speech but she hurtled past, tears leaking from the corners of her eyes.

'Lady Takeda?' He stopped and Amaya heard him confront Akio. 'What has happened, Lord Izumi?'

Akio shouted over his shoulder as he continued his pursuit. 'Her father's dojo has gone up in flames.'

The sound of the city folk chattering and squawking their dismay was distant to her. Even in the street the smoke was heavy. Amaya pushed through the growing swarm of people and stepped through the large wooden gate to her estate. The heat washed over her skin. She looked at the glorious garden, it was choking in the smoke which poured from the dojo just out of sight.

'No!' Amaya stumbled as she ran forward in desperation.

'We have water! The rest are coming behind me now!' a man shouted out somewhere beyond Amaya's vision.

The dojo gave a mighty crack as the wood began to weaken and break under the heat. Amaya stumbled under the force of the bang which followed. Thick smoke and flames licked the ground and began to spread up the wooden veranda to the rest of the house.

'I will help you,' Amaya yelled, following the man, desperate.

'Lady Takeda,' Akio said, loudly, but Amaya was deaf to everyone. She rushed forward and snatched the first pail of water from one of the men. More followed, but she took the lead.

'Father!' she cried, launching the water at the dojo. She was pushed back by the wall of heat which seemed to melt the air around her, burning her skin. She threw a hand up to shield her face.

'Amaya! Get back, you will be killed if you get any closer.' Akio ran forward. Abandoning proprieties, he threw his arms around her waist, lifting her up easily and hauling her back. The pail clattered to the floor and she struggled, kicking her legs and pounding at Akio's arms. The smell clogged her nose and throat; burnt wood, charred tatami, crisped paper. Shun had arrived and was standing at the entrance to the garden surveying the scene, a silent watcher, his face severe. Then, with purpose, he sped forward and joined the men from the town. Bucket after bucket he brought forward and emptied upon the raging dojo. He began to carry two at a time and launched them with precision at the most intense blazes.

'Let me go.' Amaya was fiercely angry, and her tears were dark with soot. They fell, like blackened rain, onto Akio's arms. Amaya's resisting subsided as she watched the fire devour her memories hungrily. 'Father,' she whispered, to herself.

The men from the town began to douse the fire. Great sails of steam rose into the air, like gigantic ghosts, as the fire was suffocated of its vicious life. Amaya slumped into Akio's arms and sank to the floor. Her chest heaved as he sat too and held her still. She continued to watch until the dojo was a damp, black heap of charcoal, steaming and creaking in death.

One of the men walked toward them. He removed his conical hat, pulled the makeshift mask from his mouth and looked down at Amaya's upturned face, fixing her with a weathered pair of eyes.

'Thank you. Thank you for all your help,' Amaya said, her voice a croak. She stood but her legs would not support her. Akio stepped closer, so that her back leant against him.

'We are sorry we could not do more, Lady Takeda. Your house, the damage.'

'None of you were injured. Everyone is safe.' Her voice was flat.

The man bowed low and gestured for the others to follow him. Amaya watched them depart, leaving only her, Akio and Shun. Hastily, she wiped her face.

'Amaya!'

She turned at Kyo's voice. He sprinted across the garden tripping over his own feet, his face white. He was shaking his head, looking frantically around.

'Kyo, where's mother?' Amaya said, quietly.

Her brother's lip trembled, and his eyes blinked rapidly. 'She returned home no more than an hour ago. She wanted to watch some of the fireworks from home. That is what she told me.'

Amaya heard no more. Voices and sounds were muted by her terror as she turned her head in the direction of the dojo and strode toward it. Staring hard she scoured the black remains of her father's destroyed legacy. Twice she swept her eyes over the fallen construct, but it was on the third look that her eyes found what she had hoped they would never see.

'Mother.' Amaya stumbled forward; the wood hot beneath her feet.

'Amaya!' Akio yelled.

She stopped and gazed behind. Her brother had collapsed. Shun and Akio were kneeling over him.

'Kyo,' Amaya said, into the smokey air. She turned around and lurched to her brother's side.

'Lord Izumi, my mother.' Was all she could manage of her request. Akio nodded and looked to Shun. The two men moved out of her sight towards the dojo as she and her brother cradled each other.

CHAPTER SIX

The unavoidable truth that she had lost her mother began to gnaw at Amaya that evening as she sat out on the veranda alone, watching the insubstantial clouds crawl across the face of the full moon. The scarlet trees and red pagodas were all the same dense black against the star-lit sky. The sun no longer shone across Chuto, and Amaya felt cold. She wrapped her arms around herself tightly and lonely tears made their way down her cheeks. Unable to stop them, she stared ahead, blinking them free of her eyelashes. The scent of smoke was still heavy in her hair and clinging to the silk of her kimono. She had washed her face and applied new make-up for her journey back to the palace, but now she thought her efforts futile; the tears were mocking her feeble attempt. The happiness that Kyo was alive and safe comforted her but she had lost two very important things. Her home was now an empty house. The dojo, gone. Her mother, like her father, was dead.

'Lady Amaya,' Akio said, quietly, stepping up beside her.

She hurriedly dabbed her eyes on her sleeve as he approached. He lent on the narrow, wooden pillar, which was between himself and Amaya, keeping his face forward. 'You can cry, Amaya. Do not let me stop you. There is no shame in these tears.'

She glanced at him. Her mother had always encouraged composure in a woman.

When Amaya complained to her mother about bettering her own appearance, her mother had countered that make-up was important. 'A woman will not cry when wearing make-up,' Megumi had claimed. 'It has a double purpose: to enhance one's beauty and to shield the lady from showing weakness to those who would seek to exploit it. It is your painted shield. A tool you should use.'

Amaya had argued. 'I never cry. I won't. I will be strong and prove them wrong.'

'Then you had better keep your make-up perfect,' her mother had replied with a smile. 'Amaya, everyone cries.'

At the thought of her mother's words Amaya let the tears fall again. Akio reached around the pillar and placed a hand on her slender shoulder. She didn't care that he could feel her shudders. He stood with her until her eyes were dry and then she allowed him steer her back into her quarters, mute and shivering.

Amaya refilled Kenta's tea cup. It had been a week since the fire and Kyo was recovering slowly. However, Amaya saw the agony her brother was in, despite his efforts to stay brave. His sobs late at night when he thought no one could hear were as harrowing as the dreams of the fire that plagued her own sleep. She battled with sporadic episodes of grief; a feeling she was horribly familiar with. Strangely, tears had not fallen since that first evening when Akio had been with her. Amaya believed it was because she had no more to give. It felt like her heart had hardened a little more, ossified against the pain; finding a new focus in discovering how such a thing had occurred. She had written to her uncle, explaining what had happened. Explaining she knew it was no accident.

'Amaya, will you please sit? Have some tea.'

Amaya jolted, shaking her head as if a fly was bumping against it. Her eyes found Kenta's. 'Yes, thank you, Kenta.'

He moved closer to her, his expression anxious. 'I understand, you know.' His hands found each other and began to writhe in his lap. 'I understand your loss.'

Amaya gulped down the jagged pebble of sadness.

Kenta had never spoken of his mother. 'That is why I feel comfortable with you. I know you can truly sympathise.'

He nodded, glad that she had accepted his words. 'It will be all right, Amaya. Time really does heal.'

Amaya didn't want to argue, or to take Kenta's comfort from him, but she had not forgotten her father's demise, and she knew her mother's would be the same. Both so violent, so unfair. She remained haunted by what she had seen. Suddenly, she realised that Kenta too had not forgotten, nor had it become easier with time as he was claiming. She reached a hand towards him. 'You do not have to uphold this pretense with me. We can speak of these things to each other.'

He stared at her, his frown trying to push away the pain, but it seeped into his kind eyes all the same. 'Thank you, Amaya.'

She was glad for the tool a woman could use; Kenta had no such make-up.

The Emperor straightened. 'I am ashamed that this has happened. First you are attacked, and now your home and family. Will you allow me to repair your estate? It will not replace what you have lost but it will help a little, I hope. Of course, yourself and Kyo will live within the palace now. It is not safe elsewhere. At least I can have my Censorate guards watch over you.'

Amaya bit her lip. 'Kenta, an offer such as that, it may aggravate the situation.'

His face fell a little. 'I thought you would say that, which is why I have employed the local workers where you live to carry out the work on your estate. I remain anonymous, and they are being paid very well. It is selfish of me, but I need to do something.' Kenta's face was fearful.

Amaya didn't voice her discomfort at such a gift and so replied, 'as long as your name is not known. It is not selfish, Kenta. You are being more generous than I can articulate.'

His eyes relaxed onto his cheekbones and he gestured Amaya to take a cup of tea. 'You probably think I am ridiculous.'

'I do not think you're ridiculous. Perhaps silly for risking the accusation of favoritism.' She sipped her tea through a smile as Kenta watched her.

'You are the first person to call me silly. Not even my mother called me silly.'

They laughed into their drinks. It felt oddly foreign to laugh, but Amaya was glad of it.

'Your mother must have been a very patient woman.' The moment of light-hearted chatter was a relief for Amaya.

'My mother was a very patient woman indeed. With three children, she was very busy, but being the wife to a heinous man was not easy. She cared for me and my two siblings with true devotion, even the children my father sired with his concubines received her affection. She had a lot of it to give.'

'I wish I could have met her.'

Kenta drew in a deep breath, letting it out with a loud *whoosh*. 'Oh, I wish you two could have met.'

'What happened, Kenta? That night.' Amaya's trepidation was clear. 'You never speak of it. Perhaps it would help relieve you.'

He shook his head slightly. 'My mother was murdered during the attack on the palace when my father was assassinated. I witnessed her death as Sen cut her down with my own katana. She died protecting me.'

Amaya looked at him directly. Hoping he could see the support in her gaze.

'She was a good woman, like your mother. I know my erratic behavior worries you. I admit that I still do not feel like the Emperor, I am still acclimatising to this position of power, but I strongly believe I am not suited to such a role. My brother Junpei, although brash, would have taken far quicker to this position. He was raised for it and I was not.'

Amaya studied Kenta's lineless, gentle face as he sank momentarily into his thoughts. His eyes were searching, seeking something which was not in front of them. Their dark hue showed a depth that Amaya wished to glimpse, but before she could comment on his statement he continued.

'It is getting late, I think sleep is what we both need.' He rose to his feet offering his hand to Amaya. 'I feel refreshed after your company, Amaya. Thank you. I needed to speak of it. I will be able to speak of it more so. Just give me time.' The look of sorrow lessened as he smiled at her. Bidding Kenta goodnight, she left.

Her mother had been buried in the palace temple and was placed beside her father. Amaya was relieved when Kenta permitted her mother to rest in the palace graveyard. Thinking of the temple and shrine drew her attention back to Ueten and, strangely, Amaya felt herself understanding the Spirit of Light that some believed she spoke for.

'Akio, would you mind if I visited the shrine briefly?' She glanced across the desk which had recently become her home. Akio provided a solace for her, and she sought it every day, often finding herself in the Archives without consciously deciding to go there.

'By all means. You have been working all morning. I believe you have written more documents than I have.' He indicated the stack of rolled scrolls beside her.

'I did all those?'

He laughed. 'Yes. So please take your time. Return whenever you need.' Akio waved her away, his smile fortifying her. She stared a little longer, absorbing it, before leaving.

'Kannushi Masato,' Amaya called out into the shrine. The candles were still lit and flickered welcomingly. The old priest appeared, his usual convivial grin in place. He clapped his hands together as he hurried to greet her. He wasn't wearing his hat, and his bald head gleamed, the light of the candles throwing the wrinkled skin into relief and catching the few remaining strands of coarse, white hair.

'Lady Takeda, I thought you would come again.' He grasped her hands and squeezed them gently.

'I have come to pray.' Amaya felt her eyes grow hot and looked away.

'You can pray whenever you feel the need to. How is Kyo?' Kannushi Masato inquired.

'He is still in shock. He has moments of muteness, but cries at night. He shares my quarters and has been spending a lot of time with Lord Hiroshi. He is a good tonic for Kyo it seems.'

'That man is a good tonic for most. Kyo is surrounded by people who care, he will be fragile for some time to come, but his character is the kind that grows and strengthens from something like this.'

'Grows and strengthens? I hope so. I do not want his spirit to become hard and cold.'

'You should be mindful of that yourself, Lady Amaya.' Kannushi Masato's warning was clear. 'Observe your brother. You may find his way of release far better for the spirit within than your own.'

Amaya looked at her feet. 'I am trying, Kannushi Masato.'

'I know you are. Crying will let some of it go. Did you cry for your father?'

Amaya thought. 'Once.'

'And your mother?'

'Once,' Amaya repeated.

The old priest shook his head. 'Too much remains inside of you. You must allow it to run its course. Your space is not infinite.'

Amaya nodded, wanting to do as Kannushi Masato said, but not knowing how. 'I will try, Kannushi Masato.'

The two of them faced the shrine beyond the oratory. Amaya bowed and clapped twice, issuing a silent prayer. A conversation in her mind with her mother and father took place. Kannushi Masato rose to his feet and placed two incense sticks vertically in a delicate, beautiful pot, which was filled with black sand. He then gave Amaya the flame and she lit the incense. The smell began to infuse the shrine, and a musky sweetness hovered around Amaya's head, reminding her of the Spirit Festival.

'I will pray for your parents tonight and every night you are unable to come to the temple.'

'Thank you, Kannushi Masato.' She bowed once again, the long sleeves of her kimono touching the floor. After a pause, Amaya ventured a question which she had been considering. 'Was my mother murdered by those who may think I am the Prophet of Ueten?'

Kannushi Masato sighed. 'I am glad you have finally spoken of this. It shows you are attempting to shirk your doubt. Your mother was not supposed to be in the dojo. I believe this was a coincidence but no less tragic.'

Amaya exhaled. 'After what has happened, not only to myself but to others, I am willing to believe in something such as Ueten and Gekai. Unbalance, life and death. All of it.'

'But your belief needs time to grow, Amaya. Do not hurry it along. People seek answers in both the Old and New Faith, their questions are often the same, but the answers,' he bobbed his head, 'the answers rarely are; they are as unique as the person asking the questions.'

The candles betrayed a shadow across the oratory, and a man stepped forward. 'Lady Amaya Takeda.'

Amaya jolted in alarm glancing at Kannushi Masato. Her surprise, however, was free of fear. She found herself taking an involuntary step toward the man, unable not to do so. It was peculiar to experience. She stared at the stranger unashamedly, absorbing his features. She felt as if she should know him. A loose-fitting garment covered his body so Amaya couldn't tell if he was lean or slender. The cloth looked lighter than silk, but warmer, and was a dirty shade of white, hemmed and lined with blue. The bottoms of his trousers were tucked into old, black supple boots, which reached up his calves. The sleeves were held in place by protective cuffs covering the back of his hands and wrists. A straw conical hat rested on his back, the cord which held it in place, pulled across his neck. She briefly stared at his face: young but prematurely lined, bordered by untidy short hair, which looked like it belonged to the wind. His countenance was benign and truthful, yet his eyes were remote, seeming to gaze inward as well as out. In one hand, he held a long holy staff. The crescent moons stretched from the end and pincered together. Housed inside the circle, were numerous chimes. Amaya thought it looked more like a weapon than a holy staff, similar a bo staff or a naginata. However, it was the small, empty medicine gourds strung around his neck, resting on his chest, which puzzled her.

'Amaya, this is a dear friend whom I have mentioned to you once before. This is Kin Sanjo.'

Amaya's jaw slackened. This man was the only survivor of the massacre sixteen years ago. This man was the younger brother of Sen Sanjo, who had murdered all the priests and Kenta's family; the man who had founded the Senkaku Nin.

'Kin Sanjo...' was all that left her lips.

Kin watched her calmly and smiled. 'Amaya Takeda, I am finally meeting you. Lord Takeda's daughter, the Prophet.'

Amaya paused, but no fear or embarrassment came forth. She felt a strange gravitation towards Kin. She could feel his curiosity, and it echoed within her. 'Are you a monk?'

'I am a monk of sorts, a travelling monk, a wandering monk, a warrior monk. I am a priest too. I am a medicine man, scholar and bird tamer. I am also one of your Elementals.'

Amaya didn't respond immediately; she knew what it meant to be an Elemental. The Prophet's pilgrimage was to locate the Elementals and gain their support. Despite herself, she suspended her doubt, she couldn't deny this man's claim, she felt the kinship too strongly herself. And she could see in his eyes that he knew this.

Kin continued. 'It is the reason I found myself in Chuto.'

Amaya looked at Kannushi Masato. The elderly priest shook his head, a satisfied shimmer on his countenance. 'I did not summon Kin. I have not seen in him in over five years.'

'Then...' Amaya returned her gaze to the warrior monk before her.

'You have read the scroll; you are familiar with the lore. As an Elemental, I am drawn to the Prophet as much as the Prophet is drawn to me. We are kindred. There are four of us, the Four Elementals of Jiki, the Spirit of the Seasons; all of us are there to ensure your path is true.'

Amaya swallowed. 'How do you know so much?'

'One does not travel the land and remain ignorant, Amaya. Not unless they try extremely hard to. Your father, Kazu, also spoke with me before my banishment and once again the night he was murdered. When he first told me of this tale and his belief that I was an Elemental, I was only a child, my understanding childish, my belief childish, my hopes childish. Now,' Kin suddenly looked anguished, 'now I am able to see it with older eyes.'

Amaya stared at him, his voice was measured and reassuring. Her questions were fledglings, but they still needed to be answered, and her belief still needed time to grow as Kannushi Masato had said. 'I fear my eyes are still too young. My knowledge is too young.'

'Your acknowledgement of that proves you are already growing,' Kin replied. He watched as her thoughts circulated. 'To clarify, the Prophet of Ueten is not magical, but blessed. The Prophet is celestial and has the power to enact change and bring peace. Yet this potential may remain untapped as it has for centuries. Neglected or destroyed out of fear and ignorance. Spirits are manifestations of nature: the way the earth rumbles in anger because of the great salamander; or the seas lash the shore; or the rainy season drowning all who stand beneath the clouds; or the sound that water makes as it flows across the land in rivers. Ueten and Gekai are no different. I have come to understand that human nature has a part to play; we are part of the life stream as much as the sun and the moon.'

Amaya looked at Kin, he had sensed what she was thinking. 'I want to believe.'

Kin closed his eyes and inclined his head. 'But that is not the same as actually believing. Kannushi Masato was correct, allow yourself time. Your pilgrimage is also for this purpose.'

Amaya nodded, Kannushi Masato smiled and placed a withered hand upon Amaya's shoulder. 'It is the beginning of a journey for you, Amaya. Perhaps what you have been praying for has come true. You have been given a voice and it is time to begin your pilgrimage.'

Amaya looked down. 'I have to leave Chuto, don't I? If the Elementals do not know their identity, then I must seek them out.'

'Yes. Embarking on a pilgrimage to find the Elementals is important. Hope and corruption flourish together in the hearts of those in Akegata,' Kin spoke, seriously. 'We do not want to see another Lord Genichiro Minamori succeed.'

Amaya woke very early. A dream she could not remember had roused her. Her first thought was Kin, she couldn't shake the desire to see him again. Pushing the blankets from her legs, she stepped onto the cool floor; the reed mats felt smooth against the soles of her feet. She stepped to the window and looked out into the half-light. The shine of the sun was just below the horizon, but there were no clouds to tinge pink. Turning back to the dim room, she lit a small paper lantern. Its dull light fell onto the scroll which had revealed eons of an ancient belief to her in a few meagre hours. A belief which had faded into obscurity, yet she was intrinsically bonded to it by her heritage. Amaya picked up the parchment and glanced through the contents again, especially the part where her clan name was detailed. She traced a single finger over the characters which seemed, at the same time, so familiar and so foreign. She was taken from her thoughts when a knock sounded at the door. She slid it open a crack and saw the frame of Kyo.

'Amaya!' He had not suffered physical injury but still, the toll the fire was taking showed in the gauntness of his face. His hair, usually so glossy, was flat and limp. However, his eyes, despite being sunken, were aglow with a new fervor.

'How are you feeling?' She held him at arms' distance and scrutinised his expression.

'Better. Lord Hiroshi and I have been working on many things together.' He glanced at her hand, his gaze finding the scroll. 'Have you been thinking about Ueten? About what mother and father believed?'

Amaya nodded. 'I have. Last night I met my first Elemental.'

Kyo's eyes widened. 'Really? So soon! Who? Where are they?'

'He is resting.' Amaya hesitated. 'Kyo.'

'You have to leave Chuto.' Her younger brother stated. If he was anxious, his face did not betray the fact. Amaya paused and looked away, the sun had risen now, and the palace was stirring. She shivered slightly and linked her arm through her brother's. He was the same height as her now. She had not had the time to fully consider her choice to leave the capital, but she could not remain.

'It is all right, Amaya. You will come back.' Kyo raised his eyebrows, his mouth forming a wide smile, the first he had given since the fire.

Amaya laughed, unable to refuse her brother's optimism. 'Let us go to the Archives. Perhaps Lord Hiroshi is there. I am intrigued to see what you and he have been working on.'

The verandas, which skirted the magnificent building were empty as they walked the lengths of polished wood; the chill had chased everyone inside. They approached the corner of the archives, and the laughter was beginning to knead the tension from her heart. She stumbled back, as another rounded the same corner.

'Watch where you are going, girl.' Rai Kimura looked

down and dusted off the front of his kimono as he continued on his way.

'You seem to have misplaced your manners,' Kyo muttered, audibly. Amaya hissed for him to be quiet.

Rai turned slowly. 'Excuse me?'

Kyo's stare became steely, and Amaya didn't like the look.

'You seem to have misplaced your manners, Chancellor Kimura,' Kyo said, his tone dripping with mock politeness.

Amaya was torn between laughter and fear. Rai strode forward and gripped the front of Kyo's blue kimono, but her brother showed no timidity, instead he looked at Rai with cool disdain.

'Please let him go, Chancellor Kimura, he meant no harm.'

The three turned, Akio had exited the Archives stepping directly into the argument.

Rai looked incredulous. 'Rude and low.' He looked at Amaya and Kyo as he spoke. 'But it cannot be helped. He is an adopted orphan with little skill, and with you as a sister.'

Akio made to respond but Amaya answered heatedly, her anger piqued. 'Rather a lowly orphan than a corrupt killer.'

Silence immersed the group immediately. Amaya was surprised at what she had said and frustrated for letting anger steer her words. Echoes of her original accusation grew louder the longer the silence continued. She bit down on her tongue; words still wanted to stream from her but she could not allow them. She needed patience and hoped her slip had not cost her the diligence she had shown during her time at the palace. Rai released Kyo and pulled out a cloth to wipe his hand. 'Carelessly sprouted allegations. I did not quite catch your words Lady Amaya, would you care to repeat them?'

Amaya shook her head the smallest amount but did not speak.

Rai smiled. 'I see sense can be forced into the thickest of skulls. A wise choice, Lady Amaya.'

Before anything more could be said he turned and walked away. Amaya was shaking, irritated that she couldn't stop.

Kyo smiled. 'Do not worry, Amaya, he won't find amusement in much soon. You are the Prophet of Ueten.'

Amaya looked at Kyo, who shrugged. Akio turned his head toward her, his eyebrows raised.

'Kyo, you should go ahead. Inform Lord Hiroshi that I am on my way,' Amaya encouraged. He nodded and hurried around the corner leaving Akio and Amaya staring at each other.

'You are finding a little more belief it seems.'

'Yes, I suppose I am. It is difficult, Akio. I did not know how arduous it was to simply believe.'

'Belief is never easy, Amaya. If it were, everyone would have it. It is one of the most tested things, and it can be one of the most fragile. It takes some years to build. However, belief is not a solitary endeavor; enough people believe in you, myself included.'

'I must speak with Kenta,' Amaya said, her resolve suddenly solidifying.

Akio studied her, his expression displaying rare confusion. 'Is anything amiss, Amaya?'

She nodded. 'Yes. I will discuss it with you both.'

They walked in the direction of the large assembly hall in which Kenta spent his days receiving guests and nobles, overseeing decrees and religious rites, listening to the folk. They paused at the guarded door, there was a debate taking place inside. Amaya looked at Akio anxiously but before they could move, the door opened and a man strode out, his attempt at maintaining a stoic face cracking with each stride. He was a court official. Amaya's eyes followed him until he vanished around a corner. Kenta, who had watched the man leave, saw them.

'Come in, Lady Amaya, Lord Izumi.' His voice was measured but Amaya could hear the weariness which hounded him.

They prostrated themselves respectfully and shuffled in on their knees. Amaya could sense Kenta's discomfort at their submissiveness. His Censorate retainers could not be seen, but she knew they were hidden within the walls.

'Who was that, Your Majesty?' Amaya asked.

Kenta sighed. 'You know him by name. That was the Minister of Justice, Riku Ka. Minister Makoto Ka's son. A friend of the Chancellor's.' He smiled weakly and Amaya noticed the dark circles under his eyes.

'It seems that, despite your uncle's efforts, the rebel army have taken the Air Province, Shiroshi is an island of safety in the north but its walls weaken every day. The rebels are now making a move to completely take the Earth Province. Corruption has Akegata tightly in its jaws. They have formally requested aid. Although I wished to avoid a path to war, it seems that this corruption is forcing my hand. The Imperial army must act soon, I fear. Sooner than I would like.'

'Must they, Lord Yamashima? I think we may have another option. Another defence against the corruption you speak of.' Amaya was surprised by her own voice. Her eyes flitted around the room, and she shifted uncomfortably. She knew that the Censorate were Kenta's own men, trusted and selected by Lord Hiroshi, but she did not wish to speak of her pilgrimage in their presence. Kenta, noticing her apprehension, lifted his hand. Immediately, Amaya could hear quiet movement from behind the walls as the Censorate guards left them alone.

She drew a breath. 'I have reached a decision. I have never doubted my father and there is no sense in beginning now. Not when I could apply this apparent gift of prophecy to bolstering the peace you are setting out to achieve, Lord Kenta. I believe in the Way of the Spirits, there is no reason to doubt Ueten or Gekai and the message of balance they represent. I do not know if we should declare that another Prophet has been found, make my pilgrimage public, and await the many who would see this as a sign of true hope to rally? Or, if we should undertake the pilgrimage in secret, assess the will of the people and help them find hope independently of a Prophet or Divine Heir.' Amaya held her palms upward in appeal. 'I leave his decision to you, Kenta. You are the spearhead of Akegata's ventures; the Emperor to whom the people will turn to in this encroaching war. What say you to my musings?'

Kenta's eyes did not move from hers. 'I am continually astounded by your capacity for all things in which heart and wisdom combine. Amaya, the people of Akegata will feel the hope emanating from the Prophet of Ueten regardless of your identity being revealed. These two spirits, Ueten and Gekai, are thought to only manifest in such a way when the need arises, when the balance needs to be reset. Whilst the open knowledge of the possibility of another Prophet and Divine Heir would indeed bolster the people, you should carry out your pilgrimage in secret. At least until you have met all the Elementals. Too little is known about those who may seek to take your life. For this sole reason, I will not have you endanger yourself.' Kenta rested a hand upon Amaya's. 'A Prophet has not been seen in over three hundred years. We must tread very carefully.'

'You will not bear this alone, Lady Amaya. Your father entrusted us, and we shall continue his efforts and protect you and your pilgrimage. It was the last promise I made to him.' Akio bowed low.

'My fortune must be improving.' Amaya grinned. 'I have already met an Elemental.'

Akio and Kenta moved as one, but it was Akio who spoke. 'You have? Who? How?'

'He found me. He seems to have been aware of his identity as the Prophet's Elemental for some time; my father originally sought him out. You both know of him. His name is Kin Sanjo.'

'You have met with Kin?' Akio's tone was elated. 'Is he here? In the palace grounds? It has been a great deal of time since I last saw him.'

Amaya nodded. 'Yes, he was at the shrine with Kannushi Masato.'

Kenta leant forward, his hands upon his bent knees. 'This is wonderful. Your pilgrimage is starting strong. If Kin is one of the Elementals, I cannot worry.'

'You know who his brother is?'

'And I have never met two siblings less alike,' Akio replied. 'Kin is only two years older than myself and four years Kenta's senior. We can remember him well. He was a young priest when he still lived here, he led us spiritually and became a good friend.'

'His banishment was an injustice.'

'Perpetuated by my father, Chancellor Kimura and his supporters. The two most powerful men in Akegata cannot be contested but not all agreed with the decision. Casting out a nine-year-old boy because of an atrocity his brother committed did not sit well with some; Kannushi Masato, Lord Hiroshi, my mother,' Kenta added.

'He is the man who has been travelling the country, who we have refrained from naming. It seems he has revealed himself to you of his own accord.' Akio nodded, his eyes fixed on Amaya. 'It was something your father had mentioned but the massacre his brother committed stole the breath away from all at the palace.' His gaze seemed to retract at that moment, as if scrutinizing thoughts he hadn't pondered in a long time. 'No one knew why Sen suddenly turned on those he had been raised by. Perhaps the revelation that another Prophet had been discovered or that Kin was an Elemental sparked such an atrocity...' Akio was speaking his thoughts aloud. 'He felt his beliefs challenged?'

'Lord Akio, Sen was not the one who had a sudden and unavoidable destiny thrust upon him.'

'And yet, that may have been the very trigger for such an outburst.' Akio mused further. 'Kin's acceptance is testament to his character and worth.'

Amaya nodded. 'I felt he was a good man, his heart seemed that way. Good, but lonely, almost hungry for something,' she paused, realising that her words were too full of fondness for a man she barely knew. 'I apologise. It is simply that I felt no fear, only understanding. It sounds foolish, I only met Kin briefly.'

'He is your Elemental, Amaya. Someone who will share a connection with you for the rest of your life. Only three others will be able to comprehend such a connection,' Akio said, his smile reassuring.

'Three other Elementals,' Kenta continued. 'They may not know who they are.'

Amaya agreed. 'But where are they? The scroll is abundant in description of the connection between the Prophet and the Elementals but frustratingly ambiguous with the Prophet's discovery of them.'

'The one instruction which is clear is that you embark on a pilgrimage to locate them and hone your belief,' Akio confirmed. 'The pilgrimage is supposed to act as not only a physical journey but a spiritual one.'

'You must leave Chuto.' Kenta's face had collapsed with resignation. 'You cannot go alone, Amaya,' Kenta said, after a long pause. His eyes travelled to Akio, his expression pleading.

Amaya looked at them, and then she understood Kenta's stare. 'Akio must not leave your side. He is your first retainer and your main vassal. He has been for years.'

Kenta frowned, his smile twisting to one side. 'Amaya, I cannot accompany you myself. The most I can contribute is my best samurai and fighter. I will be able to focus on my duties here knowing Akio is beside you.'

Akio inclined his head. 'I will go for myself as well as in your stead, Kenta. Amaya, do not fret, Kenta has his Censorate guards as well as Imperial samurai. Then there is the palace itself, and all the protection it offers.'

'Thank you,' Kenta breathed, his shoulders relaxing a little. The frustration in his irises was angry, inflamed. 'However, you must document your absence for it to be legal. I am sorry. All I can do is permit you leave, but I cannot keep your leaving a secret. You may submit any reason as a cover.'

'I understand.' Amaya nodded. 'Thank you. Both of you.'

Fresh anxiety blossomed on Kenta's elegant face and he seemed unwilling to finish the dialogue between them. 'This is not safe, the nature of Ueten and Gekai is something that has not been witnessed in centuries and the knowledge and effects are largely unknown, save for the information and anecdotes documented by the author of the scroll your father protected. Most other references were burned, destroyed and damaged during the First Warring States Era by those who wanted to eliminate the Prophet and Divine Heir. Yet these spirits have shown themselves despite all this. They must be needed,' Kenta debated with himself. 'Akio and Kin will travel with you. Before the Earth Province becomes any more overrun with rebels, you should search there first, whilst there is still Imperial influence.'

'I was going to suggest that myself,' Amaya replied. 'I should depart as soon as I can.'

'Yes. I will make the necessary arrangements here. You speak with Kin,' Kenta said to her.

'And I will prepare our belongings.' Akio finished.

Amaya sat on the floor of her quarters in the Takeda estate, surveying her old room which now felt as distant as her childhood, its familiarity lost somehow. Half of her home had been saved from the fire, but a sizable amount had been claimed. Outside of her window, she could still see the remains of the dojo: dejected and dead. The new one Kenta had commissioned was yet to spring from the ashes. However, for Amaya it would be a poor constellation. The experiences she had gained in that building were tainted by the fire which had claimed it, and nothing could truly replace it. She gripped the handle of her bag tightly as the memory of that day formed in her mind. Her resolve to find the Elementals had strengthened in the last week. At times, Amaya thought she could feel Ueten, at others Gekai. Rather than dwell on the growing sensations, she allowed them to come and go, hoping to learn from them as they occurred. There was one constant however, and that was vengeance. It lapped at her thoughts, testing her resolve and reasoning. She knew she shouldn't but she could not help but revel in the feeling, stoking it and enjoying the scenarios she wished she could execute upon Rai and Sen; her own form of justice. Continuously, she had to shake the images from her mind, she knew she was not a terrible person yet she wished such brutal things on those who had wronged her; on those who had wronged the Takeda and deprived the country the samurai spirit at its heart.

She sighed and rose to her feet. As she neared the gates to her estate, a courier appeared on the street outside. He bowed when he saw her and entered. Handing her a scroll, he left quickly to continue his deliveries. Amaya recognised the elegant script of her uncle. Hastily she opened it and began to read.

My Dear Amaya,

I am appalled to hear of the catastrophe regarding the fire. Megumi's demise grieves me in a way which cannot be contained in this scroll. I will pray for you all each day. It is a blow to the Takeda family, and to you and Kyo especially, I am sure. I am just grateful that you both are safe and well. It would be the utmost tragedy if you were all to have perish. Perhaps the perpetrator is creating a symbol with such an act.

I arrived safely in Shiroshi Temple. Nothing to report from the Air Province, besides the ever-growing threat of the rebel army. My city here is becoming increasingly more dangerous; shinobi have been sighted, rebels infiltrating the castle walls as spies. So, I may be kept here a while. I am afraid letters will have to suffice for the time being as it is now not safe for even a priest to travel. I have written to the Court and Chancellor Rai as well, detailing this matter. They are aware that I will be corresponding via letters.

I hope you are coping and are not allowing grief to consume you. You have a temperament that soothes others Amaya, do not let it be destroyed because of someone's act of terror no matter how unjust and wicked they are.

Please send my regards to Kyo,

Uncle Jiro Takeda.

Amaya sighed and rolled the scroll up tightly. She quickly returned to her house and placed it on the low table in the tea room for Kyo to find should he return to the Takeda estate during her absence. Hurriedly extracting some delicate rice paper and a brush, she began to write her reply. She detailed all that had happened since the fire. She expressed her optimism and proactive decision to search for the Elementals, writing that she had already found the first of four. She released a breath as she stamped the Takeda seal upon the complete letter. Amaya hadn't realised how cathartic placing the truth on paper would be. She felt comforted in the thought that her uncle would understand her enthusiasm and, if need be, provide support. He was a priest after all, and like Kannushi Masato, he would hold belief in the spirits.

She stopped abruptly as she stepped down from the veranda into her forecourt.

'Vast improvement.' Daiki Kimura was leaning casually against the gate to her estate. His eyes scoured her from afar.

She glanced down at herself. Her thick tunic and warm hakama trousers were a plain navy, hemmed with white. The bottom of the hakama flowed about her knees, the bottoms tucked into her split-toed boots. From afar, she looked like a young man. Her cloak shrouded her katana from view, she would have to keep it concealed on her journey; only samurai and ronin could carry weapons in public. She had dressed so that no one would give her a second glance. Pushing her low ponytail over her shoulder, she glared ahead. Daiki's look still irked her. He smiled, seeming to sense her defensiveness.

'How may I help you, Lord Daiki?' Amaya asked, quietly, her eyes narrowed as they studied him.

'Myself and my brother will be accompanying you north. My father has requested it.'

Amaya halted, her hands balling into fists. 'There is no need.'

Daiki laughed, but still did not enter her property. Amaya noted a slight glimmer of discomfort as his eyes swept across the blackened ground and section of burnt veranda. 'There is every need, Amaya. It is rather dangerous in the north you see. Lord Izumi may be a skilled samurai and archer, but he is only one man. You never know when an extra samurai will come in handy.'

Amaya wanted to shout that he was no samurai, that his very nature contradicted the Way of the Samurai. 'But your brother also?'

Daiki shrugged. 'I do not question my father.'

'Someone should,' Amaya muttered, stepping forward in resignation. She would allow Rai to have is way but only so far. She would use the opportunity to discover things about the Chancellor; she could be clever too. 'But why are you here, at my home, Lord Daiki? I am to meet everyone at the main gate to the city. You needn't have come.'

'Oh, I volunteered.' He smiled, his eyebrows raised. Unfolding his arms gracefully, he walked toward her. His clothing was not as embellished as she was accustomed to seeing. Instead, he donned a simple pair of dark green hakama, a black tunic, the sleeves of which were tucked into brown protective arm cuffs, which reached his elbows. In fact, the only detail Amaya could see was the sigil of his clan; the Kimura tree and moon were beautifully embroidered in gold on his chest and on each of his cuffs. The other piece of his outfit, the one which Amaya couldn't help but admire, was Daiki's katana. He tapped its hilt, sensing Amaya's stare. The movement drew her eyes to his face, so different from Shun's that Amaya frowned. Both were tall, but where Shun was striking, Daiki was elegant. Where Shun was broad and muscular, Daiki was lean and agile. Shun's eyes told of a tortured person. Amaya faltered. Strangely, Daiki's bore the same affliction.

He shifted. 'I know I am handsome, many women tell me so, but do you really have to stare, Lady Amaya?'

Amaya struggled with the instinct to strike him. She walked past, wanting the company of the others. Daiki followed, and she could feel his silent laughter.

'No need to be so fierce, Amaya. It is all in jest.' His voice mocked.

Amaya spun around, causing Daiki to stumble slightly to avoid collision. 'You will show me more respect. If you have no manners, I will gladly teach you some. Your father seems to have neglected you in that regard.' She glared at him disdainfully.

A spark of anger flashed across the surface of Daiki's dark eyes, but he riened it back, replacing it with amusement. 'And I expect the same, Lady Takeda. I am not my father. I have not wronged you. Please accept my deepest apologies if I have offended you. I did not think you so fragile that you could not suffer lighthearted joking. I assure you, you will find me the essence of solemnity from now on. Shall we?' He gestured for them to continue forward, the main road now within earshot.

Amaya didn't speak, she was unsure what response his words warranted. She snatched a glance at him, and true to his word his face was still, unmoved by his usual aloofness, and Amaya briefly saw relief upon the otherwise inert visage. The change came a little too easily Amaya thought.

Akio, Shun and Kin were waiting for her by the main gates as planned.

'Lady Takeda, are you ready?' Akio said, lightly, but his eyes found Daiki and held him under a curious inspection. Daiki gave Akio a cursory nod before approaching Shun.

'Hello, brother.' His grin was high-reaching, genuine.

Shun bowed his head respectfully, his eyes unwavering in their scrutiny. 'Thank you for escorting Lady Takeda from her home.'

'You are infinitely more grateful than Lady Takeda was.' The smile, which was still upon his refined face became empty, but before Amaya could respond, Akio stepped forward. No longer in the formal clothing of the Secretariat, he seemed carelessly handsome. He took her small bag.

'I still cannot believe we are going,' Amaya said, bowing and taking her belongings back from Akio. 'I can carry it, Lord Akio. Thank you.'

Akio and Shun were both dressed in the same billowing hakama pants as Daiki, except Shun's were blue and Akio's black. Both of their tunics were white. The same sigil that Daiki bore was emblazoned on Shun's chest, but Akio had the discerning heron of the Izumi clan upon his. About his waist, was the black silk sash he had offered at the shrine months ago. Trailing along its length were the numerous autumn leaves, falling in golden stitches. Tucked into this sash was Akio's katana. However, he had an addition to his person, a polished bow and a quiver of arrows strapped to his back.

'A bow, Lord Akio?' Amaya questioned.

'Lord Akio is a fine archer,' Shun commented. 'I try to have him train the new recruits when possible.' The General inclined his head politely.

'In fact, I prefer the bow to the katana,' Akio said, smiling from Shun to Amaya.

'I think it a coward's weapon. Never near true danger, out of arms reach as it were,' Daiki chuckled, his fingers grazing his katana. Amaya faced him, his rudeness silencing her.

'I do not disagree with you, Lord Daiki. However, it is merely a personal preference. I of course seek the sanctuary of my books over the dojo. Neither weapon is better than the other in my eyes. They both ultimately share the same purpose.'

Daiki raised his thin eyebrows. 'Such a shame that your

talent with a katana is unused, Lord Akio. I have heard of your skills. I would gladly go into battle alongside a man with such battle prowess.'

'I was not under the impression there was a war to be fought,' Akio replied, graciously.

'Not yet,' Daiki teased. 'But one would be foolish to ignore the rumbles of the storm in the Air Province.'

'Let us not talk of this now,' Kin interrupted, speaking for the first time, his voice saturated with warning. He was staring at Amaya. She thought she had hidden her anger at Daiki well. 'It is not a conversation to be had in the street.'

'I apologise, Eisen,' Akio said, inclining his head at Kin, using the alias the three had decided upon.

'You have my apologies too, Kannushi.' Daiki bowed in Kin's direction.

'I am not a Kannushi, and you may call me Eisen.'

Daiki faltered. 'Thank you. Eisen it is then.'

'Let us leave then,' Shun said, motioning for the road beyond the gates. His eyes had not left his younger brother, and Amaya was startled to see pity permeating the torment.

As the group left, Amaya slid her hand beneath her cloak and wrapped her hand around her katana.

'We are going to the Earth Province, so we shall take the northern route below the mountains,' Akio said, indicating the path to their left.

Amaya nodded. 'Do we aim to go as far as Rikujou? That city is near the border to the Air Province.'

'Yes, that is our destination.'

'Will we be able to approach Rikujou? It is so near the border. The Air Province is where the rebel army are congregating. We know they are already spilling into the Earth Province. My uncle has also expressed concern,' Amaya questioned.

'It will be safe if we travel as nomads, hinin even,' Shun said, reassuringly.

Amaya looked up at him and nodded, his assurance

oddly placating. 'We head for Rikujou.'

The late autumn wind lashed at their faces and caused their cloaks to fly behind them as they entered the shelter of a bamboo grove. The bamboo shoots whistled and swayed causing many leaves to fall about them like red rain. Amaya struggled at times, as if the wind that slithered through the grove was forcing them back. The chill on the gusts promised snow.

'The town, Kusamachi, lies on the other side of this woodland. We can rest there for the night and leave before light. It will take at least three days to travel to Rikujou from there,' Shun said.

The bamboo became thicker and more difficult to navigate. Amaya turned and found herself next to Kin. His face was hidden from the moon's light in the shadow created by his large conical hat. The bells of his long staff tinkled as they moved. He had completely closed his cloak to the wind.

Her eyes fell on a regal bird perched on his shoulder. 'What is he called?' Amaya asked, pointing at the silent hawk.

'She is called Taka.' As Kin spoke, Taka opened her wings slightly.

'She cannot enjoy being in the woodland. There is nowhere to fly.'

'Hold out your arm, Amaya,' Kin said.

Amaya obeyed. At once Taka left Kin's shoulder to land on Amaya's arm. Even through her clothing Amaya could feel Taka's talons.

'She likes you.'

Amaya glanced about. 'Do they not recognise you?'

'Shun and Daiki?' Kin frowned. 'Daiki does not. He is your age, too young to remember the incident let alone the face of a nine-year-old who is now a man. Shun, however,' Kin stared ahead, where Amaya could detect the General's broad back as he stalked through the woodland, Akio beside him, 'it would not surprise me if Shun knew my identity.'

'But you must be so different from when he last saw you

and he would surely say something if he did recognise you.'

'Shun is quiet, reserved. He is also honourable. I know you can sense that Amaya, you just refuse to acknowledge it because of who his father is,' Kin said, not unkindly.

Amaya sighed, squinting in the dimming afternoon light. 'I cannot deny he is wholly unlike his father.'

Kin fixed her with a stare so like his hawk's.

'You were banished because of Shun's father and Emperor Kado Yamashima,' Amaya continued. 'Yet you bear no ill will.'

'I was happy to travel Akegata, and because of my exile, I have discovered and learnt many things.' Kin's narrow features broke into a small smile.

'But you have had to hide yourself and never return to your home. Even now you must travel under a different name.' Amaya shook her head.

Kin smiled at her words. 'In truth, the Air Province is my birthplace. I would not have discovered myself and become a physician, amongst other things, if I had stayed in Chuto all my life. As a medicine man, I was able to approach people and be accepted in small towns and villages. Most had been forgotten, and illness was worsening. So you see my banishment was a positive thing to some and myself.'

'I admire your approach,' Amaya said. 'You truly are wise.'

'Yes, Eisen is wiser than us all, I fear. There is something very sage about him.'

Amaya turned at the voice, unhappy at the intrusion. Daiki had stayed at the rear of the convoy, his abilities trusted by Shun entirely. She hadn't realised that she and Kin had fallen behind so much.

'No need to fear, Lord Daiki. I have taken unfortunate situations and grown from them. Every person has that potential. Many are ignorant to the potential lessons, or worse they choose to ignore it.'

Amaya returned her gaze to Kin, her awe mounting.

'Oh, I agree. There are too few who seek it. Many mistake simple knowledge for wisdom,' Daiki commented.

Kin laughed. 'You have your own philosophy, I see.'

'Nothing more than common sense.' Daiki gave a small grin again, his eyes finding Amaya. 'And my common sense is screaming at me as I speak. I will leave you both to your conversation.'

Amaya hesitated but did not reply for fear of exposing her uncertainty. She watched Daiki as he veered away from them.

'You do not like him,' Kin stated.

'I have yet to discover anything to like. He has been nothing but rude and abrasive.'

'He was not always so unpleasant.'

Amaya felt her eyebrow rise with her disbelief. 'He has no manners, no pride, no honour.'

'These things I see are very important to you, Amaya. They are not all there is to a person's existence.'

'I am aware,' Amaya replied slowly. 'That does not make them any less important. But to lack them entirely?'

'It cannot be easy having a tyrant like Rai Kimura as a father,' Kin replied, steadily.

Amaya regarded his statement. 'No, I suppose not.'

Kin ambled away from her after that, seeking a break in the canopy so that Taka could stretch her wings. Amaya could hear Daiki close by, striding quietly through the grove.

However, it was Shun's voice that broke her reverie. 'We are at the edge of the wood.'

Amaya pushed on and stepped out into the evening moonlight. She hadn't realised how dark the bamboo woodland had been until her eyes began to adjust. Akio tapped her shoulder lightly and pointed just off to their right. She followed his gesture and saw, in the near distance, the soft lights of Kusamachi wrapped in the arms of a shallow valley. The group stopped in the nighttime stillness, looking down at the soft glow from their position on the hillside whilst the wind played with their garments. Daiki fiddled with his katana, the chink of Kin's holy staff, the rustle of Akio's quiver of bows was all that could be heard.

Akio leant closer to her. 'There are several Ryokan inns here. We should have no trouble in finding one.'

Silently, they descended the grassy path, which crossed the grid of terraced rice paddies, the glow of Kusamachi shimmering on the waters' surface.

The streets were still and Amaya could see no one, but she could hear laughter and shouting from the izakaya taverns which lined the small, dusty streets. The food eateries were open and busy too. She could see the backs of many people through the material flaps, hunched over their food. The smell of dashi broth and yakitori sauce drifted out, born on the rice's steam. Lights spilled onto the road alongside the sound of merriment. As they continued to walk further into Kusamachi, Amaya saw a restaurant which was bustling. She could see the owner: a woman who was smiling and serving the numerous customers. Amaya turned, feeling her hunger wake as she smelt the various spices which infused the surrounding air.

'Shall we eat?' Akio said, staring at the place.

'Not in there,' Daiki said, shaking his head.

Amaya stared at him. 'But the other places do not smell half as good.'

Nodding in agreement with Amaya, they all entered the small and homey store, Daiki trailing in reluctantly behind them.

'Welcome, come in.' The woman turned, gesturing them a low table near the slatted, open window. She had pretty face and a friendly tone. Amaya thought she must be slightly younger than her mother, Megumi. The thought was enough to rouse vivid images in her mind, and her mother's smiling face seemed oddly intrusive, as if her gaze undid much of the healing Amaya had attempted over the past two weeks. With huge effort she pushed the vision away, to a distant corner she reserved for all that caused her pain.

The group of five sat comfortably on the floor cushions and looked at the various meals available.

'I recommend the Hiyashi soba,' the woman spoke, placing earthen handmade cups on the table and filling them with bitter-smelling tea. Her round face was shining slightly, evidence of a busy day, but her eyes had no lack of energy as her smile pushed them up into crescent moons.

'That sounds perfect,' Amaya said, trying to shake the creeping cold from her body.

'Would you all like the same? I have just cooked a fresh pot,' the woman said loudly over the din of noise that filled her restaurant.

'I could not refuse such a temptation,' Kin replied, removing his hat and letting it hang down his back.

Soon, steaming bowls were placed in front of them and, picking up their simple wooden chopsticks, they began to eat.

Amaya continued the conversation with the woman, whose name she learned was Inari, whenever she had a free moment from serving. She garnered that Inari was the chieftain of the town, or at least that was how the townsfolk regarded her. Several times throughout the evening Inari would be approached with a question or request, and Amaya enjoyed watching the ramen maker help each person. The trust displayed upon each face, both young and old, was unhidden. Inari's own countenance was a warm and open one, embracing the loyalty of the villagers.

The night was a dense black now and the same stars which Amaya always saw looked down. Patrons began to leave, only a few inebriated ones remained. They were donned in travelling cloaks Amaya noted.

'They come from every corner of Akegata,' Inari commented, following Amaya's curious stare. 'Kusamachi is positioned on one of the main trade and travel routes from Chuto to the north.'

'Do you ever get any trouble?' Shun asked.

Inari shrugged. 'No more than the next place. We get undesirable folk as well as honourable ones.'

'You mean hinin?' Amaya questioned, thinking of those who travelled exclusively, lived nowhere and everywhere at once. Hinin had always intrigued her but asking questions about the people who were considered below the ranks of society, lower even than merchants, was not something she had been permitted as child.

'Yes. Them and others, like ronin, medicine men, monks, priests. So many kinds I could not list them all.'

'You must learn a vast amount from working here.'

Inari chuckled. 'Some of the people are clever, some bring news, some have heads as empty as some of the court officials, and they only bring hearsay.'

Akio laughed loudest. 'I have met my fair share of those.'

'What kinds of court officials do you meet, Inari?' Kin asked, taking a sip of Sake. 'Samurai? Lords? Governors?'

'Nobles like that tend to travel in disguise. Sometimes I get an inkling they might be noble; there is refinement about one or two, but you never question your customers. Discretion is an unavoidable part of my service here. For the most part, I remain unobtrusive and, thankfully, unnoticed. Left to go about tending to my business and the village.'

'Of course,' Kin smiled.

'You five are definitely more interesting than the usual rabble,' Inari commented.

'I shall take that to be a compliment. Have you always lived in Kusamachi?' Amaya asked.

'Yes, since I was married. My husband was the leader of the samurai battalion which was once stationed here. I was originally from the south, from Kasaichi. I am still very fond of that city.'

Akio agreed. 'It is so alive.'

'You all strike me as Chuto folk. Except you,' she looked at Shun, 'you have the look of the Water Province about you.'

Shun shook his head but did not respond. Inari seemed not to notice Shun's discomfort, or she had and was being sensitive to it. Amaya thought the latter.

Inari continued, 'but if you are from Chuto, why are you here in Kusamachi? The nearer you travel to the Air Province the more trouble you will encounter.'

'We are aware of the danger the Air Province poses. We are travellers, if we are careful no harm will come to us,' Amaya said. Her eyes were beginning to feel dry with tiredness.

'Then your plan is to travel even closer to the Air Province? Their army has already dispatched troops as far as Rikujou, that much is known on the road. They have control of the river Dao. Although no one has acknowledged this fact openly,' Inari said, sadly.

'How have you so much information?' Amaya asked.

'Like I said, the hinin, actors and bards, they bring much news as they travel. They wander each province and gather firsthand events. Although they are outcasts, their knowledge cannot be faulted; they have no reason to lie. Also, my husband's letters were detailed in what had occurred. When the Air Province began to occupy the north of the Earth Province the entire battalion left to defend the border and aid the Governor of the Air Province in his battle to stop the rebel army spreading.' Inari's voice had grown feebler, but anger governed her expression.

'I heard of the Kusamachi Battalion's advance,' Shun spoke, quietly.

'Then you know of the slaughter which happened. Only a few returned alive and my husband was not one of them. The Earth Province is greatly weakened. The castle here has remained empty since then. It has not been rebuilt since the fire which destroyed it.'

Amaya sighed, Chuto had not been attacked since the assassination of Kenta's father.

'The person responsible for the instigation of the civil

war has yet to be identified,' Inari said, angrily.

Akio nodded and pulled his drink toward him. 'Various representatives from the Air Province have been interrogated but no information has proved useful. It seems that everyone in the Court is claiming ignorance,' Akio said, hollowly. 'And there is only so much which can be done with such little evidence. There are those who strive to correct all that has gone awry.'

'Who are you all?' Inari said, looking at the five, her expression suddenly scrutinising. Amaya looked at Akio who nodded.

'We are those who strive,' Amaya said, smiling.

Inari opened her mouth but before she could reply one of the group of men nearby stood. Inari bowed apologetically and rushed over to settle the bill.

'She is very kind,' Kin said, glancing at the owner.

'And very knowledgeable. Hopefully we can ask her some further questions,' Akio mused.

Amaya was half-listening, her eyes remained on Inari. Two more of the five men had risen to their feet, and Amaya did not like their postures. She squinted, wishing she could hear what was being said, but muffled voices were all that she could distinguish. The man nearest Inari reached down. Amaya lent forward her heartbeat elevating horribly. Realising what was occurring, she leapt to her feet, sending her Sake into Daiki's lap. He shouted out in annoyance, but Amaya was deaf to his complaints. She jumped over the table and in a few quick strides reached the men. Inari glanced back at her, and her expression was terrified. She shook her head at Amaya, her gaze beseeching her to stay away.

The man had pulled a slender short sword from his waistband. 'We will be taking our leave. Without payment. But you will pay for your insolence.' His face was dirtied, his nose squashed against his round, flat face. He lifted his blade, a laugh forming in his throat.

Amaya did not wait. 'There is no honour in theft. You

should not ignore the law.' She snatched a chopstick, gripped the man's free hand and pinned it to the table with the thin piece of wood. He screamed out in pain and his peers drew their blades. Inari's expression had become dark, and she reached beneath her obi belt.

The man grunted and swiped his blade through the air. Amaya pushed Inari away and felt the blade tear her own clothing. She shook her hand a little and felt the dagger she had concealed beneath her sleeve slip into her fingers. She danced around the man and between the low tables, aware of his advancing comrades. Pushing down upon the chopstick and twisting it, the man dropped his blade, his free hand desperately seeking to pull out the piece of wood. His small eyes were livid.

Amaya turned but was met with the point of another katana. Breathing deeply, she stared at the man holding it.

'That's one of my guards you have injured,' he growled. He twisted his wrist but before he could lunge, Amaya felt a great wrench at her arm. She careened back, unable to stop herself.

'Amaya, what are you doing?' Akio had a hold of her, his katana was drawn.

'They were going to hurt Inari,' Amaya replied, heatedly. 'Their behaviour must be corrected. It is unjust to let them take advantage in such a humiliating way.' She felt no regret in her actions despite how hasty they were.

'We knew,' Akio replied, his eyes trained forward. 'Daiki had already marked them as bandits the moment we entered.'

'And what? You were all going to wait?' Amaya felt a sting of embarrassment that she had not been so vigilant, that Daiki had been the one with such sharp eyes.

Akio didn't reply but kept a hand across her chest protectively.

Shun was stood between Inari and the men but he had not drawn his katana. Kin was on his feet, his staff clenched in both hands. The crescent points looked far more intimidating now. Only Daiki remained seated, unmoving, nonchalant. He drank his Sake lazily, observing. Amaya shook her head in disdain, but her attention was taken by Shun's deep voice.

'There is no need for violence. I apologise for my friend's temper. If you allow us, we will tend to your wound. He is a medicine man,' Shun said, calmly. 'There is no need for more dishonour. Simply, reimburse this gentlewoman for the food and drink you have indulged in.'

The men laughed, spittle flying into Shun's face. 'We do not need your charity. We own this road and all trade that occurs along it.'

Amaya comprehended who the men were. The Kaminari bandits which terrorised the roads were known throughout Akegata, and Daiki had recognised them in the first instance. Amaya now understood why he had seemed so unwilling to enter.

'The Emperor Yamashima owns this road, and all the roads in Akegata,' Shun pressed, wiping the saliva from his cheek with his gloved hand.

All the men gaffawed 'That child-Emperor? He could not own a puppy, let alone protect a country. Who are you anyway, the Emperor's tongue?'

Shun looked down sadly and sighed. 'No, his General.' He slid forward with purpose. Amaya was startled by his agility. His muscular frame gave the impression of strength and stamina, not speed. She hadn't even seen Shun draw his katana, but there it was, a length of shining, deadly steel. He took two paces forward, parried his blade easily, shifting to the side as he did so. Using its length, Shun carralled two of the men through the open doors. The others pursued into the night. Through the open windows, they could easily be seen. Shun's opponent's blade passed him by inches but Shun did not flinch, his face remained impassive as he brought his katana down in a long slashing movement. The man's face froze with a look of shock as he was cleaved from collarbone to stomach. Blood pooled on the dust road instantly with Shun in the centre of it breathing steadily.

The remaining four men advanced on him but Shun, like a statue, did not move. One man broke free of his comrades and, shouting like a lunatic, lunged at Shun. The General merely flipped his katana at right angles to his arm and dropped low. The attacker's blade missed but Shun's did not. He pushed up from the ground hard, his blade almost entirely severing the man at the waist. Shun let out a growl as he broke free of the body, and returned to the same standing position as yet more blood created a scarlet pool about him.

'Remain still,' Akio said, and Amaya watched as he resheath his katana. 'Shun does not require our help. He is one of the Five Masters after all.'

Amaya felt her mouth open a little, and she stared at Shun again. He was patiently waiting but the remaining three were not as quick to hurry forward as their companions had been.

The man who had claimed to be the leader of the others grit his teeth. 'I am not a man to throw my life away foolishly.' He clicked his fingers and retreated, his remaining guards trailing behind him. Shun straightened up and wiped his katana clean before returning it to its sheath. He turned around and ducked back into the store. 'Are you harmed?' he asked Inari. She nodded but her face had paled and was speckled with blood. Shun steered her to a seat.

'Well done, brother,' Daiki said, lightly, stepping down from the platform on which their table was situated.

Shun gave him a cool look. 'Thank you for your support.'

Daiki raised his hands comically, palms upward. 'Why waste energy? Would there really have been a point in any of us stepping in?' He looked at his brother expectantly. 'You are skilled, dear brother.'

'As are you. You can help, so next time please do not sit by idly. Akio, Eisen and even Lady Amaya were prepared to fight.' Shun's voice was low, the usual rumble in place.

Daiki rounded on Amaya. 'Ah, yes. Lady Amaya. Quite the spectacle you caused on this secret journey. You are proving to be an interesting companion. I may enjoy this trip yet, with that unpredictable hot-headedness of yours.' He grinned, and his handsome face seemed almost fiendish.

But Amaya didn't have a moment to reply.

'Thank you,' Inari said, quietly, finding her voice. 'Please do not think I am without skill. I have had to defend myself many times. I am a samurai's wife after all. This village's inhabitants try to hone their skills every day.' She bowed low.

'I hope we have not caused more trouble for you,' Kin said, worriedly, walking to her side and offering her a cloth with which to wipe her face.

'No, no. I truly believe they were fearful. The General...' She looked up at Shun. 'They will not come back here but they may try to attack you on your travels. You must be cautious.'

'Of course. Inari, how long have incidents like this evening been happening?' Akio asked.

'On and off since the Kusamachi Battalion perished. There are no soldiers stationed here anymore. All ryokan on main roads suffer. Kusamachi perhaps more so because of the trade we have access to. We manage.'

'The Emperor will hear of this,' Akio promised. 'He is trying to rectify his father's mistakes against many obstacles. All he asks of his people is patience.'

'If he is different and better than his father, I will gladly give it to him,' Inari said.

Amaya beamed at her, feeling an overwhelming gratitude. Kin placed his hat on his head and picked up his staff. 'We will help you clean, but after, we need to find a place to rest tonight if we want to leave early,' he said, to the group at large.

'I can accommodate you. I wish I could do more to repay you. I only have two spare rooms.' Inari looked at Amaya and the four men. Amaya opened her mouth slowly, feeling her cheeks grow warm.

'That would be a lot of help, Inari. Lady Amaya can take one room and we will take the other,' Akio said, kindly, smiling at Amaya.

When they had finished scrubbing and washing, midnight had been and gone. Daiki couldn't have looked more disgruntled at having to perform servants' work, but the others had graciously taken up various positions, and the job had been finished quickly. Kin had seen to the dead men's burial, the others had attended to the mess.

The group followed Inari through the sliding doors at the rear of the store and entered her living quarters. Amaya appreciated the humble warmth and followed Inari to the room she would occupy for the remainder of the night.

'I will bring you some linen sheets in a moment. First, I will show the others to their room. I am sorry I cannot offer you more, Amaya,' Inari said, clasping her hands in front of her, bowing.

Amaya stuttered, 'Inari, you have helped us. This is more than we expected when we came to Kusamachi. I am grateful for your generosity. Thank you.'

Inari bowed and exited the room, leaving Amaya alone. She looked around. It was a very plain room she thought. An indoor altar was tucked into the far corner. Several candles were lit and, in their light, Amaya could see a folded apron, a pair of slippers and an origami frog. She advanced on the altar and crouched down. The slippers looked like they had been pink, but the silk had faded to a soft rosy grey. The design was somewhat outdated, but Amaya enjoyed the pattern; cherry blossoms were embroidered in golden thread, and birds in black. The slippers were no bigger than Amaya's hand, and very dainty. *Hardly worn*, Amaya realised. As she scrutinised them, Inari entered with Amaya's blankets.

'Those were my daughter's, and the apron belonged to a dear friend named Baba. She was the previous owner of this ramen restaurant,'

Amaya was unsure of how to respond but Inari continued. 'They were killed. Murdered by shinobi from the Hidden River Village when they raided Kusamachi whilst the troops were in the north.' Inari picked up a menko card from the black lacquer box which was next to the altar, her pretty face overshadowed by grief. Amaya's heart was hurting, she didn't know how she should comfort Inari.

'I am sorry. You have suffered a lot of pain because of this war.'

'I have accepted what has happened to my family. I plan to continue living my life enough for the four of us, carrying them in my heart.' Inari gave a small smile, her open face pale as she struggled with her memories. 'I will leave you to sleep. You have an early start. If you need anything, please ask me.' Inari bowed.

Amaya could not sleep that night. She held her father's katana close, finding a familiar comfort in the hard object but it did not prevent Inari's misfortune hounding her mind.

She rubbed her eyes and opened the window. The cold of early winter was already upon the Sky Province. The taverns had closed and the people of Kusamachi were sleeping. For a while, she thought of Inari's daughter and imagined losing Kyo. She quickly shook that from her mind. She thought of Kenta and hoped he was not agonising over events he could not undo. Thinking of the news Inari had delivered threw into relief the strife the young Emperor had before him, news which had not even surfaced in the courts. She wondered how much more she would uncover.

Closing the window, she walked across the room and slid her door open silently. She nearly tripped. Asleep on the reed mat floor was Akio. His back was against the wall, his knees bent and his head forward, resting on his folded arms. Amaya could see the rise and fall of his chest and grinned. She crouched and watched him for a moment. Even in sleep, his expression was gentle. Shaking herself free of her reverie, she rose and then left to fetch some water.

'Cannot sleep, Lady Takeda?'

Amaya jumped. 'You as well, General Kimura? Please refer to me as Amaya, we are travelling companions now.' She smiled as she took a seat beside the stoic Shun. She watched him in the dim light of the single lantern, his face was still young but so different from his father and brother's.

'You look nothing like your father, Shun,' Amaya said, quietly.

He turned to face her. 'That is not unusual, I am not his real son. Lord Kimura adopted me when I was a young boy, just before Daiki was born. Inari was right when she said I have the look of the Water Province about me. That is where I originate from, although I barely remember it now.'

Amaya was taken aback as she recalled Rai's own words regarding Kyo. She titled her head to one side. 'I cannot believe that Rai would adopt someone. Do not think I am being rude.' Amaya did not know how to finish the sentence which she had begun.

'My father is full of surprises, Amaya.' Shun smiled ruefully and finished his drink. 'Daiki is his blood son, five years younger than me. Yet he does not despise me.'

'Why would he? Because you are to inherit the Kimura clan?'

Shun nodded, he did not seem happy at the thought. 'Daiki is forever seeking our father's approval but has never once been bitter towards me. He has only shown me the love you would expect a brother to show. By blood rights the Kimura clan should be his. I do not understand why my father would not name him as heir of the clan. And yet Daiki is incredibly loyal to him despite it.' Shun shrugged and fell back into his thoughts.

'I can understand why you are the one my father chose to be the Master of the Sky Province,' Amaya said.

Shun turned in his seat. 'Your father was an incredible man. I will never forget the lessons he taught me. The lessons he taught all the soldiers. He was worthy of being one of the

Five Masters. Far more worthy than I. I miss him deeply.'

'My father would not have chosen you were that the case. That I can promise you,' Amaya replied, seriously. 'Do not waste the opportunity he has given you.'

'Opportunity?' Shun said, incredulously. 'I never desired such a title.'

'Yet you accepted it,' Amaya retorted, not harshly. 'General Kimura, you are more reserved than anyone I have met in the samurai class; you have managed to shirk the arrogance that plagues many men. You are more patient, calm, honourable, but I can sense the disquiet you house, and I think my father wanted you to use this title as a way of overcoming the grief that eats at you so that you can let your attributes shine. You will pass your skills on to another, not just your skills in combat but your skills as a person. You have the chance to choose the next Master of the Sky Province. Choose wisely, as my father has done.' Amaya studied the General, his strong face had a kindness that Rai's had never had. She looked at his dark, angry eyes and saw desolation lingering alongside the premature sagacity. 'Do you know, Shun, I think if you smiled more you could be very handsome.' Amaya grinned as Shun twitched at her words, his cheeks turning pink. She leant forward and saw the corners of his stern mouth rise a little.

'Very handsome indeed. My brother was very popular. Almost as popular as I, if truth be told, before he became the embodiment of seriousness.' Daiki entered the room, and took a seat on the other side of his brother.

'Why are you up, Daiki?' Shun questioned, his eyes not leaving the empty cup in his hand.

'No doubt the same reason you are both up. I am uneasy but perhaps it is the hostility towards me from a certain travelling companion which has chased sleep away.' He chuckled at Amaya but did not elaborate further.

'You make it too easy, Lord Daiki,' Amaya countered, unable it seemed to let his hidden jibe go. She inwardly chastised herself for allowing him to rile her.

'You wound me, Lady Amaya.' He placed a strong hand over his heart.

'*You* are welcome, Lord Daiki, but your abrasiveness is not,' Amaya reasoned, studying his features. Shun remained silent as the argument unfolded, Amaya could sense his agitation acutely, but Daiki continued.

'We should all get some sleep.' Amaya placed a hand under Shun's elbow, pulling him to his feet. She glanced at Daiki but he remained seated and showed no sign of heeding her suggestion.

'Goodnight, Amaya Takeda. You can sleep safely, knowing I am keeping watch.' Daiki saluted his brother, and Amaya was taken aback by the sincerity of the smile he gave him.

Amaya had slept for a few hours and was woken by a knock on her door.

'Come in,' she said, sleepily, hopping on the spot as she tried to pull her happi top into place. The floor was cold beneath the soles of her feet. Akio entered causing Amaya to sway dangerously as she hurried to secure the ties.

'Sorry. I thought that you were Inari,' Amaya said, embarrassed.

Akio turned abruptly to face the door. 'I wanted to let you know that breakfast is ready. Inari has kindly cooked for us.' Akio walked out the door closing it quietly behind himself. Amaya let out a deep breath, shaking her head and laughing to herself. She quickly pulled on the rest of her clothes. Tucking her billowing trousers into her split-toed tabi socks and picking up her bag, she left the room and entered the store. Laid out across the small bar were many plates of homemade food.

Inari smiled and beckoned Amaya to come over. 'Come and sit, Amaya. You have time for breakfast.'

Amaya grinned, it seemed Inari was in good spirits. Amaya's admiration of Inari's resilience became stronger and she took a seat between Shun and Akio.

'Where is Eisen?' Amaya questioned, immediately feeling Kin's absence.

'It seems you are beginning to realise the senses of Ueten,' Kin spoke quietly to Amaya, as he entered the store. He then continued to speak to the rest. 'I was exploring Kusamachi and have good news. I have managed to find us some transportation.'

They all looked at the white-garbed warrior monk.

'You have been busy,' Akio grinned, offering him a seat.

'I have obtained some horses. Reasonable price and in good condition for their age.'

'That is good news, Eisen,' Inari spoke handing him a bowl of food. 'Here, eat this.'

Kin bowed his head in thanks.

The breakfast did not last long, and Amaya was sad when the time came to depart. Inari's domestic chatter had successfully removed them all from the matter at hand.

'Inari, thank you for your kindness. It was more than we could have hoped for,' Amaya said.

Inari took her hands and beamed. 'I am glad to have met you, Amaya. I hope you all stop by again.' She stood at the entrance to her store as they all bowed.

'We may well take that offer, Inari,' Akio replied. They approached the horses and mounted them.

'Lady Takeda, can you ride a horse?' Shun said.

Amaya raised her eyebrows. 'Of course.'

Shun nodded and squeezed his legs, sending his horse into a quick trot. The group waved to Inari, who slowly became smaller as more distance grew between them.

CHAPTER SEVEN

The border to the Earth Province was coming closer and Amaya felt uneasy. The mountains to their left stretched into the sky, towering over them like the spine of some gargantuan creature which would stir at the slightest noise. Amaya had felt the very ground beneath her feet shake several times throughout her life, and pictured a slumbering being stirring below the soil and water and cities. *Gekai*, she thought to herself as imaginings of Ueten and Gekai came forth. Her mother had told her as a child that if she wasn't quiet at night and didn't go to bed sensibly, that she might wake the beast beneath the earth.

Amaya's hands were slick against the reins. Despite the Face of Winter fast approaching, she felt overheated. They had been riding hard. The long wall which marked the border snaked its way through the grassy, hilly countryside and up the mountain's craggy feet. Amaya could see the moss and vines creeping up the stones; nature reclaiming what was once its own.

'There is the entrance,' Kin called out to the group. They came to a halt and followed Kin's outstretched finger to the gap in the wall. It was reinforced with two large red wooden poles that indicated it was a legitimate entrance to the Earth Province.

'There should be sentries,' Amaya said.

'There has not been human presence here or on many northern outposts since the Kusamachi Battalion perished. They were the last strong force between the capital and what lies ahead, and now they have gone,' Shun said.

Amaya frowned, the true severity of the civil war was becoming more and more apparent the further they travelled north. The citizens in Chuto had truly been blinded by festivals, politics and their own lives. Amaya could not pretend she had been any different. She kicked her heels lightly, sending the horse into a canter. 'Let us go through now. Shinobi and other outlaws live in those mountains,' Amaya shouted behind her. The others caught up as they passed into the Earth Province.

The landscape was the same as the one behind them. Amaya thought it should have looked different somehow once they passed through the gate. A insubstantial droplet landed on her cheek, more followed until the air was unbreathable in the sudden icy rain. The smell of decaying foliage and mud filled Amaya's nose and mouth as the group set forward at speed.

After they had ridden for some leagues, Amaya was completely drenched. Her clothes stuck to her clammy skin and felt heavy. Her long, black hair had fallen in bedraggled stands, clinging to her cheeks and neck uncomfortably.

'The Dao River is up ahead,' Akio yelled to the group, and they slowed their pace. The uneasiness Amaya had felt before, slithered back into her thoughts and she found herself looking in all directions. Inari's words presented themselves in her mind, she had said that the Dao was under the control of the rebel army and the nameless warlord who led them.

'Shall we continue up the river or stop at Kawazoi, the town at the foot of that mountain?' Akio questioned. The group's silence was broken by the slapping of the rain against the sodden grass and their steeds' shuddering pants.

'How long would it take to reach Kawazoi?' Amaya replied.

'A day's ride, but it is off our course,' Daiki said, loudly.

'If we continue to the river, we could board a boat. That would take us closer to Rikujou and allow us to rest,' Amaya suggested, thinking of the river ferries her uncle had told her about.

'Haste is necessary when traversing these places,' Kin replied. 'Lady Amaya's idea is sound.' The group pushed forward through the wind, water spraying up from the horses' feet.

They had entered a forest of beech trees at noon and now, in the late afternoon, Amaya's discomfort was beginning to worsen, and she pulled to a stop.

'I think we have strayed from the path, Akio.' She turned in her seat and surveyed the forest. Each direction looked the same. Beech tree after beech tree rose from the leafy floor and towered above, their grasping branches forming a broken canopy which swayed with the wind and sprinkled droplets from the earlier storm. Amaya could hear the flow of water nearby.

She dismounted her horse and clambered through the leaves and over small hillocks, fighting her way through soaking twigs and bracken, her senses converging on the gushing. She saw the water; it streamed roughly over rocks and weaved its way out of sight. Drawing closer, she crouched beside it and reached into its ripples. It was warm. She let her hands linger in the spring water.

'Amaya.'

Amaya started in surprise. She turned and saw Akio approach.

'Please do not vanish like that.' He smiled and then looked at the steaming creek. Daiki, closely followed by Shun and Kin, came into sight pulling Akio and Amaya's horses with them.

'Amaya has found this stream. I believe if we follow it, we will find the Dao River,' Akio said, as he formed a foothold for Amaya to mount her horse.

The group slowly meandered through the trees and over rocky mounds, following the stream. Amaya felt sore from the uneven ride but was distracted from the ache when she heard the deep bellow of a bear from where they had come. A sulphurous aroma saturated the area, but Amaya didn't mind it. She thought it might conceal their presence. As they proceeded, the stream became wider and faster. The trees began to thin out and Amaya could see beyond the edge of the forest. Gradually, the sound of many voices reached her ears.

'People,' she said, warily. Amaya looked at the clandestine pontoon which had appeared, shrouded by the trees of the forest which continued to stretch along the river's banks.

Shun spoke in a low tone. 'We must approach openly. They may be the ferrymen of the boats which sail to the coast.'

Amaya nodded as the group continued and left the protection of the forest. She could see a group of men beside the boat. They were yelling at the workers who were loading large boxes onto the deck. Others on board were strapping them down and recounting their cargo. Amaya could smell their exertion from where she was. One of the men on the riverbank looked up and noticed the group. He shouted to his men who immediately stopped their work and picked up their weapons; each figure straightened and fixed their attention onto the approaching group. Shun held out his hand and the others halted. Daiki stopped alongside his brother, his eyes trained forward.

'We only want transportation,' Kin shouted.

The man who had spied them looked to his fellow beside him expectantly and spoke in low tones which Amaya barely caught.

'We do not take passengers,' the man, who had alerted the others, said in an odd gruff tone. Amaya squinted trying to scrutinise the stranger. He was dressed in strange clothing, his skin was olive and his hair black and curly, but his features were wholly unfamiliar.

'See his looks? He is not from Akegata. He is a foreigner,' Amaya spoke in hushed tones. She had never met a foreigner before, but her father had spoken of the ones he had met. 'All foreigners are as different as you or I, Amaya,' her father had said, in answer to her question. Once, she had seen a Great Ship on her trip to the north of the Sky Province when she was younger. However, she had only seen the crew from a distance. 'These foreigners are pale skinned, like a doll, Amaya. Their wide eyes are all manner of different colours, like their hair. Several men I saw had locks of red, as red as fire.' Amaya had gasped at the idea of red hair and colourful eyes. 'They sound like Oni from Demon Island.'

Her father had crouched down next to her, pointing at the vessel. 'They call that ship a carrack. Last month, we had merchants from a land where their skin was tanned gold, their eyes bronze and chestnut, with tall noses and hair black as lacquer.'

Amaya pulled herself from her memories, her father's voice disappearing with the phantom of his face. Akio continued, staring at the stranger. 'More importantly what is the weapon he is carrying. It is not a katana or a bow. I have not seen foreigners carrying such an item before.'

Shun frowned and yelled out to the man. 'There are only five of us. We do not need passage as far as the coast, our destination is Rikujou.'

The man took another few paces forward, his weapon still raised. Amaya squinted so as to study it, but it was too distant.

'We can pay you,' Daiki added. Silence followed as the man turned to his comrade and a rapid but hushed conversation took place. The man turned back to face them and gestured for them to approach. The workers on the riverbank and on the boat lowered their weapons and continued with their task.

'We will take two of your horses as payment,' the smaller man explained.

'This way,' the foreigner attempted, clearly uncomfortable with the language.

Amaya tried to place his face, but it was unlike any she had seen. His nose protruded from his face like a hook, creating a distinct profile. His eyes were unusual, large like a horse's and lighter in colour. He turned his head, and even in the dim light, darts of green broke the bronze surface of his irises. She stared at the weapon hanging from his belt. The length of it was a hollow, steel tube resting in a wooden sheath, the end curved downward. On the top side was an odd protrusion of brass. Also, in brass were intricate floral engravings set into the wooden base. Amaya began to doubt that it was a weapon at all; it did not seem sharp, it was not like any blade she had ever seen, and it was too short to be a yari spear or bo staff. She saw that the other men were compiled of Akegatans and other foreigners; they were carrying katana.

She ascended the ramp on the main deck, staring at them inquisitively. Each set of eyes stared back but told of nothing. She soon realised as she passed by the many men that she was the only woman. The boat was of a moderate size but the cargo of heavy boxes overtook the space. The man pointed to a gap between the boxes and the railings. The smaller man interpreted the foreigner's hurried speech. 'You sit there until we reach your destination. We will arrive there after sunset.' With these last words, the and the foreign leader departed.

The last box was heaved into place and the enormous black sail was unfurled with a snap. Amaya felt the boat begin to drift away as the wind caught the heavy fabric and lent the boat its speed. The men descended to take up their oars and standby should the wind fail. The river was wide, and the banks were hidden by winter-stripped trees and shrubs which were once red or green. Amaya watched the water as the speed increased. Icy spray found its way through the railings and flecked her face. Returning her gaze to the forest, she caught glimpses of monkeys and heard the shrieks and knocks of the Picus birds hidden amongst the dense trees, hammering their green heads against trunks.

'I am going to check our horses. The one's they aren't keeping,' Daiki informed the group. He stood somewhat unsteadily as the boat swayed. 'They cannot be enjoying this ride, but I love it. Boats are superior.'

The crew had remained hostile and had not approached them since they had left the pontoon hours before. Amaya turned as Akio handed her a flask.

'The temperature is cooling with every league,' he said, rubbing his hands together. 'You should keep warm.'

'It is a beautiful forest here, even when staring at the Face of Winter. It makes me realise how much of Akegata I have yet to see. So many hidden secrets.'

'Secrets I am sure you'll have plenty of time to explore,' Akio replied, straightening up and squinting at the riverbank.

Amaya faltered, 'I hope so. That would be a true blessing.' Strangely she thought of Gekai as she contemplated discovering Akegata later in life. 'I am going to walk further down the boat,' Amaya said, 'stretch my legs.' She rose stiffly to her feet and walked along the railing towards the bow. The wind was harsher nearer the front, but movement was bringing life back into her deadened legs. Amaya remained there staring at the river. She peered over the edge and watched the water part and stream down the length of the boat. She thought it remarkable how a powerful river could be so silent. *The dragon river-god must be sleeping,* she pondered.

'Are you hinin?' An odd voice came from behind her.

She turned and found a foreigner standing close by, but it was not the leader who had granted them passage. This one was taller but not as interesting to look upon. He clearly understood and spoke more of her tongue than the leader.

'Yes. I am a singer. From Chuto, travelling to Rikujou for work,' Amaya recited the prearranged fabrication, hoping the man could understand her.

'A singer?' His eyes widened happily. He reached for her arm, his rough hands closing about her wrist. 'I have heard of singers and other trades. The Water Trade. Are you from a Yūkaku district?'

With a sudden horror, Amaya realised the mistake he had made. 'No, I am not the kind of woman you assume.'

He yanked her close to him, towards the crates before she could say more.

'Please, let me go. You have misunderstood me. I am a singer, a bard, nothing more. I do not provide the pleasures you are looking for.' Desperation made her voice rise. The foreigner was incredibly strong, his hands like solid iron around her small wrist. With her free hand Amaya reached for her hidden katana but was freed from having to reveal her weapon.

'In trouble already. You are a tiresome guest.' Daiki had emerged from the other side of the boat. Amaya glanced at him, her hand lingering by her side. The foreigner had also turned at Daiki's interruption, and Amaya could see that he was not happy.

He waved his other hand violently through the air, gesturing for Daiki to leave them be. 'Mine,' he growled at Daiki.

Daiki held his hands up in defence, his expression humoured. 'Ordinarily, I would not deprive you. A man has his desires, but unfortunately, she is my travelling companion, and is indeed a singer. And a singer only.' Daiki stepped forward now, his eyes serious. The look was not lost on the foreigner. Daiki pointed from Amaya and then to himself.

'Your wife?' The foreigner asked after a moment's pause.

'Yes,' Amaya seized the opportunity, nodding fervently. The man grunted his annoyance and thrust Amaya forward. She collided heavily with Daiki's chest, but he remained firm, one hand finding her back and steadying her.

'You have my thanks.' Daiki nodded politely to the foreigner who turned and disappeared. 'Your husband?' Daiki stared at Amaya, laughing. 'That must have pained you to say.'

'I was hoping he would respect that at least,' Amaya said, nettled.

'It seems he did. Still, best to stay with your own group until we alight. Another foreigner might not be so understanding, and your husband might not be there to aid you.' Daiki walked away, leaving Amaya solitary between the crates. She shuddered at the thought of what might have unfurled had Daiki not arrived, and hastily left the shadows, continuing to bow of the boat. The beauty of the journey was tainted now, and she couldn't help but flinch every time a person passed her by.

'Your husband is a handsome man. Very handsome.' A delicate but husky voice sounded from behind Amaya.

'Oh, yes. I suppose he is.' Amaya relaxed when she realised it was a woman, an Akegatan. *Where has she been this whole time?* Amaya watched her.

'Still, I find mine infinitely more attractive.' The woman had long, rippling ebon hair which she had clasped low in an old style. The fringe was blunt, but it made her eyes seem bigger. She was as petit as Amaya but very round at the belly.

'I am with child.' The woman tapped her stomach, her eyes shining. She took Amaya's hand, steering her toward the railing. The skin on her palms was rough for a woman's.

'Who is your husband?'

'The foreign leader, Afonso.' The woman stared out across the river, her cheeks red. 'My name is Kaori.'

'It is good to meet you.' Amaya bowed. 'How is it you came to marry a foreigner? I have never even met one before.'

Kaori shrugged. 'Luck. Punishment. Duty. Love. Take your pick.'

Amaya frowned at the bizarre words, and Kaori laughed loudly again. Amaya noted something peculiar in the sound, and suddenly she didn't feel altogether safe around this woman.

'Will you have children one day?' Kaori asked, directly, her eyes holding Amaya firmly.

Amaya stuttered. 'Perhaps.'

'You would have beautiful children I should think. Especially with that husband of yours.' Kaori raised her eyebrows. 'You are very pretty. Big eyes. Knowing eyes.' She leant close to Amaya; her hand snaking up quickly, her fingers caressing her cheek. Amaya stepped back. Kaori's hand remained in the air, but her eyes never left Amaya's.

'No one will take my child from me,' Kaori said, quietly.

'Who would want to?' Amaya said.

'Everyone. And no one. Him. He thinks I do not see it.' Kaori gripped the railing and lent backward, throwing her head back and releasing another laugh. 'But I, the Torima, shall not allow it.'

Amaya simply stared. The woman was unhinged, yet there was something childlike in her character. 'Your child will be safe with you I am sure.'

'Of course she will,' Kaori said, snapping her head back down to face Amaya.

'She?'

'I know it is a girl. I can feel it.'

'That's good.' Amaya didn't know what else to say.

Kaori shrugged. 'I would not mind a boy, but girls are clever in a different way to boys.'

Amaya laughed a little but did not respond.

Kaori smiled widely. 'I have enjoyed talking with you.'

'Ayane. My name is Ayane.'

'Yes, I am sure it is. Well, Ayane, I must see to my husband. Even with a belly this big he still has an appetite to satiate. A woman's work is never done,' she giggled and walked away, leaving Amaya stunned.

After another hour or so Amaya felt certain it would be time for them to disembark but a shout from below broke the hush. Immediately, the crew came to life and the sound of feet running on the deck erupted around Amaya. She turned in bewilderment, the sudden burst of noise causing her to adopt a defensive stance. The far bank, which only moments before had been still in the moonlight, was lined with Kaminari bandits who had appeared from nothingness. Amaya squinted and watched as numerous fire arrows were released upon the boat. Screams from the oarsmen below deck rent the air. Amaya's inertia was shattered as an arrow embedded itself in the deck by her feet. She stumbled back frantically looking around for her comrades. The deck continued to burn as more arrows pierced the ship. She gazed at the river and saw the bandits climbing into small boats which had emerged from the reeds. A moment of gratitude; they weren't shinobi. Indeed, if they had been, nobody would have heard them until they had boarded and begun slitting throats.

A man pushed Amaya to one side roughly. It was the foreign leader, Kaori's husband, Afonso. Amaya gripped her arm where he had pushed her; the wound from her attack at the palace still ached. She could not remove her stare from him as he raised the mysterious weapon to his shoulder and pointed the tip forward toward the nearest boat of bandits.

All seemed mute as Amaya watched Afonso use the strange weapon, fascinated. He ignited the small wick which crackled and was devoured by the flame quickly. The one thing she did recognise was the smell of gunpowder. She saw his finger resting upon a small curved piece of metal on the underside of the weapon. He closed one eye, and Amaya followed his gaze. He pulled his finger back, and a thunderous bang saturated the air. A cry left Amaya's lips as her hands went to her ears. All sound was briefly muffled, and a dull ringing began. She crouched down instinctively. Her breath was lost as one of the bandits was thrown off his feet, blood spraying the water. He fell from the boat and Amaya did not see him re-emerge. She gazed at the bandits as they scoured the boat for the source of the deafening sound. She could not move for fear, her eyes focused on the bloody water and her stomach lurched.

Another piercing crack issued, and Afonso's body jolted with the power. Another bandit screamed and held his stomach trying to stem the flow of blood which washed over his hands and drenched his clothes. Amaya looked on in morbid enthrallment. More men approach the railings, all carrying the same terrifying weapon, and the once calm river was in turmoil with the thrashing of arms and legs and ripping of the air. The blood on the water's surface seemed almost pink in the moonlight. The cacophony deafened her to all else, even from her own voice, and the acrid stink of gunpowder was a blanket about her.

Pushing up, Amaya found her feet and scrambled away from the side of the boat and the firing weapons. She found herself buffeted by the frantic crew who all assumed position against the bandits. However, some had made their way on to the deck. Their eyes roved above their masked mouths and they held their short swords aloft. Amaya knew she must return to her group, but blaze and bandit hindered her path. Rushing forward, she used her shoulder to clear a path. Yet she was pushed back and jostled whenever she made progress. Her tanto dagger slipped from her sleeve and into her palm, ready. As she rounded a flaming stack of crates, a group of bandits thundered across her path screaming maniacally. Two stopped and faced her, lingering in their murderous thoughts. Amaya's chest was already heaving with exertion, but she would not stop moving forward. Gripping her small blade, she took just one step forward when a familiar sound shattered the space around her.

The bandit nearest to Amaya lost half their face in the explosion which ripped through skin and bone. Afonso was positioned to the right of Amaya, his weapon smoking in bloody murder. Blood flecked Amaya's face and side. A detached eye swam in puddle of crimson, staring up at her. The other bandit reeled back, looking from his fallen companion to Afonso, who was preparing his weapon for a second assault. However, Amaya moved first, driving her blade deep into the bandit's back. She heaved upward until she felt him fall limp and collapse to the ground. Afonso only paused for a moment; his eyes narrowed, his expression grateful.

'Lady Amaya!'

Amaya was grabbed from behind and Afonso moved on. Shun gripped her wrist tightly and dragged her to the stern where Kin and Akio were waiting. The fire began to engulf the ship despite the crews' efforts. Amaya recoiled as a man staggered forward his chest on fire, an arrow protruding from his sternum. The cabin was alight with red and orange as the arrows danced around them. The screams of the horses were the most piercing in the night's chaos. Flashes of the flaming dojo enveloped Amaya's mind. Akio pulled her close to him as the ship creaked nastily and the sail disappeared in a wall of fire. The crew began to cough and retch, their eyes watering as the thick smoke clouded the boat. Both crew and bandit could no longer see.

'They are using gunpowder. They must have some stored aboard,' Amaya yelled over the shouting.

'This way, quickly. When the fire reaches the gunpowder, the explosion will leave nothing,' Kin replied, beckoning the group to follow him to the other side of the ship away from the arrows.

'Where's my brother?' Shun shouted, turning on the spot, his eyes searching for Daiki.

'I have not seen him since sunset.'

'He is probably with the horses,' Akio said. 'I will go.'

'It is impossible to get below deck,' Amaya shouted, her hand reaching for Akio's arm. Her feet were hot, the fire raging below was consuming the innards of the boat. Planks began to fall away under the heat. The ship leaned to one side creaking in pain, and Amaya found herself scrabbling to stay upright. Shun gripped her arm and heaved her up.

A crack as loud as any thunder filled the air; the boat was splitting. The sudden lurch sent Kin and Akio over the railings to the river below. Amaya shouted out in shock and ran to the edge, Shun still holding her arm. She looked down to the frothy water but could not see anything.

'Shun! What shall we do?' Amaya turned to him, her expression desperate.

'Can you swim, Lady Takeda?' Shun said.

'Daiki...' Amaya's sentence faded.

Ignoring her, Shun kicked away a fragment of the railings. She stood beside him not taking her eyes from his dark ones, and without hesitation they both leapt from the edge of the boat, Shun still holding Amaya's hand.

  As they plunged below the surface of the murky freezing water, Amaya's hand was ripped from Shun's grasp, and the sounds from above were muffled to near silence. A strange sensation numbed her body as she floated below the surface for a moment, suspended in the icy comfort of the soundless water. Keeping her eyes closed, she gathered her bearings and the disorientation diminished. Her breath was short and with one hand on her katana she kicked forward wanting to put distance between herself and the blazing ship. The thought of the unknown cache of gunpowder spurred her on. Her chest stabbed with pain and she flailed her legs, her breath burst from her lungs in bubbles which fought each other as they rose. Her kimono and cloak weakened her by the moment. Using just one hand, her chilled fingers struggled with the clasp about her neck. Her legs kicked violently as she fought to rid herself of the weight of fabric. The instant it was loose, she dragged her arms through the water, pulling herself upward. Amaya broke through the surface, her mouth opening wide as she drew in air. She did not look back but struggled toward the shore. The yells and bangs were still loud behind as she reached out and grabbed a handful of reeds and pulled herself into them until she made contact with the solid riverbank.

  The explosion was incredible. The blast rippled across the frothy water, pushing her hard against the damp soil, and everything was illuminated for a moment in a bright light. Splintered wood and shattered metal burst outward. Amaya could hear the shrapnel bombarding the reeds and water alike. She gripped the shrubs and heaved herself from the cold water once the last splash had sounded. Crawling to a tree, she fell against it unable to control her rapid, pain-filled breathing. The silence which followed the explosion was so peculiar that Amaya thought she had gone entirely deaf. Her ears rang and her vision swayed languidly.

She lay still for a moment allowing the dizziness to ebb away, but it was soon replaced by uncontrollable shivering. The excitement had left her limbs and Amaya could feel weakness steeling over her. She scoured the bank but could not see far, trees and tall shrubs obscured her sight. Looking back, she watched as the ship and its cargo disintegrated, the screams dying away with it. The pieces of boat looked like small, fiery islands. Curling into a ball and tucking her hands under her arms she allowed herself to rest. She could not control the convulsions that racked her body as she gulped for breath The sting of gunpowder infused the air about her as she closed her eyes.

Amaya felt heat. Her eyes were still shut, and she was aware of dancing light across her eyelids. For a wild moment, she thought she was still on the ferry, and that the fire was still raging. However, her ears adjusted, and she could hear the crackle of a small fire and the smell of beech wood. Her eyes were heavy, and the lids seemed stuck together. She reached a hand shakily to her face and rubbed her eyes open.

'Amaya? How do you feel?'

Amaya recognised the voice, and it soothed her panic. 'Kin.'

His form came into focus, sitting anxiously next to her. 'I am glad you have woken. You have been like this for over a day,' he said rearranging the blanket that covered Amaya. She struggled to sit up.

'Where is Akio and Shun? And Daiki?' Amaya said, slowly realising the absence of the others.

Kin drew a breath. 'Shun left to find Akio this morning. Shun and I located each other first and then we discovered Daiki alive. After the three of us rejoined, we stumbled upon you, but we have not yet found Akio.'

Amaya assessed Kin's countenance. Her throat became strangely solid and her eyes stung as she comprehended what he was saying.

'I did not know what to think when you and Akio were thrown overboard,' Amaya said. She looked at the fire hoping for a distraction. The screams from the ship echoed in her mind as she gazed through the smoke. Hanging on a low bough, just beyond the fire's reach, were her clothes. Gasping, she glanced under the blanket. Relief ensued; she was not completely undressed.

Kin gave a small sigh. 'We had to get you out of the wet clothes. They were practically frozen onto you. The Face of Winter is looking further and further south with each day.'

She gave a small smile and remembered something important. 'My katana, Meiyo, do you have it?'

Kin pointed, she followed his hand and saw her katana leaning against a tree.

'I did not know you had brought a katana, Amaya,' Kin said, quietly.

'I did not think it important to mention. Women are not allowed to carry weapons, so I thought it best to keep it out of sight from strangers. I did not wish to draw attention,' Amaya explained.

'A wise decision but I do feel more at ease knowing that you can protect yourself. I should have expected as much, you are Kazu Takeda's daughter, after all.' Kin smiled knowingly and looked upward, the night had finally taken the sky.

'Where is Taka?' Amaya realised that Kin's hawk had not been present since before they had boarded the boat.

Kin lowered his gaze. 'Taka is soaring above us now, she proves a useful eye in these situations. She is guiding us to Rikujou.'

Amaya cocked her head to one side. 'I did not realise. She must be very intelligent,' Amaya replied, in awe.

Kin nodded. He made to reply but stopped abruptly and rose to his feet. 'Someone is aproaching.'

Amaya clutched the blanket tightly and rushed to her clothes. They were dry and crisp. She pulled them on hastily as Kin held out a burning branch, casting light in front of himself. Amaya then heard footsteps, clumsily stumbling through the bracken. As she narrowed her eyes, she could make out three figures.

'Oh!' Amaya yelled out. She ran to meet the three, but her happiness was flattened. Shun's face was grim and haggard, Daiki's exhausted, and hanging between them was Akio. His feet were dragging, and his body was unmoving. Shun and Daiki pulled Akio past the silent Amaya and placed him on the ground by the fire. They looked up at Kin who fell to his knees and began to examine Akio closely. Amaya watched as Kin turned his back to them and focused, she could not see what he was doing but she could not tear her gaze from Akio's white face. Helplessness blossomed from the ashes of hope and she felt her eyes brim.

'He has a heartbeat. A very faint one,' Kin said, without stopping his work.

Shun sat down heavily and lent his head back upon the tree with exhaustion, whilst Daiki remained afoot, uneasy, his gaze upon the man he and his brother had rescued. Amaya touched Akio's hand. She had never felt a living body that cold. His skin was grey and his lips a deep blue. She did not leave his side, and she did not remove her hand.

Gradually, colour began to spread across Akio's face with the aid of the fire but his expression remained passive and inert.

'Thank you for finding him, General Kimura, Lord Daiki,' Amaya spoke, quietly, bowing low.

Shun faced her, his black eyes acknowledging her thanks. 'Lord Izumi is a good friend.'

'And we cannot have the Secretariat die, can we?' Daiki said, taking a seat. He too looked moments from sleep, his eyes ringed in dark circles, and his hair loose and dishevelled. 'Lord Yamashima would never forgive us.'

Amaya stoked the fire with dry wood. 'I need to keep the fire going. We need to dry out the clothes.' Amaya's voice was hollow. She felt that she could do nothing for Akio. Shun and Daiki had found him and brought him back. Kin was working on his broken body. She had done, and could do, nothing.

'Thank you,' Shun said, passing her more wood.

Kin sighed and looked up. 'We have to wait for him to regain consciousness until I can properly assess his condition. If he makes it to morning, he will have passed through the most dangerous time.'

Kin rested against a large log, closing his eyes. Amaya watched him fall asleep, realising how he had worked to save both herself and Akio. She turned to Shun who had closed his eyes too, his breathing now steady. Only she and Daiki remained awake, but he did not make any base comments as she would have expected. He merely watched nothing, his hand never leaving the hilt of his katana. She continued to feed the fire.

Amaya didn't remember falling asleep. The warmth of the fire had diminished with its flame and the campfire was now a small mound of embers but the wind was no longer vicious. Amaya sat up as the events of the previous night forced her awake. She glanced around, Shun, Daiki and Kin were not there. Turning her head, she saw the still form of Akio. She crawled on her hands and knees, moving to his side and leaning over his quiet body. A sigh of relief escaped her as she saw the rise and fall of his chest; he had survived the night. Colour had returned to his face also. She stroked his cheek with the back of her hand gently to be sure; it was warm. Akio reached up, his fingers finding hers.

'Amaya?' he spoke, his voice barely audible. She smiled down at him, her black hair touching his face as she lent in to make out his words. She placed an arm around his back, helping him up to sit up.

'I am glad you are unhurt,' Akio said, strength returning to his voice. Amaya busied herself, feeding the fire until a healthy flame flurried and hastily skewered a few fish which had been caught that morning, sticking them over the fire.

'You scared us, Akio. We could not find you for two days. When I woke up you were not here,' Amaya said, softly.

Akio frowned. 'What happened to you, Amaya?'

'Shun found me unconscious by the river. He and Kin helped me recover. Shun and Daiki found you, and Kin worked all night. We thought you were going to die,' she said, seriously. He watched her and smiled, relief sweeping his frown away.

'Thank goodness for our companions.'

Amaya nodded in agreement.

'Where are they now?' Akio continued, looking around the small camp.

Amaya shrugged. 'I only woke a moment ago, they were not here.'

'Their belongings are here so they cannot have gone far,' Akio said, reassuringly. He gazed past Amaya. 'Kazu's blade, Meiyo.'

Amaya turned and her eyes fell upon her weapon. 'Yes. My father's katana.' Amaya felt no worry in telling Akio the truth, it had been he who had returned the blade to her after all. He nodded and held out his hand. She leant back, picked it up and passed it to him. 'It is all that is left of my father's legacy now the dojo has gone.'

'It is a fine katana.' Akio turned it in his hands, marvelling at its design. 'Many a time in training I clashed my blade against this one.' The gleaming navy sheath was only disturbed by swirls of silver. Near the hilt, the Takeda clan mon could be seen: the four diamonds locked together. 'Sparring with your father are some of my fondest memories. It is a katana befitting the master of the Seishin no Ken style. The name is perfect too.'

'Meiyo,' Amaya replied.

'Honour.'

Both Akio and Amaya turned. Shun and Kin appeared from behind the surrounding beech trees each carrying a few small sacks.

'Lord Akio, I am glad you are awake. You too, Lady Amaya,' Shun said, relief breaking through his usual seriousness. Amaya stood and walked towards them, holding out her hand she relieved Kin of a bag.

'Where is Daiki?' Shun questioned, his eyes searching the trees which surrounded them.

'I am here, brother.' Daiki stepped into their circle. 'Keeping watch over the sleeping babes as you instructed.' His eyes fell on Amaya, then shifted slightly to Akio before returning to his brother again. Amaya squirmed but did not voice her discomfort on Daiki overhearing her conversation with Akio.

'What have you been doing?' Amaya asked the other two.

'We lost all our provisions on the boat. So, Shun and I ventured out and found a small town further down the river. We managed to barter some belongings,' Kin said, pulling out a box. 'How about we have a drink of Sake?'

Amaya grinned. 'One glass in celebration of our safety and Akio's recovery.'

Kin passed out small cups and they all sat in the quiet created by the cocoon of trees, sipping the rice wine.

'We made an interesting discovery whilst in the town.' Shun broke the stillness. Amaya and Akio looked up. Kin's gentle expression became grave as he pushed his conical hat from his head.

'Some of the men from the ship had survived and were there. We heard a worrying discussion.'

Kin glanced at Shun and looked down at his feet seemingly happy to let the General tell the tale. Akio frowned and Amaya's momentary celebratory mood vanished with the smoke of the fire.

'It seems a good number of those boxes were recovered from the wreck. Each box was full of those weapons we saw being used. They are called Firearms; powered by gunpowder, firing a small lead ball at great speed. They are deadly weapons to samurai and archer alike.' Shun rubbed his face in agitation.

'Those weapons were almost magical; I could not even see it. Who would invent something that destroys lives so easily? There is no honour or grace in those things.'

'There is no true grace in death, and honour disappears with the person, Amaya, whether delivered by a katana or a Firearm,' Kin said, sharply. Amaya felt slightly taken aback but found herself pondering her own words.

'Why bring them to Akegata?' Akio said.

'A foreign race has formed an alliance with the leader of the rebel army. They were allowed entry to Akegata as part of a trade. Firearms would be supplied to the rebel army and the foreigners allowed a foothold in the new society of Akegata, a foothold in trade from Kasaichi Harbour in the Fire Province,' Kin continued.

Akio looked outraged. 'Those weapons in the hands of the rebel army? Lord Kenta must be informed. Even the Imperial army cannot defend against such weapons. How have they managed to smuggle such cargo through Akegata past the checkpoints? Surely the Ito Merchant's Guild would prevent such a transaction? Which port did they arrive at?' Akio's eyes were alive with questions.

'Should Lord Kenta be informed of this by bird, Akio? It would be too risky,' Kin suggested. 'Especially if there are those who know of these weapons within the Court.'

Akio shook his head. 'I believe the Emperor should be informed by us directly, rather than information passing through another party. It will have to be documented if he is told now. That may be a disadvantage.'

'You mean in case those who should not be made aware of the information discover it?'

'Correct, Lady Takeda. We still have time,' Shun said, joining the conversation. Amaya looked at him. His expression was as grave as the others', his tone serious.

'I take it back, Lord Akio,' Daiki whispered. Amaya

started; she had almost forgotten his presence he had been so silent.

Akio looked quizzical. 'What is your meaning?'

Daiki uncrossed his arms, an elegant movement which Amaya was slowly becoming used to. 'I mean that I retract my remark about the bow being a coward's weapon. I believe we have a true victor for that title, these Frearms.' Daiki's voice held no jest.

However, the moment Daiki had spoken, Rai Kimura's weathered face had entered Amaya's mind, at once putting her on edge. She wanted to turn around at that moment and return to the palace, to Kenta. She did not want him exposed to Rai whilst he was alone.

Kin was gazing at her, his expression comforting. 'Do not worry, Amaya, all is well at present. You have an important part to play yourself, you must avoid distraction. Kenta is more than capable.'

'We had better hurry to Rikujou then. We cannot allow a new regime to begin. I will not live in a country run by a dictator who uses weapons like that and condones the current Court.'

CHAPTER EIGHT

The shrubbery had started to thin out, but reeds still lined the banks of the Dao River.

'We should take this road. We will be in Rikujou in under an hour,' Kin informed the group as he looked up at Taka circling above.

An hour passed and, as Kin had predicted, around the next river bend they saw before them, stretching out across the flats, Rikujou. It dominated the countryside with its far-reaching streets which crisscrossed around the shrine at its centre. Even from where Amaya stood, the shrine was huge; its red hue stark against the leafless city trees and the earthen browns of the many houses. That day had been the coldest Amaya had felt so far and as her gaze travelled beyond the city, she saw another surge of rain clouds trolling across the sky. She was not sure how long it would be until the next downpour. The clouds looked furious in their mottled purples and grays; everything felt closer under the dense shroud.

The slope leading to Rikujou was gentle. Her gaze rolled over the drained terraced rice fields which descended either side of them; the sporadic trees which were home to no life; the odd traveller or farmer making their way to an unknown place. The salt-laced wind gushed in from the east and Amaya's cloak billowed violently in its tugs. She had taken to keeping a hand held to her hood to prevent it from falling. She could hear beside her Kin's holy staff, its metal adornments chinking loudly.

'Amaya!' Kin pushed her to one side roughly. Several carts sped by, the men whipping the reigns unrelentingly. She watched as five carts passed, followed by one large palanquin born on the shoulders of several muscular men. She squinted and noticed the large boxes which weighed the carts down.

'Those crates!' She gasped turning to face the others. They continued to watch, until the carts and the palanquin reached the entrance to Rikujou.

'Look, gatekeepers. Will we be able to gain access?' Amaya wondered aloud; her tone worried as she watched the guards interrogate the visitors.

Daiki stared at the huge red wooden gate. 'Wait.' He walked at the front and met the sentry. Amaya watched as he talked to the guard but was unable to hear the conversation. She raised her eyebrows as the gatekeeper waved to the other guard to let them through.

'What did you say, Daiki?' Akio asked, surprised.

'One military soldier to another. Favour for a comrade,' Daiki said.

'We should find the foreigner,' Amaya said, not forgetting the cart which had passed them by.

'I agree,' Kin replied. 'But first we should find a place to put our belongings and rest.'

Akio nodded. 'I think we would all do well with a rest.'

Amaya didn't voice her agitation but could not stem her desire to seek out the foreigner and the strange weapons he carried. Her curiosity had already been peaked, and so had her fear.

'I remember a small Ryokan near the city shrine. We will find a warm welcome and discretion there,' Kin replied to Akio. However, his eyes were on Amaya. 'I will lead the way.'

As the group strode the length of the wide main street, Amaya caught snatches of peoples' conversations, and they all seemed to be about the same subject: the civil war. Many were expressing their opinions on who they believed to be behind the threat. Several voices hissed the feared word 'shinobi' and once Amaya almost stopped to listen as one young man mentioned the Senkaku Nin. She glanced at Kin but could not be certain if he had heard the whisper about his brother's organisation. No laughter, whether an adult's or a child's, disturbed the onerous atmosphere. The children visibly clung to their mother's kimono or father's hakama, their small features displaying the anxiety which the adults carried in the tone of their voices. As Amaya glanced around, she realised that she could see no orphan children slipping around legs, scurrying to search for a meal, or to search for their friend or sibling or pickpocket an unsuspecting traveller. She felt suddenly uncomfortable. The more she looked the more she picked out samurai carrying katana. They speckled the milling crowd in twos or threes but none of them bore the Imperial mon, and with a jolt Amaya realised that they were all rebels. Her hand slipped beneath her coat and she gripped the hilt of her katana, hoping to draw comfort from the touch.

They drew closer to the shrine's main gate. Amaya's attention was stolen from the crowds. The trees which surrounded the shrine seemed diminutive to the front gate's two-tiered design. Amaya felt her lips part slightly as she gazed through the gateway to the oratory. She could feel its enormity; its black and red wooden pillars stretched high until the curved lip of the roof stretched across. Dangling from the rafters, were lanterns as big as children. Amaya could see priests around the entrance to the main building, they seemed insects in comparison to the shrine they worshipped in. Shifting her gaze, she saw several pagodas, each with five eaves intricately carved and painted. They were amongst the brown-leafed trees, red towers of wood. The building's grandeur was divine, yet Amaya felt it somehow humble.

'It really is beautiful. I think more beautiful than Chuto's shrine,' Akio said.

'It is one of the largest in Akegata. Many travel here. There are more buildings around the main house and the lecture halls are to the right.' Kin pointed to an area of twisted, mossy trees. Amaya could just see the buildings which lay behind them. 'The Ryokan is this way.' Kin beckoned the others to follow.

Amaya tore her eyes from the shrine as the group walked down the street which skirted the shrine perimeter. She saw the Ryokan; a large wooden building. It had two floors, the second fringed with a balcony. Its walls were pale, the wooden beams and pillars black. The tiled roof swept down before curving upward, the corners taking the outline of trees. Before Amaya could study more, she was ushered inside where whey were greeted by an elderly man.

'Welcome,' he spoke, in a raspy voice, bowing low. Behind his aged, bulbous eyes, Amaya could see the humour of a child. He was bent double and his legs were incredibly bowed, reminded Amaya of a frog. She bowed in return.

He looked up and gasped as he rushed forward far faster than Amaya would have thought possible. 'I haven't seen you in over a year!'

Kin smiled taking the old man's hands in his own as greeting. 'I have been travelling around Akegata. I am glad to see you are still with us, Goro.' Kin grinned as Goro gave a wicked smile.

'You are in luck, I have a suite that can accommodate you all. Of course, it has partitions, all accessible with sliding doors. So, you may have your privacy, young lady. It must be difficult to travel with a guard of four men.'

'Thank you, Goro. That will be most welcome,' Amaya said, smiling at his informal manner. Goro clapped his gnarled hands and a young woman appeared. She was shorter than Goro, perhaps only fourteen years of age but she had the same bulbous eyes.

'My granddaughter, Tamiko, will fetch some tea, whilst I show you to your rooms. Tamiko prepares all the food in this Ryokan. You'd struggle to find more delicious cuisine in the main stretch.' He grinned warmly at his granddaughter and offered the group slippers. Opening the sliding doors, he gestured them inside. Amaya gazed around the room. It was immaculate; the tatami reed mats which lined the floor were smooth. She could see a low table in the centre surrounded by soft zabuton floor pillows. The doors to the veranda were open and the small rockery and water feature were visible. She wondered how long until the water froze over, and the knock of the bamboo would cease and render the garden silent.

'This is an exquisite room, Goro. Thank you.' Amaya bowed again.

'This room is for the gentlemen. Let me show you your place, young lady.'

She followed Goro to the right of the living quarters. He slid open the papered door to reveal another smaller, but flawless room. Amaya's eyes fell onto the futon in the centre and the small, low table.

'I have been airing this suite for new visitors but with these braziers you will soon warm up. Please feel free to make yourselves comfortable. My granddaughter will bring the tea in a moment. It's Oolong tea, from across the sea.' With these last words, Goro bowed and exited the guest room. Amaya placed her belongings next to her futon and took a seat at the large low table in the living quarters. She was joined by the others; Akio taking the seat to her right, Kin to her left, and in front of her the two Kimura brothers.

'Goro seems very accommodating. Do you know him well, Eisen?' Akio questioned Kin, breaking Amaya's pondering.

Kin nodded. 'I always meet with him when I come to Rikujou. He is an old friend who has helped me many times in the past but be wary of his humour, it can be quite direct. It took me a while to get used to it.' Kin smiled. There was a knock at the door and Tamiko entered carrying a tray of cups and a steaming teapot, followed closely by her grandfather.

'Thank you, Tamiko, Goro,' Shun said, as the young girl placed the tray upon the table and poured the brown tea carefully. Her round face blushed at being addressed and she seemed unable to speak, but her shy smile spoke of her gratitude.

'Well, we will leave you now. Just ring the bell if there is anything more you need.'

The group gave their thanks to Goro and Tamiko as they left the room and slid the doors closed. Amaya wrapped her hands around the warm cup and lifted it to her lips. 'I think we should take this opportunity to look around Rikujou whilst it is still daylight. I am interested to seek out that foreigner and to see what his business is here.' She did not voice her want to begin the search for an Elemental but she knew she had no need. Kin and Akio understood, Shun and Daiki did not know the truth behind her trip.

'You're right, Amaya but I think we should rest for now. We can begin our search with fresh eyes and alert minds,' Akio said. Amaya's anxiety was not placated.

'We will go through the town and collect some more provisions. You can stay and sleep a little,' Shun said.

'Perhaps we should all rest like Lord Akio suggested.'

'We have enough energy to get some more provisions. We won't be long,' Shun said, rising to his feet. Amaya looked up at him and nodded. Akio, Daiki and Kin also stood and slid the door shut.

The silence which surrounded Amaya was sudden. She realised that she hadn't been alone on the journey thus far. She felt at ease in the Ryokan and so unpacked her things to occupy herself. Hiding her katana behind a screen which captured an old folktale in faded colours, she opened the door to the garden slightly and sat at the small table with her tea. She felt tired but knew she would not be able to sleep. Cradling the warm cup in her hands, she found thoughts of her mother slither into her mind. Amaya's lips pressed together but she could not avoid the sadness. She thought of Kannushi Masato's words, *too much remains inside you.* Shaking her head, she poured the rest of the liquid down her throat, enjoying the slight tingle the heat left behind, and rose to her feet. She plucked her cloak from the screen, wrapped it about herself and left for the city in need of a distraction.

The streets were busier than she would have expected of a city with rebel occupation, but the atmosphere was laden with unspoken trepidation. Amaya felt sickened at the sight and so extracted her pouch. Looking into the leather bag she saw the small scroll of haiku which Kyo had written for her about their father, and the golden broach bearing her family mon which her father used to wear. She only had a few ryo coins on her person and needed that for the journey back. Akio carried most of the currency.

The shrine appeared on her left; flashes of red broke through the trees of the garden and Amaya hurried on, eager to pray. She passed under the enormous gates and continued onto the wide path, which flowed directly to the shrine. There were many people on the walkway, Kannushi and worshipper alike but each seemed detached from the beauty of their surroundings. Sandalwood permeated the air delicately; at some points the scent was more intense, at others it mingled with patchouli and something else. *Fireworks,* Amaya thought, frowning at the peculiar addition.

'Do not anger this man, my Lord.'

Amaya looked up, and her eyes widened. The small man, who had translated aboard the ferry was walking towards her in deep conversation with a taller, younger man. He too had a familiar face. Amaya swallowed, she could not veer away now without the action seeming strange, and so she continued, her pace unbroken. She held her breath as they drew closer, willing the man not to recognise her.

'He must be careful not to anger me,' the taller man replied, his head high.

The translator sighed. 'These foreigners are different from Akegatans. Their honour is different.'

The other man laughed. 'You mean they have none. No matter, I will speak with this foreigner. Afonso?'

Amaya released her breath as the men passed, completely unaware. She slowed her pace, and very carefully turned to pursue the two. They took a left path, which Amaya knew led to the lecture halls. Pagodas could be seen looming above the canopy of twisting trees. Careful not to lose sight, Amaya allowed distance to build. Once through the copse the men came to a halt beside the nearest large pagoda. There, in the entrance waiting, was the foreigner who had chartered the ferry.

'The firearms are here. He says he has kept his promise, and now it is time to sign this treaty. His men are here.' The translator spoke after the foreigner had muttered at him. Despite the translation the threat was evident.

'I understand, but you must understand I need to relocate the firearms at once. I have men to take them.' The Court Official seemed impatient; his tone was aggravated despite his obvious discomfort.

The foreigner looked enraged as he replied, attempting Akegatan. 'Why your leaders not come? I travel far.' The foreigner broke into his native tongue, and looked to the small man, who breathed deep and began to translate what the foreigner had said.

'He said that he has crossed a vast ocean to form this allegiance and neither of our warlords can bring themselves to meet him in person. He wants you to know that the firearms will remain in his custody until you can arrange a meeting. He wants to meet one of them in person. He has heard of Akegata's honour code, but he states,' the man cleared his throat uncomfortably, 'excuse me, my lord, he states he has yet to see a single sign of this Akegatan honour.'

The younger man stepped closer, his eyes narrowed. 'Very well. You keep the firearms, but do not move them from Rikujou.' He allowed the interpreter to translate, before continuing. 'And one other thing this foreigner should keep in mind; he has taken one of our own as his wife. A woman by the name of Kaori. As I understand she is carrying his child. Some whispers say that she is an undesirable, a shinobi, not someone any Akegatan samurai would touch. However, she is his woman, and we have her.'

The foreigner had twitched at his wife's name, concern sneaking into his otherwise menacing countenance. Amaya recalled the woman she had met aboard the ferry, her youthful yet maniacal laugh, her long hair and large eyes beneath a blunt fringe.

The Akegatan continued no longer caring to veil his obvious implication. 'She is in my custody. Now, show me the firearms.'

With this the conversation ended and the men bowed to each other curtly. The younger Akegatan departed first, the foreigner watched him disappear into the pagoda his expression barbarous. He turned abruptly and entered the pagoda in pursuit, the translator trailing behind in his wake.

Amaya followed, the dim entrance of the pagoda before her. Slowly, she looked inside, blinking as her eyes adjusted. Piles and piles of crates were stacked high, filling the room. Some were open, their contents being inspected. To the right, Amaya could see barrels which commonly stored gunpowder. She now understood the smell of fireworks. Shock wormed its way into the cracks of her fear. She did not want to be seen but was gripped by a reckless idea. Keeping her back to the pagoda wall, she skirted the edge until she drew level with the crates. She could no longer see the few people stationed beside them, but she could hear them. Stepping with purpose and care, she edged forward, drawing close to the large boxes. The top was loose. Silently, Amaya lifted a firearm from inside. It was much heavier than she thought a hollow tube would be. She arranged her cloak about it, pressing it to her body. The weapon was cumbersome, but she was able to slide it through her waistband. It pulled against the fabric and was heavy against her hip.

Stumbling through the trees, she reached the main path and fled along it to the gates. Breaking out onto the street, she lost herself in the crowd of people. The number of boxes had overwhelmed her, and her thoughts had spiraled. *How many of the pagodas were filled?* She hissed inwardly. The cold metal of the firearm sent a shiver along her arm. She scurried on, her attention on reaching the Ryokan and delivering the stolen firearm. *There may be more making their way here even now.* This thought scared her, but she was saved having to dwell further. A boy, a little older than Kyo, knocked passed her and she almost spun about from his speed.

'Sorry,' he shouted over his shoulder before darting down a side street.

Amaya groaned. She knew her pouch was missing before she checked. Putting her worries of the firearms aside, she broke into an awkward run, dashing down the road the boy had vanished along. She reached the end, but the boy had truly gone. 'No,' Amaya said, feebly. Straightening up she scoured the road, looking to her left, then her right and finally back along the road she had sped down. Two men were walking toward her. The temptation to ask them for help was immediately quashed by her own reasoning; she did not want to be seen by anyone. She turned left and cried out as another man she had not seen stepped in front of her. Amaya noticed his blade, but it was not a katana, it was a ninjato short sword. She staggered back. 'Shinobi,'

The man did not speak as he reached for her. Amaya tripped into a run towards a closed gateway to a house. She knew she could not fight unarmed. She glanced back but as she turned around, she stifled a shout. A fourth man had dropped silently from the roofs above to land before her.

Her father's words regarding shinobi blundered into her mind as she tried to recall any weaknesses he may have described but only the fear their description had inspired came forward.

'They do not use katana?' Amaya had asked her father, disbelieving the fact.

Kazu had shaken his head. 'They can, but they favour other weapons: ninjato short swords; shuriken; kunai daggers; sais; kusurigama.' Kazu drew a picture in the dirt of the flower-bed which they sat beside. 'That is what a shuriken looks like.'

'It looks like a snowflake. Or a star,' Amaya commented, crouching beside her father.

'A deadly star. This,' Kazu drew another diagram, 'is a kunai, and this a Kusurigama.'

Amaya scrutinised them. 'They have so many interesting weapons.'

'And they are very skilled without weaponry too. With weapons, without weapons, the Way of the Shinobi is entirely different to the Way of the Samurai.'

'Is it true that they can vanish into shadows?'

Kazu raised his eyebrow. 'That sounds like magic. Do you believe in magic, Amaya?'

She nodded her head vigourously. 'There's magic in everything.'

'There is?' Kazu said, sitting back and folding his arms in front of his chest, a smile lingering about his mouth. 'There is,' he finished.

'Yes. I mean, fireflies are magical, cherry blossom is magical, when the leaves turn in autumn, that's magical. Shinobi must be magical too.'

Kazu laughed. 'Magic is seen differently by everyone it seems, but it is there, whether we see it or not. However, shinobi practice arts which utilize nature in more dishonourable ways. More ruthless and clever ways. To a shinobi, the Art of Battle lies in opportunity and secrecy, not honour. That concept is a hindrance to them ultimately.'

'They sound like cowards.'

Kazu sat down cross-legged. 'Not all of them, but many are. They are cowards that you will run from should you ever meet them.'

'I never run from cowards. I will stand and fight them.' Amaya thumped the ground with a small fist sending soil across the images her father her drawn moments before.

Kazu didn't smile or laugh. 'No, Amaya. You will run because your life is valuable. You don't want a coward to claim your life, do you?'

Amaya bit her lip and shook her head slightly. 'No.'

'They use shadows to sneak up behind their opponents, or to disappear completely,' Kazu suddenly crouched on his feet and slowly shuffled towards Amaya. She watched him, fascinated. 'They can melt away with the rain in a storm. They can fly as smoothly as a hawk upon the strongest of winds and walk on the stillest or most tempestuous of waters. They can explode with fire like the great mountains.' He imitated his description with his hands. Amaya jumped, thrilled at her father's regalement. 'They are everywhere and nowhere at once,' Kazu finished. 'But is it magic?'

The memory sent a chill through Amaya's body. 'Run' had been the only instruction her father had ever given her when speaking about shinobi. She glanced at the men's belts; kunai, shuriken, the chain of a kusurigama.

She took a deep breath, gripped the firearm tightly, and bolted towards the two men. Momentarily, taken aback they stopped. Amaya took advantage of their hesitation and crashed through them. Their hands snaked out and one of them caught her arm. She was whipped around violently, almost thrown from her feet. The firearm flew out from beneath her cloak, but the men were intent. She grappled with the one who had her in a tight grasp. The other three circled about her. Amaya kicked her legs outward, making contact with the nearest one and knocking him back into the wall of the house. The shinobi who held her, twisted her arm until she cried out.

She leant forward as far as his hold would allow and then brought her head back sharply. She felt the man's nose break against the back of her head. He merely grunted in pain before shoving her against the dirt road. She squirmed and writhed but he pinned her with his knee. None of them spoke. She thought of Meiyo lying in her quarters and wished she had brought her blade with her. The unmistakable chink of metal sounded, and Amaya struggled even more. With a savage pain in her side, she felt the tip of a blade pierce through her clothes and skin. A warmth seeped from her abdomen and began to soak her clothes. The blade was pulled abruptly before it could be pushed further into her body. Her eyes were streaming with the pain as she looked up. The man crashed to the floor beside her, an arrow protruding from the nape of his neck. His last breath came in a gurgle.

The other men stopped in alarm and looked around seeing no one. At once they scattered and fled down the street and out of sight. Amaya rolled onto her side. The ache became a severe cramp and she screamed out, unable to keep her agony silent. Gripping her stomach, she felt the blood still issuing slowly from her shallow wound. Her breath was now coming in short gasps as the grit of the road filled her mouth. She thought of Akio but instead saw a pair of small feet running towards her, kicking up dust as they pounded the floor.

'I'm sorry. I'm sorry.'

Amaya looked up and her vision swam languidly, her stomach was starting to numb and the sensation began to deaden her legs. It was the boy who had stolen her belongings. His dishevelled, dark hair caught in the breeze as he crouched next toward her. He was clutching an oddly shaped bow and a few arrows. Amaya nodded in response, her voice failing her. The boy turned her over and tugged at her clothes until Amaya felt the cold air against her skin.

'The wound is not deep,' he muttered, more to himself. 'Poison,' the boy continued as he smelt Amaya's blood. He reached beneath his ragged cloak and extracted a large bag. 'It smells like Toad's Eyes.' He rummaged for a moment, and then shrieked out. 'Open your mouth.' He instructed, gently tipping Amaya's head back. She did not protest. The boy's eyes were earnest, kind, and scared. She obeyed him and let him pour a small amount of liquid down her throat. He clamped her mouth closed as the taste seized her. Her wretches sent stabs of agony through her side, but she swallowed before her vision blackened and her mind soon followed.

'Wake up. Wake up! You need water.'

Amaya felt a sting on her cheek. Another came, and then another. She reached out preventing a forth strike. 'I'm awake,' she groaned, opening her eyes. The boy was hovering over her anxiously, hopping from one foot to another. He held out a leather flask of water.

'Thank you,' Amaya said. She stared from the boy to the room she was in. 'Where am I?'

'My house,' the boy replied, crouching beside her, relief pushing the fear away. 'Are you cold?' He stood and strode to the opposite side of the room, returning with a blanket. 'Here.' He draped it over her shoulders.

'Thank you for helping me,' Amaya continued.

He shook his head. 'It is my fault.'

'Were those shinobi your friends? Did you instruct them to attack me?' Amaya questioned.

The boy looked stunned. 'No. No, of course not.'

'Then it is not your fault. Your only crime is stealing my things.' She offered a weak smile. 'A small thing comparatively.'

The boy reached into his pocket and pulled out Amaya's pouch. 'I haven't taken anything from inside it. I did not know you would pursue me.'

'There is an important item inside.' Amaya placed the flask upon the ground and took the broach from inside. 'This was my father's.'

'He is dead?' The boy questioned, his expression solemn. 'Mine is too. And my mother.'

'My mother also,' Amaya replied, quietly. 'What is your name?'

'Tomio. Tomio Umeda.'

'I'm Amaya Takeda.'

'Takeda? Takeda!' Understanding broke across his face. 'The Seishin no Ken style.'

'Yes, my father was Kazu Takeda.'

'I'm sorry,' Tomio repeated, bowing his head over and over before finally prostrating himself.

'Please.' Amaya held her hand up to stop him. 'You saved my life. How is it you had the antidote to such a poison?'

'My father was a doctor. My mother a nurse.'

'What happened to them?'

'They refused to create poisons for the rebels,' Tomio replied, his tone dark.

'And they were killed for that?' Amaya shook her head in disbelief. 'I'm so sorry.'

'I wanted to help but...'

'You still want to help?' Amaya shifted in her seat, wincing as she did. Tomio nodded and sat back on his heels. Amaya's eyes travelled around the room. The more she stared the more she picked out the odd contraptions, large and small, lining the shelves and hanging from the beams which stretched across the single space. 'Did you make all of these things?' Amaya asked, awed.

'Yes. They aren't perfect, though and I cannot afford new materials.'

'Who taught you this craft?'

'Nobody.'

'You taught yourself? Tomio, that's wonderful,' Amaya said, truthfully. 'You have a rare skill.'

Tomio did not look convinced as he scratched his head. Amaya was gripped by a wild yet strong thought. 'Tomio, will you return to Chuto with me and my comrades?'

'To the capital?' Tomio half shouted. 'I have never left Rikujou before.' His hand went to his mouth in excitement, and Amaya could see his thoughts battling with each other behind his dark irises. 'Is it possible?'

'I should think so. We could use a talent such as yours. You may be able to help.' Amaya felt surprised at her own words. She could not fathom her reasoning, only that she wanted Tomio to accept her invitation. She did not want to leave without him.

'Where are your comrades?' He asked.

'They are in Rikujou. Perhaps in the Ryokan we are staying in. They will be wondering where I am.'

'Can you walk?' Tomio asked her. 'Let me help you.' He held out a hand. Amaya took it. His palms were rough, but his skin was warm to the touch. A heat seemed to extend between them. She stared at him briefly before rising. Then together they left his home and walked into the dusk.

CHAPTER NINE

Tomio slid open the door to her quarters. The room was filled with the flickering of the braziers, their warmth reaching into her clothing, causing her to sweat. Amaya looked around, in a shadowy corner sat Daiki. Amaya felt her chest tighten as he stepped forward.

'Amaya. Where have you been?' He faltered, his eyes raking over her and Tomio. 'Are you hurt?'

'Where are the others?' She asked, trying to steady her breath.

'They are out searching for you.' Daiki's eyes fell once more upon Tomio. 'Making new friends, I see.'

Amaya sighed, struggling to maintain her temper. She felt so weak. 'I will explain, but only after the others return.'

'Amaya was attacked, she was stabbed,' Tomio spoke up. 'See.' He held a hand up. It was still stained with Amaya's blood.

Daiki moved forward fluidly, his hands finding Amaya's arm. 'Sit down. You should have spoken up.' His touch was unexpectedly soft as he steered her to the zabuton cushions lining the low table. 'Fetch some water,' he instructed Tomio. The young man obeyed, leaving the room.

Amaya freed herself of Daiki and sat down gingerly. 'I owe that boy my life.'

Daiki was frowning, his usual amusement fading behind concern, and annoyance. 'Where were you wounded?'

Amaya didn't trust Daiki's newfound worry. 'Tomio has treated my injuries. The worst was the poison.'

'Poison? Only two types of people use such a weapon.

Women and shinobi.'

Amaya frowned. 'Well, it was no woman.'

Before Daiki could make his reply, the door opened. Tomio entered followed by Kin, Akio and Shun.

'We found this young man looking for water,' Kin said. 'He approached me and said you were attacked.'

'Amaya.' Akio strode passed Daiki, knelt beside her and held a hand to her forehead. 'You're feverish.'

Tomio and Kin stepped forward. Shun remained in the doorway, his eyes on his brother. Amaya studied the two and Shun's gaze found hers. 'General Kimura, I am fine. The young man, Tomio, has treated my injuries very well. So please do not look so grim.'

Shun's frown did not subside but the glare softened the slightest amount. 'Lady Takeda, the implications of an attack here...' He shook his head, retreating into his thoughts.

'Tomio, is it?' Kin asked, turning to the boy. 'What antidote did you use?'

'The poison was Toad's Eyes.'

Kin nodded. 'How did you have an antidote for such a potent poison?'

'My father was a doctor,' Tomio repeated what he had told Amaya.

Akio had released an audible breath. 'Toad's Eyes is a poison used only by shinobi.'

Tomio nodded. 'My father used to treat soldiers who had been attacked by shinobi. I have many of his medicines left.'

'You are a very quick thinker, Tomio. You did indeed save Amaya's life.' Kin bowed his head. 'Thank you.'

'Where were you, Amaya?' Daiki questioned, abruptly. Akio turned his head, one hand remaining on Amaya's arm.

'I went to the shrine to pray.'

'You were told not to leave the Ryokan,' Daiki snapped.

'I didn't think shinobi would be in the streets of Rikujou, especially with so many armed soldiers scattered about.

Rebel or Imperial, shinobi are disliked by all,' Amaya muttered, stung.

Daiki stepped next to his brother, pulling a fresh rice ball out from the pouch about his waist. 'And that is your trouble, right there: you didn't think. Who do you think shinobi are? You have probably met many more than you realise. Why, you're probably even friends with a few, and you wouldn't know it. Not all of them traipse around in dark clothing.' He glanced at Shun, whose face had fallen stormy at the mention of the shinobi.

'I saw the foreigner,' she interjected, before Daiki could berate her any further.

'The one from the ferry?' Shun questioned.

Amaya nodded. 'Yes, and they are here. They are storing the firearms in the pagodas. Perhaps every outhouse of the shrine is filled with the things.' Amaya's fear was apparent. 'We have to return to Chuto at once. We must inform His Majesty.' Her heart dropped with a sudden recollection. 'I had a firearm. I had one.'

'What do you mean?' Akio questioned.

'It slipped from my waistband during the struggle against the shinobi.'

Tomio cleared his throat. 'I picked it up.'

Amaya beamed. 'Where is it?'

'At my house. I can go and fetch it,' he replied, a smile appearing.

'I'll go with him,' Daiki added.

Amaya stared at him but did not raise her voice in protest. Tomio was looking up at him, and his face bore no fear.

'The foreigner and his translator met with a Court Official,' Amaya added. 'The rebel army have formed an alliance with those across the sea.'

Akio's back straightened. 'What did this Court Official look like, Amaya?'

She lifted her eyes in thought. 'He was around the same age as Shun. Broad but soft. I could not get close enough to see properly and his back was to me. I say he was a Court Official because of his clothing. He was dressed in a kimono which had been made in the Fire Province, the silk was definitely from Kasaichi. However, he didn't look like a Fire Province native. He wasn't the leader of the rebel army, the foreigner was angry about that,' Amaya paused. 'The alliance isn't a smooth one.'

'Were threats exchanged?' Shun questioned.

'It seems the foreigner has actually married an Akegatan woman, named Kaori. It was also my understanding that she is a shinobi. I met this woman on the ferry. She was with child.'

Shun frowned deeply. 'A foreigner with such weapons and shinobi connections. That combination is dangerous. Shinobi are the worst of the hinin.' Shun's usually controlled anger seemed on the surface, filling his eyes and posture alike. She stared at him, pondering the depth of his apparent hatred toward shinobi.

'But,' Amaya licked her lips, 'the Court Official said that he could arrange a meeting with one of the rebel leaders.'

The group quietened. Akio ran his hand through his hair distractedly, pulling it back down over his face. Amaya felt as though she could see his thoughts as he sorted through ideas and plans.

'This changes everything. A leader being aided by subordinates is one thing but to actually have two leaders. This changes everything,' Akio commented, finally. 'We leave for Chuto, at once.'

The group agreed with silent nods, immediately readying their things.

'It appears that Tomio is quite skilled,' Amaya said, before he and Daiki left the room. 'He is returning to Chuto with us.'

Kin stared at her, happy. 'Skilled?'

'Yes, he has an incredible collection of items he has designed and made himself. He could go far in the capital under the right tutelage. Perhaps the Ito Merchant's Guild.' Amaya grinned at Tomio.

'An innovator?' Daiki said. 'I can show you some samurai houses with secret designs which you would find very interesting.'

Tomio's eyes were now as round as his face. 'You can? Like a samurai's closet?'

Daiki handed Tomio a rice ball, his casual grin freeing his face of his earlier annoyance. 'That and other tricks. Have you heard of a Nightingale floor?'

Tomio almost slipped over. 'Yes! I haven't seen one though.'

'You will if you come to the capital.' Daiki grinned.

'Amaya, I would like to come with you. But,' he looked suddenly apprehensive, 'I can't read or write well. I can't do much really, besides make things.'

'That is a talent, Tomio. A great one. There are not many who can claim to be innovators,' Akio said, lightly. 'The Emperor will welcome you.'

Tomio nodded, trusting Akio's statement.

'Tomio, do you have siblings? Friends?' Shun questioned, his face softening somewhat.

The boy shook his head. 'My parents are dead. All my friends have gone.'

Akio turned to face him fully. 'Gone? What do you mean?'

Tomio tilted his head in thought. 'All the children I knew, the orphans I mean, have gone. They aren't here anymore.'

Amaya straightened. 'Where are they?'

'Not in Rikujou,' Tomio confirmed with a shrug. 'Kaito and Yuno, a brother and sister who were my friends, accepted work with a group of bards. Reika left with some actors before them, and Ryū was taken by a tall ronin. There have been more, but I can't remember their names.'

'All children?' Kin probed.

'A lot of the orphans in Rikujou, yes,' Tomio replied.

Nobody commented as Daiki steered Tomio from the room, but Amaya knew they were all considering the bizarre exodus of the orphans, especially as Rikujou had so much to offer a child who would otherwise starve. Large cities attracted many strays, there was always someone to steal from, someone to take pity, someone to adopt you if you were lucky. Amaya thought of the children in Chuto, her father had taught many of them before his death.

'Your pilgrimage is one Elemental closer to completion, Amaya,' Kin said, quietly, so that only she and Akio could hear his words. Confusion clouded her mind briefly but all at once she comprehended what Kin was implying as he gazed at the closed door. Akio was already wearing a smile when one broke across Amaya's face.

Amaya nodded in thought. 'I felt something earlier today, but it was a physical reaction more than anything. A heat.'

'Your affinity to Ueten is growing. That young man came straight to me without hesitation the moment I entered the Ryokan,' Kin continued. 'And I knew at once. A *heat*, as you described it.'

'How can you know? How are you so sure?'

'You have read that the Air Elemental was the one with a *voice that carries on the wind*? Well, it seems my voice really does carry on the wind.' He laughed, and the sound echoed that of Amaya's own happiness.

'We have to explain to Tomio,' Amaya commented.

'You think it safe to travel on these roads?' Amaya asked, staring along the small track that trailed the mountains' feet, shrouded by beach trees.

Akio, who was beside her, nodded. 'This time of year, not many others use them. The threat of snow keeps people on the main roads.'

'Shouldn't the threat of snow encourage us to do the same?' Amaya replied. Her disquiet hadn't abated for three days, since they had veered onto the hidden track.

'It's not going to snow,' Daiki interrupted, looking over his shoulder. 'Rebels and checkpoints litter the main road. I know this path well enough. We will drop south by the afternoon; from there it will be just one more day until Chuto. Do not fear, Lady Amaya.' The laugh in his voice was clear.

Amaya swallowed, a frown tugging at her eyebrows. She addressed Akio. 'There is something about this road. It's secret for a reason.'

'It may be that it is used mainly by hinin,' Akio replied.

'Hinin. Shinobi. Senkaku Nin,' she added, her voice low.

Kin was the one to offer a whispered response. 'My brother's organisation rarely travel as one group.'

'How much do you know about the Senkaku Nin? I thought all records were outdated.' Amaya asked, her eyes travelling past Kin to Shun, who was at the rear of the group. Tomio was tottering along beside him and had been for most of the journey.

'I haven't spent sixteen years travelling aimlessly. I've been investigating, tracking.' Kin's expression was suddenly tempestuous. 'For a long time, my sole goal was to find my brother.'

'To what end?' Akio asked.

Kin shook his head, his gaze abruptly far off. 'To speak with him. To kill him.'

Amaya felt an overwhelming longing which didn't wholly belong to her. She rested a hand on Kin's arm. 'You'll see your brother again, and he will have an answer for you, whatever shape that answer may take.'

Kin gave a wan smile, placing his free hand on top of Amaya's.

'Shun.' Daiki's voice came cutting through the hush. 'Come here.' He had stopped, his hand held up in a gesture for the group to stop. Amaya watched Shun pass by, and took a step forward but Akio's hand clasped gently around her wrist. 'Wait a moment.' He walked forward to join the two brothers, gripping his bow and pulling an arrow from the quiver.

'Amaya, what is it?' Tomio was looking ahead fretfully. His hand had instinctively sought out his own bow strapped to his back.

'A bear?'

'You know it's not a bear, Amaya,' Kin said, quietly. 'You've been feeling as uneasy as myself and Tomio have the entire time we've been walking this track.'

Amaya stared at Kin and Tomio, incredulous. 'You didn't say.'

'Nor did you.'

'I understand, Amaya,' Tomio whispered, leaning closer to her. 'Kin told me of the ancient belief in the the Prophet of Ueten, and of Gekai's corruption.' The smile on his face warmed Amaya, and she felt an incredible surge of happiness. 'Your capacity to believe is greater than mine, Tomio. I am hoping my Elementals will aid me in reaching complete acceptance of my role. I want to be useful to Akegata and those I love.'

Amaya looked towards Akio and the others, but her attention was quickly taken by a sound further along the road, beyond the bend. She walked forward a few paces. First the head, then the shoulders, and lastly the body of a man appeared. He was walking slowly, a strange limp in his gait. Akio's bow was raised and steady, and Shun's hands rested on his katana. Daiki drew his and began to walk forward.

'Wait,' Amaya called out.

Daiki stopped, and turned his head. 'Why?'

'Don't go near him.' Amaya strode forward. Akio and Shun fidgeted as she passed them by, but she held a hand out. 'It's fine.'

Daiki let out a noise of irritation. 'He could be dangerous, Amaya. You know the ilk of people who use these roads.'

'Yes, I'm aware but mountain villagers do as well. Sir?' Amaya spoke up.

The man stopped. His whole body seemed drained, his

back was hunched, his legs wobbled and he seemed to have difficulty in focusing on Amaya. 'Don't,' he said simply. 'Don't come near.'

Amaya's nose wrinkled, as a bizarre acrid stench reached her. She glanced back and her eyes picked out what it was which had caused Daiki to pause. The cold temperatures meant that there weren't many flies, but the smell of decay was now strong. Amaya looked up at Daiki who was still beside her, although his knuckles were white.

'Are you sick?' Amaya questioned the man.

He nodded. 'Yes. Many of us are. This is where we come.'

'Where you come?' Amaya took a tentative step toward him and heard Akio shift behind.

'To die,' the man clarified. 'The further into the mountains you travel the closer to the illness you will get.'

'What kind of illness is it?' It was Kin who spoke now.

'We don't know. None of us are doctors.' A racking cough erupted from his chest, breaking the odd quiet of the area. The man fell onto one knee. 'Please, leave me be. Don't go any further along this road.' His face was taut with pain, as his hand feebly massaged his chest.

Amaya pressed her lips together, her hands reaching toward him. 'Let me help.'

Another hideous cough broke from the man's mouth. Blood sprayed his chin and tears leaked from his cracked eyes. Daiki darted forward his katana raised, but it was Akio's arrow which struck the man down. The fletching was all that remained visible. The sickly man was dead before he hit the ground. Amaya did not make a sound, she just turned her head, her eyes wide until they met with Akio's. His expression was the most serious she had seen yet. He returned his bow to his shoulder and walked forward. 'Help me.'

Daiki was the first to move, he hitched his cloak about his mouth protectively, securing it in place and looked back.

Shun moved forward, and together the three hoisted the corpse and placed him beside the others at the roadside grave. Amaya watched on, her heart still trembling. As Daiki made to take the lead once again, he paused. His eyes were filled with the same solemnity that his brother often had. 'Akio did what must be done. That man was suffering, Amaya. Would you have had him linger in that state?' He didn't wait for a reply before stalking off and taking the lead.

Akio didn't speak as the group followed, and Amaya didn't question him. She understood, she hadn't needed Daiki to explain. In silence she stayed by Akio's side, hoping that she could assuage the discomfort he felt at having to act the way he had. Keeping one eye on his profile and the other on the uneven path they followed and she kept pace with him.

'It's so big,' Tomio said, his eyes wide as he gazed upon Chuto. The palace stood at its centre; a gold, white, and black heart. The cold afternoon sun was catching the very highest roof of the palace; a sharp, bright glare which Amaya couldn't look at directly. The capital grew the closer they approached, until it stole the entire horizon from them. When they reached the gates, they were welcomed by the guards. Amaya desperately wanted to hurry to the palace, the need to see Kenta and inform him of the situation had grown steadily more difficult to subdue. However, the group's progress through the streets of Chuto was slow. Many people were milling about, preparing for the coming winter and, later, the New Year. Tomio did not seem to mind, his eyes roved around the stalls and over the different people, gazing at them with hungry fascination. At last, the palace rose before them, a splendid mark upon the pale sky. Amaya looked through the colossal gates to the palace estate as they entered and realised how much she had grown to like it.

'This is where I leave you. It's been enlightening. Tomio, I will come and find you, then I will show you everything I have told you about, as promised.' Daiki smiled and ruffled Tomio's hair. Then, checking himself, he bowed curtly.

'Thank you for accompanying us, Lord Daiki. I was

never able to thank you for helping me on the ferry.' Amaya recalled.

Daiki hesitated, not glancing up from his bow. It was the first time Amaya had seen Daiki uncertain, his usual facetiousness failing him.

'Yes, thank you, Daiki,' Kin continued in the silence.

Daiki left the group, and Amaya stared after him.

The group ascended the stone stairs which led to the palace entrance. Amaya had barely climbed the last vast step when a pair of arms were thrown about her shoulders. 'Amaya!'

She turned and embraced Kyo. 'I've missed you. Very much.'

'I have been working with Lord Katou and His Majesty. Helping him with scripture and practicing the Seishin no Ken technique. Although he isn't as good as you,' he whispered in her ear.

'That's wonderful. Hiroshi Katou is a good man. I am glad you have been in such good company. What did you do with him?'

'I have been working with the Censorate, Amaya.' His eyes were fiery. 'I saw them training,' Kyo looked about furtively and then lowered his voice again. 'They practice more than just the Seishin no Ken style. However, I have been working on the investigations with Lord Hiroshi. We are gathering evidence, Amaya. There have been some interesting developments.' Kyo drew a breath, his gaze intense. 'Evidence father had uncovered. It has remained hidden until now. It seems that another was helping father.'

Amaya looked around. Shun was close by. 'Later, Kyo. Tell me later.'

Her brother nodded. 'Lord Hiroshi wishes to give me a position in the Censorate. He wants to train me personally.'

Amaya felt her eyebrows rise and her jaw drop a little. Kyo had grown up a lot in her absence, and he was bearing the Takeda name well. 'I am so proud, Kyo. You will make a brilliant investigator. The Censorate will be lucky to have you within their ranks.' Amaya smiled and embraced her brother again. 'We bring news that the Censorate will find very useful. Where is His Majesty?'

'In the Censorate building with Lord Hiroshi,' Kyo replied. 'I will take you there.'

The group followed Kyo. 'Lord Kenta has been spending a lot of time in the Censorate and with Lord Hiroshi. I think some of the Court Officials are not happy with the amount of time he is spending there, but Lord Kenta is determined.'

'I'm not surprised,' Akio said, frowning. 'Has he been sleeping?'

Kyo twisted his mouth to the side. 'I don't know. He is always in the Censorate before I arrive in the morning and stays after I've left.'

'He's becoming obsessed,' Amaya sighed.

'He's dedicated, Amaya. A much better approach than the one he had before meeting you,' Akio said.

Amaya remembered the despondency and denial Kenta had displayed. He had even hidden his identity when they had first met. 'I do not want him to make himself ill.'

'He has been talking about you often. He'll feel much better now that you are back,' Kyo said.

'Not after the news we deliver, I fear,' Akio muttered, gravely.

Kyo looked from Akio to his sister, his eyes travelling over Kin, Shun and finally Tomio. 'Is he?' Kyo questioned.

Amaya nodded. 'I believe so. This is Tomio. Tomio, this is my younger brother, Kyo.'

The two young men bowed to each other. 'I would be happy to take you around the palace,' Kyo offered an overwhelmed Tomio.

'Lady Amaya, do you need me in the meeting with His Majesty?' Shun's voice surprised Amaya.

She considered him, and strangely a desire to have him stay came forth. 'Thank you, Shun. Your account of events would be useful.'

Shun remained still, surprise clouding his usual stormy expression. He bowed his head. 'Thank you, Lady Amaya. Thank you for your trust.'

Amaya inclined her head, oddly happy. 'I am willing to show you the trust my father clearly felt you deserved.' Her eye caught Kin's.

Once outside the grand sliding doors of the Censorate building, the group were met by a Censorate member. Kyo stepped forward to greet him. 'Master Hidetaka.'

'Lord Kyo.'

Amaya stared at the soldier as he bowed at her brother, and then to the rest. He was donned in the dark green and black robes of the Censorate. The bottoms of his trousers were tucked into split-toed shoes, the same as shinobi footwear, and his sleeves were kept in place by elbow length cuffs. The ebon conical hat was resting upon his back but the collar, which was usually lifted to conceal the mouth, drooped down revealing his whole face. Master Hidetaka granted them entry and accompanied them inside.

'Captain Sano and His Majesty are awaiting you, Lady Amaya. We spied you on the road this morning.'

Amaya nodded. 'That's quite a network you have.'

'Thank you, Lady Takeda. The Censorate serve only His Majesty.'

Amaya made a noise of encouragement, but her gaze wandered to Shun. He didn't seem at ease as they strode through the dark building. The corridors seemed at times wide, at others narrow. Amaya considered a trick in the lighting, or perhaps a purposeful element in the design of the Censorate building. Each weave and meander of the hallway led them further into the complex. The walls were papered in black, with huge white chrysanthemums detailed on each panel. Amaya could not be sure where the doors were. The domed lanterns, which illuminated the walk, were painted white and green with the imperial mon emblazoned in black.

A purposefully confusing labyrinth to keep people out. Or perhaps, she considered, to keep people in.

Kenta was in the entranceway to a large room, apparently about to exit. He was flanked by numerous Censorate guards, Hiroshi Katou and the new Captain of the Censorate. Hiroshi saw them first and stared warmly at Amaya, his toad-like features boggling at her. 'Welcome back, Lady Amaya.'

'I am glad to be back.' Amaya bowed.

'Amaya,' Kenta said, stepping forward without thought. He checked himself and hesitated. 'Welcome back, all of you. This is Captain Sano, the newly appointed leader of the Censorate.'

Amaya inclined her head. Captain Sano returned the gesture, his sharp eyes lingering on her face. They were the kind of eyes which scrutinised everything, Amaya thought.

'I hope you bring news.' Kenta looked at the five, and as Kyo's had done, his eyes lingered on Tomio. Amaya gave the smallest of nods, confirming Kenta's unvoiced question.

'We bring other news, Your Majesty,' Akio continued.

Amaya observed Kenta's face and was saddened to see lines of exhaustion and worry veiling his kind and spirited glow.

'Many things have happened. Would you permit us to tell you the details immediately?' Shun said, rather directly. Amaya stared at him, but Kenta did not seem perturbed.

'I would not have it another way, General. You can speak freely here.' Kenta twitched his fan as he spoke and reentered the room behind him, gesturing for the others to follow. Amaya passed Captain Sano as she entered the small chamber and he studied each as they passed him by. His eyes appeared constantly narrowed, as if nothing escaped them, not even a breath or a thought. He wore a pointed beard, which joined the hair upon his cheeks roughly. He was not as broad as Shun, but he was older. Amaya thought his face seemed prematurely aged. However, he contained a strength which was not overly visible, but it was strength nonetheless and Amaya was glad that it was a strength loyal to Kenta. Captain Sano's attire was the same as the other Censorate guards, bar one difference: his black conical hat had a single, thick white line streaked across it. The Captain and General bowed respectfully to each other; a quiet understanding passing between them.

Shun moved forward. 'The rebel army is strong, Your Majesty. From our questioning we believe their numbers to be higher than first thought, and they have a strange weapon in their possession. A dangerous weapon known as a firearm. They have hundreds, maybe thousands. These weapons are far superior to any we have in our own arsenal. They outstrip the yari spear and bow in both speed and range. Their only weakness is that they are slow to prepare but with such numbers that does not truly matter.' Shun then proceeded to take out the firearm Amaya had snatched from the shrine. He laid it out before Kenta, who picked it up and studied it carefully. For a few minutes, nobody spoke, but the Emperor's face grew steadily more tempestuous.

'We happened to discover these weapons by chance, when taking passage on a boat. There were boxes and crateloads of them. The ship was attacked by bandits and it was during this attack that we witnessed the power of the firearm.'

'Where have these come from?' Kenta questioned, running his hand over the length of hollow metal and wooden stock.

'We encountered a foreigner. His looks were different to that of the people of Akegata. We believe that he is the one who has brought these weapons into our country,' Amaya added.

Kenta looked at her. 'What did you see, Lady Amaya?'

Amaya frowned at the memory of the murdered bandits. 'The firearms are powered by gunpowder. Lead balls are fired from the ends of these tubes at such a speed you cannot see them.' Amaya pointed to the firearm's end. 'The man I saw use the firearm pointed it at the bandit and pulled on this small piece of metal.' She indicated the place before continuing. 'The lead ball pierced the bandit's chest. There was a lot of blood and he died quickly, perhaps even instantly. Not all deaths were as clean.' She recalled the bandit who had his face blown away; his solitary eye in a pool of blood. 'It is ingenious, but with this ingenuity all honour has been lost. Daiki was correct when he said it is a coward's weapon.' Amaya trailed off, her eyes glazed as she remembered the blood spilling over the boat, the blood that could not be stemmed as it poured from the bandit's wound.

Kenta's mouth was open, his expression shocked. 'You should not have had to witness that, Lady Amaya. I'm sorry.' He looked at her, his expression morose.

She continued. 'I would rather witness this than remain ignorant. The leader of the rebel army has formed an alliance with this foreigner; a foothold in a reformed Akegata in return for the use of the firearms and military support in the coming war. I heard this in Rikujou from the men directly involved, and from the foreigner himself.' Amaya continued to tell Kenta of the conversation she had overheard. 'Lord Kenta, there are two rebel leaders.'

The Emperor swallowed, his jaw tightening. They all waited for him to speak.

'This knowledge could stop the civil war from worsening if we are able to retrieve the firearms before they fall completely into the hands of the rebel army, or at least develop defences against them. Two rebel leaders only provide two opportunities to bring their agenda to its knees. Akio, I will need you to document this information and keep it stored in the Archives.'

Akio bowed his head. 'I will do so at once.'

'I will help,' Amaya added.

'Two leaders?' Kenta mused aloud, in his own thoughts. 'Two. Or perhaps only one but the other believes they are equal in this exploit. This kind of pairing rarely ends favourably for one.' Kenta paced momentarily, before spinning on his foot to face the group. 'The rebel army believe there are two leaders, but I believe one of these leaders is being used.'

Amaya nodded slowly, understanding Kenta's logic. 'Only one can truly triumph and sit in a position of power.'

'We will prepare for all eventualities. The Censorate will redouble their efforts in the northern territories.'

Captain Sano inclined his head, acknowledging his master's order. 'Very good, my Lord.'

'What of your army?' Shun questioned.

Kenta studied him. 'I leave them in your capable hands, General Kimura. I trust you to look after them and direct them accordingly throughout the nation.'

'Yes, my Lord.'

'Allow us to aid you, General Kimura,' Amaya offered.

'You have my thanks, Lady Amaya.'

Hiroshi drew in a breath. 'General Kimura, we understand that your father must be involved in the preparations. He is the Minister of War after all.'

'I would be at ease if you would join me, Lord Katou,' Shun requested, inclining his head politely.

Lord Hiroshi nodded. 'I will, General Kimura. If I may request Kyo's presence also. He is a promising investigator and has a nose for corruption in particular.'

'Of course.' Shun looked at Kyo, his expression gentle. Amaya remembered that Shun too was an adopted son, like Kyo. She watched Lord Hiroshi and the General, her curiosity piqued, but before she could contribute any further, Shun turned to Kenta.

'If I may be dismissed, I will begin implementing plans at once.'

Kenta nodded his permission and Shun left, the leather skirt of his lamella armour rustling softly with each long stride. Kyo and Hiroshi bowed at the door, before following Shun.

'Why does Shun want Lord Hiroshi beside him?' Amaya questioned.

'He is the Advisor. Acting as mediator in certain meetings can prove useful,' Akio replied. 'Perhaps Shun is uncertain of his father's reaction and wishes Lord Hiroshi to support him.'

'Or perhaps it is simpler than that. Shun may find it difficult to contest a decision his father may make,' Amaya said.

'Something tells me Rai is not going to agree with his son but will use him all the same,' Akio muttered.

Amaya looked back at the door, her thoughts following Shun. A comment Kin had made surfaced *'It can't be easy having a tyrant like Rai Kimura as a father'*. Guilt pressed upon her stomach nastily as she debated her judgement of Shun, and even Daiki.

'Something else happened.' Kenta's voice was low.

'There was shinobi involvement,' Akio replied.

'Which clan?' Kenta's anger rolled out upon his words.

'The Shizukawa, my Lord,' Tomio spoke for the first time.

'From the Hidden River Village,' Kenta confirmed. His hand went to his mouth in speculation. 'They are based in the Earth Province. Word must have reached them of your arrival.'

'Who would have informed the Shizukawa shinobi?'

'Another avenue we must investigate it seems,' Akio growled, his anger as clear as Kenta's. 'Someone is trying very hard to prevent you from succeeding, Lady Amaya.'

The colour in Kenta's cheeks disappeared. 'How did this happen? How were shinobi able to get so close to you?' He looked at Akio. His gaze was not accusatory, rather surprised.

Amaya raised her voice. 'It is my own fault. I entered the streets of Rikujou alone, but if I hadn't then we would not have a firearm, nor would we have the information regarding there being two leaders. Nor would I have discovered Tomio.'

Kenta chewed the inside of his cheek. The motion made his cheekbones become even more prominent. 'Still, Amaya you cannot afford to place yourself in danger like this. Not now.' Kenta's tone was heavy with worry.

'I understand but it is difficult to sit idle.'

The Emperor's eyes slipped into shadow. 'I know that feeling all too well, Amaya. I am shackled by royal responsibilities. Inhibited from truly protecting those I care about. This impotence is hard to bear but bear it I must. All I ask is that you relieve my worry a little by not placing yourself in unnecessary danger.'

Silence ensued and Amaya looked at her feet. 'I apologise.'

'Lord Kenta, danger is about us regardless. A place that was safe yesterday may not be tomorrow. On the move is the safest. It is you we worry about,' Kin said, speaking up.

Kenta glanced at the three in front of him, and suddenly his shoulders slumped. 'The Censorate are becoming strong. I have managed to create that haven, at least. Lord Hiroshi and Captain Sano are irreplaceable.' He waved a hand about the room. 'The investigations have picked up again. Old leads are not yet cold.'

'Kyo mentioned that my father had been gathering evidence of some kind. He said another person had been helping him before his death.'

'Yes. It seems that both Lord Hiroshi and Lord Takeda were investigating the rebel army and their unknown leader. Of course, Rai Kimura and Sen Sanjo were their main suspects, but letters detailing another's involvement have surface. They had been hidden all throughout that time. Hiroshi believes that your father hid their identity right before his death.'

'I remember the morning of the day he was murdered. He seemed distracted, in a hurry. An odd urgency.' Amaya said.

'He must have obtained empirical evidence damning Rai. That or he had discovered the identity of the second leader,' Akio said.

'Still, the other person helping your father and Lord

Hiroshi remains unknown to us,' Kenta continued. 'This person was most certainly a spy for your father.'

'They are dead?' Amaya thought aloud.

'Perhaps, but I think not. Your father was murdered, Amaya. This other person did not want to fall victim in the same way. If they had been killed, we would know.'

'Then they are biding their time,' Akio suggested.

'All we can do is await contact from them if they are still alive and investigating in secret. We will simply have to wait, but I am not relying on their reappearance. I cannot afford to. Akegata cannot afford to. I must begin to arrange my own defences; the Censorate being the first. Now we have Tomio to help us.' Kenta turned to the warrior monk, Amaya's Air Elemental. 'Kin is right regarding where it is safest: on the move. Amaya, I would like nothing more than to have you protected here but I know you would never agree to such confinement.' Kenta laughed. 'You will continue your search once you have rested. Where will you go next?'

Amaya paused and considered her choices. 'I will go south to the Fire Province.'

'Of course,' Akio said, folding his arms. 'Kin, you are originally an Air Province native. Tomio is Earth Province.'

'All that remains is the Fire Elemental and the Water.'

'Seems such an easy task,' Amaya sighed. 'But finding two individuals in such a vast area is not so easy.'

'Do not forget, Amaya. Ueten calls to them, as do I.' Kin raised his eyebrows. 'It will not be effortless, no pilgrimage ever is. Previous Prophets did not have to hide their lineage and affinity to the Spirit Ueten.'

Amaya made a noise of lighthearted protest. 'Who will be my companions on this next stretch?'

'Perhaps a smaller group would be more conspicuous. A pair perhaps,' Kin said. 'However, it cannot be me.'

Startled, Amaya faced him. 'What do you mean?'

'The whispers of the Senkaku Nin have not escaped me. I have questions looming which may impact many things.'

'You intend to search for your brother?' Akio asked.

Kin nodded, gravely. 'For sixteen years, I have been hunting him and his organisation. The name Senkaku Nin is being spoken more and more. I cannot ignore this. Especially in light of things.' He looked at Amaya.

'I understand,' she whispered, and she truly did. 'Then it will be Akio and I?'

'A disguise will be necessary. Not siblings, your looks are too different. Newlyweds, perhaps,' Kenta suggested, after a brief hesitation.

'A fine cover,' Kin agreed.

'When will you depart, Kin?' Akio asked.

'In two days. First, I must speak with Kannushi Masato.'

CHAPTER TEN

The next morning Amaya's eyes stung with tiredness. She hadn't slept well, her mind was unable to keep at bay all which had occurred, both in Rikujou and in the palace. She felt uneasy at Kin's decision to pursue his brother alone but the fact that she and Akio would travel together provided a small comfort. Constantly there, however, was the tale of Ueten and Gekai. Like the incessant drone of a cicadas, it managed to cling to each thought she possessed. *Was it real? A message? An outdated belief? Or something beyond her understanding?* 'I'm not monk,' she said aloud, after her thoughts grew too wearisome. Finding Tomio had augmented her belief in the tale but she could not deny that doubt still lingered, or at least how she was to interpret it. If she was indeed the Prophet of Ueten, the mother to a Divine Heir, why had she not been able to save her father? This was a question she pretended she could not hear because attempting to answer it brought only anguish. She relied on her mother's words, which had been echoed by Kannushi Masato; they acted as a mantra, a compass amidst the anger.

The smell of winter was all about now. It permeated each room regardless of closed windows and doors. Amaya knew that soon the chilled winds would creep south, and the capital would feel the glare of the Face of Winter. Pushing her blanket away, she rose from her futon and reached for her clothing. She half made to grab her zabon trousers but reminded herself that she was at the palace. Looking about she could not see a kimono.

'Lady Takeda?' A voice from beyond the closed door

sounded. Amaya knew the voice.

'Please enter, Takako,' she called to her maid.

Takako entered, and folded over her arms was a kimono. The maid smiled at Amaya, bowed, and then entered. She busied about, poured Amaya tea and laid out the various pieces of the garment. 'Winter is definitely here,' she hummed. 'You know, I do not mind winter.'

Amaya sipped the warm Genmaicha tea, her favourite. 'It's too cold for me. I much prefer the spring or autumn.'

'I love tsubaki blossom. It only flowers in the winter,' Takako explained. 'But I do enjoy the smell of sakura in the spring, and all the sweets the use its delicate flavours taste delicious. Here.' She gestured for Amaya to approach. 'Your brother has been very busy in your absence. Such a kind boy,' Takako continued as she wrapped and tucked the dark green kimono about Amaya.

'He is,' Amaya agreed, holding her arms up. 'I think he will do well in the palace. Lord Katou has taken a liking to him. I believe my brother will join the Censorate.'

Takako gasped. 'That is wonderful. His Majesty's own guard. What an honour.'

Amaya chuckled at Takako's enthusiasm. 'It is an honour indeed. Kyo, an investigator.' Amaya chuckled at her own happy incredulity. 'Takako?'

The young maid made a noise of acknowledgement as she secured the obi belt about Amaya's waist.

'Have you heard of of Ueten and Gekai?' Amaya ventured, keeping her tone nonchalant.

Takako paused, her eyes travelling upward in thought. 'I'm not certain. It sounds familiar. Is it a story?'

'Yes,' Amaya replied. 'A story about two Spirits of the Old Faith.' She continued to recount the tale to her maid. Takako listened in silence, whilst she pinned Amaya's hair.

'That is fascinating, but it's quite sad.'

'Oh?'

'Yes, if the story is true, I think of Ueten and Gekai as

spiritual siblings. It is sad what happened to them.'

'I suppose it is,' Amaya said, quietly, falling back into her thoughts.

'The ladies of the castle are all in a commotion,' Takako said, with the sense of being all-knowing. She giggled and leant in closer. 'Lord Daiki has been betrothed to another.'

'Excuse me?' Amaya said, a little louder than she had meant, turning in her seat.

Takako paused. 'Yes, I do not know to whom, but it is the latest news in the servants' quarters. Many of the noble ladies were hoping they would be lucky enough. They would often talk about him to their ladies-in-waiting. You've never mentioned him, though.'

'There are other more suitable men in the Court I should think.' Amaya commented.

Takako laughed. 'I'm sure there are, my Lady. Are you thinking of a particular gentleman?' The maid laughed again, her eyebrows rising nefariously. 'I apologise if I have overstepped my bounds, Lady Amaya.'

A strange sound escaped Amaya's throat, but she shook her head. 'No, Takako. I have no one to speak to of such matters. However, there is no man. I have not the luxury of such frivolities.' She hoped the lie was well concealed. She daren't say openly that Akio had been the person she had thought of instantaneously, despite her own words. The idea and image of his face had surprised even herself. Amaya frowned, wanting to deflect attention from her discomfort. 'Such a sudden announcement. Daiki Kimura's engagement.'

'Oh, it hasn't been announced yet, but it will be soon.' Takako grinned. 'I am interested to discover who the lucky lady is. She will be the envy of all the palace.' She began to apply the make-up which had belonged to Amaya's mother.

'Lucky? I do not know if it's luck.' Amaya closed her eyes as her maid swept black across the lids.

'Oh, but Lord Daiki is very handsome, skilled, and truly kind.'

Amaya frowned. 'Lord Daiki? The Chancellor's youngest son? Daiki Kimura?'

Takako nodded. 'Yes. The Chancellor's son, the General's brother. There,' Takako said, placing her hands on her hips and standing back to admire Amaya. 'You look beautiful.'

'Thank you, Takako, but you are obliged to say that.' Amaya said with a laugh. 'Now, I must go to the shrine before the day begins.' She clapped her hands.

'Take your cloak.' Takako handed it to Amaya. 'It isn't warm enough to walk about without it.'

Amaya reached the top of the shrine steps and pulled her cloak tightly about her as a gust flurried down the paved walkway. Takako had been right; the air was noticeably cooler. She stopped only to cleanse her hands and mouth at the temizuya basin. The face of the shrine was in morning shadow, the sun rising behind it. As she approached the oratory, two silhouettes became apparent. Amaya slowed her pace. She was certain the shorter of the two was Kannushi Masato. Entering the shadow cast by the shrine, her eyes were able to detect more detail.

The second, taller man had his back to her. He pulled down his billowing hood slowly revealing a bald head. It was covered in a striking black tattoo which reached down to the back of his neck, the tendrils of ink finishing in a point. His clothing was covered by a simple threadbare cloak of dirtied white and black, hemmed in old fur. Protruding beneath the cloak, which did not quite reach the floor, were muddied black boots; fitted and split-toed like a shinobi's. She squinted, her eyes travelling back to Kannushi Masato whose posture was rigid. Amaya approached gradually.

'The Prophet of Ueten is the only reason you would return. You wish to see if it is true, Sen.'

Amaya stumbled, scurrying to the side at the name. Sen. She bit down on her tongue, unsure of what to do or where to go. So, she remained still in the shade of the nearest pillar.

'Prophet? Divine Heir?' Sen's derision was barely contained. 'I would be more intrigued in the Prophet of Gekai, a far more effective and relatable spirit. A Prophet is nothing more than a mouthpiece if anything at all; they are manmade. That, to me, is dangerous.' He waved the idea aside, as if it no longer entertained him. 'Can I not visit my home city, old man? Why would you assume such terrible motives?' Sen replied, his smooth voice laced with hidden menace.

'You are not here to see your brother, that much is clear.'

Sen laughed. 'I have no desire to see that boy. Although, he has been searching for me for quite some time, I hear.'

'He would be forced to kill you if you were to meet, and I will not allow him to become like you, Sen,' Kannushi Masato said, stepping down from the shrine stairs.

Sen laughed quietly, a rough sound. 'He would try to kill me, Kannushi, and he would fail. Like our father did. Like countless others have.'

'Do not try to be smart. I knew your father a long time before you ended his life. He had no time for you in his final years. Only your brother cared enough to try to help you, and you destroyed him, crushed his spirit at nine years of age. A worse fate than your father suffered at your hands.'

'You think so?' Sen said, in amusement. He laughed loudly causing Amaya to flinch. 'Kin has a weak mind, susceptible to weak ideas spouted by weak people. Prophets, Divine Heirs, some inclination that a goddess-given right places them above others. Kin should be grateful for the words I left him with. It has given him a strength he would not otherwise possess.'

'It is you who are truly weak, Sen. You are limited. Restricted by your own jealous ambition.' Kannushi Masato held his hands up to his eyes mimicking blindness. 'It saddens me. I've watched you since you were born, I knew you as child, and never did I imagine you would become such a monster. Such hope I had for you, my child.'

'Sentimentality,' Sen hissed.

It was Kannushi Masato who laughed now, a toad-like chuckle. 'Sentiment has nothing to do with it. Look at yourself; founder of the Senkaku Nin, you must be proud.'

Sen did not reply, he remained unmoving.

'You have failed, Sen. And will continue to fail.'

'Failed?' Sen cocked his head to the side. 'I have not failed, and nor will I. Kazu Takeda was not the only intellectual to have read the Ancient Scriptures. I discovered far more in my years away; far more than Lord Takeda ever did. The solitary thing I have not done is fail.'

'No,' Kannushi Masato muttered. 'The first failing was mine: when I failed you, I failed us all. However, can you not feel your failure, taste it? Every breath you draw is filled with failure. You have chosen to step out of Ueten's light. The powers you sought then will never be yours.'

Sen shook his head and let out a sigh, before taking a deliberate step forward.

Panicked, Amaya made to step forward too, but Sen pivoted on his foot, his cloak hissing through the cold air about his feet. 'Do show yourself. It is rude to listen to others' conversations.'

Amaya advanced, her fists clenched beneath her cloak. Kannushi Masato's expression hardened with dismay.

'Could this be?' Sen said, softly, his scrutinising eyes finding Amaya's. 'Kazu's well-kept secret finally out in the open.'

'What brings you out to the shrine this early?' Kannushi Masato said, quietly.

'I have come to pray for my parents, Kannushi Masato.' Amaya kept her eyes upon Sen.

He stared at her unashamedly without a blink or waver. The glow from the steadily rising sun consumed the shadows about them. She could see Sen's face clearly now, striped in sunlight and dancing shadow. His eyes were snake-like, pervasive and artful, resting just below sculpted eyebrows. His cheeks were hollow, emphasizing the indentations either side of his mouth, which seemed constantly on the edge of a smile. Kin shared the same indentations, the same jawline. Amaya could see that they were brothers.

'Such a dutiful daughter, praying for her parents. Tell me, Lady Takeda, do they answer your prayers?' His voice was ice, but his lingering gaze abruptly scorched Amaya so intently she averted her eyes from his. She rotated her arm a miniscule amount but enough for her kaiken dagger to slip from her sleeve into her palm.

'Come now, Lady Amaya.' Sen held his hands up and shook his head. 'So hostile for one so young. The death of your father has had quite the impact, and to have lost your mother too. In a tragic fire, I hear.' His head tilted, waiting for his goad to pull Amaya forward.

'Do not speak of my parents.'

'But why not? Why not?' Sen leant forward, his voice nearly a whisper as he dragged out the words. 'I can see ugliness inside you, Lady Takeda. There is no hiding it from me. Perhaps you are more Minamori than you realise, Prophet.' He smiled.

'Amaya, please.' Kannushi Masato twitched his head in the smallest of shakes.

She swallowed the anger which had flared, her chest burning with the taste of it, but she did not move.

'I will leave you to your prayers, Lady Amaya, so you can put away your blade. You're not ready yet and I am far from finished with you. Such expectations I have for your future.' He turned to Kannushi Masato, suddenly disinterested. 'Send my adoration to my brother, will you,' he laughed, and then vanished with the sway of a shadow and flash of sunlight.

Amaya blinked, her eyes searching him out in disbelief. 'Where is he?' She questioned, when she could not detect him.

'He has gone,' Kannushi Masato breathed.

'How?' Amaya walked forward, her eyes still scouring the grounds. 'He disappeared, Kannushi Masato. Disappeared.'

'Some trick no doubt.' He joined Amaya, steering her

into the shrine. 'His shinobi talents have grown considerably it seems.'

'Kin must be told,' Amaya said, turning about. 'I will return.' She did not wait for a response, instead she hurried back down the stone steps and towards the palace.

Without thought her feet took her to the Archives. 'Akio,' she shouted out, disregarding proprieties. 'Akio.'

'Lady Amaya?' Akio's face bore alarm as he looked up from his desk. Kenta was beside him, his expression equally as bemused. 'What is it?'

'Sen. Sen Sanjo is here.'

Kin appeared from behind an aisle, the scrolls which were clutched in his hands, spilled to the floor. 'What did you say?'

Amaya stopped and turned to him. 'Sen was at the shrine.'

'I will send Censorate members to the shrine to help Kannushi Masato,' Kenta began.

Kin interrupted and his voice shook with hatred. Fear and anger resounded about the Archives and Amaya's stomach twisted horribly. 'Kannushi Masato may already be dead. I will go.' With these words Kin turned and ran, his conical hat bouncing on his back, his medicine gourds rattling, his staff clenched in his hand.

The Archives were hushed for a moment but then Kenta spoke to the seemingly empty space above. 'Inform Captain Sano. Have Censorate soldiers sent to the shrine and to the perimeter gates of both the palace and the capital. I want this man captured. He is not to leave Chuto.'

Amaya heard the softest of sounds in the panelled ceiling as the hidden retainers obeyed. Kenta turned to Akio, but he was already moving.

'Amaya stay with me,' he ordered, not harshly. She nodded but her heart was struggling to remain still. Her terror for Kin caused it to hammer, harder and harder, until she threw her hands in the air.

'I must fetch my katana, Akio. Please,' she added. 'I can protect myself well. Just put a blade in my hand.'

He pressed his lips together, wanting to protest. 'Very well.' He looked to Kenta.

'Go, I have my Censorate guards with me.'

Akio nodded abruptly and then gestured Amaya to follow. Once outside, Amaya did not slow her pace; she rushed on towards her quarters, desperate to hold her katana. She vowed to herself never to leave it again.

'Nothing, Your Majesty,' Captain Sano reported, reluctantly that afternoon. 'I apologise.'

Kenta paced the small room. Amaya couldn't be sure if it was the same space as the last time she had been in the Censorate building, it was very disorientating.

'Even the city gates?' Kenta asked, after a moment.

Captain Sano nodded curtly. 'No trace, My Lord.'

'It is not surprising. My brother has talents most cannot claim to have. He has been collecting and honing these talents for sixteen years.' Kin was sitting but his feet could not stay still. He lent his arms upon his knees and they bounced with his agitation.

Amaya's legs almost twitched as his did. 'We will find him.'

Kin looked at her. 'I will find him, Amaya. I do not want another to have to suffer at his hand. This is my duty.'

'I would ask you not to bear such a burden by yourself, but I understand your desire to do so,' Akio sighed. Amaya looked about desperately, the need to aid Kin swelling beyond what she would have expected.

'My brother has shown himself. Finally.' Kin shook his head. 'We have no more time. I leave today whilst he is still in the Sky Province.'

'Take what you need,' Kenta said, his hand coming to rest on Kin's shoulder.

'Thank you, Kenta. Amaya,' he faced her, 'I'm sorry to

leave you so suddenly, but I will return. Allow your belief to guide you.'

Amaya knew he was referring to the Elementals she had yet to discover. She nodded but couldn't keep the sadness of his departure at bay. She nodded again when no words came to her. Then Kin rose to his feet and left.

'He will be fine,' Akio reassured her. 'You can feel him, yes?' He touched his own chest. 'You have the connection that Prophet has with her Elementals.'

'It is a bizarre feeling. I can sense Kin more so than Tomio.' She hadn't considered the fact until that point.

Kenta elaborated. 'Kin was your first Elemental, the Air Elemental. His voice, his influence, is the strongest, the most far-reaching.' He inclined his head. 'You both must prepare to leave tomorrow. However, this evening, the Chancellor has an announcement. We must appear at ease and continue as normal,' Kenta said.

'We will attend,' Akio replied.

Later that afternoon, Amaya sought out the confines of the palace dojo. As she slipped her feet from her geta sandals and stepped onto the wooden floor she felt an old, welcoming sensation creep up her legs and into her body. She had barely practiced in the months which had passed, especially since the fire had claimed the place she loved to train in the most. With the thought, images soon followed until her mother's face was stark amidst the flames of her memory. Closing her eyes, she drew a deep breath, allowing the sweetness of the cedar and the lingering scent of sweat distract her. She pulled her cloak off and brushed her hand along her katana. When she slid her feet into the stance of the Seishin no Ken style, she was startled to feel her eyes brim. She hadn't realised how much she had missed the Way of the Samurai and was painfully ashamed of her neglect as the Assistant Master. She moved slowly at first, allowing her body to awaken. Then, steadily and without thought, her pace increased. She was comfortable in this skin and felt beautiful when she danced the Seishin no Ken. Bringing the katana down in a final crescent sweep, she ended her session.

Outside it was darker than she had expected and with anxiety she recalled Kenta's request to attend Rai's meeting. She tugged her cloak into place, ensured her katana was hidden and made her way to the palace. She did not care that she was in hakama, or that her face was flushed with exertion.

The small assembly room was filled with Court Officials, and as Amaya gazed around, she saw all Six Ministers, including Kannushi Masato. He saw her as she entered and hurried to greet her.

'Amaya, my dear.' He looked at her curiously. 'You've been in the dojo I see.'

'Do you know what the Chancellor's announcement is concerning?' Amaya questioned at once, her eyes detecting an large number of nobles and samurai.

Kannushi Masato shook his head. 'No, but we will soon find out.'

'This is strange,' Amaya continued, the peace that the training had brought began to dwindle. 'More people should be privy to the subject of today's meeting.'

'Lady Amaya.' It was Akio who now spoke. He too bore the expression of someone slightly lost. 'Kannushi Masato.'

The two bowed to Akio as he came to a stop beside them. Amaya looked up at his face, his charm was masked with the same suspicion Amaya felt, and his eyes moved constantly.

'Is Tomio here?' Amaya asked.

'I passed him in the hallway a moment ago. He was on his way to greet Mari Ito of the Ito Merchants Guild as arranged. Your brother was escorting him. They seem to have found a friend in each other.' Akio responded, but he did not remove his eyes from the crowd. 'There.' He tilted his head. Amaya followed his gaze, her eyes coming to rest on Rai and Daiki. The two were settling at the head of the room. Soon everyone began to take a seat and Amaya found herself chivied into one beside Akio. 'Where is Lord Kenta?' Amaya hissed.

Akio leant closer to her, craning to look around. 'There he is. He is joining Rai and Daiki.'

Amaya saw the Emperor now and his face was placid, she could not read his expression because it was not one she had seen before.

Rai stood once everyone was seated. He smiled over the crowd and bowed. 'In this time of upheaval, it takes every ounce of one's faith and hope to remain strong. We must find pleasure in the smaller things in order to weather events such as war and illness. I am happy to be able to bring a small morsel of light. It is my hope to set an example to those who war amongst themselves unnecessarily, by means of a truce. It is my hope to bury old animosities in the name of reconciliation. My son,' Rai gestured to Daiki, who knelt beside him. Amaya studied his comely face; his expression grim; his eyes staring beyond the room, as if he'd rather be elsewhere.

'Daiki,' Rai continued, 'is to be married. It is his marriage which will act as the vehicle of this truce I spoke of. It is my hope to put to rest an old feud the Kimura clan has shared with another once-prestigious family.'

Akio shifted next to Amaya and at the same time Kenta turned his head to Rai, his expression grave.

'The family I speak of is, of course, the noble Takeda.' Rai's black eyes found Amaya, his smile wide now.

Amaya felt her mouth open a little. She flinched as though someone had struck her. Her hand went to her stomach as she comprehended Rai's announcement.

'Daiki will be wed to Lady Amaya Takeda. It is time for the Kimura and Takeda to reconcile. United we are stronger. Lady Takeda, please come to the front.'

Amaya's breath quickened; her throat constricted with the urge to vomit. She felt Akio's hand, it rested on the small of her back. 'Go, Amaya. Act the part now. Do not worry, I will never let this go ahead.' Akio's whisper bolstered her steps as she stood and strode forward.

The silence of the room was heavier than before and Amaya could feel each pair of eyes following her as she walked through the middle of the chamber. She willed herself to remain calm, to act the part as Akio had instructed. Rai welcomed her by taking her hands in his, but his grip was hard and cold. Amaya could feel the threat in the squeeze he gave. He then began to clap, slowly at first and then, as more people joined, the tempo increased like some peculiar tribal beat. Amaya looked to Akio whose hands rested in his lap. Kannushi Masato, too, was still, unmoving. Kenta's eyes were upon Rai, but they soon found Amaya. He gave the smallest shake of the head.

'It seems we are to be married.' It was Daiki. Amaya hadn't seen him stand and join her. 'The lie you told on the ferry is no longer an untruth. Rejoice, Lady Takeda, my dear.' He took her hands and bowed his head. His palms were rough - a samurai's hands - but far warmer than his father's had been.

Amaya merely stared at him, unable to speak for fear of only rage spewing forth. She was not confident she could stem it as Daiki's nonchalance washed over her. Managing a smile, she faced the room, allowing the comments of those around them to reach her.

'The Kimura and the Takeda,' one man said, incredulously, shaking his head.

'A formidable union. This is truly an example to follow.'

'But what of the Takeda?' Another spoke.

Amaya shivered with the words. Daiki stared; he had felt her tremble. 'Soon only your brother will hold the Takeda name now. I hear he is proving his worth in the palace, perhaps he is worthy of the name Takeda.'

'Do not forget my uncle,' Amaya finally spoke, her jaw tight.

Daiki raised an eyebrow and laughed. 'Jiro? No, he's not forgotten at all.' He released Amaya's hand. 'Who do you think my father asked in regard to our union? Rules must be followed, Lady Amaya. Your parents are dead, your uncle is the next Takeda who can be approached with such a request.'

The breath Amaya drew was sharp, almost painful. 'My uncle would never agree to this. I cannot believe it. I will not marry you,' she hissed the last part.

Daiki leant in so that his nose almost touched her cheek. 'You do not have a choice, Amaya. I certainly do not. Try to exercise obedience for once; you may find it a refreshing change.'

'Obedience I have. Just not towards your father.'

Daiki clenched her wrist tightly and held his breath. Amaya waited for his next stream of ill-mannered words, but they did not come. Instead, he released her arm gently and stepped away from her. 'I did not request this.'

'Is there nothing you will not do for your father? No order too unseemly?' Amaya susurrated at Daiki's retreating back.

Slowly, the crowd dispersed, the room emptying gradually until only a handful remained. Amongst them, Amaya could see Kenta and Kannushi Masato. She looked for Akio but could not detect him amidst the remaining few.

'Lady Amaya,' Kannushi Masato said, simply. 'This is unexpected. Completely unexpected.'

Amaya felt her face grow hot. 'Rai is truly trying to destroy the Takeda.' She let out a humourless laugh. 'Well done, Lord Kimura. I have been completely ambushed with this announcement.'

'His intentions are disguised under the pretence of something that should be a joyous thing,' Kenta added. 'There could be myriad reasons behind this match considering your shared lineage.'

Amaya shook her head. 'Where is Lord Akio?'

'He is furious.' Kenta's tone was low. 'As am I. Akio is going to nullify this union at once.'

'How can he do that?' Amaya whispered, unable to stifle the flash of hope.

Kenta looked at her a little awkwardly. 'It will not be announced formally but there is only one way to extract you from this marriage union.'

Amaya nodded, her chest swelling at the prospect. 'Anything.'

'You will have to be wed to another of equal or higher social standing. We must make it appear as though it has been arranged far longer than your betrothal to Daiki.'

'Higher than the Chancellor's son? Who?' Amaya faltered, uncertain again.

'Akio Izumi, of course,' Kenta replied, 'If there was another way, Amaya, I would choose it.' Kenta's eyes pleaded with her.

She held her hands up to stop him, her eyes stinging with the threat of tears. 'I am grateful that Lord Akio would sacrifice himself in such a way.'

'Sacrifice?' He let out a small laugh, which Amaya couldn't quite understand in that moment. 'As long as you are promised to another, especially one of such social standing as Akio, no other can touch you. It is a means of protection at least; a shield against Rai Kimura's true intentions.'

'So, what is Lord Akio hoping to do?'

'He is forging documents which will detail your father's agreement with his own father regarding your marriage.' Kenta swallowed.

Amaya stumbled a little. 'He can't. Forgery of such a thing is punishable by death under the Ten Laws of Akegata.' She turned to pursue Akio but Kannushi Masato gently held her hand.

'Perhaps not death, but something one would find worse: a loss of honour. He and his entire family will be shunned. Let Lord Izumi do this for you. To watch you marry Daiki would be more than he could bear.'

Amaya halted, frowning as she contemplated the meaning behind Kannushi Masato's words. 'I would rather none of you to risk yourselves on account of me. I know all too well the toll a loss of honour can take.' She paused. 'I'd rather marry Daiki than be the cause of pain to any of you.'

Kenta raised an eyebrow, forcing amusement into his eyes. 'And be Lady *Kimura*? Under the control of Rai Kimura. It is not something you could endure. I would not expect you to endure such a thing. And nor would Akio.'

Amaya shook her head, her gaze dropping to the tatami floor.

Kenta's gaze soothed her, as he spoke, 'Akio will not fail.'

'Lady Amaya,' Shun called out.

Amaya turned, and stopped mid-stride. 'General Kimura,' she smiled. It had been only a day since her engagement to Shun's brother.

Shun bowed low. The silence was awkward, and he looked on the verge of uncomfortable speech. 'My brother has a good heart.'

Amaya started in surprise. 'Please, General Kimura. You do not have to console me.' She looked kindly at him, a strange want to reach out overwhelmed her.

Shun looked up, his tortured eyes struggling to find something in hers. 'I apologise, Lady Amaya. My father has acted unkindly, to both you and my brother.' He sucked in the end of his sentence. 'I am to leave the palace shortly.'

Amaya frowned. 'So soon? Where are you going?'

'I am going to the Air Province to join my men.'

'It is so dangerous there. Would the Earth Province not be safer for you to command from?'

Shun shook his head. 'I will place myself in the same danger my men face. I wish to help Akegata as you are, Lady Amaya. I may discover more regarding the two leaders if I am closer to the source of conflict,' Shun said, quietly.

'Please do not act recklessly, Shun.' She stepped forward. 'My father entrusted two important things to you: the title of General, and the title of Master of the Sky Province, making you one of the Five Masters of Akegata. Ultimately, you are the one to continue the Seishin no Ken style in his stead. I would hate to see his protege perish.'

Shun's back tightened, his shoulders reached his ears and his tan skin reddened. 'It is you who he has placed his hopes in.'

'I am the Assistant Master of the Seishin no Ken style. I have seen you spar; you move exactly like him. Exactly.' Amaya nodded, hoping that the action would strengthen her words.

'Thank you, Lady Amaya, but I believe it is more than simply the Way of the Samurai your father believed in. He believed you hold something few do.' He bowed so low that his katana pointed skyward. Then he left Amaya to continue her way. She watched the tall General as he descended from the veranda and paced through the bare garden. The shrubs were so fragile in winter yet Shun's large form, donned in the heavy gear of combat, did not seem out of place as he marched. *He knows of Ueten and my identity as the Prophet*, Amaya decided after debating Shun's last words. Oddly, she was not disconcerted by the fact, simply curious as to how he knew.

Akio was still behind his desk, his hand moving fluidly over the parchment, when she entered the Archives. On hearing her he looked up.

'Please, rest. You haven't slept, have you?' She settled opposite him.

He pushed his tousled hair back from his face, the dark strands sticking between his fingers. Amaya watched his face unashamedly, finding the tiredness beneath his eyes endearing. The fingers of his scar tugged a little at his mouth as he leant his head back. She half moved her hand to touch it.

'I will not rest until the document is complete, Amaya. The longer it is left, the more unbelievable it will be. I will not allow that man another opportunity to exploit you.'

'Rai will persevere, as he always has. You are risking so much.' She waved a hand over the parchment. The ink was still wet, it glistened in the pale light and Amaya could smell the faintest aroma of cinnamon mixed in with the charcoal of the ink stick.

Akio looked at her resolutely. 'To see you married to another...in such a manner,' he rested his elbows on the table heavily, visibly composing himself behind his interlocked fingers before continuing. 'Every day is a risk in the palace. If you are shackled to Daiki, you cannot search for the remaining Elementals and continue your Pilgrimage.'

Amaya felt a strange disappointment. Her hands were upon the desk, and they balled into fists at Akio's words. 'I trust you can help. However, if it seems you may be discovered, I want you to cease.'

Akio reached out, his free hand resting atop one of hers. 'Lady Amaya, I can make no such promise until you are released from this absurd contract.'

Amaya's nod was slight, her eyes held Akio's and she felt her breath quicken. 'Do not ask me to watch you endanger yourself.'

Akio permitted a small laugh to escape him. 'Lady Amaya, do not think me selfless. I am not only doing this for your sake but also for my own.'

Amaya lent back, to see Akio's face in its entirety. 'Lord Akio, I came today to release you from any duty you feel you may have towards me. I would not want you to marry against your will, or in circumstances such as these.' The words Kenta had spoken to her the previous day had not left her mind.

Akio's hand stopped, the brush hovering over the ink well; a single drip descended, barely disturbing the tiny dark pool. 'Forced?' His swallow was audible. 'Lady Amaya, although the circumstances are not as I would have liked, I never thought I would be so fortunate as to marry for love.' His eyes moved from the parchment directly to Amaya.

'I too wish you to marry for love. Few are fortunate enough, but you are removing such a choice for yourself by doing this.'

Akio placed the ink brush upon its stand. 'Amaya.' His laugh was tinged with exasperation.

Amaya's eyes widened as he dropped proprieties for the first time.

'Amaya, you misunderstand what I have said. I *am* marrying for love.' He reached his free hand across the table, placing it atop hers.

Amaya's skin prickled with a pleasant heat, which swelled the longer his hand remained on hers. She did not want to say aloud what Akio had stated for fear she could be mistaken.

He saved her from her difficulty. 'I am saying that I love you, Amaya. And nothing brings me more happiness than the thought of sharing my life with you.' He exhaled his humour gently, 'if that is acceptable to you?'

'Acceptable?' Amaya felt blissful tears rise, teetering upon the ends of her eyelashes. She dared not blink. 'I believe I have wanted this for some time. I believe I have loved you for some time, I just did not know it until your words.' She placed her hand upon each cheek, they were burning, but she relished the feeling. 'I am so full of love even my face is brimming with it.'

Akio laced the fingers of his hand through hers, his back slumping with relief. 'You have made me feel like a whole man, Amaya.' He stared at her. 'Kannushi Masato shall marry us.'

'At the earliest moment.' Amaya heard her own giggle. Akio laughed harder. Through the laughter and ecstatic tears, Amaya could not stop gazing at her husband-to-be; never did she think she would feel such delight when only a few hours before such dread had occupied her every waking moment.

CHAPTER ELEVEN

'Chancellor Kimura, the document is legally binding. This pledge was drawn between Lord Izumi's father and Kazu Takeda over six years ago.' Hiroshi Katou sighed as if preparing for the outburst. None came, however.

'It was folly to think that Kazu would leave such a lovely daughter without a suitor. Lord Akio is a fine match.' Rai bowed his head, but Amaya could not see his expression. 'I find it strange that Jiro Takeda was unaware of this union, however. Perhaps he and his brother did not share all Takeda business.'

Amaya remained stoic, not wanting to disturb what appeared to be a peaceful resolution. Akio was beside her and this gave her courage to refrain from speaking. His very presence calmed her.

'Lord Kimura, it is a heartfelt apology I wish to give for this confusion. Will you allow myself to announce the change in events? To save you from having to do so.' Akio bowed.

'Of course, Lord Izumi.' Rai's voice was flat. 'Congratulations to you both. I wish you many happy years together.' With these last words, he bowed and rose to his feet. 'Excuse me.'

Amaya watched Rai's shadow fade away behind the closed screen door. 'Akio. Lord Hiroshi. Thank you.'

Akio dismissed her gratitude with a playful wave. 'We have a wedding to prepare.'

'In such a short time. You will need every available staff.' Hiroshi puffed, rising to his feet. 'Please allow me and Kannushi Masato the honour.'

'I could not deny your aid. We must be married tomorrow if we are to leave as planned. I have asked Takako to lead in the bride's detail.' Amaya offered.

'Good, good. Then it will already be completed, no doubt.' Hiroshi was still chuckling as he departed.

Akio turned on his knees so that his face was opposite Amaya's. 'I am happy, Amaya. Truly.'

Amaya nodded and took his hands in her own. 'I did not think marriage would be a part of my life.'

'Surprises are not always so terrible.' He leant forward, his nose brushing hers. 'I do love you.'

The following morning, Takako had proved Lord Hiroshi correct. She had swiftly attended to the details of the wedding through the previous afternoon, all through the night and in the morning. Her lady-in-waiting had finished Amaya's make-up and hair, and was already busily wrapping Amaya in her white shiromuku gown. The purity and sturdiness of the fabric felt like a reflection of Amaya's feelings in that moment; the fortune in marrying Akio was not lost on her and she felt a resounding jubilance. There was an undercurrent of yearning for her mother and father which burned through her bliss, however. It dissipated in a moment as Kyo entered holding her fan; the fan her parents had given her as a child. He stopped at the entrance and admired her. 'Amaya, you and Akio are beaming as much as each other.'

'You have seen him?' Amaya questioned excitedly, motioning for Kyo to place the fan upon the table.

'Yes. Lord Kenta and Lord Hiroshi are with him.'

'Of course,' Amaya fell quiet. Both she and Akio were orphaned; neither had parents to attend their union. It would be a very quiet and private event, but Amaya felt better for that fact; no unwanted prying eyes from those who cared nothing of their future.

'Amaya, would you permit me to step into father's role?' Kyo's voice was straight-forward but careful. 'I would not want to intrude.'

'Kyo, I could think of no one I would want by my side during the ceremony.'

Kyo bowed his gratitude. 'I shall oversee the final preparations for the ceremony. Amaya,' he stopped at the door, 'you were always meant to be a bride. Akio's bride. You have known each other for many years. Perhaps not in person, but through your letters you know each other's souls. I'm certain of it. When you first met him and the stories from that time, even mother said that Akio had stirred something important within you. For him, I always feel it was there. He has loved you for a long time, Amaya.' Kyo almost skipped from the chamber in his glee.

Takako laughed affectionately, pausing to watch Kyo hurry away. 'He is a good brother, Lady Takeda. An incredible spirit.'

Amaya was still watching the door as Takako approached her. In her hand, she held the tsunokakushi headdress. It was the same pristine white as her gown. Gently, Takako placed it atop Amaya's sculpted hair and clasped ivory flower pins to adorn and secure it in place.

'There.' Takako stepped back to reveal the mirror behind her. Amaya stared at her own bright reflection. The early winter sunlight softly gleaned the fabric, catching the white embroidered birds upon her collar and folds of the shiromuku. Her obi belt was fastened in an elaborate bow which swept out behind her like the wings of a heron. Amaya had requested the unusual knot to symbolise Akio's family name and crest; the name she would be taking: Izumi. Her ebon hair glinted silver beneath the white tsunokakushi; the rouge of her lips the only colour.

'The last piece.' Takako whispered. She passed Amaya the small, ornate kaiken blade. The sheath was a pale red ochre inlaid with the crest of her clan: Takeda. It had been her mother's.

Amaya bowed as she received it and slid it slowly into her belt and out of sight. 'Thank you for all you have done, Takako. You have helped make this day as wonderful as if it had been planned for a year.'

'No less for my Lady. Now, go. They will all be assembling.'

Amaya ascended the final step of the stone stairs which led to the shrine; Kyo's arm was under her elbow, warm and supportive. 'A little further, and then you will be a wife, Amaya.' He squeezed her gently.

Amaya pressed her lips together feeling the paste upon them. 'My entire being is tingling, Kyo.'

'The offerings have been placed at the alter, the ceremonial cups are prepared – the same as Akio's parents used – and Kannushi Masato is ready to lead you to the shrine. Akio is – .' Kyo stopped as the two reached the summit of the steps, the beginning of the flagged pathway to Amaya's future. Kannushi Masato was a few steps away and beside him, Akio. He was donned in a black kimono top with striped hakama. The seven pleats of the samurai were defined in the fabric which rippled in the chill of winter. In his hand was a familiar fan. Amaya noticed the exception and grinned; it was her own favourite fan, the one her father had given to her as a child. She glanced at her brother and raised her eyebrows.

'I did not think you would mind.' Kyo whispered, nudging her forward.

Akio had not removed his gaze from Amaya since she had appeared at the top of the steps. His dark irises glittered joyfully, gratefully as he took his place beside her. The four begin the short trip to the temple alter to begin their wedding before the gods.

Hiroshi Katou and Kenta were waiting within behind a narrow table adorned with seasonal fruit, vessels of Sake and the rings. Amaya only had time to give a nod of her head before she and Akio were steered to the centre of the quietly beautiful hall. Kannushi Masato began the purification and motioned to the nuptial cups set out on a tray. San San Ku Do was the physical symbol of exchanging their vows: nine sips of sake from the three different cups. Kannushi Masato filled each delicately. Amaya knew what each represented and felt no reluctance as she and Akio knelt and gathered a sakazuki cup each. In unison, in comforting silence, they took their first three sips: the three couples – parents and now herself and Akio. The second: the flaws of hatred, passion and ignorance. And, finally, the third: freedom from those three flaws. Amaya felt the smallest of twinges as she recalled, very briefly, the vow of vengeance she had made to her father's ascending spirit the final night of the Spirit Festival. She could not honestly commit to the just cause she believed herself pursuing; the flaw of hatred would be a difficult thing to relinquish and Amaya chastised herself for such a weakness.

The black lacquer sakazuki cups lay empty upon the tray as the two rose and approached the alter. It was the first time Amaya had heard Akio's voice since the day before.

'Some, who do not know us, may feel pity; we do not have our parents to share this day with. Yet, my gratitude is filling my heart today that there is no room for sadness. Thank you, my mentor, Hiroshi Katou, you have instructed me in such nuanced ways and prepared me for everything a young man could need. Kannushi Masato, my spiritual guide, you have taught me the intricacies of the gods and the subtle yet important influences they have over our everyday lives. You have allowed me to explore philosophies and doubts with no judgement. To my brother in all but name, Kenta Yamashima. Your unconditional love and support has shaped who I am. I know you consider me your mentor and protector, but please believe me when I tell say that you have been that and more in my life. You have shown me god-like bravery time and again. You have displayed genuine kindness when others would not have. Thank you, brother.' Akio took a breath and his eyes finally found Amaya.

'My wife, Amaya. My wife.' An involuntary grin burst across his face. 'I cannot believe it, yet it feels written by the gods themselves. I have known you a lifetime already Amaya and your father, Kazu, deserves more thanks than I can articulate. My gratitude to you and this union is like a spring-time joy. I am grateful you have snuck into my heart and mind, Amaya, for it is clear to me that neither were whole before you entered the Archives that day seeking me out. When all else fades, the only echo left is love; touching humanity with intangible fingers and unveiling clouded eyes so that they may see the decades which await them. Await us – unpicked experiences ready to be cherished together. We are the wayfinders on this path and I cannot wait to walk it alongside you. For all of this, I thank you, Amaya.'

Amaya felt ecstatic tears cling to her eyelashes. She had never felt this kind of value as a woman and as a person. Akio passed her a small cup of sake, taking one for himself. Together, they faced the small gathering. All had their own cups, their own expressions of gratitude and love. They drank together. Kannushi Masato placed the evergreen cedar branch at the alter; the final thanks to the spirits who had blessed this union. 'You may now exchange the rings.'

Kenta stepped forward, cradling the rings in his palms. Stretching out his hands, he beamed at the two. 'This has made me so happy. The two I love the most, joined before the spirits.'

Akio took Amaya's hand in his warm one. Gradually, absorbing each moment, Akio placed the finger onto Amaya's finger. He gripped her hand long after simply staring at the band around her finger. Tenderly, Amaya adjusted the grip and traced her fingers across the back of his hand. As Akio had done, she placed the ring upon his finger, marvelling at such a thing. Strange to think that before the sun set on the day, they would be on the road, journeying to the Fire Province to continue Amaya's pilgrimage. She knew the banquet and night of the wedding would have to wait.

CHAPTER TWELVE

Akio was indeed ready when the sun began to wane. Amaya had spent the rest of the afternoon disrobing from the wedding attire and donning her travel wear. Sending Takako home, Amaya had prepared her belongings and relived all that had happened that day. She had wanted to train in the dojo but deliberated that she needed the energy for the journey south. She had run out of time.

'Will you take this?' Kyo asked, helping his sister with the last of her things. He was holding the scroll of Ueten and Gekai in his hands.

'Yes,' Amaya replied, simply. 'You've gotten taller,' she said, truly scrutinising him. 'Kyo, I'm sorry.'

Bemusement broke across his face. 'Why do you say that, Amaya?'

'I am sorry I have been away. I have neglected you. Mother only recently died. I have been selfish.'

Kyo abandoned his task and walked to her, pulling her into an embrace. He had indeed gotten taller, he seemed to look at her from above now. 'You're speaking nonsense, Amaya. You think you are being selfish? That couldn't be further from the truth. You are being selfless.'

Amaya laughed, and looked at her brother. 'If you insist.'

'I do,' Kyo said, seriously. 'We all need you to succeed. Your pilgrimage is to discover your Elementals and evolve spiritually. Being such a mirror for Ueten will no be without severe challenge. You are battling with your own belief; an entirely different battle to the one in the Air province. Shirking doubt and vengeance, breaking the chain of retaliation is not something a weak person can do. It is not something which will happen quickly.'

Amaya shook her head, awed. 'You sound wiser than Kin.'

Kyo looked suddenly bashful. 'It is not wisdom. Just the observation of a brother who cares for you. Still, I am trying in my own way to help. Soon I will be an official investigator of the Censorate.'

'Yes!' Amaya said, clapping her hands. 'You will come of age is in less than a week.'

'I will discover the identities of the rebel army's leaders and the one that aided father years ago when all this began.'

'I have every faith that you will,' Amaya replied, sincerely. Kyo handed her Meiyo, and she took the katana in both hands, her eyes on her brother. 'I will rid myself of this doubt and vengeance. It is all I can do for everyone. For the Takeda and for Akegata.'

Akio met Amaya beside the gates of Chuto. The sun's belly scraped the horizon to the west. The light threw pinks and oranges across the sky, tainting the few clouds a dark purple. The wind which scurried along the streets and pushed Amaya forward was icy, and she knew that snow may fall on Chuto before her return. She tightened her cloak and tipped her conical hat further over her eyes.

'Ready, wife?' Akio asked, twisting his ring around his finger. Amaya could only see his mouth, his eyes were in the shadow of his own conical hat.

Nodding, she gestured for them to leave.

The evening came quickly, devouring the dusk just as Amaya and Akio reached the path which led along the fringe of the mountain forest. Amaya had not ventured south of the Sky Province, only having family in the north. She had heard many things about the people of the southern territories and had seen many a painting of the famous mountains of the Fire

Province and the coastline of the Water Province. The largest river was also in the Water Province, and everybody throughout Akegata believed the water-god dragon dwelt there.

'Is it true that Fire Province natives are passionate and reckless?' Amaya questioned, thoughtfully.

Akio laughed. 'I am from the Fire Province. You have also met Shin Nakamura and his wife Emi. She is from the Fire Province originally.'

'Oh yes,' Amaya said, remembering the open and cheerful Emi. 'I liked her very much. Lord Nakamura was also very kind. I am sorry I did not get to see more of them.' The horror of the fire, which had claimed her mother's life and taken the dojo from her, burst into her mind as savage as the flames had been that day. It had overshadowed all that had occurred at the time, including her first encounter with the Nakamura clan.

'And you will meet them again,' Akio replied, gently nudging her shoulder. 'They are to receive us when we reach Kasaichi.'

Amaya bit her bottom lip happily. 'That will be wonderful.'

'It will not take us long to reach the city if the weather holds. Snow shouldn't fall in the south for at least another month, but we will still need to find sheltered accommodation, the nights are now too cold for out of doors. Perhaps the Face of Winter will show itself earlier this year.'

'You know the road well?'

Akio nodded. 'Yes, very. I've travelled it many a time. I believe there is a quiet ryokan beyond the foot of the next mountain. We won't make it before dark, but it is almost a full moon.' He pointed to the pink and lavender sky. Amaya could see the moon, a pearlescent phantom in the twilight, hanging above the mountains.

The forest to their right was black; a dense impenetrable black which felt like it was drawing them into its depths. Occasionally, a protruding branch would snag at

Amaya's cloak. She didn't flinch, but it made her steadily more uneasy and she found that her hand was never far from the hilt of her katana. The moon was fat, and its shivering light made the shadows seem even darker, giving them life and movement which verged on the unnatural. The sky was sprayed with stars and Amaya found herself remembering the old legend and how Souzou, the Spirit of Creation, had painted the Milky Way. Seitan had been born of the stars themselves. Amaya imagined her to be beautiful, too bright to look at directly. However, it was their children, Ueten and Gekai, who truly intrigued her. She thought their tale a tragic one, as her maid, Takako, had said.

'Amaya.' Akio's voice interrupted her thoughts. He touched her arm gently, steering her down a short, narrow path. They had arrived at the ryokan. The silence with Akio had been so comfortable that she hadn't been aware how long she had let it go on for.

'So soon.'

He laughed. 'You were in your thoughts; I did not want to disturb you.'

Amaya felt her cheeks grow warm. She pulled off her conical hat at the same time as Akio did. He reached out his arm and slid the door open. The interior was dimmer than Amaya would have expected of a ryokan; only a single brazier lit the small entrance.

'No shoes,' Akio commented to himself as he closed the door quietly.

'Welcome.' A woman appeared from the corridor to their right. She bowed low in greeting.

Amaya and Akio responded in kind and removed their shoes. The tatami mats were old and rustled softly beneath her feet as she stepped up. It smelled a little damp, like an aged mountain, Amaya thought.

'We seek a room for the night if you have one,' Akio spoke up.

The woman eyed them both. 'We have a room suitable. Please follow me.' Her voice was cracked despite her youth, and Amaya noticed the darkness ringing her eyes. She looked exhausted. Akio gestured for Amaya to follow the ryokan owner. The hallway they were led down smelled as the entrance had done and was lit just as poorly. The warmth was frail, as if it would scurry away with the slightest wind. Amaya frowned. It was a well-used road with many potential customers, yet the ryokan was hardly maintained. The doors were all closed, but no light flickered around the cracks and the stillness spoke for the emptiness.

'I hope this is to your liking,' the woman said, revealing a moderate room.

'Thank you,' Akio replied, smiling gratefully. 'You are very kind.'

The woman bowed again as they walked inside. 'May I fetch tea? The night is cold.'

'Yes, that would be most welcome,' Akio answered.

Amaya waited until the woman retreated and closed the door. 'The whole place is empty.'

Akio nodded, and then walked to the window. He opened it and looked out briefly. 'It is.' When he turned around, he was wearing a frown. 'We will leave at dawn.'

Amaya's stare travelled around the sparse room and at last fell upon the two futon which lay side by side. She quickly made her way to the table. 'If we make good time, we will be in Kasaichi in two days?'

'Yes, at a brisk pace.' Akio confirmed, sitting opposite her.

The woman announced her return and brought in the tea. 'Please ask if you require anything else.'

'Again, thank you.'

Amaya looked at her face once more and was uncertain of the expression. Before she could scrutinise further the woman left. 'Is she ill?' Amaya wondered, aloud.

Akio poured the tea, his face serious. 'Her behaviour is peculiar.'

'I thought all ryokan owners would be like Inari or Goro,' Amaya said, thinking back to her previous experiences.

'The ones I have met usually are.' Akio was uncomfortable, Amaya could see it clearly. She joined him at the table, accepting the tea. Wrapping her hands around the simple cup she allowed her hands to warm up. Akio too was rubbing his hands and breathing in the fragrant steam.

'Akio?' Amaya ventured. He looked up at her, inviting her to continue, a small smile tweaking his lips. 'I have been trying to repay the words you gave at our ceremony. Yet, none are sufficient. I do not want you to think I am mute. Here is where my unvoiced feelings reside. The feeling is raw, new-born and exhilarating. It is almost made of light yet too strong for anything to conquer...'

'I know, Amaya.' Akio leant across the table and cupped her face. 'I also know it occurred far sooner, quicker, than we could have imagined. I plan to take my time and discover you even further. We have many years ahead of us.'

Amaya held onto her cup as she slowly drained it, until the heat had finally gone. She and Akio spoke about the civil war and the two leaders. They speculated and organised their thoughts, and Amaya couldn't help but notice that they were the same as one another's. Her grins, frowns, smiles, laughs were shared by the man sitting in front of her.

Their cocoon of harmony was rent apart. A wailing scream echoed throughout the vacant ryokan, quickly muffled by the tatami floor and papered hallways. Akio was standing in an instant, Amaya soon behind.

'Stay here,' he instructed.

Amaya made to protest but Akio gripped her shoulder. 'I will call out should I need you, Amaya. So please, remain quiet. You may be my element of surprise.' He scooped his katana from the floor by his feet, secured it into his waistband and dashed from the room without a sound.

Amaya remained exactly where he had left her. She continued to watch the door, her heart the only sound she could make out in the new stillness. Its beat gnawed at her nerves, fraying them steadily. It was the second louder, longer scream which shocked her legs and body into movement. She grabbed her katana and ran from the room, her footsteps soundless, her movement fluid. She stuck to the walls as she ran low, poised. Her hand did not leave the hilt of her katana and her eyes were trained ahead. Low voices reached her ears, and so she slowed her pace and came to a stop at the door to the room they originated from. She threw it open.

  Akio was standing in front of the ryokan owner, his back to her. She was on the floor, blood issuing copiously from a slash to her arm. Akio was facing a man who was dressed in black and dark indigo clothing. He wore a mask across his mouth and nose. Only a pair of deep-set murky eyes could be seen. Amaya's gaze returned to Akio, he looked at her and fear broke out over his face. The man twitched his head in Amaya's direction.

  Amaya placed her hand upon the hilt of her katana but before she could draw it a kunai blade was brought up to her throat roughly. She stopped and kept her chin up away from the small dagger. As Akio turned to Amaya's aid, the masked man raised his short ninjato sword, the tip pointing at Akio's chest. Amaya shook her head, silently pleading Akio not to move.

  'Rin, hold the girl there. I will kill him then we can interrogate her.' The man's voice was gruff and wheezing. His eyes did not leave Akio. It seemed he was aware of the danger Akio posed.

  'Yes, master.'

  Amaya frowned in surprise when the person behind her spoke; it was a young woman who was holding her at knife point. Rin's tone was as harsh and abrupt as the man's but it clung to a young feminine pitch. Recognizing that the man and Rin were shinobi, dread crept into Amaya's veins but she was determined not to panic. However, despite her attempt, her feet wanted nothing more than to take her far away, as her father had once instructed her to do if she should ever encounter these people.

'Are you from the Kageyama Clan?' Amaya blurted, wanting to remain in the same room as Akio for as long as possible. She felt the girl's grip flinch indistinctly. The man didn't answer, so Amaya continued. 'Why are you attacking this woman?' Amaya felt her confidence stirring with each moment she spoke; they had not killed them yet.

'Quiet!' Rin squeezed Amaya's arm against her back at such an angle Amaya thought it would snap. She winced and held her breath to stop herself yelling out but was forced to release her own katana. She looked around the room; a narrow mirror showed herself and Rin in its smooth surface.

She saw the young shinobi's longer blade just behind her own left hand. Both of Rin's hands were occupied so Amaya slowly inched hers toward the ninjato sword. Her fingertips brushed the handle.

'Rin! Attention!' The man snapped. Amaya moved quickly and grasped the hilt, pulling it from the sheath and raising it so that the point cleared the scabbard and stopped just in front of Rin's abdomen. The man swore loudly as Rin froze, both girls at a stalemate.

'You are trained in combat,' the man said, looking at Amaya. He lifted his blade. 'Your quick thinking has only saved yourself.' He raised his weapon and moved toward Akio. Amaya had a moment to act, with a flick of her wrist she threw the short sword as if it were a yari spear. It pierced the man's jugular and he fell to the ground. Disgusting gargles issued from his throat as blood pulsed and pooled about him. His eyes rolled as he watched her, disbelief etched across his features. Amaya braced herself, waiting for Rin's blade.

'Master!' Rin shrieked out.

Ignoring the pain in her arm, Amaya forcefully pushed back against Rin. Collapsing on top of her Amaya felt her wrist crack and the dagger flew from Rin's hand. The young shinobi struggled out from beneath Amaya, but Akio had already closed the distance between them, his katana raised.

'Stop!'

Amaya, Akio and Rin paused. The ryokan owner, cradling her injured arm, stood. 'Don't kill her.'

Rin jumped up nimbly and ran from the room and out of the guest house. Amaya stared at the place where the shinobi had been moments before. Akio returned his katana to its sheath his eyes still on the door Rin had fled through.

'What did you mean by that?' Amaya said, to the woman.

'Why was she and her master trying to kill you?' Akio asked, his tone gentle as he bent to aid the woman.

She nodded at Amaya as she answered Akio's question. 'It is as your wife said, they are of the Kageyama clan. Shinobi mercenaries, trained in their Hidden Mountain Village.'

'I still do not understand. You said not to kill her after they attacked you,' Akio responded.

'She is a respected fighter in the Kageyama clan. She and her master lead the raiding groups. By killing him you have condemned not only my husband and I but other ryoken along this road,' the woman said; her fear vicious. She raised her uninjured hand to Amaya.

Amaya frowned at the woman's change in tone. 'I saved my husband's life and he saved yours.'

'An entire family was murdered further down this road for defying the Kageyama. The Kageyama clan earn money by protecting this road and that family did not pay. Rin, her master and a few others descended from the mountain that night and slaughtered the man and his wife, their two children and all of the guests staying there. I could not watch you bring that upon my family by killing Rin. She is the daughter of the Doyen; the head of the Kageyama clan. And you have just murdered his brother.' She pointed to the dead shinobi at her feet.

'Have you not asked for help?' Akio said.

The woman laughed bitterly. 'Of course we have. That is why Rin and her Master were here today. I recently requested help from the Ito Merchants Guild, as well as requesting aid from the palace over a year ago. That was clearly a mistake.'

'How long has this been happening?'

'Years. Since the first threat of civil war.'

'It's no longer a threat, I'm afraid.'

'So I've heard, but the new Emperor's gaze is firmly fixed north. He is ignoring the pain the Fire Province is suffering and has been suffering. He is unwise and wants to hide from the responsibilities his weak father has left him. He cannot understand a country he has never travelled. He cannot understand the troubles peasants suffer. I don't think he even tries. He just leaves it to his advisors and Court Officials.'

'How dare you,' Amaya growled, surprising herself. 'I am sorry your situation here is dire but do not accuse His Majesty of disregarding his country. He does care, very much. The civil war is almost upon Akegata. Not only the Sky Province but all other provinces will be reduced to nothing. If these rebels were to attain victory, Akegata would become a country of bloodshed again. With no monarchy and only Warlords fighting for supremacy, what do you think will happen? Have you considered that His Majesty may be addressing the greater problem to prevent the rebel army from destroying everything?' Amaya took a deep breath as the images of the firearms careened through her memory. 'Well, have you?'

'Amaya,' Akio didn't finish as Amaya left the room, unable to look the woman in the eye, ashamed of her own outburst.

Akio entered their quarters a short while after. He watched Amaya silently. 'I have treated her arm the best I can. I am unsure of how we should move on from here. The woman and her husband are in danger of being attacked by the Kageyama clan again,' Akio said quietly, picking up his bag.

'We are leaving here tonight. We cannot stay, I must help Kenta. You heard what that woman said. What if there are many people who feel the same? I did not realise how little support Kenta has. People like her will happily place their loyalty elsewhere. The court is corruption incarnate and the people of Akegata are losing faith in him because of the mistakes his father made, without giving him a chance to rectify them. Kenta wasn't even supposed to be Emperor. He had everything taken from him in that assassination, not only his family but his freedom too.' Amaya began throwing belongings into her bag.

Akio grabbed her wrist not unkindly. 'Amaya, please calm down. I understand. Kenta is my best friend and I've watched him suffer many things from childhood. He is not weak, and he can weather this if we remain with him. He is a far stronger human being than most people I know. He has his mother and sister to thank for that. And his father.'

Amaya laughed hollowly. 'His father?'

'Yes. With Kado Yamashima providing an example of how not to be, Kenta will never become that way.' Akio's grip on her wrist loosened and he placed his hand on her shoulder instead, a smile on his face. 'It is you who needs to have more faith in this country, Amaya.'

Amaya nodded and took a deep breath feeling her eyes sting. 'We should still leave tonight. I think that Rin would rather have revenge for her master than kill poor ryokan owners. Where would the Kageyama clan get their money locally if they murdered every family on this road?'

Akio nodded and sat down on the floor heavily as Amaya continued to pack.

Amaya and Akio bowed low as they left the ryokan and took to the path. They had decided to travel on the smaller forest roads at the foot of the mountains.

'We have to be careful of earthquakes, Amaya,' Akio said, as they cut through the cedar trees. Amaya nodded, weaving her way towards the shrouded path ahead. She had experienced the shaking of the ground before but only once had there been a truly terrifying time. Many of the capital's homes had fallen into dust, the same had been reported across the Sky and Fire Provinces. Her old teacher had said that the biggest catfish in the world lived beneath Akegata, in the ground. Whenever it was disturbed, it would stir and cause the ground to quiver. Amaya thought of the old story and wondered if it was in fact Gekai causing the ground to tremble.

'Nobody has used this road for a while.' Amaya mused, as she looked left and right down the abandoned track. Shrubs had started to reclaim the ground and she could see many animal footprints and scratches in the dirt.

'Well, at least we won't be seen by people,' Akio said, quietly. They began to walk, the path rose and dipped over the roots of the mountains and Amaya was glad to be wearing more comfortable clothes. Despite the chilled air, Amaya's hair stuck to her neck and forehead. She pulled the ribbon loose and refastened her tresses high atop her head. The trees were naked in suspended death, and the Face of Winter was finally turning to stare at the huge mountains. Snow blanketed the crags and stones which were not covered by trees and Amaya wondered how long until the path she and Akio walked along would remain untouched. Looking upward, she found a clear sky, pale and blanched by the shivering sun. Occasionally, a large bird circled high above and Amaya blinked every time the sun shone from the surface of a mountain stream.

Amaya had a thought. 'Isn't the Hidden Shrine located in this cedar forest?'

'Yes, but nobody has seen it for many years. It is an ill omen to see the shrine.' Akio paused for a moment. 'Sen was rumoured to be living there, before he formed the Senkaku Nin. It's still said to contain some of their power.'

Amaya looked at Akio, 'I want to help Kin overcome the fear and anger inspired by his brother. I can't pretend to understand but I was able to feel his pain back at the palace.'

'That's because he is your Elemental. You will have a connection with all your Elementals for the rest of your life,

Amaya.'

Amaya fell silent as she thought about her task as a Prophet of Ueten; he connection to Gekai and the wrath represented by that spirit. She was unsure of her aims: would she have to rid Akegata of Gekai, cleanse the nation of wounds inflicted by corruption, or simply just be a symbol the people could turn to? What would become of her should she fail? She inwardly chastised her own despondency. Akio was staring at her sadly. His eyes looked through hers, but she could not take her gaze from his.

'Do not worry, Akio.' She gave him a gentle shove. Amaya's words were stifled. Ahead, just out of sight, she could hear the tread of many feet and jovial chatter. The company she couldn't yet see were singing and laughing. Amaya stared at Akio, unsure of how to proceed. They didn't seem to be approaching, rather walking in the same direction as herself and Akio but at a slower pace.

'We have company!' A voice came from behind.

Amaya twirled about, her heart suddenly leaping from her chest. Not far from her and Akio, stepping out of the forest, was an incredibly tall man. Amaya could see that he was taller than even Shun, perhaps of the same age. His legs seemed to stretch forever beneath his rough spun zubon trousers. His sleeveless, floor-length kataginu which covered his willowy body bore a strange design; a black moth embroidered upon the white. Its delicate wings extended, the ends of which fragmented into smaller moths in flight. The garment was secured by a single black sash around his middle. The white fabric of the sleeveless kataginu was stark in its contrast to the black bottoms and billowing black sleeves of thick fabric. Akio's eyes were also narrowed in scrutiny. However, before either of them could respond, the man's companions appeared.

At first glance, Amaya estimated ten in total. They were all donned in different clothes, except for the sleeveless white kataginu with the embroidered moths; they all wore those. The tall man reached them first and it wasn't until he was close that Amaya saw the remains of white grease paint near his hairline. He had pulled his long hair back into a ponytail, but it was loose; flowing over his shoulder and down his chest.

'A travelling couple?' He guessed, his hand going to his long chin in mock thought. His slightly wide-set eyes radiated a casual inquisitiveness and one corner of his mouth curved in a smile.

'Yes. We are newlywed,' Akio replied, noncommittally.
'You are travelling actors perhaps? Bards?'

The tall man clapped his hands together, his shoulders relaxing somewhat, and he closed the gap between them. 'Indeed. I myself am an actor.'

At once Amaya understood the grease paint. She turned slightly, as Akio had done, to keep the group in view. There were eight men, including the tall one, one women and twin children. Amaya regarded the odd assortment, finding them curious.

'You are taking a very interesting route.' Another man commented, gesturing to the road. He was older than the first man but very weather-worn. His face had many lines, deep and shallow, like a map of his smiles, frowns and pain. He was muscular Amaya noted, his hands looked thoroughly used but she could not be sure as to his occupation. Most actors and travelling groups were hinin, and were generally avoided, aside from performances. Their nomadic lifestyle set them apart from society.

'I know the Fire Province well, friend. I find these back roads far more beautiful,' Akio said, his calmness soothing Amaya's tension. 'I wished to show my wife that winter can be as stunning as the other seasons.'

'Ichiro, we should perform for this happy duo,' the tall man said. 'But this young lady is worthy of a song by herself. You have found yourself a fine wife, sir,' he said to Akio, without taking his eyes from Amaya. She stared back at him, uncomfortable in his gaze but not wishing to break it.

Akio bowed his head in thanks yet did not give a response.

'Akira, we cannot linger. We must reach the Fire Province within three days; it will snow in four.' The woman stepped forward now, addressing the man named Akira, and Amaya saw parallels in their looks.

For the first time Akira's eyes left Amaya. 'Sumiko, you are correct.' He leant closer to Amaya and Akio. 'My sister is always correct. It's uncanny, and sometimes rather unsettling. A talent for fortunetelling some say.'

Amaya looked over Akira's shoulder to his sister. She was tall and lithe, but her jaw was not as pronounced as her brother's. Her eyes were the same, though; half hidden beneath a blunt fringe and encased by uncommonly long eyelashes. Her mouth looked intelligent and hard-set but as she smiled at her brother's comment only one corner lifted, exactly as Akira's had done.

'Yes, let us continue,' Ichiro spoke again. Amaya couldn't be sure who the leader was amongst the group, for only a few of them had spoken. Yet her assumption was the weathered Ichiro.

Amaya inched closer to Akio as her gaze fell upon the two children. They were truly identical, and Amaya couldn't help but stare. She had never in her life seen twins. The stigma surrounding them meant that many did not reach adolescence, killed as babes. The one closest to her, standing nearer the front, had an earnest expression but his gaze was pensive and far off, as if he was not really staring at her. However, Amaya jolted when she met the unadulterated malice in the second child's eyes. He stood a little further back from his brother, but his eyes were anything but far-off; they calculated everything with a dark glare.

'What are your names?' She bent down, addressing them both.

The nearest one spoke first. 'My name is Hisato and this is my brother Haruki.'

'Hello.' Amaya smiled widely. Hisato grinned shakily

but Haruki continued to stare.

'Sorry,' Hisato muttered, his hand rubbing the back of his head apologetically as he glanced back at his brother. 'He doesn't talk much, and strangers make him a little uneasy.'

Amaya shrugged. 'That's alright. You must always be careful of strangers. That's very vigilant of you, Haruki.' She nodded at Haruki before standing. 'How old are you both?'

'We are seven years old,' Hisato said, proudly, falling into pace beside Amaya.

'You must be the oldest, Haruki,' she commented.

Haruki looked up; his sombre expression momentarily eclipsed by surprise. 'How did you know?'

'I am an older sibling too. I can tell.' Amaya smiled warmly. Haruki slipped back into his silence, but his scowl seemed a little less severe.

Amaya returned to the adults' conversation in time to hear Akio begin the farewell.

'Do not allow us to hold up your progress,' Akio said, raising his hands in a friendly gesture. 'We wish you safe passage to your destination.'

'Oh, I was hoping you would travel with us for a spell. We are very entertaining companions,' Akira said, in an over-exaggerated display of disappointment. Amaya squinted her eyes a little, there was something behind Akira's flamboyancy which made her restive.

'That's kind of you. We would be happy to join you. Where is your destination?'

'The Kasaichi region,' Ichiro replied, nonspecifically.

'Perfect. We are also heading for that region.' Akio bowed his head gratefully. Ichiro's slim eyes loitered on him for a moment and then he returned to the group.

Soon the convoy was moving at a good pace. The hinin's need to be in the Kasaichi region within three days suited Amaya and Akio, for they too needed to make time. Amaya quickly learnt that Haruki really did not talk that much but Hisato was chatty and amiable, popular amongst all the group. Both twins never seemed to stray far from each other, or a man called Tsubasa. His hair was cut very close and Amaya imagined it had been completely shaved not long ago. Like Ichiro, Tsubasa's hands had been subjected to heavy use but his face was youthful, except for a craggy pink scar which ran the length of his right cheek. Tsubasa wore an eyepatch under which the scar disappeared, only to reappear at his eyebrow again. Like all the others he also wore plain zubon trousers and a white sleeveless kataginu; his was frayed and ripped around the shoulders.

During the second day the reason for Tsubasa's dishevelled clothing became apparent. Amaya was astonished when a huge white and black speckled hawk descended from the sky to land upon his right shoulder. The glorious bird would have dwarfed Kin's hawk, Taka, should they be side by side.

'Are you a bird tamer?' Amaya inquired, finally gathering the courage to speak. She had rarely strayed from Akio's side, content to listen to the conversations and observe the different members of the group carefully. Now, she left Akio, who was conversing with Ichiro and Akira.

The young bird tamer's voice was more of a rasp when he spoke. 'Yes, I have trained birds since I was a child.'

'I have never had the opportunity to keep birds,' Amaya said, staring at the fearsome creature.

'They are incredibly intelligent. You cannot keep them.' Tsubasa's tone was not unkind. His eyes swept over his winged companion, before pointing to his marred face. 'I tried to keep him once.' He smiled and lifted his eye patch. Amaya suppressed a shudder. There, where his eye should have been, was a deep reddish hole. Scar tissue spread from it like a web. He replaced the patch and continued. 'If they could talk, they would have many sights to describe to you. They have an omnipresence that most can only hope for. He is my eye in the sky.'

Amaya marvelled but then a small face appeared on the other side of Tsubasa. It was Hisato.

'Tsubasa is teaching Haruki and I about bird handling. It's really difficult.'

'I'm sure it is, Hisato but if you keep practicing then you will succeed.'

'I hope so,' Hisato said, concerned, his eyes on Tsubasa. 'I want to be like Tsubasa.'

'Both he and Haruki work well with birds. They make fine pupils but Hisato daydreams too easily and loves to climb. I think he is trying to reach the sky to be with the birds.' Tsubasa looked down at the boy whose face had collapsed into worry. It quickly transformed into determination, and his mouth screwed up in a silent vow to try harder.

'How about Haruki?' Amaya questioned.

'Haruki is a quiet boy. He and his brother have suffered the same but as you can plainly see Haruki has chosen to use his past as fuel for darker thoughts.' Tsubasa's tone was grave, and Amaya looked back to Haruki where Hisato had joined him.

'With Hisato beside him, he won't ever stray too far,' Amaya said, as she watched a small smile break through Haruki's austere expression in reaction to his brother.

Tsubasa shrugged and nodded his head slightly. 'Hisato is a good tonic for him. Take him away and I would rather not like to think of the effect on Haruki.'

'They are very close to you, Tsubasa. I have seen them; they do not like to be far from your side.'

'It's to be expected. I was the one who found them and brought them to the group. They tried to outsmart me when we first met in the Earth Province.'

'Outsmart?'

To Amaya's surprise, Tsubasa laughed. The sound was as rasping as his voice. 'Yes. You see, I did not know they were identical twins. They were starving on the streets of a small town they had wandered into. You know the prejudice society holds against twins, they were despised and so they began to use it to their advantage. It was that or starve. One thing hinin do not do is discriminate, unlike the elite of society.' He checked himself. 'So, I caught them almost before their trick had begun. Anyone else would have been fooled. Hisato immediately apologised for his behaviour, of course, expecting a beating from me but Haruki reacted defensively, an ingrained reaction I think. He stood there and waited for punishment. I saw the potential of having such a pair in our group and so they joined us. I have been caring for them ever since and keeping them out of trouble. They make for a great magic show.'

Amaya nodded, laughing at the thought of Hisato and Haruki in a magic show.

Tsubasa didn't talk about the twins after that but his silence emphasised their importance to him. Amaya could see his attention in the furtive glances he gave.

The afternoon of the second day was drawing near when Amaya noticed one of the group was missing. She looked around for the young man she knew was named Ryota but was given no time to dwell on his absence because she was approached by Akira.

'Cho.' Akira had addressed her intimately the moment he had learnt her name, or rather the name she and Akio had allocated to use on their travels. Akio had taken the pseudonym Naoki.

'Hello, Akira,' Amaya said, her eyes directly searching out Akio. Amaya had made an effort not to be alone with Akira since they had started travelling together. Her disconcertion regarding the actor had only grown, and his outwardly insouciant teasing disposition only made her more uneasy, for just below it, Amaya sensed a snake-like virulence.

'Would you permit me to accompany you for a time? It seems your husband is otherwise engaged.' Akira stepped aside, offering Amaya a clear view of Akio in an animated conversation with Sumiko.

She narrowed her eyes, trying to determine Akio's body language and when she couldn't make out anything to rouse concern she sighed and turned her attention to Akira.

'I would be happy for your company, Akira.'

Akira fell in step beside Amaya and next to him she felt like a child, fully able to appreciate his stature. As usual, Akira was on the edge of inappropriateness, never straying too close but always close enough that she would touch him with a simple misstep.

'We will reach the Kasaichi region in the next two days,' Akira said, lightly. His strides were long and precise, his gait elegant. The white sleeveless kataginu flurried lazily as he moved, the design upon it flashing in and out of sight.

'Then my husband and I can let you continue on your way,' Amaya responded, smiling politely.

Akira's face dropped, his eyebrows rising sadly. 'Why so keen to leave, Cho?'

'We also have pressing matters, and I would hate to think that we held you from yours.' Amaya looked up at Akira. He shrugged casually and nodded his head.

'What is your group called?' Amaya questioned, her eyes caught by the design upon his kataginu again, the one which they all wore.

'Some refer to us as Kawarakojiki.'

'Riverbank people?' Amaya said.

'Yes,' Akira confirmed. 'We are not welcome anywhere, except when we perform, so the riverbank becomes a beautiful place to rest our weary heads.'

'That sounds a little lonely for me. Pleasant but lonely,' Amaya commented truthfully.

'Not lonely! Far from it, Cho. We are cohorts. The freedom to wander Akegata as we please, bringing the people pleasure in the form of drama and music and magic.' Akira waved his hand through the air dramatically, his face aglow.

Amaya frowned, *cohorts*, she thought to herself. She gazed around briefly, only managing to glimpse a handful of the group. 'It must be fulfiling for someone who loves the arts as much as you do.'

'It's one of many loves,' Akira said, grinning wickedly.

'The others are?' Amaya questioned.

'I'm a fanatic of tricks and skills. I'm rather good at throwing stones.' Akira's hand went to his pocket and extracted a small black stone no bigger than a beetle. Amaya felt intrigued despite herself. Akira held the stone between his thumb and middle finger, lifted his arm slightly, palm side up. He tensed his wrist for just a moment, then flicked it forward. Amaya's eyes were slow to catch the movement but an instant later a snow monkey fell from the tree a few meters ahead, dead.

Amaya felt her eyes open wide, and she ran to the convulsing animal. She knew it was no longer alive, yet the death throes made her feel queasy. The small hole in the creatures head now started to issue blood, front and back where the stone had entered and exited cleanly. The eyes, so much like a person's, stared up at her in surprised accusation.

'Did you have to kill it?' Amaya asked, trying to ignore what Akira had just displayed.

'Would you have preferred I merely broke its leg? It didn't feel a thing, I promise you,' Akira said, his usual joviality suddenly stilted.

'Stop showing off, Akira.' A voice meandered its way into their vicinity.

Akira turned his refined face to look down upon Seiji. 'Ah, Shamisen! I thank you for playing to our guests last night. I'm sure sleep would have evaded them otherwise,' Akira complimented.

Amaya recalled the previous evening; she had been agitated and disturbed at the thought of sharing a roadside camp with the Kawarakojiki. However, the moment Seiji had plucked the first note of his lullaby, Amaya had felt the disquiet float from her mind. Seiji had a wonderful voice too which complemented his playing. Amaya and Akio had very quickly fallen asleep against each other.

'You really do play well, Seiji,' Amaya said, echoing Akira's compliment.

'Your words are too kind,' Seiji replied, bowing his head slightly.

Amaya's eyes looked down to the dead monkey, the image of Akira's technique tumbling through her mind. As a distraction, she forced herself to look at Seiji again. He was a taller than she was but barely passed Akira's shoulder. However, Amaya knew he was only fifteen, and a few more years may see him as tall as Shun. Seiji's pronounced nose gave his face a more mature look which had caused Amaya to judge his age incorrectly at first. His eyes had an internal stare and seemed to be continuously reflecting upon something. As Seiji turned his head in response to something Akira said, the sun shone strangely from the red silk tie which secured his short hair. He wore it in a half ponytail, but a few stray strands fell about his sharp face.

'The Change is my favourite time of year,' Seiji said to Akira's statement which Amaya hadn't heard.

'The Change?' She questioned, thinking about autumn.

'Yes, I always try to be in the mountains when it is occurring. Alas, The Change was brief this year. The Face of Winter is reaching into the Fire Province with each day.'

'Do you not travel all together?'

'Sometimes, sometimes not,' Seiji replied, adjusting his brown braided belt which held up the white kataginu. He had purposely let the white garment slip from his arms, so that it hung loose about his waist, reaching his knees.

'Some of us perform in different places,' Akira elaborated, but his eyes had turned sharply to Seiji. 'Seiji is our newest member, but quite the talent. I think he is aware of it, though,' Akira whispered audibly behind his hand.

Seiji laughed; the sound as melodic as his singing. 'It's never a bad thing to be confident in one's own strengths. Why, you just displayed your confidence to Cho.' Seiji pointed back in the direction of the dead monkey, raising his eyebrows as if to emphasise his point. 'My display is just more pleasant for others.'

Akira drew a deep breath and shrugged, defeated. 'Indeed, I cannot argue with you, Seiji.'

Amaya did not detect annoyance between the two, just a friendly rivalry. Seiji reached behind his back and unfastened his shamisen. Then he pulled off his gloves with his teeth. Amaya noticed that his hands were paler than the rest of his tanned skin.

'Why do you wear gloves, Seiji?'

'I earn my living with these fingers, Cho.' He grinned and plucked a few strings harmonically, sending a shiver through Amaya. Still, as Seiji walked away surrounded by his music Amaya couldn't rid herself of the foreboding Akira's action had incited.

That evening Seiji didn't play, and Amaya wasn't visited by sleep until well after night had fallen. Akio too seemed unable to drift off. The Kawarakojiki members sat around, dotted on the fringe of the small fire created to keep animals at bay.

Amaya rolled onto her back, her arm coming to rest against Akio's. 'Akio, are you awake?' Her whisper was almost mute. She saw Akio give the slightest of nods. 'I want to talk to you. I will wander a little into the trees, nearer the road. Join me,' Amaya breathed. Again, Akio nodded.

As he had indicated he would, Akio appeared next to her. The moon's light intermittently breached the lazy clouds, but the gleam was still too dim to see any details of his face, and she found herself picturing them instead. From his defined jaw and clear skin, to the arch of his eyebrows and the curve of his smile.

'What's wrong, Amaya?' Akio questioned, leaning close so that she could hear him better.

'There is something odd about these people.'

'They are hinin, Amaya. It wouldn't be unnatural for you to feel uneasy around them.' Akio tried to reassure her, but Amaya knew his mannerisms and inflections too well.

'You're not comfortable either, Akio,' Amaya said, her

whisper a little accusatory.

Akio sighed in the dark. 'No, I am not entirely comfortable, but they are travelling the road we are also travelling. It seems less suspicious to play an innocent married couple and accept their offer to travel together, rather than deny them when there is no good reason to. We have one more day at most, then we can separate from them.'

Amaya groaned. 'Did you see what Akira did today?' Amaya asked, the image of the monkey making its way into her thoughts.

'Yes, I did. I haven't let you out of my sight the entire time we have travelled. I have never seen anything quite like what Akira did.' Akio trailed off into thought.

'How does an actor know how to do that?' Amaya hissed.

'Actors don't,' Akio replied. Amaya watched his silhouette twitch at the same instant she heard something. Before Amaya could ask, Akio leant her against a tree bringing his face very close to her own, so their noses were almost touching. She felt her chest swell and the tips of her fingers and toes tingle with each breath that escaped his mouth and brushed over her.

'It isn't safe to wander too far from the fire.' The voice, although quiet, broke through Amaya and Akio's silence like a shout. Amaya recognized the voice, it was Ichiro. She heard the man falter as the clouds parted and revealed the moon which in turn revealed them. 'I'm sorry. I seemed to have disturbed you, but it really isn't wise to leave the fire, you could get hurt.' Ichiro's tone did not display any embarrassment he might have felt.

'Of course, how foolish of us. It's just that I haven't spent time with my wife these past two days,' Akio explained, feigning awkwardness. 'We will return momentarily.'

'Be sure you do. My watch will end soon, and Seiji's will begin. He might mistake you for thieves. The young ones always act first and check later.' Ichiro stared for a moment, his hand at his side, before stalking away. Amaya jolted. His hand was resting upon the hilt of the longest katana she had ever seen; a Daito katana. He disappeared into the foliage.

Amaya didn't need to say a word, she knew Akio had seen what she had and was equally as shocked.

The dawn of the third day came too quickly for Amaya, who felt as though she hadn't rested at all. Her dreams had been fleeting and staggered, blending into one another. The consternation she had felt on seeing Ichiro's weapon had not left her whilst she slept. She had dreamt of it, and of Akira's stone, and the dead monkey. In fact, as she rubbed her eyes, she recalled that the monkey in her dream had worn a human face, Akio's face. The bizarre image followed her into the late morning when they stopped to eat.

'I hear the tactful Ichiro mistook you both for bandits last night,' Akira laughed as he swaggered over to where Amaya and Akio were, and leant against the tree they were sitting beneath.

'No harm,' Akio said, lightly.

'We will be separating late this afternoon I am told. Such a shame. You have been a refreshing change.'

'We are grateful you allowed us to accompany you,' Amaya said, craning her neck to see Akira's face. 'Between your acting, Seiji's shamisen and Sumiko's singing, we have had a very interesting trip.'

'It's my pleasure,' Akira replied swooping into a low bow. His head remained up, his eyes on Amaya. As she gazed at Akira, a movement just beyond his shoulder caught her eye. Ryota, the missing member, had returned.

Akio seemed to have spied the young man's return too. 'Your young friend has come back.'

Akira glanced back and straightened up. 'So it seems.' With a flash of his teeth he turned about and sauntered over to him.

Amaya was overcome by an anxious curiosity. 'Akio, I have to know what he's saying.'

Akio frowned, his eyes on Ryota. The young man was being interrogated by Ichiro, but they were too distant for either Amaya or Akio to hear. As Amaya watched the conversation unfold it was clear that, despite Ryota's young age, Ichiro respected him.

Ryota's face caught the light in such a manner that his features seemed almost sculpted. Amaya was surprised to see that he had astonishingly exquisite eyes which sat symmetrically above his pronounced cheekbones and were a little obscured by stray pieces of hair falling from the mass of dishevelled black. He wore his sleeveless white kataginu as a cape which he seemed to have adjusted by adding a fabric neckpiece, at that moment it was pulled up over his mouth and nose.

Amaya stood and walked into the trees, holding her hand out discreetly to make sure Akio knew not to follow her. She looped back around so that Ryota and Ichiro's voices were clear.

'It's true, she is pregnant,' Ryota confirmed. His voice was surprisingly soft but his eyes, which Amaya could just see, were steely and vapid.

'Where is she now? Where did you take her? Did she survive the wreckage?' Ichiro questioned.

'Yes, she survived. Of course she survived but she is with them now,' Ryota answered curtly.

'At least she is safe and cared for. I will pay her a visit before the next full moon. You will do the same. She must be monitored. She is too volatile to be left unwatched.' Ichiro finished.

Just then Ryota's eyes snapped up, looking beyond Ichiro's back to where Amaya stood. She didn't flinch but carried on walking with purpose, feigning concentration on her task. Gradually, she meandered her way back to Akio whose back was tense.

'Well, I know why Ryota left. Nothing worrying. He was checking on a comrade of theirs, a woman who is pregnant.'

'Where is she?' Akio probed.

Amaya shrugged. 'All he said was 'she's with them now'.'

Akio screwed his mouth to one side, his forehead creased. As he turned, she caught the edge of his scar which snaked up the side of his neck.

'We must leave sooner.'

Amaya took her eyes from Akio and followed his gaze. She hadn't heeded it before but strapped to Ryota's back was a katana. 'Now we know at least two of them carry weapons. What kind of Kawarakojiki carry weapons?' Amaya mumbled, stirring uneasily.

'The kind that can kill with a single stone.' Akio's eyes had moved from Ryota to Akira.

When the convoy started to move again Amaya found herself staring at each member of the group with renewed suspicion. Ryota had a katana strapped to his back; Ichiro, a Daito on his hip. Her scrutinizing stare next found Sumiko, but she had no visible weapons upon her personage. Indeed, Sumiko and Akira both seemed unarmed, but Akira had shown that he required no weapon aside from a simple pebble. Again, the face of the dead monkey blundered into her head. Sumiko's long sleeved fabric cuffs were wrapped around her slender forearms at present. Amaya had seen her unravel them until they almost touched the floor. She had explained how she incorporated them into her dances.

Lastly, her eyes found the little twins, and of course they were weaponless. *What combat could they possibly know at their age?* Amaya thought, trying to assuage her unease. Hisato chatted animatedly, his arms forming images which Haruki must have found amusing because he was wearing a rare smile. Tsubasa was just behind them, a smile also upon his face as he watched them. Hisato turned and started to walk backwards facing both Tsubasa and Haruki. He continued his conversation with the same enthusiasm. Seiji wondered through her line of sight, breaking her scrutiny of Tsubasa. The young musician appeared weaponless with only his shamisen slung over his shoulder but Amaya's doubt and fear were mounting with each minute that passed. She stole a glance at Akio, he still had both his katana and hers looped into his belt, shrouded by his cloak. The more she stared at the Kawarakojiki, the more potential dangers she saw.

Ryota had remained with the group, but very rarely interacted with any of them, though he was friendly enough when approached.

'I've never seen an actor with a katana before,' Amaya said, as she and Akio passed Ryota.

Ryota turned and met her eyes with his vacuous ones. 'That is because I'm not an actor.'

'No?' Amaya said, surprised at Ryota's admittance.

He reached behind himself and tapped the hilt of his katana. 'I use this for my magic tricks. I'm not an actor or a musician.'

'A magician,' Amaya said, her eyes flitting between Ryota and his katana.

'What kind of tricks require such a fine weapon?' Akio questioned.

'Ah, a magician should never give away his act.' Ryota tapped his nose, an eyebrow rising teasingly.

'A fair statement. I would much rather keep the illusion in any case.' Akio returned the young man's smile, but Amaya saw the doubt plainly in the squint of his eyes.

If Ryota had noticed the look he made no indication he had done so. His eyes found Amaya one last time and she witnessed curiosity in his gaze. Instinctively, she stepped a little closer to Akio, feeling safer as she did so, but maintained her intrigued stare. It was Ichiro who broke the quiet.

'Ryota, we will reach the fork soon. Naoki has informed me that they are to take the southern path which joins the main road again.' Ichiro nodded respectfully at Akio.

'Ichiro is correct. Myself and my wife will leave you soon.' Akio looked up, and Amaya knew he was reading the sun. Something she had never learned to do. She made a note to ask him to teach her.

'I am sorry I have not been able to talk with you more,' Ryota addressed Akio. 'Sumiko and Seiji have informed me that you are quite the genius. Very knowledgeable.'

Akio faltered for a moment, unsure how to receive the compliment. 'Thank you but I'm sure their words are exaggerated. I am no more than a farmer from the Earth Province.'

'From what has been described to me, I'm sure you could get a job in the Court with your talents,' Ryota smiled, his beautiful eyes glimmering.

'I wouldn't want to work in the Court, I'm content with a simpler life,' Akio laughed.

'Couldn't agree more. I do hate complications,' Ryota replied. 'Please excuse me.' He bowed curtly and left with Ichiro.

Amaya turned to Akio, her eyes still on Ryota's back. 'What a strange thing to say. You don't think he suspects?' Amaya frowned.

'No, but he was definitely probing for details. I'm glad we are leaving them soon.'

'So am I. I have never been around or experienced the company of such people before. It makes me realise how ignorant I am of some things.'

'Amaya, you are from the samurai class. How would you ever have firsthand experience of hinin? You were raised away from such people.'

'Well, now I have had my first contact, I will be sure to remember each and every one of them. Even the nameless pregnant woman who we did not see. I'll remember her existence.' Amaya stole a glance at each of the Kawarakojiki. 'I wish we could take the twins with us, though.'

Hisato and Haruki were walking in silence now, obviously tired.

'I knew you would. They are good children, but they have found a home amongst these people, and I'm sure Tsubasa would never let any harm befall either of them.' Akio gestured to the bird tamer, who was still only a few paces behind the boys.

Amaya still felt a twinge of remorse regarding the twins when the fork in the road appeared. The whole group came to a stop.

'Well, friends, I have enjoyed your company.' Akira's customary grin illuminated his face. His hands reached out quickly and gripped Amaya's. She saw Akio twitch at her side but he controlled his discomfort. 'Cho, your beauty has inspired me. I will be sure to dedicate my next performance to you.' He kissed her hand delicately with cold lips. 'Naoki, you take good care of your wife.' Akira smiled again but his eyes did not.

'Thank you all for allowing us to accompany you, and showing us some of your talents,' Akio said, politely. 'Hopefully we will meet again.'

'Oh, I'm sure we will,' Seiji replied, plucking a few strings on his shamisen.

CHAPTER THIRTEEN

The sun had passed its apex long ago and the light was dimming rapidly when Kasaichi stretched out before them. Amaya had never visited the capital city of the Fire Province before, but she had heard of the canal system which weaved throughout it. Akio had confirmed that Kasaichi had some of the most beautiful bridges in Akegata and suggested that the two try a boat ride before they leave.

'Aside from Chuto, this my favourite city,' Akio explained. 'It's very alive.'

'I am excited to see it,' Amaya said, bouncing slightly on her feet, unable to maintain composure. 'Will we go directly to Lord Nakamura's estate?' She questioned as they approached the main gates.

Akio nodded, his expression elated. 'I hope they are well.'

They had passed through the last of the farmland where the rice fields were as barren as the trees and shrubs that sporadically fringed them. The sun was bloody in the purpling sky; it was hanging above Kasaichi bathing it in a rouge glow, and Amaya thought it looked aflame. The main street extended before them and even as Amaya watched, more and more lanterns were lit like little stars popping into existence in the very street. They proceeded and came to the first bridge.

'This is the largest canal, and it actually encircles the whole city, feeding the smaller canals. The design is rather like a wheel and its spokes.'

Amaya was too awed to reply immediately. She strode to the edge of the wide bridge and leant against the thick wooden railing. The red of the paint was bright even in the early evening light. Below, the water was dark, the early evening sky captured on its surface.

Akio walked to join her, a smile growing. 'In late summer, there are so many fireflies along the canals,' Akio said. 'And in the spring almost all the canals are lined with sakura or ume trees. It is beautiful. This year was the first I didn't go to Kasaichi for the sakura viewing festival.' Akio leant against the railing now, staring at the canal.

'Let's come back here next spring,' Amaya said. 'I would love you to show me, and I wouldn't want another's company.' However, even as Amaya made the request, she knew that even next spring was an uncertainty.

Akio faced her. 'I would be glad to show you Kasaichi in every season. We can start now with winter.' He held his hands up, as if presenting the city.

Twilight had come and Akio was anxious to reach Shin Nakamura's home. Amaya had to apologise numerous times because she could not help but stop to watch or taste or try the many things which gave Kasaichi a nightlife different to Chuto. The beef offered to her by a jovial merchant had a flavour which she hadn't encountered elsewhere, the brown sauce that soaked the meat was sweet yet light and the meat itself seemed to melt upon her tongue. Every other store displayed crab.

'This is the most superior,' Akio stated, holding out a long crab leg. 'The season for catching this kind of crab has only just begun. This may even be the first catch.'

'It's so rich and sweet,' Amaya said, sucking out the flesh. Her eyes opened wide. 'It's completely different to other crab I have tasted.'

Eventually, Akio succeeded in steering Amaya down a smaller street but only once she had had three more crab legs. Halfway down the quiet road Amaya read a sign beside a large estate.

'This is the Nakamura residence,' Amaya said.

Akio nodded and proceeded casually. 'I have been here many times. Kenta too, before he turned eighteen and was confined to the palace.'

Braziers lit the path which wound through the garden and over the bridge towards the veranda. The veranda itself skirted the house and was illuminated by small lanterns of either red or white. As Amaya and Akio made their way through the dark garden, a figure appeared at one end of the house. She spied them and paused for a moment.

'Shin! Come quickly! It's Akio and Amaya!' As Emi shouted the message, she stepped down from the veranda a little awkwardly, gripping hold of the thin wooden pillar for support. 'Akio, we were worried. We expected you this morning.' She wagged a small finger at him.

'And we would have arrived then, but we met some interesting folk on the road. I had to let Amaya sample the delights of Kasaichi.'

Emi frowned. 'You've been eating crab. I can tell.' She bowed to Akio, a laugh brewing beneath her smile. Then she rushed at Amaya; it was a slow sort of rush. 'I am so happy you're here.' She took Amaya's hands in her own, and it was as Amaya laughed and offered her own embrace that she realised Emi was different. Amaya held a hand to her mouth as she stared at her new friend and the swell of her stomach.

'Yes.' Emi chuckled. 'I am going to have a baby. Me!' She shook her head as if hearing the news for the first time herself.

'That's wonderful,' Akio said, his grin wide.

'Come, come, it is cold. Shin must not have heard me.'

Once inside the well-lit room, Amaya was able to see Emi clearly. Her round face seemed rounder for the glow in her cheeks which housed charming dimples when she smiled. Her eyes were brimming with excitement. The pale blue of her kimono was patterned with silver bamboo, which were thrown into relief every time she moved.

It was as Amaya admired Emi's obi belt design that Shin entered the room.

'Akio, dear friend. I am glad you made it safely.' Shin bowed low before giving Akio a wide, mischievous grin. 'Lady Takeda.' He turned to face her and bowed again. 'I hope the journey was not a tedious one. The mountains can make it more tiring.'

'It is the first time I have seen the Fire Province. Had I been on horseback or in a palanquin I would not have been able to appreciate it. I had good company too.' She glanced at Akio.

'Quite. Congratulations are in order, old friend.' Shin embraced Akio and placed an affectionate hand upon Amaya's shoulder. 'It was sudden, but not wrong.'

Emi puffed. 'I am just sad we could not attend. I adore a wedding of love. It is so rare.'

Amaya straightened up unable to prevent the pleasant heat she could feel filling her cheeks. Shin laughed but Emi's chuckle was filled with harmless teasing. She gasped a little and then hurried from the room without explanation. Shin and Akio seemed not to be concerned, and Emi's sudden disappearance was explained when she returned with tea. The group sat upon plump silk cushions which were scattered around a fire pit. The coals within burned steadily adding to the heat provided by the braziers. The walls were patterned in bright designs which danced with the shifting light. Painted Koi seemed to swim, birds fluttered and the bamboo patterns swayed.

'Shin, as I mentioned in my letter, we are not planning on staying for any length of time in Kasaichi. We must return to Chuto before winter fully reaches the south.'

'That gives you no more than a week. Will you allow me to help you whilst you are here?'

'I merely wish to remain unseen. We do not want our presence known.'

'Lord Tozen is currently away, so many of his attendants have gone with him. I have ensured that no other visitors will be arriving or travelling through the city. You should remain unrecognized, as long as you do not stray too near the castle.'

Akio nodded, relief showing plainly upon his handsome face. 'Thank you, Shin, but I thought you would be away. The last I heard you were near the coast.'

'I only returned two days ago.' He glanced at Emi, the rascally grin returning. 'I think I will remain in Kasaichi for some time.' Shin couldn't seem to keep the smile at bay. 'I must now be the dutiful husband and father.'

Emi dashed at him, unashamedly placing her arms about him. She squeezed him tightly and Amaya felt her shoulders tense and her heart tremble. A smile slowly found its way onto her face and she looked at Akio. He was already glancing at her.

That evening Akio and Shin talked at length, and Amaya was happy to see Akio so animated in his reminiscing. She could sense that he missed his childhood friend a great deal, and this thought led her to Kenta; trapped and unable to visit his loved ones freely. *He has so few loved ones*, Amaya mused sadly. An Emperor must be so distant; this thought saddened her further. *Dear Kenta.*

'Amaya let's leave these two to talk. You must be exhausted. Would you like to use the onsen? It may relax you. I was thinking of taking a bath myself.'

Amaya relished the idea of a hot spring. It felt like an age since her last time. 'Thank you.'

Once undressed, she and Emi stepped out into a secluded part of the garden. Amaya could already smell the sulfurous water, and shortly after she saw it. A small but pristine onsen was tucked away between rocks and trees. The occasional belch of bubbles enticed Amaya, and she stepped down into the pool. The effect was almost immediate, her limbs tingled with gratitude. The days she had travelled seemed to evaporate with the steam 'You have a wonderful estate, Emi.'

'Thank you. I have servants to help during the day, but I try to keep it as well as my mother did. Will you and Akio live in his estate, or your own?'

Amaya spluttered on the hot water. 'Akio and I have had no chance to discuss where we will live.'

Emi clapped a hand to her mouth. 'Oh goodness, I forget how recently you were wed. I feel as if you have been married for years. You both seem very at ease with each other.' She nudged Amaya with her shoulder. 'He speaks of you often. Even when your communication was just on parchment. There was an affinity there.'

'He was my first friend before and during my stay at the palace. I did not even realise that my fondness was love until our hands were forced.'

Emi nodded. 'I apologise, Amaya. I am always too blunt. I am glad to see Akio so happy. To see you so happy.'

'No, no. I thank you for it. I love that quality. It is one that I wished I possessed.'

'It's gotten me into trouble.' Emi giggled.

'I had never considered marriage. Not since bringing shame to my clan.'

'Marriage has been second to all else in your life.' Emi commented, her accuracy uncanny. She sat up straight, her expression amusingly serious. 'It is time to envision it. You are an adult, Amaya, with a great deal of love to offer a person. You and Akio will have a happy marriage.'

Amaya laughed despite herself and deviated. 'What will you name your child?'

'Kohaku,' Emi said, simply. 'It is a perfect name, for a boy or a girl.' Her smile pushed her cheeks up so that the dimples blossomed.

'I like that,' Amaya replied, sincerely.

'What will you name yours? I mean when you have children.'

Amaya went to respond but the reality and uncertainty of her future stifled her words. 'I do not know.' She finished, hoping Emi hadn't noticed her momentary lapse.

'Kasaichi needs more children?' Emi commented.

Amaya frowned quizzically.

'The city isn't as alive with children as it used to be. It was Shin that commented on it.'

'I saw some families milling the streets.'

'Not many. The orphans have all but up and left.' Emi shrugged. 'Shin told me that only last week he saw a large group of them march north through the gates.'

Amaya looked down in thought. Something stirred in her mind, and then Tomio's voice grew clear. 'I have heard of similar movements elsewhere in Akegata.'

Emi raised her eyebrows. 'In the north?'

'Yes. In Rikujou. A young friend of mine told me that children were being offered work, or simply being removed from the streets and taken.'

'Where?' Emi's expression was now clouded with a frown.

'I really don't know.'

That night Amaya slept the best she had since before the fire in her estate. She lay awake in the heat of her bed for a time, next to Akio and his peacefulness, until she heard the rest of house moving about. She pushed the heavy covers from her body and allowed herself a long stretch, her arms falling heavily when she was finished. With her refreshed body she felt alert and ready to explore Kasaichi with Akio.

'Good morning, Amaya.' Emi smiled, her hair still mussed at the back from sleep.

'I slept so well,' Amaya said.

'It is nice to have female company. I never had a sister, and only a handful of female friends but they have all married and left Kasaichi. So, thank you for indulging me.' She placed a tray of miso soup and rice on the table. Next to it, she placed a bowl of tangerines.

Amaya stayed talking with Emi much longer than she had meant to. The moment Emi had brought out her books and poetry collections Amaya was absorbed. It wasn't until her stomach growled that she realised it was past lunch time and they had devoured the tangerines.

'Emi, I would very much like to see Kasaichi. Akio said he would show me today.'

'Let's all go together. You and Akio, my husband and I.' She pursed her lips together, her look mischievous.

Shin had demanded that Akio and Amaya stay with them for the duration of their stay in the Fire Province which Amaya was more than happy to agree to. Emi barely contained her elation, displaying it with an impulsive grab of Amaya's hands. However, when presented with the suggestion of accompanying Akio and Amaya around Kasaichi both Shin and Akio agreed that it was too risky to be seen together.

'It would draw attention to Akio and therefore yourself, Amaya,' Shin explained. 'From what Akio has confided in me, you are both travelling in disguise. It would be prudent for us not to be seen together. Ordinarily, I would be happy to. However, Emi is more than able to go with you both, as I'm sure she wants to.' He smiled at his wife. Emi, whose face had become crestfallen, suddenly brightened again. She clapped her hands and chivied Akio and Amaya from the house.

The streets of Kasaichi were just as busy during the day as they were at night. The city was at its fullest; the shrieks of traders and shopkeepers over their neighbours was accompanied the melodic sound of bards singing and playing their instruments. At several points, Amaya had various food stuffs thrust into her hand to try, and before she had reached the end of the street she was full. As she, Emi and Akio crossed a high arched bridge the castle became visible through the hundreds of trees which shrouded it. She was sad that she couldn't see more. Amaya hadn't realised how much she missed female company, and Emi was proving to be a staunch friend.

'Here,' Amaya said, extending her hand to Emi. 'A toy for your baby, when he or she is born.'

Emi's eyes glimmered happily as she accepted the spinning top. Its design was bold and simple with blue and red stripes but beautifully crafted. 'Thank you. The first gift.' Emi drew Amaya into a hug. They continued their exploration of the streets, Emi exclaiming at the many sights as if it were also her first time to see them, and Amaya couldn't help but be caught up in her excitable mood. She pulled on Akio's arm as the crab stand from the previous evening came into view. Leading him to it, she selected three legs. Emi was engrossed in conversation with the dango stand owner and so she offered Akio the third. She caught herself still holding Akio's arm but before she could release it he placed his hand on hers. They remained that way, arms linked, for the rest of the afternoon. Emi's expression displayed nothing but elation. Amaya caught her looking many times, a ridiculous grin stretched over her round face.

'I must gather some provisions for our journey home before all the stores are emptied.' Akio said as the afternoon waned. He stared at the crowds swarming around each stand. 'Will you wait for me in there?' Akio pointed to a ramen restaurant. With the early winter cold chilling the evenings, Amaya was more than happy to sit. She waved Akio farewell, finally releasing his arm, and ducked into the store followed by Emi.

They were greeted enthusiastically by the owner, who steered them into a seat which overlooked the street. The window was open slightly, releasing the aroma of food. He brought blankets and tea, adding that he would await their call. Amaya sat, her legs crossed under the thick cover. Emi glanced at the choices of food and pointed out the one she wanted before excusing herself.

Amaya found herself pondering her reason for being in Kasaichi: finding her next Elemental. She thought about how strangely fateful finding Tomio had been. The pale sun shone upon her face through the crack in the window and the breeze which entered was cool, but she lingered in it. The sun somehow felt different in the Fire Province. She closed her eyes and smelt the surroundings.

'It smells different too.' A voice broke her trance at the

same instant their shadow blocked the sun.

Her eyes popped open, not daring to believe her ears. 'Daiki.' She half shouted.

'Good day, Lady Amaya.'

Amaya didn't care to hide her incredulity. 'What are you doing here?' She had dropped all politeness in her shock. Her eyes sought out Emi, but she was still away.

'Business. The more intriguing question is why are you here?' Daiki raised his eyebrows.

Amaya was wholly speechless. She couldn't believe that her identity had been discovered with absolutely no means of rescuing the situation. So, she just leant back, allowing Daiki to watch her satisfactorily.

'Nothing to say, Amaya?' He said, through a grin. He turned in his seat slightly so that half his fair face was blanched by the sunlight.

'You look exhausted, Lord Daiki. How long have you been away from Chuto?'

'I have been on the coast, not in the city but I am exhausted. These Fire Province people are far too excitable for my taste. They favour Kasaichi over the capital,' Daiki scoffed. 'Give me the refinement of Chuto any day over this madness.' He gestured to the heaving street beyond the open window. 'There is something about the City of Fire, though. I cannot deny it.'

'Kasaichi is lively, full of energy. I have grown very fond of it.'

Daiki shrugged noncommittally. 'You still have not answered my question.' He turned his stunning face back to her pointedly, his devilish eyes probing.

'Akio has business here. I was asked to accompany him.'

'So soon after your marriage? I'm certain newlyweds have much more appealing things to do.' Daiki was clearly reveling in his mockery.

'Believe what you will, Lord Daiki.'

'Hello.' Emi had returned, her surprise at finding Daiki

plain upon her face.

'Daiki Kimura.' Daiki introduced himself and bowed his head respectfully. 'You are Lady Emi Nakamura.'

Emi faltered slightly. 'Yes. How do you do?' She bowed also, returning to her seat. 'I believe we met during the firework festival.'

'Yes, I think we did. Very briefly.' Daiki grinned at Amaya.

'What brings you to Kasaichi?' Emi enquired.

'Business,' Amaya replied on Daiki's behalf, not caring to keep the exaggerated mystery from her tone. 'No doubt following his father's instruction.'

Daiki's chortle was marred with almost invisible irritation. 'My father does not control my every movement. But, it is as Amaya said. Business takes me from my beloved city. I will be returning soon.'

'I hope you have enjoyed Kasaichi, Lord Kimura,' Emi replied kindly, but Amaya could see the curiosity beginning to show. Despite her carefree spirit, Emi was not unintelligent, and was privy to most of Shin's arrangements. Daiki was not among them and Amaya could see that much in her friend's expression.

Daiki's mouth twitched slightly, but his attention was taken. 'Are those Akio's business associates?' Daiki asked, nodding in the direction of the street.

Amaya had to lean forward over the table to peer out of the half open window. Her eyes found Akio immediately, but it took her a moment longer to register who Daiki had referenced.

Her stomach knotted horribly. 'Something's wrong.' She craned her neck to see the smallest member of the few which were standing around Akio. She cried out, her hand going to her mouth.

Daiki jolted in surprise, his facetiousness breaking beneath concern.

'They are Kageyama shinobi. I recognise her.' As she

said it, the small figure turned slightly and Amaya's fears were confirmed in a blink. Rin Kageyama and four of her clan were slowly and subtly edging Akio down the street. She starred fiercely at the young shinobi and what felt like the beating of a hundred butterflies rippled across her chest. Ignoring the sensation, Amaya leapt from her seat and rushed to pull her bearskin boots on. A strong hand gripped her arm.

'Release me.'

'Be silent,' Daiki hissed. 'If they are Kageyama, you had best not reveal yourself. Think, Amaya. They are shinobi.'

Amaya paused, but her worry for Akio spurred her limbs into action again and she wrenched her arm free of Daiki's grip. 'I will not leave him. They will kill him but it's me they want. I was the one who killed one of them two days ago.'

'Then count yourself lucky and save yourself. You are not stupid, Amaya, and neither am I. This could be a trap for you. I cannot let – '

Amaya stared up at Daiki but all she could see was his own discomfort. 'Are you willing to let the Secretariat die? Raised in the samurai class, educated in the Way of the Samurai. Where is your honour?'

'I have enough of that and more,' he snarled, irritated by her insinuation.

'I've yet to see it.' Amaya breathed the words heatedly. She swallowed. 'Help me. Please. Shun wouldn't hesitate.' Amaya saw the flash of bewilderment on Daiki's face.

He growled in annoyance. 'Fine.'

'Thank you.' Amaya truly felt the gratitude. She turned to Emi whose flushed face had paled.

'Amaya, I will inform Shin.' She glanced outside. 'You are going to go even if I ask you not to, aren't you?'

'Yes, Emi but Daiki is going to help me. Please inform Shin at once. I am sorry to leave you like this.'

Emi waved her hands. 'Hurry up then. I could not bear anything to happen to Akio.'

As Amaya hastily left the store, the only comfort she

had was that Akio had his katana. At least he was able to fight should it come to that. For a moment she considered leaving Daiki and pursuing the Kageyama alone, but the idea was fleeting as she watched Akio, now in the distance, joined by yet more Kageyama. Daiki had remained silent his eyes focused, watching their quarry as carefully as she was.

'Where did they go?' Amaya asked, panicked, as the shinobi vanished.

'I saw. Follow me,' Daiki said, picking up the pace. Amaya glanced at him, his comely face unusually serious, before willing herself to trust him. She knew that there was no one else to help her at that moment.

Amaya and Daiki managed to keep the Kageyama in sight through the city, but with a nasty start Amaya remembered the stories she had heard about shinobi.

'Daiki, we have to retrieve Akio before they leave the city.' Her panic was barely contained.

He held up a hand to quiet her, his eyes still not moving from their aim. 'We won't be able to get him in the city.'

'But once they are in the open.' Amaya shook her head.

Daiki's jaw clenched in annoyance. 'Amaya, have a little faith. I can track them if we lose sight. I am not inexperienced.'

'They are shinobi. It's impossible. You know as well as I the methods they use. Especially the Kageyama. This is their terrain.'

'I am aware. I have come up against these people before but you forget, they have a captive. They will be travelling slower.'

'Just don't let them out of your sight, and I will do the same.'

As Amaya had predicted, the moment they were beyond the city walls the Kageyama flitted in and out of sight more and more frequently as they passed through the rice fields. Their movements were so fluid that she and Daiki struggled to keep up. Her eyes had become accustomed to discerning them from the surroundings but as they ducked down into one of the many rice fields they didn't reappear again.

'Daiki,' Amaya hissed fearfully, her eyes roving.

'There,' Daiki muttered, indicating with a nod of his head. 'They will be in the forest soon. That's when this chase will become truly difficult.'

Amaya twitched her head in his direction. He was wearing a hungry smile, and Amaya realised that he was enjoying this challenge, but she didn't dare confront him about it and break his focus.

They increased their pace, being somewhat reckless in their movements to reach the mountain forest quickly. They ran the length of the path, not caring to duck out of sight as the shinobi had done. Amaya knew they had to recover the distance lost. They entered the forest and Daiki bent low; his face close to the floor. He stood and without speech made his way through the trees. Amaya stared at the floor herself but could see nothing to indicate the Kageyama's movements. Still, Daiki had purpose in his step, so she followed him, ignoring the shrill caveat in her head

The stopping and starting continued well into the early evening. Amaya's adrenaline had still not left her body, but it seemed Daiki's prior weariness was slowing his pace. She rested a hand on his hot back. 'If you think it's possible, we can take a moment.'

Daiki looked up from the ground where he was studying the leafy, uneven floor. His expression still bore the hunger she had perceived earlier.

'I cannot allow shinobi to capture our beloved Secretariat. What would my father say?' Daiki's eyebrows rose again but Amaya saw the same agonized gleam in his irises that Shun wore so plainly.

'I meant that I am tired. I haven't got your stamina, Daiki.'

He regarded her for a moment, not believing what she was saying. 'No more than a few minutes. We really will lose them otherwise. They are doing a very good job at covering their tracks.'

'Not good enough.' Amaya grinned.

Daiki flashed her a smile of his own, and it was uncommonly guileless, completely transforming his face into one that she hardly recognized.

'What is it?' Daiki asked, apparently detecting Amaya's wonder.

'You just looked a little different then,' Amaya said, feeling foolish.

Daiki wavered briefly, his eyes striped by the shadow of his hair. 'Don't tell me you you're falling for me too. Just when I thought we could get along.'

It was Amaya who hesitated now but rather than the expected anger or annoyance, she found herself laughing. 'Flattering yourself, Daiki? I am a married woman.'

Daiki screwed his mouth to one side, relief crowding his expression. 'And there I thought I was sure to get a scolding from you.' He batted his hand through the air.

Amaya only had a moment to enjoy the new understanding which had budded between them before a bizarre bird call issued from above their heads. Daiki's eyes immediately lifted to the canopy but before he could say a thing they were descended upon from all sides. Daiki drew his katana in a violent circular motion, sending the dead leaves upon the ground into the air, shrouding him and Amaya from view. She felt him push her. 'Run.' Daiki was smiling.

'Wait,' Amaya started but he pushed her more roughly.

'Do not tempt me to use you as leverage for my own escape,' Daiki whispered. 'I would be happy to.'

Amaya stumbled back, believing that Daiki may well do exactly as he had threatened. He raised his katana but the shinobi merely encircled him, never straying too far from the shadows. At times they were the shadows themselves, at other times they disappeared into the dark entirely, only to reappear somewhere different. Amaya hated the terror they catalyzed within her. However, Daiki showed none of the fear she felt. The three shinobi closest to him were suddenly thrown back, ploughing defined lines in the forest floor as they became the victims of Daiki's brutal slash. Amaya was getting farther from them now, but the sounds reached her clearly and her terror formed a nasty amalgamation with self-disgust. She had left Daiki.

Wheeling about, she sped back the way she had come, pulling Meiyo from beneath her cloak. Amaya saw Daiki's face fill with panic as he glimpsed her from between his attacker's arms. Two shinobi advanced and Amaya drew in a breath grasping her katana in both hands, her feet sliding into place. She tightened her grip as the first approached from behind. The shinobi in front of her gave away his comrades' movements and she swept her foot around, bringing the katana up and back in a swooping slash. The shinobi's ribs splayed apart but Amaya did not pause. She allowed the momentum to carry her through the brief shower of blood until her blade met the second shinobi's ninjatō short sword. The clang was grating as her katana bit through the rust upon her opponent's blade. The shinobi snaked out his free hand, her throat his aim. She jumped back avoiding his grasping fingers but before she could move further, she was shoved to the floor.

She felt dirt embed itself into the skin of her cheek and her mouth fill with decaying leaves. Something was on her back. Amaya still gripped her katana in her hand but was unable to wield it. Struggling, she managed to roll onto her back. Rin was on top of her, and her expression was enraged. Amaya looked around and saw many other members of the Kageyama clan coming from the trees. Daiki was surrounded and blood streamed down his face. Amaya thrust her hips upward abruptly, unseating Rin.

The young shinobi sprang nimbly to her feet and backed away, blade raised. Amaya adjusted her grip on her katana and faced Rin. An old feeling coursed through her limbs, a feeling she used to have when fighting her father. Blood seeped down her face and beneath her collar. Her eyes met Rin's and she felt an overwhelming and bizarre urge to stop the fight, but Rin dashed forward lifting her blade. Amaya shifted her foot slightly gaining the advantage, Rin veered away from her a moment later. Amaya frowned at the action and moved accordingly.

'Amaya!' Daiki shouted. She moved swiftly, ducking low and spinning on the ball of her foot. She brought Meiyo diagonally upward. The young man who had crept up behind her jumped back, barely avoiding Amaya's blade. She titled her head to one side, glancing back. She had heard the light footfalls of someone close behind her. She smiled again as she felt her senses heighten; she could not battle the inappropriate joy she felt in a battle for her life. Watching the man in front of her, she pulled a pointed hairpin from her braid and brought her blade up high. She thrust it down under her arm and felt the tip pierce flesh. The young man in front ran forward, his face half masked like the others. Amaya pulled her weapon from the body behind and ran forward. An instant before the inevitable clash, she was brought up short.

Someone was gripping her cloak. Amaya brought her foot up high and kicked the man in the face violently instead. He fell to the ground, his nose indistinguishable.

'Stop.' A deep voice came from behind. 'Stop or this man will die.'

Amaya sucked in a breath. Her chest heaved as she slowly turned. Daiki was enveloped by many men, two on each arm, and there were chains of a kusurigama weapon about his ankles. The man who gripped her clothing was huge. His body was solid, immovable and his expression was icy.

'Father, it is this girl who murdered my master, your brother.'

Amaya looked to one side and saw Rin. She replied venomously, 'because he was about to murder my husband, the man you have captured.' She looked up at the Doyen.

'You are a skilled fighter, girl,' he said, quietly taking her katana from her and passing it to his daughter. 'But your katana technique cannot defend against the Kageyama. Our methods are very different, and superior. You are hindered by honour.' He nodded to the men who surrounded them. Amaya did not protest as they grabbed her roughly and marched her and Daiki into the trees. However, her eyes did not leave her father's katana.

'Where are you taking us?' Amaya demanded.

Daiki threw his lean shoulders back, dislodging the shinobi's hold on him. 'I don't need you to manhandle me. I'll come.'

Amaya tried to memorize the route they were taking, but it was impossible. Every tree looked the same and no one spoke as they moved through the cedar forest. They crossed small tributaries; passed steaming hot springs. Amaya managed to look up a few times, catching glimpses of monkeys but her head was pushed down roughly after the third or fourth attempt. Slowly, the ground became steeper and, at times, Amaya had to use her hands to climb large rocks and slopes. She caught a hint of wood smoke on the breeze coming down the hill. She looked up for the first time in a few hours. Daiki too seemed to be smelling the air.

The group descended into a small dip which was encased in bamboo, and Amaya saw it; the Hidden Mountain Village. She was pushed roughly to her knees and felt the grit embed itself into fresh cuts. She looked up and saw Rin standing over her.

'Father,' Rin began.

The Doyen turned and faced his daughter. 'Silence, Rin. I will decide what to do with them.' With these words he paced into the nearest quarters.

Rin turned back to Amaya and smirked. 'It seems your husband is popular already,' she said. Amaya turned her head sharply. Akio was on his knees beside a small bamboo dwelling, hands tied behind his back, several women around him.

'What do they intend to do to him?' Amaya questioned.

'Nothing, yet. He hasn't killed one of us. It is you who is

the murderer.' She looked down at Amaya and raised her foot bringing it down upon Amaya's shoulder heavily. She fell back, a splintering pain rippling down her torso.

'How brave of you,' Daiki spoke, breaking the silence he had kept for the entire journey. 'Attack a defenceless woman who is bound and on the floor. If this is the Kageyama then I am disappointed.'

Rin rounded on him. 'There was no need for you to get involved. You did this to yourself.' And as if to emphasize her point, she punched him squarely in the stomach, forcing him to one knee. 'I will not make the mistake of underestimating her again. She murdered my master.'

Amaya was watching Akio, he turned his head as if sensing her stare. His entire body collapsed when his gaze fell upon her. She mustered a smile and nodded her head the smallest amount. His eyes then found Daiki and bewilderment joined his anxiety.

'Take her to the hold,' Rin said to two men, pointing at Amaya. She did not struggle as she was hoisted to her feet and dragged to a small, solitary hut. Daiki was standing to his feet, his face livid. Akio had stood also. Both were looking at her, willing her to remain calm.

They opened the door and shoved Amaya inside a single room. Almost all light was exterminated as they closed the door and barred her in. She allowed her breath to return to normal and her eyes to adjust but the space was black. There was no covering on the floor and the dirt crunched softly under her feet as she inched forward. She could only see a sliver of fading daylight from the crack around the door behind her. There was no place from which she could spy and so she hovered in the middle of the space. It was colder in the Kageyama Clan's village higher up the mountain. Amaya sank to the floor, her back against the wall farthest away from the door, and drew her knees up to her chest and rested her chin on them. The day's walk had exhausted her and she could not stop herself from drifting into a light, guilt-ridden sleep.

Amaya was woken by the scream of a hawk. It had interrupted a nightmare she could not quite grasp onto, or perhaps the bird cry was part of her dream. The night air wrapped around her. She could hear in the distance the gurgle of a hot spring and shivered, imagining the warm soothing water against her chilled skin. It reminded her of Emi and Shin and hope teased her until sense stamped it out. Her friends would be worried but with no information they could do nothing. Scooping her arms under herself she brought her hands to her front. The room was already becoming suffocating and so she tried to steer her mind elsewhere, beyond the four walls. The palace came first and then Kenta. She lent her head back, irritated that she had been captured. Her imprisonment had emphasized the growing sense of desperation in locating the remaining Elementals. The rope caused her skin to redden as she tried to twist her hands free, but she stopped as someone approached the door and opened it.

Amaya realised how dark her confine really was. It was night outside yet she could plainly see a petit slender silhouette against the moonlight.

'Rin.' Amaya watched the figure step into the small room.

'I have brought you water.' Rin placed a large cup on the floor and stood still.

'Thank you.' A mixture of resentment and interest overcame Amaya.

'Here.' Rin's tone was impatient as she bent down and loosened the bonds. She pushed the cup toward Amaya.

'Where did you learn to fight?' Rin asked, bluntly.

Amaya looked at her and frowned. 'Are you surprised? I learnt from my father.'

'Women are not traditionally taught combat, and you used the Imperial army's technique; the Seishin no Ken style,' Rin said, leaning closer to Amaya.

'Yes. My father is Kazu Takeda, the innovator of that technique.' Amaya licked her lips, unsure that she should have revealed that truth. She hadn't intended to but she felt compelled.

The young shinobi fell silent in thought but an accusing frown fell upon her brow. 'There was something slightly different in the way you moved yesterday, different from the usual stance.'

Amaya smiled as she watched Rin, the moon casting a soft light across her face. A hardened expression swamped her otherwise gentle features.

'You noticed. I am surprised. I have not abandoned the development of my father's technique. I wish to keep evolving it as he would have done.'

'Your father is dead then?'

Amaya nodded and looked down. 'But he lives on in his katana technique. I practise in his dojo,' she said, ignoring the memory of the fire.

Rin looked up quickly. 'You are not who you say you are. Your father is the innovator of the Imperial Way of the Samurai, you are a skilled fighter, you have your own dojo.' Rin paused before rising to her feet and leaving the room. She slammed the door and locked it. Amaya stared at the dark space where the shinobi had been crouching. Rin's sullen eyes and her harsh tone incited Amaya's fascination; she wanted to know as much about Rin as Rin did about her.

She was woken a second time by a dream that eluded her. She could also hear movement outside of her prison and looked toward the door. An unbroken line of light told Amaya it was daybreak. Picking up the cup of water left by Rin, she gulped down half the content and breathed deeply, continuing to listen to the movements on the other side of her door.

The day trickled by and nobody entered the room. She strained to listen, hoping to hear Akio's voice, or Daiki's. She felt as if she and Akio had parted many months ago and wanted to hear his comforting tone and see his familiar face, to be sure he was unhurt. Slowly, the light framing the door faded and night fell again. Amaya stood to relieve some of the day's stiffness.

Three more days passed, and no one had visited her. She had finished the cup of water two days ago, and her mouth was as dry as the dirt under her feet. She had taken to walking every so often to keep her blood moving but now she felt so weakened, she slumped against the wall of the small shack. However, she refused to cry out, to call for sustenance, she would not give the Kageyama shinobi the satisfaction. She distracted herself with internally reciting the words from the scroll her father had discovered and protected. She found that it was her father's voice which recounted the information; like a night time story when she was a child. She wrapped her arms around herself and rested her head on her knees wondering if the Kageyama could sense her unease as she drifted into a turbulent slumber.

Amaya's head bobbed with a heavy sleep. Suddenly every muscle in her body convulsed. She felt a hot pain course through her veins causing her to collapse sideways onto the floor. She tried to stifle a cry of agony as images of a valley she did not recognize and people she had not met flew through her mind. The smell of blood filled her nostrils as if it poured from fresh wounds and the sounds of screams crashed into her ears; a cacophony of war music and dying horses. Three faces stood out in the blurred visions of war; Rai Kimura's smiling face; Sen, unsmiling, satisfied; and lastly Kenta, elegant and kind but his eyes stared without seeing as bloody chrysanthemums blossomed across his white kimono until he was drenched. A soothing flutter shivered through her body and she felt the hopeful presence of Ueten, clear and uninhibited. Another searing wave pushed forward, and fear erupted, pursued by panic. Gekai.

She fell still as the pain subsided. The images stopped as abruptly as they had arrived. Amaya continued to breathe deeply, her body exhausted, as she lay on the floor. *Am I asleep?* Her face felt wet and she realised she had been crying. Wiping her tears away she sat up, fear once again creeping back into her mind. A film of cold sweat covered her body and she started to shiver.

She jumped as an angry voice broke out.

'Get out of my way. I want to see her.'

'Your father has decided her fate, Rin. She will die in there, gradually, with only loneliness for company,' one of the men outside said. Amaya heard a dull crunch, and the door opened quickly. She caught a glimpse of a man lying on the ground unconscious, his comrade bent low over him. Rin marched toward her clutching something. She thrust Amaya and Akio's bag under her nose. Amaya pulled herself into the new situation, but her head continued to throb.

'What is this? Palace paperwork, seals and a transcript? How important are you?'

'As a woman you should know the answer to that question, Rin,' Amaya said, her tone irritated as she looked past Rin to the man. 'Isn't he supposed to be your friend, one of your clan?'

Rin faltered and glanced behind her. 'He is a shinobi. That is all.'

'You sound like a member of the Shizukawa shinobi clan. Disposable asset, is he? Was I not kidnapped by the respected Kageyama clan?'

Rin looked affronted. She threw the bag onto the floor and sped forward. With rapidity she lifted her fist and hit Amaya in the face. Amaya was thrown back against the wall and tasted blood in her mouth. The cut on her face from the ambush days before reopened.

'A girl of wealth should not speak about what she does not know.'

'You assume that I am wealthy.' Amaya laughed. Rin pulled out a book from the bag and Amaya recognised it as the journal she sometimes wrote in. She had taken to keeping accounts, and her latest entries were of the Kawarakojiki people. Amaya looked Rin in the eye.

'I believe you are wealthy, or at least once were, but I

know you are definitely not married as you claim to be.' Rin smiled. 'So, who are you?'

'I am Cho Satou, married to Naoki Satou.' Amaya braced herself, she knew Rin had all the information.

'Do not lie, *Amaya*. Why are you in the Fire Province with no official clearance from the Emperor? There are no documents here. As a woman in the employment of the palace you cannot leave without permission.' The young Kageyama's eyebrow raised in what Amaya thought looked remarkably like disdain.

'Why are you interested in who I am? Am I not to be killed on your father's request?' Amaya said, raising her voice. 'You should hold no interest in me.'

Rin flinched and opened her mouth to speak. 'You, your fighting is familiar. I saw it.'

'Rin!' A loud bellow came from the doorway. Rin turned around to confront her father as Amaya looked up into the man's furious face.

'You have entered this place against my simple instructions.' His statement rumbled.

Rin held up her discoveries and Amaya watched the Doyen rift through the journal and paperwork.

He looked up suddenly. 'You are of the Takeda clan. Could you be the princess of the Takeda clan?' The Doyen's tone was not kind, his eyes narrowed in dislike. Amaya nodded in resignation.

Rin looked from her father to Amaya, 'Doyen, do you mean that this girl's father was the one?'

'Rin, I told you to forget. Death happens in our world often. You are not a Kageyama shinobi if you cannot control your emotions,' the Doyen said, loudly and Rin fell quiet.

'Where is the man you kidnapped in Kasaichi?' Amaya said, speaking to the Doyen. He looked down at her, his expression angered.

'Did you give her this water, Rin?' He asked indicating the empty cup.

'I did. I was hoping to ask her questions.' She drew in a breath.

'Do not go behind my back, Rin. You know the punishment and it is hard to enforce when my own daughter cannot control herself. Stop behaving like a disobedient dog, my brother trained you better than this.'

'Sorry, father.' Rin bowed low but remained in the doorway. The Doyen took a step toward Amaya. He kicked the cup at her.

'Killing you will be appropriate for the damage your father once caused my clan,' the Doyen said, waspishly. 'Stand.'

'You knew my father?' Amaya said.

'I knew your father; a cold man,' the Doyen hissed.

'He was not cold.'

The Doyen pushed her against the wall by her neck. 'You will be killed tomorrow. Beheading seems the most fitting for your disposal. I cannot have Takeda clan filth in my village. We will send the palace your head with the regards of the Fire Province.' The Doyen turned and left the small room. Amaya heard him shout to his men outside. 'The dogs will have a good dinner tomorrow.'

Amaya was once again left in darkness. She slid down the wall to the floor, her temper growing alongside her curiosity. She wanted to ask Rin questions of her own. From the Doyen and Rin's reactions Amaya understood her father must have fought with the Kageyama clan in the past. Amaya continued her silent debate well into the night.

She roused herself from thoughts of Rin as she remembered the sudden outburst of pain she had experienced moments before the shinobi had entered armed with accusations. Closing her eyes, the image of Rai Kimura's face came into her mind. She had felt Gekai and had seen Rai, and Sen. She had a fleeting and terrifying thought that the two men had met but discarded the idea. She pushed the hideous image of Kenta's bloodied face from her mind, never wanting to see it again. Daybreak would make itself known soon; the birds were already waking.

A soft rustle just beyond the door caused Amaya to shift around. She frowned and sidled closer, leaning against the wood, pressing her ear to the cold surface. Closing her eyes she strained to detect more. It was quiet for so long Amaya began to think she had imagined the delicate noise. Her back tensed. Again, a distinct but almost silent shuffle came from just beyond the door. A frown spread from between her eyes as her confusion and curiosity battled. Amaya pushed herself even closer, her entire body now in contact with the slatted sliding door, as if it would help her distinguish what was occurring outside in the near dawn.

'Amaya.' The voice was so quiet, Amaya held her breath.

'Akio.' She knew it was him. He was on the other side of the confine. He moved a little and Amaya could hear the scuff of his face on the door. She pressed closer, a ludicrous thought that she could touch him through the solid partition.

'I'm coming in.'

At once Amaya stepped back, her hands balled, her chest tight. The grind of the door caused her to wince, but the moment Akio crossed into the room she released her anxiety in a single long breath. Without thought she strode forward and embraced him. 'You are unhurt?' She asked.

Akio enclosed his arms about her shoulders. 'Yes, I am unhurt. And you? Amaya, I am so sorry.' He handed her a flask of water.

She accepted the drink and gulped it in one long draught. Then she leant back, craning her head in order to look at his face. It was still too dim and so, holding him by his arms, she turned him about until his face fell into the early light. His eyes were wide, pained. His mouth a straight line, its corners unmoving with his upset. He swallowed with difficulty, unable it seemed to elaborate.

'You have nothing to be sorry for, Akio. I was not going

to allow the Kageyama to take you. Not when it was my own fault they were pursuing us. Do you really think I could leave you?' Her question was almost a challenge.

He shook his head, his hand lifting to her face. His own grew closer until his breath warmed her cheeks. Their embrace strengthened but he pulled away, lifting a finger to his lips. Her gaze lingered on his alert eyes. A dog gave a single whining bark.

Sweeping her behind him protectively, Akio faced the door. 'They will know I am missing. This is the first place they will come.' He passed her something. 'Meiyo.'

Amaya received her katana, a smile pushing tears of relief into her eyes. 'Thank you.'

'Follow me. I have observed the Kageyama, and I know the exit from the Hidden Mountain Village. Stay close to me, Amaya. I will get you away from this place.'

Akio left the prison first, Amaya close behind. She glanced at her feet. To the left and right were the shinobi guards. Both were dead. The feathered end of an arrow protruded form each neck, like odd jewelry. Akio pulled to arrows free, wiped them roughly on his hakama and replaced them in the quiver. Lifting her eyes, she glanced at his frame silhouetted against the sun which was only just breaking above the horizon, casting the palest oranges and pinks above them. He had murdered for her. He had killed. A disturbing flurry of guilt shivered through her body at the thought but it was quickly thrust aside by Akio's voice.

'Amaya, step back and do not move.' Akio's instructions were clear, and final. Amaya stared about and terror plummeted into her stomach. Kageyama were looming in the shadows; they *were* the shadows. Amaya hadn't realised the fact at all, but Akio had. She had little time to marvel at their skills before Akio advanced on the nearest and most threatening darkness. He was not waiting for them; he was not allowing the shinobi the advantage of the first move. She felt a surge of panic but as she glanced at Akio's face she felt the sensation subside. He had turned his head, and Amaya saw the determination his features carried. His eyes were imbued with a wildness she had not yet seen in him, and his jaw was taught with his focus. There was no fear present; Akio seemed serene.

He pulled his bow from his back and plucked two arrows from the low-slung quiver. He notched both at once, his fingers splayed upon the bow, the index pointing out. He did not pause to take aim, his body moved with instinct, trusting his eye. The arch of his back and pull of his arm was strong and purposeful. The arrows found their marks, and two shinobi crumpled to the floor before they had even left their shadows. Akio had not delayed and nor had his face changed. The placid fury was still there, still guiding him. He extracted the remaining two arrows as several shinobi darted forward, their speed causing Amaya's panic to roil in her chest once again. However, the urge to leap to Akio's defence was numbed as he parried a shinobi's ninjatō short sword, plunged the arrow through his attacker's throat and yanked it free in one motion. He notched the bloodied arrow, the second clamped in his teeth. Rotating at the waist he lifted the bow and pulled his arm, strength and certainty filling his every motion. The twang was immediate as he released the arrow. The way the shinobi fell was almost humourous; mid-dash as if all movement had been suddenly stolen from him. He crashed to the floor, his face hitting the ground with a crunch.

Akio was forced to draw his katana, Shinka. The blade of the nearest shinobi's kusurigama reeled past Akio's face but as the shinobi yanked it back the blade scraped Akio's cheek. Without even a grimace he slid his feet forward, carrying himself to the shinobi in a few moments, and Amaya felt her fear subside with each of Akio's steps. The Kageyama's eyes were wide in surprise; Akio's face was so close to his. The smallest of movements from Akio's blade ended the shinobi's life in a shower of scarlet which drenched both Akio and the shinobi. The tip of Shinka appeared, jutting out from the man's mouth in a gurgling red fountain. Akio's grace was different to her father's or Shun's. His agility was more dance-like than Daiki's playful footwork. It was instinctual. An innate ability resided in Akio and Amaya could not help but be enthralled in a way she had not been previously.

As he pulled his blade free, he crouched low, his arms behind him, his legs coiled. Amaya felt her mouth open in wonder; Akio's eyes had been closed, and still were. His head twitched as the remaining shinobi approached. Amaya wanted to cry out but found that her faith in Akio kept her voice tethered. She watched on. He opened his eyes the moment only a meter separated him and the two advancing Kageyama. Bow in one hand, katana in the other Akio turned, his foot sweeping the floor in a crescent movement. The shinobi jumped, predicting Akio's attempt. Amaya tilted her head in awe as he simply hooked his bow over the shinobi's head and pulled him close and into the path of the second shinobi's ninjatō blade. Only a flicker of shock at killing his comrade was emitted. Akio gripped his katana, its tip pointing at the dawn, and thrust it upward into the bowels of the remaining shinobi.

The corpse slumped, and Akio kicked him over, wrenching Shinka free. He looked up at Amaya, and his face was haggard. His eyes were so wretched that Amaya felt like she had been slapped by his stare. She could see now why he had refused a role in war. He detested himself in this skin. He hated that his talent in killing was so great, that he was so gifted in murder. Akio extricated his bow, returned the unused arrow to the quiver and stepped over the bodies towards her. His chest and face were sprayed red, his eyes swimming in the colour with a melancholy Amaya hoped would vanish.

The ground shuddered violently, and Amaya staggered. All was quiet for a moment as she steadied herself and glanced at Akio in confusion but then shouts and screams broke the early morning silence. The ground gave another tremendous tremor and Amaya was thrown sideways. She struggled to stay standing as the noise of the grumbling earth swelled. She heard resounding thuds and the creaking of trees as they were shaken from their homes. More screams and cries rendered the air. Rocks pitter-pattered into the village from the mountain and Amaya threw her hands over her head.

A hand snaked out; Rin grabbed Amaya's wrist, wrenching her forward. 'Come with me, you are not escaping,' she said, looking around. Amaya felt someone snatch her other hand and turned. Akio had a hold of her, his expression still stark with the anguish of the fight he had just taken part in. Amaya wrenched her arm from Rin's grasp and ran, Akio beside her. She gazed around, huge boulders had tumbled down the mountainside and crashed through homes. The Kageyama clan had scattered as the forest continued to tremble, her escape forgotten by all. She heard a piercing, ringing scream. Turning she saw Rin, glanced by a falling tree.

'Amaya, we must go,' Akio yelled out over the chaos. Amaya ran a few more paces before she groaned in frustration and confusion. She glanced back at Rin who lay unconscious on the ground. A few other broken bodies lying around her.

'Akio, we have to help her. I cannot leave her here to die,' Amaya said, surprised at her own words. She did not question herself as she sprinted to Rin. Akio nodded and with Amaya's help hoisted the young shinobi onto his back. Amaya could hear shouts from men as they left the village quickly and vanished into the trembling cedar forest.

CHAPTER THIRTEEN

The Kageyama's Hidden Mountain Village was behind them, and the ground had stopped shaking but Rin had not regained consciousness. Amaya felt gratitude for the fact. However, she had been trying and failing to ignore the person who she had left behind.

'Akio, we have to help Daiki?' Amaya said, when they paused for their first break. Amaya felt her legs tremble, the starvation was making each step harder than the last. 'He helped me follow the Kageyama so that we could take you back, but we were ambushed and brought to the village. I shouldn't have left him.' Amaya sat down heavily, willing herself not to cry.

'Half the village was destroyed by that earthquake, Amaya. We barely escaped ourselves. I cannot risk you re-entering such a hostile place. Daiki has most likely done as we have and run.'

Amaya nodded, imagining that Akio's words were fact rather than a hope.

'If we return, we may be recaptured or killed. Also, Rin needs my attention. I only hope there is something I can do,' Akio said, trying to reassure Amaya.

The door of the first ryokan they found was slammed in their faces. Akio, who had been carrying Rin on his back, lowered his head sadly. 'I thought this would happen.'

'No one will take us in,' Amaya groaned. 'Let me at least carry the provisions and the katana, Akio.'

'Not the katana. If we are stopped and you are carrying them, there will only be trouble.'

'I'm sure they'll just ignore the shinobi you're carrying.' Amaya laughed despite the seriousness of the statement.

However, Amaya's premature prediction proved false. The second ryokan they approached did not suffer the same scruples as the first, and on entering their room it was plain to see why. The house was very old, and tatami mat by tatami mat it was falling apart.

'They really need our coin, or they would have turned us away.'

'Then let us be quick about it and relieve them of our presence,' Akio said, as he lowered Rin onto one of the futons carefully. He busied himself with water and a few ointments he had kept on himself.

Amaya looked at the young shinobi. 'She's younger than me, I think,' Amaya leant closer. 'If it were not for the severity of her frown, she would have a pretty face. Everything about her is small. It's astonishing to think of the strength she has.'

'She is a shinobi. Size is often deceptive where they are concerned,' Akio said, ripping up one of his garments and emptying the hot water into a small bowl. 'Their methods of training are intense, brutal.'

'But they have the endurance and stamina to show for it,' Amaya replied, sitting cross-legged and aiding Akio in his task.

'They have a lot more than that, Amaya. They have certain techniques which some, like Shun Kimura, find dishonourable.'

'And you?' Amaya questioned, watching Akio clean the wounds on Rin's face and arm.

'I myself find them fascinating.'

'I thought I was the only one who had that curiosity.' She had kept the secret intrigue which shinobi incited to herself.

'I find them fascinating because they are smart, not bound by honour or other social confines,' Akio commented, holding his fingers to Rin's wrist.

'But honour helps to make us human,' Amaya argued.

'Of course, I do not doubt that. Honour is something which one must have to function as a person. It is balance that is missing for both shinobi and samurai. Shinobi operate in shadow and darkness, like the roots of a great tree. The samurai operate in the open, like the leaves. The roots and leaves despise each other and so the tree cannot grow. Cooperation, genuine and trust-filled, is what may never be achieved. At least not in my lifetime.'

Amaya pondered Akio's words carefully. 'Perhaps it might.' She glanced again at Rin, her small face bruised and lacerated. 'Akio, there's something odd about her. I have ignored it but the need to save her at the Hidden Mountain Village confirmed my suspicions.'

Akio tilted his head to the side, clearly curious. 'You believe she is your Fire Elemental, don't you?'

Amaya grinned, thankful she didn't have to voice the sporadic thought. 'Yes. Perhaps. I am unsure, Akio. I do not understand it myself. I had a strange feeling, I needed to help her, she needed to be saved. I do not know why.' Amaya stared at Rin again as Akio bandaged her wrist. She noted how pleasant Rin looked when her expression was not twisted with frustration and anger.

'Whether it is your benevolent nature or Ueten's, the outcome is the same. There.' Akio pulled the cover up to Rin's chin, and then turned to Amaya. 'Your turn. Come here.' He gestured for her to sit beside him. She obeyed, shuffling on her knees stiffly. Sitting back on her heels she lifted her face.

'Your lip,' Akio muttered, anger accenting his tone. 'Tell me if I hurt you. It's not deep but it will sting a little.'

Amaya nodded and kept still as Akio washed her cut and cleaned the dirt from her face. She studied his expression carefully. Myriad emotions fluttered across it, and each one made her want to wait for the next. The melancholy and sad, the angry and anxious, the relieved and concerned. She felt her breath quicken and spoke to distract herself from her thoughts. 'I had a strange dream.' Amaya didn't know how else to name it, and so she continued to explain to Akio what had happened to her whilst confined.

'I wish I had been there with you. That must have been terrifying,' Akio said, his face grave, his hand pausing. 'Gekai. You felt Gekai,' Akio stated plainly, his thoughts appearing on his face.

'Yes, then I saw Rai and Sen. I also saw a valley I have never seen before.'

'I think that something bad has happened in our absence.' Akio's voice was quiet, and Amaya knew he was thinking, as she was, of Kenta and the others.

'Here.' She took the cloth from his hand and rinsed clean water through it, before wiping the muck from his face. Akio fell into silence and watched her, as she had watched him. She made certain to keep her touch light. Her fingers traced his jawline, distinct and strong. They swept over his cheeks and across his brow. She stopped momentarily but Akio's hand reached up and encased hers. His fingers were warm, their touch purposeful. Amaya didn't move away. Akio turned his head towards her, and she inched nearer to him. Then, at the same moment, they leant forward. Their lips met in a gentle, delicate touch which sent a ripple through her entire person. The kiss became stronger the more they lingered.

Rin stirred, causing Amaya and Akio's time to evaporate. Rin blinked and winced slightly as her eyes roved in their sockets. Her gaze fell upon Amaya and she sat up quickly. At once, she moaned in pain and clutched her side falling back onto one elbow. She tried a second time to move but again was knocked back by the pain, her small face contorted in a silent cry.

Amaya placed a hand gently on her shoulder. 'Please, do not move so quickly. You have been hurt in the earthquake.'

Rin slapped her hand away. Amaya watched as the young shinobi quickly looked around taking in her surroundings. Her eyes found the door first, then the window and the closet. Finally, their gaze rested on Amaya's katana which Akio had removed from her when they laid her down. She had the appearance of a trapped animal. 'Why did you bring me here?'

'Because you were injured. I do not know why I considered it. If I'd known you'd be so ungrateful, I would have left you behind,' Amaya said, irritated and hurt.

'Have some tea and food, Rin. Your body is weak, you must regain some strength,' Akio said, in an authoritative tone, pushing the tray across the low table. She paused and stared at the tea.

'It's not poisoned,' Amaya said, taking a sip herself. Rin hesitated for an instant and then drank and ate greedily.

'Did *you* treat my wounds?' She asked quietly, her sharp eyes finding Amaya.

'No, Akio was the one who treated you. His father was a physician.'

'Why?'

'You could thank us,' Amaya said, looking away.

Rin threw the cup down. 'I did not ask for your help! I would never want the daughter of my father's rival to help me,' Rin added in hushed tones. She lifted her arm gingerly and rotated her shoulder, letting the movement loosen her stiff joints.

'Can you tell me how you know my father?' Amaya said, in a direct manner, ignoring the accusation of rivalry. Rin paused, some rice half way to her mouth. She placed the rice back into the small bowl and lowered her eyes. Her expression seemed agonized and Amaya realised that she was trying to contain her temper.

'Your father was the one who murdered my brother,' Rin said. Her words echoed around the small room and Amaya faltered as Rin looked up. 'He beheaded my older brother in a skirmish that broke out on a road during an ambush. Your father was accompanying the Governor of the Fire Province when my clan ambushed the convoy. We were aiming to take money for a contractor,' Rin said, staring at Amaya with steely eyes. 'I watched the whole thing in its entirety. That is how I recognised your fighting technique. I never forgot the way your father moved.'

Amaya thought back a few years and suddenly remembered the day her father brought home a bloodied and bawling Kyo. She contemplated the timing of this event and the ambush.

'Rin, was it you who had to destroy your brother's body?' Akio questioned.

'Yes. I see you are familiar with the shinobi traditions. I did not have to, I chose to.' Rin looked at the window. Amaya watched her and realised that she had never allowed herself to cry for her brother.

'I understand the Way of the Shinobi but you must grieve for your loss, otherwise it becomes an infection,' Amaya said, inching closer to Rin. As she did so she understood that she had not once grieved, not in the way she was encouraging the shinobi in front of her to do.

Quiet,' Rin said. 'You have never had to dispose of one you love. You know the methods the shinobi use to destroy evidence. Our fighting skills are secret, and a corpse can give away those secrets if examined.'

'You must give up your revenge,' Amaya said, her tone stronger.

Rin faced her with furious eyes. 'You speak of these things? You, who murdered my master; the very man who taught me from infancy. He was my guide and mentor.'

'I was protecting Akio and the ryokan owner. You holding a knife to my throat left little time to query the situation,' Amaya said, in angered tones.

'I have lived with the shame of wanting revenge for my brother, yet my clan still love me. I will not give up.'

'I am afraid you have lost your chance. My father, Kazu Takeda, is dead. I told you this.'

A stillness spread uncomfortably throughout the room.

'Good,' Rin said, finally.

Amaya bristled. 'Good? My father was doing his job that day. He was a very worthy man and a gentle person.'

'Gentle enough to develop a katana technique that would be used by an entire army?' Rin spat back, standing to her feet. Akio rose sharply and stood between the two.

Amaya clenched her fists tightly, trying to tame the fury which beat at her stomach. 'Rin, your clan are criminals and you cannot deny that. You can't. What my father did was his duty. I do not agree with killing needlessly but I do agree with protecting. My father was protecting not only the money but the innocent people travelling with it. You were willing to kill that day for money; for whoever had hired your services. Where is the honour in that? My father killed to protect the Governor and the convoy of people who stood in your way. I am sorry you lost your brother, but every person alive has, or will, lose someone of great value to them. I do feel vengeful for the circumstances in which I lost my important people but I have come to realise that there are bigger and more pressing matters to take care of.' She stopped, breathless. Rin was watching her closely.

Akio placed a tender hand on the small of Amaya's back. 'It is true, Rin. Amaya can comprehend what you feel but you cannot seek revenge on Amaya. It was not she who killed your brother.'

'I know,' Rin said, awkwardly. 'Why did you save me? We have no relation to each other. Our only connections are hatred and distrust.'

'I believe that we do have a connection to each other, besides hatred and distrust,' Amaya said, grudgingly.

'You are not making sense.' Rin became impatient and inched toward the door; a movement not lost on Amaya.

'Have you heard of the Prophet of Ueten, and of Gekai?' Akio interrupted.

Rin paused. A bewildered expression flourished across her stern face. 'I have but it may be a little different to the narratives you have encountered. Shinobi history is never officially recorded; we do not deserve such recognition.' Rin snorted in derision. 'Kageyama children are told about Ueten and Gekai as part of our history.'

'Your history?' Amaya questioned.

'It has long been understood and passed down by our clan elders. In the days of the Prophets, the shinobi were not divided into clans as they are now. We were one. We were powerful. We were the shadows of the nation. The history of Ueten, Gekai and the Prophets teach us that no one is impervious to being tainted. It teaches that uncontrolled emotions, whether happiness or anger, often lead to fractures which cannot be repaired. The scars of the First Warring States Era are still upon the geography of this land as well as the contours of each Akegatan's heart. None know this more than the shinobi. We were splintered beyond repair and have learnt from that experience.'

'You believe shinobi have suffered?' Amaya questioned.

Rin considered the query seriously. 'No, not suffered. We were enlightened. It is true, we are despised by the samurai class who deem our ways dishonourable. The people of Akegata fear us, perhaps rightly so. However, they only fear what they do not understand. The samurai would not be enjoying their seat at the top of the world were it not for the undeniable skills of shinobi and they cannot abide it. We do not seek loudmouthed acknowledgement as samurai do, but we do deserve a quiet respect and reverence. We earned it during the First Warring States Era.'

'Earned it?' Akio asked, as invested in Rin's rendition as Amaya. 'From the accounts I have read, the shinobi and samurai fought equally during that time. There are records that the shinobi profited from the war.'

Rin sighed but not in anger or upset. 'Eventually, shinobi did profiteer as mercenaries but not until hundreds of years into the bloodshed. As the samurai were loyal to Empress Mimiko, so were the shinobi loyal to Lord Genichiro Minamori. He was our blood.'

'Blood?'

'His mother was from the shinobi brotherhood; she and her samurai husband gave birth to Minamori no Genichiro a man who blended both samurai and shinobi ways.'

'Genichiro of the Minamori.' Akio mumbled. 'How do I know this name?'

'The Minamori clan eventually became the Kimura clan; that much is documented in the Archives of the palace.' Rin replied.

Amaya's blood suddenly slowed in her veins and her head swam as she grappled with a comprehension just coming into her focus. 'Akio, that must mean my ancestors stem from the same clan as the Kimura; we share a connection to the Minamori.'

'This is certainly an unexpected link and it would explain much of what we had discovered, such as why the shinobi aided in the assassination of Emperor Kado Yamashima if this shinobi version of the history behind the Prophets was known to others. Yet the link itself is so distant and you could not be more opposite to the likes of the Kimura clan. Your Takeda heritage is not simply samurai, Amaya. You also have shinobi lineage too. Rin, why is this shinobi loyalty to Lord Minamori important?'

'The shinobi were charged with his protection and the samurai were charged with protecting Empress Mimiko. We formed the roots of the Empire, the samurai the leaves. When the Prophet was declared, the expectation was that Mimiko was to marry him.'

'The Empress would not have married a man so clearly not touched by Ueten's light.' Akio posited.

Rin snorted. 'Genichiro Minamori was not always so twisted. He was a great man, a great samurai, a great shinobi. The palace Archives are sorely lacking in Ancient Scripture, it seems. Parchment is not the only means of recording events that have shaped our world.'

Amaya squinted in thought, pondering what Rin could possibly by implying.

'Regardless, the shinobi have not discovered what befell Lord Minamori, but the Prophet of Gekai was thrust upon Akegata. There were those who attempted to control him, assassinate him, but this only spurred him deeper into that Gekai's clutches. Mimiko became his biggest adversary in trying to prevent his path and, so, he sought to separate all samurai and shinobi from Mimiko. Genichiro's own sister was a retainer to Mimiko and loved her dearly. This is where my shinobi elders believe the age-long rift between samurai and shinobi began. Some shinobi remained staunchly by Lord Genichiro's side, some openly rebelled and followed his sister and others sought to repair the growing hostilities. That is told to shinobi children as the beginning of Gekai and when the clan elders realised a fact which had been misunderstood through history.' She hesitated and eyed Amaya with renewed and surprised interest. "You are descended from the Minamori? You have an interest in the Prophets? Are you –?' Rin lashed her body around as if struck.

Akio spun about, and Amaya straightened. Members of the Kageyama clan swarmed into the room. Amaya lunged for Meiyo but withdrew her hand quickly as a shuriken throwing star flew close by, slicing through her skin.

'Do not move.' It was the Doyen. Everyone halted, including Rin. He walked forward and took a small knife from his belt. 'I have come to collect my daughter now she has woken, and you will suffer for her kidnap as she will suffer for regaling clan lore to outsiders.' He raised a kunai dagger his focus on Amaya. Akio made a small movement and a silent shinobi cracked the back of his legs, forcing him to his knees. Amaya shook her head, panicked that Akio would be hurt. There were too many of them to contend with in such a confined space, and she knew that Akio understood the danger of struggling now. The Doyen lifted his hand and threw the kunai. Yet instead of feeling the blade she heard the clink of metal close to her face, and on opening her eyes she saw two daggers on the floor. The Doyen's expression bore only lividity which he focused on his daughter. Rin, her arm still raised, fell to her knees.

'What is the meaning of this, Rin?' The Doyen said, quietly.

'Amaya and Akio helped me recover from my injuries.' Rin's voice was tight, and Amaya saw that she was struggling with what she had just done. Her hands were shaking.

'Your betrayal is immense, Rin, but you are my daughter.' The Doyen seemed unsure himself. After a moment he flicked his hand and his men left the room, leaving through the window and door.

'I will spare you, Amaya, as you have spared Rin,' he said, through gritted teeth. 'Rin, you are a traitor, and as such will never succeed the Kageyama Clan. You are banished from the Hidden Mountain Village. If you do not want to perish then leave the Fire Province and never return. That is the price for her life and your treachery.'

Rin looked up, her eyes full of tears but her father's only held disgust. This was the greatest punishment she could have received; a dream had been snatched from her. A life had been snatched from her. A family had been snatched from her. *Death would have been more favourable*, Amaya thought.

Rin bowed low. 'I am sorry for my actions father and I accept your punishment.' Before the Doyen could speak Rin leapt across the room and out to the garden, vanishing over the wall into the cedar forest. The Doyen looked at Amaya once more. 'Between you and your father I have lost both children.' With these final words he left.

Amaya and Akio sat down and did not speak for a few minutes. Amaya felt that she was waiting for Rin to come back. Akio slid the door closed and the room dimmed.

'She will not return,' he said.

Amaya lent on the low table. 'She did not finish her explanation. We did not discover what the shinobi elders cam to understand.' She buried her face in her hands. 'I am so certain that she is my Elemental. It's such a strange feeling, Akio. I hate her, yet like her all at once.'

'She could not fathom her need to stop her father from killing you, I saw the confusion in her expression. Time is what she needs. She has a good heart, beneath it all. She has grown up in a very different world than either you or me.' Akio sat next to Amaya and smiled. Amaya lent sideways and placed her head on his shoulder. He brought up his hand and stroked her hair softly.

She and Akio were ready to leave within the hour, seeing no reason to linger. They paid the bemused ryokan owner in full and left swiftly.

'I wish we had horses,' Amaya said, in frustration, looking down the long road that stretched over the hill ahead.

'We can take the most direct route but we will have to travel through the forest at points. If we move fast and quietly we should pass unnoticed.'

Amaya and Akio travelled for three days with little rest. Feet dragging and fatigue hounding their every step, Amaya requested a stop. They were almost at the boarder to the Sky Province and decided to travel the remaining stretch of the journey the next day. Amaya watched as the moon grew steadily brighter in the waning light. It lay close to the land, luminous even though it was only a crescent. They settled near the roadside, out of sight behind some spindly shrubs. The moment Amaya sat down she felt her limbs relax and yawned despite herself. It was cold. The ground was cold, the air about them was cold, the light was cold. Amaya drew her knees up to her chest and rummaged for food in her bag. Akio set about making a small fire.

Once the pieces of kindling were sputtering into life and gradually consuming the wood on top of them Amaya felt the heat sneak its way beneath her cloak and seep into her skin. Akio took a seat beside her, throwing his thick cloak across both their shoulders. The warmth from his body chased away the bit of chill that the fire could not. He began to doze as Amaya studied the map, chewed on an onigiri and listened to the stillness. Akio fidgeted in his sleep, his head eased back against the tree they leant against. Amaya watched his face; in sleep he looked so rested. His eyelids were not moving with dreams or nightmares. The light of the moon threw delicate shadows down his cheeks, over the bridge of his nose and across his intelligent mouth. His lips were parted the smallest amount and his breaths were deep and quiet. As gently as she could, she slid her arm through his and lowered her head to rest upon Akio's shoulder. Sleep soon found her too.

She was woken by a noise beyond the tree line. Dawn was approaching but the sun had yet to break free of the land. Listening closely, she could hear hooves and the footfalls of a group of people. Careful not to disturb Akio she crept closer to the edge of the road and looked through the gap between two trees. A small convoy passed by and she saw, through the crack in the largest palanquin curtains, a face. It was Daiki.

She felt her stomach clench with relief and shock. He was alive and travelling with a group of Court Officials from the Fire Province. Fighting the urge to call out to him she watched the carriage dissolve into the dark. Then dawn became still again and she returned to Akio, nudging him awake. His hand went at once to his katana, his face alert, the peace of sleep gone.

'A convoy just passed by. It was Daiki and Court Officials from Kasaichi,' Amaya said, collecting her things as Akio rose to his feet.

'At least we know he is alive,' Akio replied. 'But why is he travelling with Court Officials? I am intrigued to know what his business was in the Fire Province. Shin stated that he had no plans to receive nobles.'

'He told me he had been at the coast,' Amaya replied, remembering Daiki's words.

Akio looked at her sharply, his frown deep. 'We must reach Kenta at once. Daiki would have been in the Fire Province on his father's orders, no one else's. What could Rai have wanted in the south?'

Amaya shook her head. 'Perhaps Lord Hiroshi and my brother have uncovered more evidence and information whilst we have been away. Together we may be able to shed some light on the situation.'

The sun steadily rose, marking their time as they walked through the Sky Province. They passed groups of hinin consisting of peddlers, medicine men and on occasion a singer or two. These sightings led her thoughts to digress to the Kawarakojiki.

'Amaya, have you thought more about that vision you had in the Kageyama village?' Akio asked, breaking the reverie Amaya had been wallowing in.

'Yes, but I still do not recognise any of the faces, besides Kenta's, Rai's and Sen's.' She faltered, herself remembering a glimmer of the dream. 'Except for one face. I did not know who it was but that was because he had no face. Yet I sensed I knew them somehow.'

Akio frowned and stepped next to Amaya. 'I'm sure this will make sense soon, it is Ueten and Gekai's influence. The Old Faith is full of the influence of those Spirits.'

As the sun dropped low, they went over the peak of a small hill and Chuto emerged before them, the rooftops glowing in the late afternoon sun. The capital spread out over the countryside, the palace dominating the centre. It was glorious even at a distance.

'The gates are ahead. Let's not keep Kenta waiting. I'm sure he will be delighted to see you,' Akio laughed.

The gates loomed higher the nearer they approached, and Amaya could see two imperial guards leaving their posts.

'Are they coming to greet us?' Amaya questioned. She looked up at Akio who was frowning.

He moved nearer to her. 'Give me your katana.'

Amaya obeyed, and Akio slid Meiyo into his waistband. They continued forward, the two guards advanced, their hands on their blades.

'Lady Amaya Takeda, you are under arrest,' the nearest guard said, seizing her arm. Amaya yelped as he tightened his grip.

Akio moved forward and took ahold of her hand. 'For what reason are you arresting Lady Takeda?' He demanded, raising his hand. Amaya heard the ringing of metal as the other guard drew his katana and placed it between Akio and the guard who held Amaya.

'Please, Lord Izumi. You may return to the palace, but Lady Takeda will have to accompany us. I am not at liberty to discuss the reasons,' the guard said, clearly uneasy. Akio paused and Amaya stopped struggling.

'She is Lady Izumi, my wife. Who authorised this arrest?' Akio looked at the two guards, his expression furious. Amaya bit her lip, fearful that Akio would act irrationally.

'Akio, go to the palace. I will be fine.' Amaya said, imploringly.

'I will return and inform His Majesty.' Akio bowed curtly and departed, hurrying toward the palace.

'Lady Amaya, you will be kept in the city prison. You will have your own cell,' the guard said, grabbing Amaya's arm and steering her through the gates towards the city penitentiary. 'You will be comfortable.'

The narrow and secluded street which led to the entrance of the jail was heavily guarded. Amaya held her head high as she was marched forward down the stairs to the dark cells, she refused shame. It was a little warmer below ground but the damp clung to her skin causing her to shiver.

'Is this my cell?' Amaya said, despondently, looking into the dank hold which was carved into the earth. She was shoved through the metal barred doorway. The guard locked the gate and left without another word. Amaya walked to the centre of the room. The only light came from the sparsely placed paper lanterns which lined the aisle running between the cells. She saw a blanket; it was holey and damp. As she bent closer to look, she felt her stomach lurch; it smelt rancid. She imagined a person had died whilst wrapped in it. There were chains hanging from the wall. Amaya turned away from them and walked back to the locked gate. She craned her neck to see up and down the aisle. She couldn't see or hear any other prisoners. Even the guards had vanished.

Amaya watched the daylight fade as night arrived and she was reminded horribly of her imprisonment at the Hidden Mountain Village. The soft, flickering glow of the lanterns made the empty cells seem even more barren and cold. For a moment, she stood still, unsure of what to do. She paced around her prison for much of the night, unable to ignore the restlessness. Eventually, Amaya could walk no more, and tiredness forced her to sit on the cold floor. She leant sideways against the metal bars and faced the stairs, willing her eyes to close.

Cold, moist stone made her jaw ache as she shifted. She had slipped to the floor in sleep. Straining her ears, she was certain she had heard the strum of a shamisen but now the cells were filled with silence. *Seiji*, she thought.

After some time had elapsed, a guard emerged and clanged her cage. He passed a cup of steaming tea and a small cracked bowl of rice to her.

'Please, can you tell me when I might leave? Or at least why I have been imprisoned?' Amaya shouted after the guard. He stopped, his back to Amaya, and said nothing before he continued to climb the stone steps. She looked at the food and drink. Using her fingers, she hungrily ate the dry, flavourless rice. The hot, bitter liquid left her tongue tingling after each hurried gulp. After she had finished the tea she kept hold of the cup until its warmth had gone.

As the afternoon of the next day came, Amaya began to feel caged, angry. She kicked the cup across the floor. It bounced from the walls and spun to a stop beside her.

'You had better watch your temper, girl.'

Amaya sat up at the sound of his voice. Her fear and anger worsened as she looked up at Rai Kimura.

She threw herself at the bars, surprising even herself. 'You are the reason I am locked up in here. What are you trying to prove?' Amaya hissed under her breath. She watched Rai carefully, analyzing him, as he paced before her. Her breath caught short as she remembered seeing his face in the apparition she experienced in the mountains and as she recalled, with disgust, her ancestral link to the murderer before her.

'Forging documents.' Rai shook his head. 'Whether I am the reason or not, Lady Takeda, you broke the law. Anybody else would be punished accordingly, why should you be any different? Unless you are special in some way.' He laughed. 'You should have married Daiki.'

Amaya let her arms fall to her side. 'I have forged no documents. My betrothal to your son could not happen.' The lie came easily to her. She knew who would be punished and the sentence he would receive. She could not allow Akio to be executed.

'It cannot happen now. I could never marry Daiki to a criminal who has, no doubt, already lost her virtue.' Rai clasped his hands in front of him, shaking his head once more.

Swallowing the reply she wanted to give, she instead responded. 'I am of the samurai class. You cannot simply imprison me without warning. I must be released.' Amaya did not relish summoning the privilege she had but she could see no other avenue open to her in that dark cell.

A flash of rage blazed through the calm in Rai's stare. 'You lost your samurai status when you made a personal attack on me and the Court. That was as good as treason and you are lucky that, as a child at the time, you were not made to commit seppuku. Hiroshi Katou also pleaded for your mother's life then. You truly do not comprehend the severity of your mistake'

'If I am no longer of the samurai class, why have I been permitted to work alongside his majesty? To marry Lord Izumi? To continue to pen decrees in the Archives?'

'Because I have allowed it. Me. Your every movement has been because I have allowed it.' Rai hissed through the bars.

Amaya gripped the bars. 'I will not fear you, Rai. You are creating this illusion of control, but I am in prison for a reason. You are scared and cannot let me remain free. Something about me terrifies you.'

'You couldn't scare a child, Lady Takeda. You have no power in these waters. Your friendship with the Emperor will only damage him eventually. Forgery is a severe crime. However, as the merciful Minister of Justice, I shall lesson the punishment from execution to labour in the Yukaku District. You will work off your debt to society there.'

Amaya's gaze bore into Rai's. 'You would have me as a prostitute? You are that fearful? I wanted you stopped as a child and my ambition has not changed. It has had many years to evolve beyond childish fancy.'

'Ambition or vengeance?' Rai questioned. 'Can you afford such a thing, Lady Amaya?'

'If it means I attain justice. Until you can provide your justification for my punishment, you are compelled to release me.'

'You will be released when deemed appropriate. I will deny you your freedom seeing as you take liberties with it. I am the Chancellor and the Minister of Justice answers to me. Your needs come second; the palace has suffered a loss and is currently in upheaval. Your brother seems at the centre of it all.' Rai smirked. 'A court assembly is to be held tomorrow at noon so do not expect visitors, and I think it best you remain here whilst His Majesty conducts the assembly. Your husband has been confined to the Archives. He is the Secretariat after all.'

'And what of Shun?' Amaya could not conceal her tone

of concern.

Rai paused at her question. 'My son and his platoon remain at the border which separates the Earth and Air Provinces, where I sent him over two weeks ago. It is time he upholds his rank as General,' Rai said, turning to leave.

Amaya yelled in disbelief. 'Why send your own son to a place that dangerous? You know the rebel army has almost completely occupied the north of the Earth Province. A General cannot lead his army if he is dead.'

'I trust my son's abilities and he follows his father's orders honourably.'

Amaya grit her teeth but did not comment. Rai said nothing more, instead he threw a scroll at her. It sailed between the bars of her jail and landed at her feet.

'That is from Jiro, it arrived the day after you left Chuto,' Rai said, and with a last look of loathing, he left the prison.

Amaya shouted in frustration and kicked the cup again. She thought of Shun, and then of Kin and panic rose in her chest rapidly. She swept the scroll from the floor and broke open the seal. The letter unravelled revealing her uncle's familiar script.

Dear Amaya,

I hope you returned safely from your trip to the Earth Province. Rikujou is slowly becoming less safe, I hope you did not encounter any trouble. I would have been happy for you to visit me, but I fear it would have been too dangerous for you to reach my estate safely.

The Air Province is still unstable and so I am to remain here. I planned to visit you this season, but matters have kept me from travelling. I know you understand, my dear niece.

I hope the dojo is nearly repaired, that will be a great comfort for you and Kyo. I understand he is working for Lord Hiroshi Katou. How proud we must both be.

I await your reply,
Jiro Takeda, your loving uncle.

She rolled up her uncle's letter and fastened it before placing it on the ground. Her uncle had mentioned Kyo and Hiroshi Katou, the kindly old advisor. Soon, her thoughts wondered to the Court assembly and the reasons behind it. Rai had aggravated her curiosity rather than give her any real information. She cursed him under her breath. *I would give anything to kill him now.*

Amaya waited dazedly as the day waned and gave way to night. Her mind was exhausted but still she could not rest. Seeing Rai in person had shaken her. She remembered the feeling of Gekai and the images of faces she did not recognise. She longed for her Elementals. She felt saddened at the thought that she had another to find and that she had lost another. Her goal was so distant, yet the civil war was so close.

'Amaya.' A whisper came from the other side of the cell bars. Amaya jumped and looked around.

'Who is it?' She scanned the dim corridor. A figure came from the shadows. 'Rin?'

'Quiet. The guards are sleeping.' Rin waved a set of keys.

'You didn't kill them?' Amaya said. Her surprise that Rin was there made words somehow difficult. Rin silently unlocked the gate and opened it a crack big enough for Amaya to squeeze through.

'No, I did not kill them. Stealth is the most important lesson we learn. Killing is second to that,' Rin said, looking up the stairwell. Amaya marvelled at her.

'Maybe you could teach me some of these famed skills one day,' Amaya said, as the two crept up toward the streets of Chuto.

'No,' Rin said, seriously. 'Only the Kageyama can know the clan secrets.'

Amaya nodded as they emerged under the moonlight.

She could see the palace in the distance and sighed. 'Thank you, Rin.'

'Where do you need to go?' Rin questioned.

'The palace,' Amaya replied, immediately. 'But getting in will be impossible.'

'I will find a way in.'

As the two neared the palace, they were brought to a stop by the perimeter wall, atop which Amaya knew patrolled both Imperial guards and Censorate soldiers. She stared up at the obstacle, her heart floundering. 'There are guards and the moat on the other side of this wall.' Amaya stated, attempting not to sound despondent.

Rin laughed. 'I said I would find a way in. Wait here. Quietly.' She held a finger to her mouth. 'Keep your back against the stone.' She didn't wait for Amaya to speak, instead she turned around and scaled the wall. Amaya felt her mouth drop as she observed the shinobi climb what, moments ago, had appeared unclimbable. Rin moved like a spider, her limbs working together fluidly. Amaya ran her hand over the stone; it was smooth. She knew it had been designed with shinobi in mind, to prevent them from entering the grounds. Amaya found herself understanding how Kenta's family had been so easily assassinated. Twilight was drawing to a close and shadows consumed the street and the wall. Rin was already out of sight.

The sounds of the city quietly hummed with the residents still out for the night. Flurries of jovial conversation, muttered talk and simple footsteps only served to heighten Amaya's unease; she couldn't keep still, shifting from one foot to another. Several times she glanced up, but nothing appeared, no sound came. She wondered where Akio and Kenta were. Rai had said that Akio was confined to the Archives but she knew she could not go anywhere near the palace buildings. As she pondered the best course of action, a hiss sounded next to her head. She whirled about. Dangling down the white stone was a rope. Amaya tugged at it and as she did, a bird call broke the stillness.

Grabbing the rope, she made her way up the wall quickly. 'How did you climb?' She asked Rin the moment she reached the top.

'A shinobi's secret,' Rin replied, arcanely.

'The guards?' Amaya said, catching her breath.

Rin shook her head. 'Sleeping soundly but incapacitating them takes longer and it's more dangerous. The living can raise the alarm quicker than a corpse.'

'The shrine is the safest place for us to reach. I cannot enter the palace. You might be able to, but I am not a shinobi. The shrine is close by, just beyond the small woodland.' Amaya pointed to their left. 'But what of the moat?' She said, looking down. The drop was high, the water dark.

Rin was frowning. 'We will walk along the wall, until we are as close to the shrine as possible. Then I will decide how to proceed.'

'Thank you,' Amaya said, placing a hand on the shinobi's shoulder. 'Thank you for helping me.'

Rin shook off Amaya's hand. 'I am trying to understand. Do not thank me yet, I still haven't decided to join you.'

Amaya didn't push her, because she could sympathise with Rin's confusion. The young shinobi was simply testing her own belief, her own resolve. Just as Amaya was doing.

Rin broke into a silent run, rippling along to wall-top like a ribbon of moonlight. Amaya followed close behind and the two girls fled along the wall, passing the unconscious bodies of the guards Rin had dealt with. The copse of tall trees came closer with each stride, and Rin slowed to a standstill. 'We can drop down here,' she said, pointing at a tree on the other side of the moat which was bent over the water like an elderly woman. Rin's dark hair was whipped about her face by the wind and, as she scrutinised the area, she pulled a few strands from her mouth and tucked them behind her ears. She extricated a long thin wire from her waistband. At its end was a three-pronged hook.

'Move,' she instructed. Amaya stepped aside and Rin began to spin the hook, releasing wire slowly. Soon a dull drone, like that made by a fat insect, rendered the air. The wire stretched in a wide circle as Rin whipped it through the air. Without warning she let it go. The hook sailed across the moat, the metal wire ringing eerily. It arched into the sky before falling gradually into the branches of the tree. Rin jerked her hand, satisfied it was secure she tied her end to the curved lip of the wall.

Rin stepped over to Amaya and passed her a sheathed tanto dagger. 'Take this. Watch what I do and copy me. I will catch you.' Her voice was brusque, and Amaya could see the awkwardness she felt in helping.

'I understand.' Amaya nodded and watched as Rin rested her own sheathed ninjatō sword upon the wire. With a short jog and a little jump she lifted her feet from the roof and took to the air. The keening of the sheath sliding against the wire caused Amaya's hairs to lift. She glanced around nervously but could see no one. Rin reached the tree and, sticking her feet forward, landed safely.

Amaya stared down the length of wire, its gradient gentle, and gripped the tanto dagger in her hands. Then, as Rin had done, she placed it upon the wire. She rocked back onto her heels for a moment and then bounced into flight. The wire sagged a little, but her descent was quick. The moon was captured in the moat, and her shadow passed over it, an insubstantial dot against the crescent reflection. She stuck her feet forward and almost at once made contact with slender branches which cracked and made way for her. She caught sight of Rin who had one arm wrapped around the trunk, the other outstretched waiting for her. She grabbed hold of Amaya's arm and pulled her to safety before cutting the wire loose.

Slowly they climbed down the tree, Amaya was unable to stem the awe as she studied the ease with which Rin moved. The young shinobi's talents made her comprehend how little she knew outside of the Seishin no Ken technique, and for the first time in her life, Amaya felt inadequate in combat. As her feet found solid earth, she promised herself to improve and train in more weaponry, in more techniques.

Rin turned to face her. 'Are you the Prophet of Ueten?'

Amaya stumbled at the bluntness of Rin's question. 'That is what I have come to believe.'

'Then the connection you believe we share is more substantial?'

Amaya nodded. 'I feel you are my Elemental. Your knowledge and understanding of the legend encourages me in that belief.'

'Perhaps I am. This would clarify all that has been happening in the Kageyama; the rumblings of changing times and the shinobi movements recently.'

'I want you to finish what you spoke of before; about what the elders came to understand during the start of the First Warring States Era.'

'Not out in the open.' Rin said, curtly.

'The shrine is this way. I can lead from here,' Amaya whispered.

They entered the soft glow of the shrine's candles and stopped in the pillared heidan. Rin gazed around the beautiful hall of offerings. Amaya watched Rin seek out the doors and windows of the large space; any rafter or crack in the floor did not escape her eye.

'Amaya?' A startled voice broke the hush of the shrine.

'Kannushi Masato!' Amaya pivoted on the ball of her foot. Rin did the same but clenched in her hand was a kunai dagger. 'This is Kannushi Masato, the priest,' Amaya hissed, encouraging Rin to lower her weapon.

Kannushi Masato paced forward, his wrinkled brow wrinkling more so with his concern. He placed a hand on her shoulder. 'Amaya, I thought you had been imprisoned? How have you come to be here?'

'I escaped, Kannushi Masato. I do not know what to do. I

know nothing of what's going on.'

The old priest looked about. 'Not here. I will hide you in the pagoda.'

They followed him in silence. Amaya noticed that Rin still had not put away her dagger, her apprehension was paramount, and Amaya could feel it distinctly.

'Who is your friend?' Kannushi Masato asked, once they were within the confines of the pagoda where the fireworks had been stored.

'This is Rin Kageyama of the Hidden Mountain Village. She helped me escape from the prison,' Amaya said.

'The Kageyama clan? What brings you to Chuto?' Kannushi Masato said, his eyes narrowing in interest.

Rin remained in the shadows. 'I am not welcome in my clan any longer.'

Amaya glanced at Rin and lowered her head. 'She saved my life and because of that action she was banished by her father.'

'You saved Amaya's life? I am very grateful. You have done a good thing.'

Deciding that haste was important Amaya spoke directly. 'I believe Rin is my Fire Elemental. She has shed much light on the hidden parts of Ueten and Gekai's history.'

He continued to look at Rin. 'Your pilgrimage is going well, Lady Amaya. Kin has been restless for a week now. I prayed for your safety but Kin's worry has been growing daily,' Kannushi Masato said.

'Kin has returned?' Amaya felt calm seep in alongside her agitation.

'He has been staying with me. He is still anxious about the presence of Sen and his involvement. He is praying that the Senkaku Nin are not part of this. That would make a very different kind of enemy. Little is known about them and it is this mystery which makes them deadly. Who can fight against that which they do not understand?'

Amaya sighed. The relief that Kin was well, placated

her somewhat. However, Rai's other fragments of information plagued her. 'Rai told me that the palace has suffered a loss and that a Court Assembly is to be held tomorrow. What did he mean?'

Kannushi Masato nodded ruefully. 'It seems you have not heard.' The old priest seemed suddenly older. 'Lord Hiroshi Katou was murdered three days ago.'

Amaya sank back against a pillar. She shook her head in disbelief as the kind wizened face of the Advisor came into her mind.

'How? I mean who would kill him?' Amaya stuttered.

'He was poisoned. A poison needle was found next to his body. The poison is unfamiliar, but it is being analysed.'

'And Kenta?' Amaya asked, quietly.

'He wanted to see you very much Amaya but in the present climate of things he could not venture into the city and to the prison. Since your departure with Lord Izumi, everyone is treading very carefully. Certain documents were discovered at the scene of Hiroshi's murder, and Kenta, Akio, myself and Kin have been examining them.'

'How is Kyo?' Amaya said.

Kannushi Masato nodded distractedly. 'He is outraged and upset. He had grown close to Hiroshi and was working with him in the Censorate every day. Hiroshi treated him like a man; he recognised Kyo's intelligence and made him an official investigator the day before his murder. So, you can imagine Kyo's reaction. He is determined to discover who the murderer is. You probably know who he thinks is behind the crime.'

'Rai Kimura,' Amaya said, her temper bubbling. She wanted to go to Kyo who had lost yet another important person.

'You cannot enter the palace,' Kannushi Masato said. 'However, it seems that Lord Hiroshi and your brother were close to discovering who the second accomplice is, the second leader.'

'How much had they uncovered?' Amaya asked thirsty to know everything.

'It must have been a substantial amount. It seems that he had help; Lord Hiroshi had been in correspondence with someone in the north for the last week, and it appears that the information provided by this person was crucial. It was the same person who aided your father, Amaya. They have finally shown themselves after all these years. Perhaps they are aware of more than those in the Censorate are and felt it was too dire to speak. With you and Lord Izumi gone, they may have felt compelled to break their silence.'

Amaya groaned. 'That is why Lord Hiroshi was killed. The same as my father. What of the letters and the documents?'

'Most have been either destroyed or taken. The attacker knew what Lord Hiroshi had discovered and wanted the evidence gone. Even if we know who the culprit may be, without evidence there is nothing that can be done. Nothing. Kyo is determined, however. So, Lord Kenta has been watching over him and forming a protective shield whilst he continues Hiroshi's work. Kyo has learnt much from him.'

Amaya continued. 'And the identity of this person who complied with both my father and Lord Hiroshi is unknown?'

Kannushi Masato nodded unhappily. 'Yes, unfortunately.'

'So why is an assembly being held?' Amaya questioned.

'Kenta will use the assembly as a means of acquiring information, but he must be careful. He has ordered all ministers, vice ministers, secretaries and clerks to be present.'

'All the personnel with a whit of authority.' Amaya pondered for a moment.

'I will be attending. I am Minister of Rites as well as the priest of this shrine. I will be able to relay everything to you, so please do not attempt to attend the assembly, Amaya. Please. None of us can afford you to be caught and given a more severe punishment,' he said, anxiously.

'Rai also told me that Shun is still in the Earth Province.'

Kannushi Masato lowered his gaze. 'Yes, for over two weeks now Shun has been in the north. We had word that his platoon was attacked. Many of his men died and many of their horses too. Their water was poisoned with an unknown substance but Shun is unharmed. The water from the river was contaminated.'

Amaya's face turned pale. 'Has Shun had the poison studied?'

'You think it the same as the poison used to murder Lord Hiroshi.' Kannushi Masato stated.

Amaya nodded. 'Yes. It's likely. It could even be the same poison used against me in Rikujou.'

Before they could continue the conversation, Rin spoke. 'Someone is coming. I can hear them on the pathway.' She dashed forward and stood beside Amaya instinctively.

'Wait a moment,' Amaya said, stepping forward. 'I know who it is.' She smiled, and a moment later Kin entered.

'I am so glad you are safe. The guards have been alerted to your escape from the prison.' Kin glanced at Rin. 'You must be Amaya's Fire Elemental.'

'Who are you? How can you know?' Rin stared at Kin suspiciously.

'Do you need to ask? I have the same feeling about you, the same feeling that you must have felt for Amaya. It is a connection we all share. The Spirits residing in us are old friends,' Kin said, stepping towards her. 'I am an Elemental, the Air.'

'It does not feel comfortable,' she said, finally.

'It will continue to feel strange until you have accepted your role,' Kin said, his voice kind.

'My role?' Rin looked up at Kin and then at Amaya. 'My role?'

'Yes. As an Elemental you are to support Ueten and help her,' Kin explained.

'I know the history,' Rin said, abruptly, her expression

pained.

'Then you must understand your importance. Not just as Ueten's aid. You have the potential to help Akegata from it's current situation,' Kin continued. 'It seems you have already helped Amaya.'

'I have had no choice in the matter,' Rin said.

'You mean you would *choose* to abandon Akegata, your home?'

Rin's face darkened. 'No, I would not.'

He smiled kindly at Rin, bowing his head. 'You do not have to do anything you do not wish to do. However, it may be wise to stay with us. You can make your decision when you are ready.' Kin raised his eyebrows. 'You would not be the only one fighting to believe. Amaya,' Kin gripped her shoulders, 'something happened during your absence. I felt your distress.'

'I had a dream whilst in the Fire Province. I saw faces but the only ones I recognised were Rai, Kenta and your brother's. There was also a face with no features,' Amaya said, hoping Kin would be able to enlighten her.

He thought for a moment. 'Well I can explain the faceless person. That has to be your last remaining Elemental.'

'I wish I knew who it was. I feel that they are close, but I felt Gekai, I felt it.'

'It was painful?' Kin asked, his expression saddened as he placed a gentle hand on her shoulder.

'Yes.'

'That is because the sense of Gekai is offensive to Ueten. They are opposites and Ueten has started to stir. Gekai has moved and Ueten has sensed that. Has Kannushi Masato informed you of Hiroshi's death?' Kin asked, in a hollow voice.

'Yes, he has explained many things. He has told me not to attend the assembly.'

'That is for the best, Amaya. I have seen Kyo and he is coping, he has matured a lot whilst you were gone. You would be proud of him'

'Still, I want to see him.'

'You will soon enough. He visits me often,' Kin said, smiling slightly. 'I think it is because he wants to ask if I sense anything about you rather than see me.'

Amaya smiled. 'Where is Tomio?'

'Tomio is safe. If he hasn't been with your brother, he has been with the Ito Merchants Guild. They are developing a defence against the firearms, using the one you secured to understand the construction behind such a weapon. Tomio is incredible; he has already reversed the engineering of the weapon and set about compiling designs for a defence. He will also begin improvements to the bows. He is quite the archer himself and seems to have already developed a bow that outstrips the ones of the imperial army.'

'The things I saw in his house in Rikujou were ingenious. I do not think Tomio is happy to be developing weapons.'

Kin sighed. 'Tomio does not agree with war. He is far too peaceful.'

'And we have asked him to put his talents into augmenting such a thing.' Amaya felt the unwelcome clutch of guilt.

'We have little choice. Tomio understands this and he would much rather help defend against these foreign weapons than watch them destroy what we have.'

Rin stepped closer to Amaya, closer to the light of the candles. 'I heard my father speak of firearms once before.'

Amaya stiffened, her back tensing. 'He has encountered them?'

Rin scratched her head. 'I'm not certain. I was not a part of the conversation and it was not my place to eavesdrop.'

'Could the Kageyama clan be involved?' Kin questioned.

Rin was suddenly uncomfortable. 'Perhaps. My father has been absent a lot, leaving his brother in charge, and the contracts he has been making have been steadily more reckless and widespread.'

'Would you recognise a poison if it was used by the Kageyama?' Kin asked.

'Yes, if it were developed in the Hidden Mountain Village, I would know it.'

'Would you be willing to examine the needle used to murder the Emperor's Advisor?' Kin asked, his tone pleading. 'If we can know for certain we could begin to comprehend our opposition in more detail.'

'If it is Kageyama, I will also make you an antidote.'

Amaya blinked. 'Thank you, Rin.'

That night Kannushi Masato returned, and by his side was Kyo. Amaya, who was on the second level of the pagoda, heard his voice before she saw him. She jumped up and ran to the top of the stairs just as he appeared at the bottom. 'Kyo.' They met halfway and embraced. 'I am so sorry, Kyo. I am so sorry.' She felt Kyo's hands grip the fabric of her happi top.

When he stepped back Amaya was able to study his face. She was delighted and saddened to see how much he had changed. His cheeks were leaner, the boyishness gone. His jaw was tighter, manlier. The look he gave was different. Amaya couldn't place it, but his irises contained something that she had seen in Shun's. However, as he stared at his sister, she watched the steeliness deplete and a little of his sweetness return.

'I have missed you, Amaya. So much.'

'We are all working hard.' Amaya promised him.

'Kannushi Masato tells me you have someone who may be able to identify the poison,' Kyo said, his voice quiet in its eagerness.

'Yes. This is Rin Kageyama.'

Kyo faced Rin, his eyes narrowing. 'Of the shinobi Hidden Mountain Village?'

'Yes, I am the daughter of the Doyen of the Kageyama clan,' Rin said, standing to her feet.

'You must be very proud to inherit a clan of murderers,' Kyo said, his brow furrowed. Amaya made to interrupt but it was Kin who spoke first.

'Kyo, Rin is not solely to blame for her clan's actions. She is Amaya's Fire Elemental,' Kin finished, quietly.

Kyo bit his lip, his fists balling. 'The Kageyama were the ones who butchered my parents and left me to die.' He was glaring at Rin who had fallen silent with Kyo's last words. No one had confronted her this way. He turned to Amaya shaking his head. 'She's truly your Fire Elemental?'

'I believe she is. Kyo,' Amaya said, as he went to speak, 'she has twice saved my life.'

Kyo stared at Rin and Amaya saw a mixture of frustration, anger and gratitude flicker across his face. And then he bowed. 'Thank you for saving my sister's life. I apologise for my rudeness.'

Amaya felt tears forming but she blinked them into retreat. Rin's eyes were wide, looking absurdly large in her small face, a moment later she bowed in return.

Kannushi Masato stepped forward and placed one craggy hand on Kyo's shoulder and the other on Rin's. 'This,' he said with a shaking voice, 'is what mends a little of my weary heart. Your capacity for forgiveness, Kyo, and your willingness to accept it and change, Rin. This is what can heal his broken land.' They all paused in the wake of Kannushi Masato's statement. The old priest clapped his hands, breaking the reverie. 'Now, I have informed Lord Kenta and Akio of your whereabouts, Amaya. They implore you to remain here in hiding until after the assembly. You will be told everything, so please do not worry. They ask a little more patience of you.'

Amaya nodded but could not shirk the agitation. Kyo spoke up. 'Here is the dart. Any help you can give would be invaluable.' Upon his palm was a small box. He passed it to Rin who took it in her hands. Prizing open the lid Amaya watched her face fall.

'I can see without even testing the poison that it is Kageyama.'

Kyo drew in a deep breath and closed his eyes but didn't

comment on the fact. 'Thank you.'

'I said I would prepare an antidote but even if you had it the poison works too rapidly.'

'What if the men were able to ingest the antidote now. Would it inhibit the poison and save the one infected?' Amaya questioned.

Rin's hand went to her mouth absentmindedly. 'It's possible.'

'Then that is what we shall do. It is better than no protection.'

'The ingredients are difficult to come by, especially in winter,' Rin said, her tone anxious.

'It is all we can do for now,' Kin said. 'It will help to have it.'

'I will detail what is needed and how it is prepared.' Rin inclined her head and hurried away.

When Rin had given the list to Kyo he had departed at once, his destination the Censorate. Kannushi Masato also left them to sleep, stating he needed to prepare for the early assembly. Kin offered Amaya and Rin the highest room on the seventh level. After they had shared a meal they went to settle for the night.

'Amaya, you wanted me to complete the history as the shinobi understand it?'

Amaya, who was leaning back on her arms, her stomach full, straightened. 'If it is acceptable.'

'The shinobi elders began to realise that Ueten and Gekai were not separate Prophets.'

Gradually, Amaya understood the gravity of what Rin had stated. 'You mean they are he same Prophet?'

Rin nodded, her expression grim. 'It first became apparent with Lord Minamoto.'

'But how is that possible? The two spirits are opposite in nature.'

'There is a very narrow line between them. All it takes is uncontrolled emotions to taint the Prophet, leading them down a vastly different path.'

'A path which breeds war.' Amaya's voice lost its strength. 'This worries me, Rin.'

'As long as you have the support of your Elementals, they will help you maintain the true course. Lord Minamori did not listen, his arrogance and jealousy had grown too strong.'

Amaya did not convey the depth of her concern; she felt ashamed of her feelings of vengeance and anger. However, alongside the shame nestled dread.

Amaya woke just before dawn. Quietly, she opened the door and stepped out onto the balcony which encircled the pagoda. Peering over the edge she saw the other balconies in the shadows. The sun was above Mount Honju, illuminating the snow and sparkling waterfalls which shone through the forest. The trees shrouded the foot of the mountain like old boots. She could see the palace to her left and some of the beautiful estate buildings. With a smile, she wondered if Akio was still sleeping, imagining him slumped over his desk in the Archives. She felt his absence acutely and compared it to the feeling she had for her Elementals. It was different. It affected her heart, not Ueten. The echo of their kiss became prominent, and she ran her fingers along her lips.

Amaya turned as Rin stirred and opened her eyes. 'You are awake,' she said, to Amaya.

'I have never seen the city from here before,' Amaya replied, as the cold breeze picked up her ebon hair and sent a shiver through her.

Rin stood and joined Amaya on the balcony. 'The assembly is today.'

'Yes. I want to go but I must stay and wait for news,' Amaya said, stiffly. She gripped the railing and leant back letting out a deep breath. 'Rin, I am grateful you helped me. I do not just mean last night. I understand you are still unsure where your loyalties lie.'

'I know that. Since we met in that ryokan, I have been

uncertain but you must understand the importance of the name Kageyama.' Rin cleared her throat. 'I do not know a life outside of the Way of the Shinobi, and it will take time to release the Kageyama from my heart.'

They turned as Kin entered the room with a tray of tea. The three sat at the low table on the floor cushions and drank. 'You will not have to wait long, Amaya. I too am curious.'

Amaya blew on her tea, steam streaming about her face. 'Let us hope progress is made.'

Noon came and went with little activity and Amaya's unease grew. Her two Elementals fidgeted, and Amaya wondered if they were sensing the discomfort. She stood and strode to the balcony. The wind had grown stronger throughout the night and carried with it the whispers of snow. The Face of Winter was almost fully upon them. As she pulled her long hair away from her eyes she gazed down. There, coming from the woods, was Kannushi Masato. Amaya dashed down the flights of stairs and burst out of the pagoda to greet him. She stopped a few meters away; his face was serious.

'What happened, Kannushi Masato?' Amaya asked, with trepidation.

'Come inside,' he said, quietly. As they entered, Kin and Rin appeared and looked at the old priest expectedly.

'Is it as you feared?' Kin questioned.

Kannushi Masato nodded. 'Unfortunately, yes. The Censorate's investigators have returned from the Earth Province, the rebel army is moving with purpose. It seems the civil war is upon us. I have also been informed that the poison used against Shun and Amaya is not the same as the one used to murder Lord Hiroshi.' Kannushi Masato paused briefly. 'However, Shun did have the poison from his camp examined and it is Shizukawa shinobi poison. For two shinobi clans to be involved shows how deep the rebel leaders' influence reaches.' Kannushi Masato sighed.

Amaya spoke slowly. 'Kannushi Masato, who was not present at the assembly?'

'Only two people; Daiki Kimura and Jiro Takeda the Governor of the Air Province.'

'My uncle,' Amaya repeated.

'Yes, he was not present and it is unknown why. Kenta's request was compulsory. I am sure he is unharmed, Amaya. We have not heard that Shiroshi city has been attacked. Do not worry.'

Amaya began to pace. 'Perhaps the snow has hindered his journey south?'

'Snow has been falling for over week in the Air Province,' Kin commented.

'Daiki Kimura was also absent, but I saw him returning to the capital.' Amaya said, recalling the convoy she had spied and Daiki's face in the palanquin window.

'When did you see Daiki Kimura?' Kannushi Masato said, sharply. Amaya explained what had happened. How she had met Daiki in Kasaichi; how he had helped her rescue Akio.

'I have met Daiki Kimura once before.' Rin's voice was quiet, but everyone faced her when she finished speaking.

'When?' Amaya asked. 'Why?'

Rin looked up as she attempted to remember. 'A year ago, now. He met with my father, but I do not know what was discussed. I could not place him at first but then I recalled when he was at the Hidden Mountain Village.'

Amaya shook her head. 'This only confirms Rai Kimura's involvement. He has been using his son, and Daiki has obeyed.'

'What would you expect him to do, Amaya?' Kin asked, gently. 'To go against your father would bring disgrace. Daiki is showing loyalty in his own way.'

Amaya felt a bizarre rumble of irritation. 'What else has Daiki done for his father? I cannot imagine. Yet he seemingly has no trouble in following orders. Who knows who he may have hurt, or even killed, so that Rai can have his path cleared?'

'I do not believe Daiki Kimura is evil,' Kin stated.

Amaya bit her tongue hoping to restore the composure she felt slipping away. 'Daiki has his own mind, his own will. What has he done with it?'

'What can he do with it?' Kin retorted, not severely.

'Help us. He showed that he is capable, yet he prefers his father's methods.'

'It was not Daiki who murdered Kazu. Your father died by Rai's own hand,' Kin replied, a little forcibly. 'Do not make the mistake of thinking him Rai's double. He is not.'

'Why do you defend him?'

Kannushi Masato and Rin were watching them in silence. The priest stepped forward, his hand reaching for Amaya. 'Amaya, Kin may be right. Do not forsake Daiki.'

Amaya looked at her feet. 'So many things to attempt belief in. Daiki Kimura may be the one thing I cannot. However,' she said loudly, as Kin made to speak, 'I will try.'

'That is all we ask.' Kin smiled. 'Kannushi Masato, what was discussed regarding Hiroshi's investigation and the remaining documents?' Kin pressed.

Kannushi Masato broke away from his thoughts. 'Akio has presented a theory to myself and Kenta: it may be Shun who has been in correspondence with Lord Hiroshi, and it was he who was in correspondence with your father, Amaya.'

Amaya sat down heavily. 'That isn't wholly unfeasible. Could it really be? I mean Shun is Rai's first son.'

Kannushi Masato raised his eyebrows. 'In name only.'

'Where is the Imperial Army?' Amaya asked.

Kannushi Masato looked pained. 'The Minister of War has been dispersing the troops throughout Akegata for the last year, as a means of protection, leaving only a few platoons with Shun in the north but now I know there is a different motive behind this.'

'Why?' Amaya probed.

'Because the Minister of War is Rai Kimura.'

Amaya looked at her feet, understanding dawning on her. Before she could speak Kannushi Masato continued.

'Kenta has already been gathering the troops which are spread throughout the country.'

'They won't make it to the north in time,' Amaya said, horrified.

'They can try,' Kin said. 'That is all they can do.'

Amaya felt a terrible helplessness loom over her, casting her thoughts and resolve into its shadow. She shook her head. 'How can Ueten help? This is war. And who am I? I am irrelevant in the face of this.'

'Amaya, do not allow your doubt to steer you. Belief can be blind but you have other senses. Use them. Listen, feel,' Kin gripped her hands. 'If you expect failure that is what you will receive.'

Amaya didn't reply. Instead she pulled her hands from Kin's and walked away, needing solitude. She had expected Kannushi Masato's news to provide answers, not more questions. Certainties not ambiguities.

Amaya woke late the next day, slumped over the table. There was a blanket draped over her shoulders. As she looked up, she saw Rin opposite her. She too was leaning upon the table with a blanket over her. Amaya rose to her feet and stretched. As she ventured through the pagoda, she could not find Kin or Kannushi Masato anywhere. Confused she returned to the room where she had fallen asleep, Rin was alert.

Noon passed and still no body had come, anxiety overpowered her and she decided to risk going to the palace. As she stepped into the woodland, she heard the footsteps of several people. She started to inch back toward the pagoda until they came into view.

Akio, Kin and Kannushi Masato appeared from the leafless trees. She smiled widely and walked to meet them. She made half a movement to reach out to Akio but stopped herself; their faces were grey.

'Come into the pagoda, Amaya,' Akio said, gazing at her.

Her heart fluttered in shallow beats. 'What is wrong?'

'An incident took place last night,' Kin said, as Rin came

into the room, her feet not making a sound.

'Kyo has gone,' Akio said, in a whisper. Amaya stepped back looking from one solemn face to another.

'Gone?' She repeated, her voice cracking.

'He was taken by somebody whilst collating his evidence. He is no longer in Chuto. Kenta had most Censorate soldiers searching the palace and city for him when it was made known he was missing,' Kannushi Masato said.

Amaya was unable to think clearly. 'Where is Rai Kimura?' She demanded.

'He is in the palace,' Akio said, stepping toward her.

'He is using someone else to cover his filthy tracks. Who is suspected of taking Kyo?' Amaya said, her anger rising. She paced forward but found her way blocked by Akio.

'Kyo will not be harmed. I do not believe that is Rai's intentions,' Akio said, in a strong voice. Amaya looked up and found herself trusting his words.

'I want to speak with Kenta,' she continued.

Akio shifted uncomfortably and Amaya saw a scroll in his hands. A strange sense of fear took hold and she spoke more loudly. 'I want to speak with Kenta.'

'You cannot,' Akio said, frowning.

'Why?' Amaya replied, her voice becoming louder still.

'He is no longer in the palace. He is leading the Imperial army and half of the Censorate soldiers to war as we speak,' Akio said, finally handing the scroll to Amaya. 'This is a message from him to you.'

'No! Why did he not tell me himself?' Amaya raged as she broke the seal and unrolled the parchment. Her fury simmered as she read the elegant scripture;

Dear Amaya,

I apologise for not seeing you whilst you were imprisoned. I wanted to see you very much, to explain everything myself. I want you to remain safe and not to worry about your pilgrimage or Ueten. Your future is important. I can picture your face as you read this, so please do not be angry. Your efforts will not be in vain, Amaya, I promise you this.

You will have heard of everything which has occurred, including what was discussed in the assembly. So, you must understand why I have decided to accompany my troops and discover the true nature of everything. I think you will come to understand. There is no more time, and few people I trust.

Hiroshi Katou has died in order to expose and prevent further corruption and I do not wish to be idle and hide whilst his sacrifice goes to waste. My presence may finally lead the rebels to expose themselves. I do not wish to echo my father's actions. I will not be a coward. However, I am a coward for writing you this letter. I would not have been able to tell you the truth about my choice to lead the Imperial Army, it would have been difficult to keep my resolve after seeing you again. I never want to lie to you. That is why I have written this letter.
I will return.

Yours
Kenta

'Coward!' Amaya screamed when she had finished reading the letter. She sat down on the floor heavily and clutched the scroll in her shaking hand. Her breath came short as her worry for Kenta swelled. 'Why could he have not come to see me?'

Akio crouched next to her and she handed him Kenta's letter, he read it quickly. 'You would have asked him to stay, Amaya. That is plain.'

'Of course, I would. He is being reckless.'

'Do you really think so?' Akio said, quietly. Amaya looked up at Akio, his eyes were shining, and she realised how Kenta's departure was affecting him. Suddenly she felt ashamed, selfish.

'Amaya, you are the only person who could have prevented him from leaving. I asked him to reconsider but he was resolute, and his reasoning is honourable,' Akio said, gripping Amaya's hand.

Shaking, she let out an angry noise. 'What if he dies, Akio? What then? Akegata needs him. We need him.'

'He knows this. He has been making this decision for the last month at least, perhaps even before you met him. He does not want to sit in a palace and command people to die. He wants to be there and experience this. Something his father could never find the courage to do. He has called upon the Five Masters to fight beside him. I believe he will come back alive,' Akio added, firmly.

Amaya sat, her thoughts shooting about her mind like stars in the dead of night. 'I understand Kenta's motives. It just angers me that he still feels he must carry the weight of Akegata on his shoulders alone. I will not let him and I know you will not either.'

CHAPTER FOURTEEN

Two days had passed since Kenta's departure. Amaya had read his letter many times and still felt resentful. She remembered the carefree yet reliable side to his nature and it saddened her that he had become so serious and isolated. She recalled how she had called him silly and smiled inwardly. She hadn't spoken much to the others and for this she felt guilty. Amaya had taken to standing on the balcony, which was where she found her thoughts could roam more easily. Her face was cold, her nose numb but she stayed there as her mind wandered. She recounted the vision, the faces she did not recognise and Rai. The pain of the people and the pain Gekai had brought her that night in the mountains felt real. Looking out at the horizon, dawn approached and with it came an overwhelming sense of helplessness. Rin walked onto the balcony, but Amaya did not look at her, instead she spoke, her voice as cold as her face. 'What's the point in being the Prophet of Ueten if I am hindered from using the qualities she possesses?' Amaya said. 'What is the point if I am unable to help those I care about?' She looked down at her hands, her knuckles were white as she gripped the wooden railings. 'What is the point?' She finished.

'I think there is a reason to it all,' Rin said, in her gruff tone. 'The point is you are still free to use this voice and power as you see fit. It is you, not Ueten, or it is both of you; you are the same. You cannot be stopped, not really. You are the Prophet. I do not think anybody wants to stop you, but you have already made your decision I think.'

Amaya replied. 'I have already made my decision.'

'Can I come?' Rin said, in the quietest whisper.

Amaya faced her, surprised. 'You really want to help?'

Rin gave a small nod.

Amaya wrote a detailed note and addressed it to Akio and Kin. She hoped that they would understand everything she needed them to do. She then wrote a second letter solely for Akio. She felt guilty for not seeing him in person and now, finally, understood why Kenta had chosen to write to her. Facing Akio would cause her resolve to waver, leaving him would be impossible.

She and Rin had packed provisions and eaten. Amaya had decided to dress in her dark blue hakama trousers which she tucked into knee-length bearskin boots. The fitted vest and billowing white kimono kept her warm. Finally, she tied her long hair into a loose plait which fell down her back and wrapped her thickest cloak about her. Rin remained in the traditional shinobi outfit of the Kageyama clan; black and indigo.

They left the pagoda and entered the woodland sneaking between the trees. As they reached the temple, they veered off to the right and continued through the wood. They soon reached the edge, where the trees stopped. A pathway, which led to some of the smaller buildings on the palace estate, stretched out in front of them.

'We will have to be quick,' Rin said, looking at the empty path. Amaya gripped her katana and nodded. They broke through the trees and ran. Entering the gardens, they hurried to the perimeter wall and scaled it as they had done when entering the palace grounds nearly a week before. Two guards were to their left, but Rin shook her head vigourously as Amaya prepared to attack. 'We cannot afford for the alarm to be raised. This is the Way of the Shinobi.' She held a finger to her lips and silently drew out wire from the pouch tied about her leg. She pointed to the bridge and proceeded to spin the wire above her head and release it. It did not catch the pre-dawn light; instead it fell in the shadow of the bridge. Amaya understood and pulled out her short tanto dagger. Rin slid along the wire first, Amaya waiting for her signal and then followed. As she made her way over the moat, she had to swallow the new appreciation for the shinobi arts. She could not help but want to learn more.

Once she had reached Rin, they entered the street. It was empty aside from a few feral cats which looked slyly at them before losing interest and sauntering off. 'The shop owners and merchants will be out soon.' Amaya warned.

'We will be gone before they are.' And with only those words Rin broke into a sprint. Amaya followed as closely as possible but Rin seemed to have an imaginary wind behind her. They reached the main gates, and only then did Rin pause. Amaya stared ahead at the wintry vista, the sun now peeking its head above the land, meek and afraid.

'The sun thinks it's too cold,' Amaya said.

'Then it's going to be very dark where we are going,' Rin replied.

Amaya and Rin continued to run for a time before both could run no further.

'The Imperial Army will already be in the Earth Province now. We have to hurry before too much blood is shed,' Amaya panted, enjoying the slow pace.

'What will you do?' Rin asked.

'I will not let this battle be the ruin of Akegata. Every soldier in the rebel army is being used by their leaders, they do not deserve death any more than the Imperial Army troops.'

'They support the cause they fight for, Amaya. Do not be naïve,' Rin said, harshly.

'I know they chose to be in this war. I also know that stopping it now will not prevent another war in the future, but the corruption must be pulled out at the roots,' Amaya finished, trying to catch her breath. 'Those who mean Akegata true harm will want to watch this war unfold. They will want to see Kenta die.'

'I'm not sure I understand.'

'The real aim is to be rid of all the corruption which has spurred this war into action. To be rid of those people who have orchestrated this war for their own selfish goals,' Amaya said, loudly. 'Otherwise, these weeds of war will keep reappearing. I will not give in to Gekai's temptation as Lord Minamori did hundreds of years ago.'

Rin remained silent for a moment, clearly pondering Amaya's idea. 'You do not have all your Elementals,' Rin said, directly.

'I will have to do what I can. I must strong in the face of corruption as many others are. They do not have prophecy but fight a worthy cause.'

'I see. You intend to kill these people, the people fueling this corruption and war?'

'Yes,' Amaya said, without hesitation, surprised at her own words. Rin stared at her and gave a small smile.

Soon they approached the bamboo grove which Amaya had travelled through during the previous summer. Memories of Kin, Shun and Akio came forward and she smiled. The weight of her task then seemed so much lighter now, considering what she was going to find on the road ahead.

'We have to go through a small part of this bamboo grove, Kusamachi is on the other side. That's where we will rest for the night,' Amaya said, stepping forward. Rin nodded and they both entered the forest. The narrow trunks remained verdant, but it was a cold green.

Amaya shivered despite her thick cloak. 'It will snow soon.'

Rin made a sound of agreement. 'Within the next few days.'

Occasionally, the wind knocked the tops of the bamboo together and created a soft hollow echo all about them as they hastened forward. The ground was hard beneath Amaya's boots and the chill began to penetrate the soles before long. The two young women wove between the bamboo careful not to make too much noise and never straying too deep into the grove's depths.

As evening approached Amaya felt comforted by the concealment the darkness offered. The imminence of winter added urgency to Amaya's footsteps.

'Where will we stay?' Rin asked, quietly.

'I have a friend who will accommodate us,' Amaya replied, pushing forward.

They emerged a short while later from the forest and looked ahead; there was a faint glow reflecting on the low clouds. As they rejoined the path and reached the top of the hill, Amaya looked across the darkening land.

'This is Kusamachi?' Rin questioned, gazing at the source of the light. Amaya nodded and began to descend toward the town. They passed through the gates unhindered and joined the late-night wanderers.

'It's a lively town,' Rin commented, as she watched people inside the numerous ryokan and izakaya. Despite the activity, Amaya felt the melancholy of war; its grip affected this small settlement and had been doing so since the Kusamachi battalion fell years ago.

'This is where we will stay tonight.' Amaya ducked under material curtains and entered a familiar place. She could smell fresh noodle soup and smiled at the memory which accompanied the scent; Akio, Kin, Shun and Daiki sitting at the bar eating, chatting, preparing.

'Amaya? Is that you?' A woman spoke, and Amaya was drawn back from her reverie.

'Inari!'

'The Face of Autumn was still upon us the last we saw each other. It is good to see you. I hope your reason for being here is not a bad one.' Inari took Amaya's hand in her own.

'The Imperial Army is what gives me purpose,' Amaya said, directly.

Inari sighed. 'They passed by Kusamachi two days ago now. They are travelling to meet the rebel army.' She gently steered Amaya and Rin towards a secluded table. 'I heard a rumour that the Emperor is with them.'

Amaya nodded.

'Why would he decide on such an unsafe course? The Earth Province is no longer safe. He should leave the war to the General, to Shun.' Inari's gaze was incredulous.

'He wishes to fight, rather than command men to die' Rin said, speaking up for Kenta.

Inari looked at her with kind eyes. 'I have not met you before. What's your name?'

'I am Rin Kageyama.' She bowed low and Inari did the same. A flicker of recognition flashed through Inari's face at the name. 'Of the Kageyama clan, the shinobi who dwell in the mountains of the Fire Province?'

Rin nodded abruptly, but Inari's gaze was without prejudice. 'I am glad to meet you, Rin. Now, you must both be hungry. Please sit and I will bring you some Hiyashi soba.'

Amaya and Rin took a seat on the floor at a low table and enjoyed warming Genmaicha tea whilst Inari prepared them dinner.

'I saw Shun, over three weeks ago now. He joined a platoon here in Kusamachi,' Inari said, as she placed the bowls of steaming soup in front of them.

Amaya looked up quickly at the mention of his name. 'Is he well?'

'Yes. He said you might stop by here at some point.' Inari looked at Amaya. 'He is fond of you, Amaya. You have a good friend in Shun and he seems to know you well,' she looked at Amaya pointedly, 'his guess is correct.'

'We won't be able to stay long, Inari. We intend to leave at dawn. We have to reach the Imperial Army camp,' Amaya said, as she slurped the noodles from the broth.

'I do not know your reasons for following them, but please do not get hurt in this battle. This war is inevitable but your presence in the Court and beside the Emperor is invaluable. Many innocent people have lost their lives, as is the nature if war. Do not let your name lengthen that list.' Inari looked at her sadly. Amaya suddenly remembered how Inari's child and husband had been murdered as a result of the civil war.

'I do not intend to get hurt. I just want to help.'

'That's what you said the last time you were here. I believe you can but only if you are wise when making your decisions. Vigilance, Amaya. Choose your battles, is this really one you want to take part in?' Inari said, as she led the two outside. 'I have something else for you; my horse. Her name is Yona.'

Amaya stared at Inari, an inexplicable gratitude overcoming her. 'Can you really loan us your only horse? You may need it yourself.'

'I wish to aid you in any way I can. Hiyashi soba for dinner and a place to stay for the evening seems like so little in the face of what you are attempting. I was unable to help my family, perhaps I can help you, and through you, help others.' Inari eyes seemed suddenly solemn, and Amaya could see her jaw tighten. 'Yona is not a big horse but you two are not big girls.'

'Thank you, Inari.' Amaya paused as a thought came to her. 'Akio and Kin might stop by here soon. Perhaps later today.'

Inari frowned. 'You did not tell them you were leaving.'

'No. I need you to tell Akio something from me.'

'Of course, I will Amaya, but shouldn't you wait for them?'

Amaya shook her head. 'Would you tell Akio I am sorry and that I understand why Kenta wrote me a letter now. That I could not face him for fear of losing my conviction.'

'I will pass on your message, Amaya..

Rin's impatience overwhelmed her. 'Amaya loves him. They are married.'

Amaya felt her jaw slacken and her eyes grow round. 'Rin.'

Inari laughed. 'I could see the bond between you both the last time you were here. It was a fledging love, but it seems that its strength has grown considerably. You do not have to be shy, Amaya. This is a wonderful thing.'

Amaya stared at the young shinobi and Inari but before she could respond Inari spoke again. 'I will pass on the words you have said. It is your love to share with him. I will not take that from you. Now, we should all rest. You both have a long journey in front of you tomorrow.'

That evening Amaya found that sleep came easily. She had thought that it would evade her, with the task at hand so daunting. However, Rin's statement about Amaya's feelings towards Akio had given her an odd relief. Something, which had been wedged within her unable to find its way out, had been freed by the Fire Elemental's brusque approach. Just as sleep stole her consciousness her stomach gave a flutter of delight and a part of her hoped that Akio would catch up to them.

'You laughed in your sleep, you know,' Rin said, over their hasty breakfast of miso and rice. Her small face was shrouded in suspicion. Amaya kept the bowl by her mouth a moment longer to conceal her grin.

Inari walked over to them, a small package in her hands. 'Something for the road and Yona is prepared.'

They walked out into the early light. Kusamachi was still asleep, not a soul walked about but Amaya knew the merchants and farmers would soon be stirring. 'Thank you, Inari,' Amaya said, pulling herself onto Yona. Rin sprang up behind her, her strong hands gripping each other about Amaya's waist.

'Just take care.' She patted Amaya's leg and offered Rin a smile. 'Look after each other.'

They waved farewell to Inari and led Yona from the stable. Trotting down the main street, the sound of Yona's hooves echoed from the still dwellings. As they passed through the northern gates, a large black and gold lacquer palanquin approached, flanked with guards who were not donned in either imperial or rebel attire, yet they each carried a katana. Amaya recognised the mon emblazoned upon the breasts of the men; an avenue of trees with a sun looming over their tops. It was the crest of the Ito Merchants Guild. The palanquin itself was adorned with brass mountings and beautiful paintings depicting children playing throughout the four seasons, and upon the door was the same crest which the men bore upon their garments. Amaya leant out abruptly and rapped on the door of the palanquin as it passed them. The men in front yelled out and turned to Amaya, drawing their katana.

'Get away from there. What do you think you are doing?' The guard shouted, angrily. Amaya knocked again on the door.

Rin grabbed her hand roughly, disbelief flashing through her eyes. 'What are doing, Amaya? You do know that the person inside is a member of the Ito Merchants Guild, are you trying to get us killed?' Rin glanced at the extravagant palanquin and swallowed.

Amaya wrenched her arm from Rin's grip. 'I'm finding out some information.'

The red silk curtain twitched slightly, and a refined woman gazed out disdainfully. Her shining black hair was elaborately decorated with a kanzashi comb, silk flowers and jade hairpins. She had on several layers of fine fabric; a noble's kimono. Her face was a clear cream and her dark eyes were symmetrically painted in colours which matched her other gold and green adornments.

'Who are you?' The woman's voice was quiet yet commanding.

'I am Amaya Takeda,' Amaya and Rin bowed their heads. 'I apologise for my brazen approach.'

'I am Mari Ito.'

This woman was not only a member of the Ito Merchants Guild, she was its founder.

'So, you are Amaya Takeda,' Mari continued, leaning forward in sudden interest. 'A young genius who works for the

Guild has told me much about you. Please raise your heads, both of you.'

'Do you happen to mean Tomio Umeda?' Amaya said, happily.

The woman nodded. 'Yes, Tomio is a very gifted young man, an asset to the Guild. I am sure there are some in palace who are frustrated in my enlisting him to the Guild. Now, why are you here knocking on my palanquin door?'

'It was Tomio I wished to enquire after. If he is well and where he is?' Amaya said.

'Tomio is currently assembling the Imperial Army's defence, I have just travelled from their camp. Tomio insisted on being present.' The woman scowled, 'I would prefer his brains to be safe and guarded but he was adamant to remain with the Emperor.'

'Did he succeed?' Amaya questioned, delicately.

Mari narrowed her eyes. 'As much as he and the rest of the innovators within the Guild could manage. They have done well considering how little time they had. Tomio proved to be invaluable. It was very wise of His Majesty to nominate him and very prudent of my partners to accept him.'

'Where are they camped?' Amaya asked, cautiously.

'Why are you asking such a thing? You cannot go there; they are too near the border now. Rikujou is no longer under Imperial rule.' She smiled slightly and Amaya bowed at the carefully veiled information.

'Thank you, Mari Ito.'

'I cannot imagine what for. Now, look after yourself and that spirit of yours. I do not believe that this is where your journey ends. You are only just exploring what you can offer Akegata.' With those words Mari clapped her hands and the men picked up the palanquin and proceeded.

Amaya stood back as the curtains closed. She admired the power this woman had and was eager to meet with her again. She and Rin watched as the carriage entered Kusamachi and went out of sight. Knowing that Tomio would be at the camp lightened Amaya's heart. She had not seen Tomio since her departure with Akio 'You will soon meet my Earth Elemental,' Amaya said, over her shoulder.

'Tomio? The person she mentioned?'

'Yes. He saved my life once, as you did.'

'Are you always in need of help?' Rin laughed.

'Only since my identity was revealed to me.' Amaya sighed.

The mountains to their left marked their progress as they rode on; they were now nearing the border to the Earth Province. They approached the edge of the forest of beech trees Amaya had travelled through on her last journey north. She stopped. 'As we make our way through this forest, we will come across the Dao River. That is where I first met the foreigner who transported the Firearms into this country. If we take a ferry down the river, we will reach Rikujou earlier, but it may be a risk,' Amaya said.

'I do not think we will encounter them. The Firearms may have already reached the rebel army. The sooner we reach Rikujou and locate the Imperial Army's camp the better,' Rin replied.

'The Firearms were also in the Fire Province,' Amaya pondered.

'In both the Earth and Fire Provinces,' Rin replied.

Amaya felt a frown descend upon her brow. 'That's strange. Why store them in the Fire Province? They would have to smuggle them through the Sky Province, and even if they used the sea and transported them by boat, the waters around Kyoshima and Teishima are dangerous.'

The further they travelled the colder it became and Amaya was surprised at the noticeable drop in temperature. The cries of winter animals shivered through the trees as they walked deeper into the forest, and in the distant mountains, Amaya heard the faintest shriek of the red-crowned crane.

'Do you hear that?' Rin said, pausing and holding up

her hand for silence. Amaya strained and heard a faint gurgle of water. She nodded and the two continued, following the sound. The noise of the water grew louder, until eventually they reached a frothing brook. Amaya dipped her hands in and felt a current of warm water.

'I think this may be the same stream which I followed to the Dao River the last time I was here,' Amaya said, dipping her hands in once more, enjoying the heat.

'If we hurry, we may reach Rikujou tonight. It is only just noon,' Rin said, peering through the bare canopy. 'Also, this is Shizukawa shinobi territory.' She looked about, uneasy. 'The Hidden River Village could be close by and we wouldn't be aware of it. I would not like to meet shinobi from that clan in their territory, it would not end well for us.'

Amaya and Rin continued into the afternoon, following the small tributary. The sound of a much larger body of water reached their ears and as they broke through the trees, they saw the secret pontoon in the distance. Amaya remembered the foreigner's boat and the masses of cargo which the men had been loading onto it. This thought led her to the bandits who had attacked the ship. She scoured the banks as far as she could see; there was no movement and it seemed Rin had not detected anything either. A large ferry was moored to the pontoon in plain sight. Amaya squeezed Yona's muscular sides and she trotted forward, down the incline to the pontoon. They dismounted and paced to the boatman.

Amaya bowed to a man who was sitting near the boarding plank. 'Are you taking passengers?'

He looked up at the two girls and the horse. 'I am but it will be extra for your horse. Where are you going? My boat goes to the coast,' he said, blowing out a plume of smoke as he puffed on a carved pipe.

'Our destination is Rikujou, so we do not need passage as far as the coast. Will it be possible to alight earlier?' Amaya questioned.

The man's face darkened. 'Rikujou? That's not a place

you should be travelling to, young lady. It is only because of the Ito Merchants Guild's presence that the townsfolk are still safe. Even so, the rebel army occupy that city entirely now and are making entrance very difficult,' he stood as another person approached. Amaya turned to face the stranger whose eyes were concealed by the shadow his hood cast. She could still see his mouth and he smiled at them. 'My destination is the coast, sir.' His voice was smooth with a slight gruff lilt.

'Very well, I will stop as near to Rikujou as is safe and then continue on to the coast.'

'Thank you,' Amaya said, paying the fee and boarding the boat with Rin. The other man paid his fare and joined them. Yona was led below deck, to a straw laden hold. The ferryman took the helm and as the wind picked up the boat sped away from the pontoon.

'Last time I travelled on this river we were attacked by bandits,' Amaya said, anxiously.

'I haven't seen any bandits for the last few weeks. Which boat did you travel on? It can't have been mine.'

Amaya faltered. 'A cargo ship. We were lucky to secure passage.'

Rin glanced at her and her eyes held a warning. Amaya looked across the river and fell silent.

The man sat behind them turned to face her. 'A cargo ship?'

'Yes,' Amaya said, keeping her voice clipped. She sighed quietly and watched the water gush against the side of the boat.

As the sun arched over them and began its descent, the light reflected dazzlingly on the river's surface. She squinted and saw a small wooden platform ahead.

'This is where you leave us,' the ferryman said, slowing next to the bank and opening the gate in the railings. 'Watch yourselves.' He lowered the wooden bridge and stood aside.

They turned to face the steep rocky path which would eventually lead them to Rikujou. They had only climbed partway when Amaya glanced back. The Dao River weaved, snake-like, out of sight, the ferry already a small dark mass in the distance, vanishing around the corner.

CHAPTER FIFTEEN

Rikujou spread out before them; a dark mass on the land, pin-pricked with the odd light. The sun was past the horizon but the ghost of it's light lingered in the sky.

'Wait a moment,' Amaya said, suddenly, as they approached. 'There will be guards from the rebel army.'

'They are already aware of us. Someone is coming,' Rin replied, and a moment later a voice reached them on the evening wind. To their right a patrolman approached. Amaya noted his outfit, it was one of battle, but it did not bare the Imperial mon.

'He's shinobi dressed in the rebel attire,' Rin whispered, disconcertedly.

'Who are you?' He demanded.

'Travellers who are seeking a room in Rikujou,' Amaya said.

'A curfew is in place. The gates of Rikujou are closed,' he stated.

'Will you not let two girls in to find a place to sleep? There are bandits in the nearby mountains.' Amaya eyed the guard.

He remained silent for a moment. 'What are your names?' He asked. Amaya said the first name that entered her mind.

'Megumi Izumi.'

'Umi Katou,' Rin said, her voice far more feminine than Amaya had heard before. The guard paused for a moment, scrutinizing them. Then he nodded and waved his hand, allowing them to pass.

'Get into a guest house now. Guards patrol the streets and won't be as sparing as me.'

Bowing low in thanks, they scurried through the gates into Rikujou.

Amaya felt claustrophobic as she and Rin strode along the main street. It was silent and almost all the houses were dark inside. Amaya recalled the busy town, full of energy despite the rebel army's nearby presence. Now, the mood had been thoroughly depressed with the soldiers' arrival. Ahead she could see the magnificent shrine. She continued right up to the entrance and paused, looking at the main building. It towered high, even above the pagodas around it. It was the central force in Rikujou and it still awed Amaya. She looked to the side and wondered if the Firearms had been moved from this holy place.

They continued on towards Goro's ryokan. Sliding the door open, they revealed a dimly lit, chilled entrance. A single bell sounded, a brief silence ensued and then an old man limped around the corner. His face was bruised and beaten.

Amaya gasped, she barely recognised him. 'Goro!'

He studied her for a moment and realisation swept across his face. 'Amaya Takeda!' He rushed forward and bowed. 'It has been some time. Please, come in.'

Amaya and Rin inclined their heads and followed Goro to a room. It was smaller than the one she had stayed in on her last visit.

'Why have you returned to Rikujou? Especially after what happened to you when you were last here,' Goro said, anxiously.

Amaya looked at his battered face. It pained her to watch him try and smile through his grimaces. 'What happened, Goro?'

'The rebel army. This is just a scratch.' He indicated to his injuries. 'Public floggings and beatings are a kindness; a lot of folk have been killed. It is too dangerous for you to be here, Lady Amaya.'

'Whilst I am staying in Rikujou I am called Megumi Izumi, and my friend is Umi Katou.'

Goro looked at Rin and bowed again. 'I understand.'

'We have some questions to ask you.'

Goro looked at her and nodded. 'Please, go ahead, I will answer them as well as I can.' He gestured them to follow him. Leading them into a small kitchen he poured tea.

'Goro, where is the Imperial Army camped?' Amaya decide it was best to ask directly.   The old ryokan owner stammered. 'Why would you want to know that?' His eyes were wide and fearful.

'I know they are on the border. I must see the Emperor,' Amaya said.

'So, it is true, His Majesty did travel with the Imperial Army.' Goro's eyes glazed for a moment as he thought. Rin sipped her tea loudly.

'Goro, do you know where the camp is?'

'Yes.' He stopped, hesitating.

Amaya leant forward, awaiting the answer. 'Tell me.'

Finally, Goro let out a deep breath and spoke as if against his better judgement. 'The camp is a few miles west of Rikujou, in the Seishin no Tani.'

'The Valley of the Spirits?' Amaya said, aloud, certain that there was some significance to the location, but she could not fathom what.

'You will not reach it before the battle begins. They plan to fight at dawn. That is why Rikujou is so quiet,' Goro said, sipping his tea.

'Dawn?' Amaya said, shocked.

'Yes, the rebel army has already started to move. The Imperial Army have only just managed to arrange themselves and there are still troops which have not reached the Earth Province yet. I hear that it is mostly the mounted Imperial Archers who have yet to join with the rest of the army.'

Amaya shook her head in disbelief.

Rin looked at her and spoke, as if she had heard Amaya's

thoughts. 'Amaya, we cannot leave tonight. We will leave at dawn. That is the best we can do. Whether we leave now or at dawn makes little difference, the war will begin before we reach the camp.'

Amaya lowered her head, she secretly agreed with Rin but her worry for Kenta consumed her reason.

After a while, sipping tea in silence, Amaya spoke. 'We leave just before dawn.' Amaya's tone was final and neither Rin nor Goro argued.

Amaya woke as the glow of the sun was slowly illuminating the sky in pinks and palest orange from beneath the horizon.

'May I come in? I have brought you something to eat and drink.' Goro's voice came from behind the door as he knocked.

'Yes, come in,' Amaya said, looking around. 'Have you seen my companion?'

Goro placed the tray on the low table and scratched his head. 'She said she would be back shortly.' Goro bowed and left the room. Amaya sat on the floor at the table and gazed out of the window. The immensity of her task loomed in the stillness and she knew that once the sun had broken clear of the horizon the battle would begin.

Rin entered the room, her footsteps making almost no sound against the tatami.

Amaya looked up at her. 'We have to hurry.'

'I bought some more weaponry and things which may be useful,' Rin said, throwing her a bag. Amaya looked inside and smiled, there were pellets of dried food, special tea, wire, blades ranging in size and more shuriken.

'Thank you for coming with me,' Amaya's gratitude was quiet but felt with every fibre.

'I am learning a great deal. I am even growing to enjoy your company,' Rin replied. Amaya thought she could see amusement behind the brash stoic expression on the young shinobi's face. They ate and drank without speaking.

'Thank you, Goro. We will be careful,' Amaya said, looking at the old man's sad face. 'Goro, Akio and Kin may pass through here.'

'You have a message?'

Amaya smiled gratefully. 'Could you instruct them to go straight to the Air Province, to Shiroshi.'

Goro looked surprised. 'Shiroshi?'

'Amaya, if you are so sure that the truth lies in the Air Province, why do you not go straight there yourself?' Rin asked Amaya as they slowed to a walk. Yona's breath issued in plumes, her nostrils flared with exertion.

'I have to be certain that Kenta is well. He cannot die here. I cannot allow him to enter this battle. Kenta's skills in combat are indisputable but without either Shun or Akio by his side, I fear for his survival. Something feels amiss about his involvement; it is too orchestrated, too exposed. He is extremely important to the future of Akegata.'

'You really believe that?'

'I believe it deeply, spiritually.' Amaya reflected on the meaning behind her own words. 'Ueten feels it.'

Rin sighed and leant back. 'So, it seems.'

Amaya stared forward and the Face of Winter stared back; its eyes open in the north, it's gaze creeping south. Suddenly Yona gave a start and, at the same time, Rin whispered, 'another horse is approaching.'

Amaya turned slightly as the sound of hooves reached her ears. The man was travelling a little faster than them but there was no urgency in his stride. Amaya pulled Yona to the side, allowing him to pass. As he did, Amaya watched him. Her mouth fell open. 'The man who was on the ferry with us!' She exclaimed, watching him grow smaller as he sped away. 'I thought the coast was his destination.'

'Do you think he is heading to the camp?' Rin questioned, her eyes on the man who was now a dark shadow in the distance.

'Why else would anybody be travelling this way?'

She squinted. The sun was now appearing. Dawn had arrived, and with it, war.

CHAPTER SIXTEEN

Amaya heard the camp long before she saw any sign of it. The unmistakable clash of katana dispersed with the loud, obtrusive cracks only a Firearm could make. The bangs echoed from the sides of Seishin no Tani; the valley walls acting like a drum. Amaya felt tears suddenly gush and tumble down her cheeks. They were tears of anger and vengeance, desperation and sadness. She urged Yona forward. The camp would be close by and she hoped that Kenta was stationed there; observing, not fighting.

'Amaya,' Rin said, quietly, squeezing her around the waist. Amaya realised that her tears had been flying from her cheeks and Rin must have felt them. Her skin stung as the wind whipped them away. She didn't speak, she feared her voice would break and she would not be able to stop her tears. She flinched as another series of cracks rendered the air, and grunted in frustration, willing the animal beneath her to go even quicker. Yona obliged and Amaya held on tightly against the wind.

As they breached the hill Amaya let out an audible noise, caught between relief and sorrow. The camp was before them. It was positioned expertly; above the Seishin no Tani at the mouth of a shallow incline; the enemy would be funneled in an attack and were also disadvantaged by the gradient. The camp's location was both easily retreated to and defended. Amaya gazed further into the valley and saw the soldiers clashing. The men, black dots upon the blanched green writhed together in a frenzy. Like a shoal of fish in a roiling ocean, katana blades flashed and glimmered; interspersed with sparks of the ignited gunpowder and delayed blasts. But it was the war cries, screams and yells of the men that caused Amaya's heart to beat heavily. She had never heard a man make such a noise.

The odd sensation she had felt that morning erupted in her chest. The grief which seemed to join her blood with every beat of her heart was enhanced by the scene that was spread out before her. Ueten's despair was her despair, her tears were Ueten's. She could smell the blood and sweat, taste the metal and gunpowder as she gazed down, horrified. Each shriek was a mother losing a son, a sister losing a brother, a wife losing a husband. Each life extinguished like so many lanterns. A blanket of death and slaughter covered the beautiful Seishin no Tani, turning the faded terrain scarlet before her eyes.

'Amaya!' Rin yelled, breaking Amaya's trance. Without hesitating Amaya kicked Yona into a gallop.

Before they reached the camp, they were approached by Censorate soldiers. Amaya clumsily dismounted Yona, Rin following.

'My name is Amaya Takeda. I am here to see His Majesty.' Amaya looked up into the soldier's confused face.

'Amaya?' A familiar voice sounded. Amaya turned quickly and her face broke into a watery smile. Stepping out from the nearest and largest tent beside the camp entrance, came Tomio. She rushed at him and grabbed his hand affectionately. His boyishness was beginning to flicker, giving way to reserved maturity. Amaya reached up and patted his lengthening hair. His discomfort at being around war and bloodshed was clear to Amaya and it sent waves through Ueten. 'Tomio, you are safe.'

'Amaya, why have you come to this place? Please do not be mistaken, I am so glad to see you, but it is too dangerous for you to be here.' Tomio bowed his head respectfully and as he rose, his eyes fell upon Rin.

'Tomio, this is Rin Kageyama. She is-.'

'An Elemental, from the Kageyama clan,' Tomio finished, raising his eyebrows excitedly.

Amaya nodded. 'She has been my companion from Chuto and has helped me many times before that. Rin, this is Tomio. He is my Earth Elemental and a new member of the Ito Merchants Guild. He saved my life in Rikujou.'

Rin bowed to Tomio but did not take her eyes from his. 'It is this person who Lady Ito referred to as the 'genius'?'

Amaya nodded. 'Tomio, how has your time with the Guild been?'

'It is very hard but that is because there has been no time to prepare. I properly studied a Firearm for the first time a month ago, the one you took during your time in Rikujou. I have been working on a defence ever since then. There are some very clever minds in the Guild, and I am eager to explore my inventions and designs.'

'Tomio, where is Lord Kenta?' Amaya asked the burning question with trepidation. Tomio did not respond immediately and Amaya bit back a groan.

'He is down there, in the Seishin no Tani.' Tomio tilted his head in the direction of the valley. Amaya turned slowly and faced the sun which was throwing its light upon the perpetually warring soldiers. The same light consumed the shadows and glinted from tears which distorted the vista before her.

'Come inside the tent, Lady Amaya. You should not watch.' Tomio's voice was soft, it had a new deepness to it, similar to Kyo's. She allowed him to show her into the tent. Rin followed slowly.

'I will fetch you some food, but it might not be palatable.'

'Just some water will be fine.'

He nodded and ducked out of the tent leaving Amaya and Rin alone. Amaya took in a deep, shaking breath and calmed herself. She could feel Ueten churning within her more than she ever had before. *Or perhaps it is the unease of my own spirit, or are they he same.*

'Amaya, can you feel Ueten?' Rin asked. She was staring at Amaya, her face creased in distress.

'Yes.'

'So can I,' Rin said, sitting down. 'This war should never have blotted Akegata's history.'

Amaya looked at her and nodded. 'I need to find my Water Elemental. I need to be able to reach the people of Akegata. If I can't, I have failed.'

'You have not failed, Amaya,' Tomio said, as he re-entered the tent.

Rin looked up at him before facing Amaya again. 'He is right. You could not have done more than you have.'

'You have had people trying to prevent you from your task, trying to wear you down. Yet you have found three of the four Elementals.'

'If logic and experience is to be followed the remaining Elemental will be in the Water Province.' Amaya ran a hand over her eyes, hoping that the person she sought would appear.

'You have found yourself here for a reason, Amaya,' Tomio said, his voice kind. 'Are you not supposed to be shirking this doubt you harbour?'

Amaya exhaled. 'I am trying. Then I think of my brother,' she could not continue and so asked a different but still unwelcome question. 'Tomio, will Kenta return here to camp?'

'Yes, he will return to camp at dusk. They will not fight through the night.' Tomio's voice was steady and confident but Amaya could sense his unease. She felt no need to draw it from him.

'Have you seen General Shun?' Amaya asked, concern and interest forming.

Tomio frowned. 'I have not seen the General since I arrived. Some say he left for the Air Province. Others say he died. That is just hearsay. I have searched the fallen each day whilst arranging their burials.'

Amaya felt a hideous jolt at the image of Shun's corpse piled alongside the others. 'Thank you for taking care of the dead, Tomio.' She placed a hand on his arm.

'I refuse to leave our men to the carrion birds and so I do what that families of the fallen cannot. I must make sure the General is alive. If all the samurai believed their master dead, then morale would suffer. In the face of Firearms, the men need encouragement. However, the rumour he is no longer here persists.'

'So, the General of the Imperial Army is not in the battle?' Rin said, incredulously. 'Who is leading and commanding the men?'

'His Majesty, Kenta Yamashima, is,' Amaya replied, wishing the fact were not true.

Amaya's patience seemed to evaporate. She could not grow accustomed to the sounds of the Firearms and still flinched with every savage shot. Maintaining her composure was all she could manage as Ueten stirred within her. She did not understand what to do but Amaya felt that the Spirit of the Heavens was trying to communicate something to her. Rin had been out to view the battle several times, accompanied by Tomio but did not share what she had seen with Amaya. The young shinobi seemed awed by the Earth Elemental's earnest nature, his sure-footedness, his willingness to help despite his innate disapproval of war.

Amaya felt ashamed. She was the Assistant Master to the Seishin no Ken style, the katana technique being used by the soldiers below. She should not waver in the face of such dishonourable weapons. As she rose to her feet, a soft drumming sounded on the roof of the tent and all about. She left and stepped into cold sleet. Looking out across the camp, she caught sight of the man she recognised from the ferry. He was in conversation with a few men, all their backs to Amaya. She removed her gaze from them, the cold sun was nearing the horizon and the rain was thick with the smell of blood. Amaya looked to her left, where the wounded were brought back for treatment. She walked towards the writhing people wanting to help but knowing she would just hinder the physicians. It did not escape her attention that almost all injuries were made by Firearms. She remained on the fringes of the growing mass of soldiers and doctors as other men helped pull them into the largest tent Amaya had seen so far. The wounded were arriving quicker than they could be seen to.

Bending down next to a man whose pain prevented even a scream, she placed a hand on his head. *I want to help him. I want to help them all.* She couldn't see where the laceration was, but blood smeared every inch of his skin and he smelt rotten. However, the eyes that peered through the red were terrified. He was young, perhaps her age. As she stroked his matted and bloody hair the horror in his eyes began to deplete. 'I am so sorry this has happened to you.' Amaya whispered to him. 'I will help ensure that no one else has to suffer this fate.'

A ghost of a smile tugged at his bloodied mouth. He could not speak, instead he raised his hand and gripped hers against his cheek.

'Here.' She began dabbing at the blood with her free hand. Despite his silence, Amaya could feel his underlying fear, it made her nauseous and continued to swell the more he looked at her. Something in his gaze softened. Was it relief she saw? Or perhaps resignation? She couldn't be sure. Instead, she held his hand and he held hers until quite suddenly his fingers slackened and his arm thudded to the wet ground with a muffled splash.

Death blossomed around Amaya and the vengeance she felt regarding her father's demise grew with each soldier's last breath. A surge of hate and desperation overwhelmed her, she wanted to run into the Seishin no Tani and join the soldiers, find Kenta, to somehow stop the bloodshed. She gripped the hilt of her katana and wrestled with her desire. Releasing an anguished groan, she relinquished her grasp on Meiyo and walked away from the wounded, the rain pouring down her neck and beneath her cloak. There, hanging above the valley of fighting men, was a rainbow. It was peculiar to behold, out of season. All in Akegata knew that rainbows were harbingers of bad luck. She had followed that belief, until she had read The Legend of Ueten and Gekai. Now, all she could see in the rainbow were Ueten's tears cascading from above.

The sound of men falling back and of the skirmish subsiding spurred Amaya on. She stumbled forward in the direction of the track, which led down to the valley. As she walked, she glanced down about her feet and realised that she was striding through rows and mounds of dead bodies. Old blood, which looked black in the waning light, stained the ground. The deceased were respectfully covered, so she could not tell if she recognised any of them. She knew that more dead bodies lined the grass of the Seishin no Tani and that the valley may become their grave. She wondered how many heads had been claimed already. Unable to stem the retch the gripped her throat, she held a hand to her nose to stem the worsening stench. She felt herself stagger and then fall to the bloody ground.

Amaya's head was pounding as she opened her eyes. She thought it was that which had woken her. Looking up, her eyes becoming less blurred she realised that she was in a tent. Its ceiling was a deep green with golden chrysanthemums embroidered across the surface. She turned her head and met a pair of gentle, kind eyes. Kenta's expression was serious. Blood and dirt splattered his elegant face and armour, and the smell of war was still on him, but he was not dead.

'Amaya?' His voice was urgent as he placed a tender hand on her brow. She looked up at him; the relief which extinguished her worry came as a muffled cry.

She stretched up her hand and placed it on his cheek. 'I'm glad you are back safely, dear friend.'

'You worried me, Amaya. I found you on the path next to the dead.' Kenta did not finish. He took a breath and issued a pained smile. 'Amaya, why did you come?' Kenta's tone was not unkind, it was filled with concern and care.

'How can you ask that? I had to be sure you were safe, Kenta. Ueten has been more active recently, I cannot ignore it. You are too important to die here. You must not go out to battle again, Kenta. Did you see the rainbow? Ueten weeps over this war.' A flash of the vision she had experienced in the Hidden Mountain Village crashed nastily into her mind bringing with it a stark image; Kenta's corpse. 'Please,' she implored.

Kenta fell silent, his hand still in Amaya's. 'I understand what you say, Amaya, but I am important here. Shun is away but the troops have their Emperor alongside them. They are fighting with such honour. If I were to sit out now, imagine how that would affect the men.' He gestured beyond the tent entrance. 'And Tomio's invention has greatly improved our defence.' Kenta stood back to show the armour he was wearing; it was reinforced with metal plates, unlike any armour Amaya had seen. The lamellar leather was almost entirely covered in bronze and gold plates. Kenta then pointed with his free hand to a large shield-like instrument which was resting against the tent wall. Amaya flinched at the dents and near-holes the Firearms had caused in its broad surface.

'You said Shun is away. Where?'

Kenta stole a glance behind him, but the tent was empty. 'He requested to travel to the Air Province. He believes something is afoot. Amaya,' Kenta shifted closer to her, 'he is the one who was in correspondence with your father years ago. He was the one who has been working with Lord Hiroshi and your brother. Shun has been helping since the beginning.'

The surprise Amaya expected did not surface. 'He believes as I do. The root is in the Air Province. The second leader perhaps.'

Kenta nodded. 'He does. He wishes to discover the truth.'

'But at what cost, Kenta?' Amaya sat up, clutching her hands in front of her bent knees. She looked at Kenta's exhausted face when he didn't answer. 'Where is Rin? The girl I came with.'

'If you mean the Kageyama girl, I believe she is with Tomio. Where is Akio and Kin?'

Amaya hesitated, 'I left the palace with Rin. I left a note before I went.'

'Amaya, they will be devastated. You should not have left in such a manner. Akio is your husband.'

'You left us in the same way,' Amaya retorted. She inwardly chastised herself for speaking so rudely to Kenta. 'I apologise.'

'You are right, Amaya, but I know I would not have been able to leave if I had seen you. I could not have left you isolated. I trust Akio; he is my best friend. The only comfort I had when I left was that he was with you. He will protect you better than any other.'

'I understand why you left in the manner you did. Do not do such a thing again.'

Kenta closed his eyes with a smile. 'How can I deny a direct request from you?'

'Kenta, I believe there will be trouble from the Fire Province.'

Kenta raised his eyebrows, his grin gone. 'The Fire Province? Arata Tozen is here now, shall I fetch him. If it is urgent, he must hear of your news.'

'No!' Amaya said, more loudly than she meant. 'I believe the Fire Province to be under the control of Rai Kimura.'

Kenta shook his head in disbelief. 'That man, he was travelling with us as far as Rikujou. How could he be sending orders from here?'

Amaya thought of her brother. 'Was Kyo's evidence ever found?'

'No, all of it was taken. Half of Hiroshi Katou's documents remain but not enough. This is why Shun has left. He wishes to retrieve your brother and bring an end to this.'

'Your Majesty.' A voice sounded from outside the tent,

'Master Akio Izumi and Kin Sanjo are here. They request entry.'

'Let them in,' Kenta said, rising to his feet.

Amaya stood too, her heart suddenly struggling against itself as she heard Akio's voice beyond the tent entrance. Kin appeared first, his long holy staff nearly touching the ceiling. He beamed at Amaya, kindness and understanding in his gaze, and removed his conical hat. Akio entered, his black eyes first meeting Kenta's, relief filling them. Then they found Amaya. For a moment Akio did not move. Amaya studied his face carefully, trying to understand the expression it bore. She felt a pang of sorrow as she recognised, amidst the allayment, disappointment. Amaya knew then that her secret departure had deeply hurt him.

That evening, Akio, Kin and Kenta exchanged their news. Amaya, Tomio and Rin listened intently and delivered their own. However, Amaya found her thoughts meandering. She would watch Kenta's animated face but could not keep her eyes from drifting to Akio. She had not had a moment alone with him to explain herself. He had shown interest in what she had to say but Amaya could sense his upset behind his outwardly talkative demeanour. Akio was listening as Kenta addressed the group. He lifted his face and met Amaya's gaze. She mustered all her emotion and hoped he could see the apology in her eyes. He stared for a moment, so intensely that she almost looked away. Then he smiled and his expression relaxed, he gave a small nod and mouthed his understanding. Amaya felt somewhat satisfied but still wanted to express herself aloud. She needed him to hear her say it. Rin's blunt statement, which so concisely described Amaya's feelings, seemed strangely adequate in its simplicity.

'So, Amaya, you believe the answers regarding the civil war lie entirely in the Air Province?' Kenta questioned, bringing her out of her thoughts.

Amaya sat up straight on being addressed. 'Yes, I do. The rebel army did not gather in the Earth Province, they grouped in the Air Province initially. This leads me to believe that the truth is there.'

'Gekai was the catalyst of war and corruption before, he is the whisper in the ears of weak-minded people now. He is the puppeteer of the easily manipulated and the saboteur of purity. Have you laid aside your own doubt, vengeance and resentment?' Kin asked. His staff lay across his lap, his hands were clasped together.

Amaya dropped her head. 'Can one ever truly break free of those things entirely? How can one achieve balance with all facets?'

Kin nodded sagely. 'That is wisdom from the Prophet.'

'Akio and you both believe there is more to come from the Fire Province,' Kenta said.

'Which means that corruption is here, in this very camp. It seems we cannot escape it. If that is the case, I strongly advise you to return to Chuto,' Akio said to Kenta.

'You know that is the single thing I cannot do, Akio.'

'You must. I do not mean as an escape from battle, I mean for you to prevent catastrophe befalling Chuto. This battle here at the Seishin no Tani may well be a distraction, from any number of things. If what Amaya and I believe means anything, then the Sky Province may be attacked by the rebels hidden in the Fire Province. You are needed in the capital, Kenta.'

The Emperor was quiet, Amaya could see his thoughts working furiously; forming and discarding solutions. Eventually he nodded, growling in frustration. 'I cannot have the capital attacked during my absence. I will return but I will have my reasons explained to my men here. I will have to take several platoons with me. The Imperial archers should arrive here tomorrow, but I will also take some back with me.'

'I have not heard from my uncle, Jiro Takeda. He may be able to shed some light on the situation,' Amaya said. 'I am also concerned for his safety.'

'Would he be able to offer us a safe house in which to stay?' Tomio questioned.

'That is my hope,' Amaya replied. 'If we can reach Shiroshi.'

'You will all be accompanying Amaya to the Air Province in a few days,' Kenta said, looking at Tomio, Rin and Kin. He then turned to Akio. 'Would you be willing to travel with them also? I am unable to go myself.' Kenta could not conceal the pain which was stark in his eyes. Amaya realised he longed to go with her but every time he was prevented from doing so, he was chained to his duty as she was to hers.

Akio nodded. 'You do not even have to ask.'

It was deep night when the group dispersed and went to their own tents. Rin, despite herself, seemed taken with Tomio. His ideas intrigued her, and she discussed the various inventions she had wanted to make for the Kageyama when she became Doyen. Amaya felt the agony which Rin was consumed by; she would never assume leadership of her clan. Amaya smiled to herself as she watched Tomio engage Rin in conversation. He somehow weathered the shinobi's passion, calming it, channeling it until words flowed unhindered. Continuous vigilance was a permanent disposition within the Kageyama but Tomio seemed to dissipate it, encouraging more smiles than frowns to cross Rin's petit face.

Amaya left them to their discussions and sought the comfort of her own tent. The silence of the night was drastically different from the sounds which had clamoured through the air during the day. The smell was the same, and this fact did not let Amaya forget the horrific things she had witnessed. A sudden flash of images blurted through her mind causing her to stagger slightly. As she steadied herself realisation stirred within her; she had seen this battle previously, there was something harrowingly familiar about it. That night in the Kageyama Hidden Mountain village, the images she had seen had been of *this* battle. She remembered the location; the Seishin no Tani, a valley she hadn't recognised. Ueten had warned her and she had failed to understand the message and convey it before the Imperial Army had departed. Holding a hand to her forehead she entered her tent. It smelt of the cinnamon incense which burned in the corner and the simple brazier warmed her.

She pulled out the tie holding her plait and shook her black hair loose. It still smelt faintly of lotus flower and tatami reeds. The black waves fell about her face and down her back as she placed the tie upon the small table. She slipped her bearskin boots from her feet and was loosening her hakama trousers when a guard announced an arrival.

'Lady Amaya, Lord Izumi is here and wishes to speak with you.'

Amaya re-tightened her hakama. 'Yes, come in.'

Akio entered slowly, the tent entrance fell back into place, blocking the moon. She looked at him, her hands clasped together in front of her chest. She thought of the hurt in his eyes and wanted to console him. He remained where he was and looked at her, with the same intensity he had done earlier that evening.

'Akio, my husband, I am sorry.' Amaya didn't finish what she had been hoping to say. In a few strides Akio had closed the gap between them. His hands cupped her face and he lowered his lips to hers. Amaya did not resist. She found her own hands lifting, his hair between her fingers.

All the comfort Akio had offered since she had first met him in the Archives came to her at once. Her grief and joy collided, and she felt hot tears fill her eyes. She blinked them free as Akio pulled away from her. He smiled and with the back of his finger wiped them away. She lowered her arms and returned his smile. He looked at her for a moment, and then wrapped his arms around her. Amaya stood enveloped in his embrace, then she lifted her own arms and pulled him close, burying her face into his neck and drawing in a breath. Earth and pine filled her lungs. Akio's hand was in her hair, cradling her as if she were a precious gift.

They remained in the embrace for several moments, until Akio leant back and gazed at her. The soft, orange glow from the brazier danced across them, casting their shadows on the tent wall. His eyes held hers and she was unable to look away, nor did she want to.

It was incongruous to feel such overwhelming excitement in a place so close to death but Amaya did not prevent it or question it. It soothed her, placated the writhing things within her which threatened to spew forth anger and vengeance. No further words were exchanged as Akio gently loosened the ties of her kimono. As it slipped from her shoulders, Amaya thought that he would hear her heart, it was beating like the wings of a dragonfly. She wrapped a finger around the tie of his kimono. He shrugged his shoulders and it fell about his waist in folds of white, grazing her exposed skin as it went. With poise she loosened her hakama and they fell silently to the floor; pools of blue fabric. Her bare skin felt alive with both the heat and cold as he leant toward her. His hand rested on her back as he lowered her onto the futon.

Ebon hair framed his face as he looked down at her and she could see her own reflection in his black eyes. The warmth from his body mingled with the winter air as he traced a finger over her lips and down her neck. Akio pulled the heavy covers around them, not once removing his gaze from Amaya's. Under her palms his back was smooth, and she placed a hand over his heart and felt it beating as frantically as her own. The pink scar which forever caught her eye covered his entire left shoulder. She touched it, unafraid. He brought his forehead to hers and then his lips before pressing his body against her.

When Amaya woke it was still night. She felt Akio's strong arm wrapped around her. His breath was soft on the back of her neck as he slept and with each exhale Amaya felt her hair move slightly. Slowly she turned to face him, she did not want him to retract his arm. She looked at his expression, and found that his refined, intelligent features were calm. A tranquillity had settled on his brow, so different from the previous night when he arrived at camp. She kissed his forehead and his eyes opened. He smiled and kissed her in return. They remained, unmoving, fingers linked together.

A piece of black fabric lay near her head. It drew her attention. She recognized it as the sash Akio constantly wore. The one he had offered to her at the fireworks festival months ago.

'You should keep it,' Akio said, running a finger up her arm.

'It is precious to you, isn't it? I couldn't take it.'

Akio nodded, clutching Amaya's hand over the black silk. 'That is why I would like you to keep it.'

Contentment clung to the corners of her mouth so that they would not fall. She nestled into his chest and gripped the black and gold silk. Akio pressed his lips to the top of her head, and stroked her hair, embracing her even tighter.

> *'As the morning mist trails*
> *Over the ears of rice*
> *In the autumn fields,*
> *I know not when and where*
> *My love will end.'*

Akio recited the ancient poem from the Collection of Ten Thousand Leaves beautifully and Amaya remained in his stillness, thinking how loved she felt. And how much love she felt for him.

The peace was shattered; a deafening horn sounded nearby. The sound of soldiers waking shattered the still air, and instinctively she reached for Meiyo.

Akio lifted himself onto his elbow, all placidity gone from his face. 'I will see what has happened. Wait here,' he said, hastily pulling on his kimono and hakama. Amaya nodded as she got to her feet. Akio kissed her quickly and ran from the tent leaving her to stand alone, the muffled shrieks of the swelling commotion outside filling the once blissful silence.

CHAPTER SEVENTEEN

Amaya fastened her ponytail, stray strands flying wildly about her face. Her first thought was to find Kenta. She slid Meiyo into her waistband as Akio's voice echoed through her mind. He had told her to stay in the tent. She paced to the tent entrance and back again but could not distinguish words from the multitude of voices outside. Taking one cautious step outside, she came to a stop in front of her tent, the moonlight reflecting from the white of her kimono and the hilt of her katana. She reasoned that she could wait for Akio there, where she could at least see the surrounding area. Most fires were out but the moonlight offered ample illumination. The commotion seemed to have moved away, towards the Seishin no Tani but it didn't sound like the battle had recommenced. It was painfully still where she stood. Panic gripped Amaya, she took another step forward into the quickening hush. *Wait here*, Akio had said. Recalling his instruction, she marched back into the tent, willing her curiosity to vanish. She wanted to aid her friends but knew that she should exercise patience.

The interior of her tent was unsettlingly still. 'I must wait.' She urged herself, pacing in a circular motion. It was as she made to walk around a third time that she noticed it; a slight mismatch in the pattern of the tent wall. It was almost unnoticeable but now that she had spied it, she could not see anything but the anomaly. She approached the area, her eyes narrowing in suspicion. *A cut in the fabric*, she realised.

The moment Amaya comprehended what she had discovered hands shot through the slit in front of her. She staggered back out of their reach only to be gripped from behind by another. They clutched at her, pushing and dragging her through the hole to the shadowy woodland beyond. One hand slapped against her mouth, stifling the scream which had nearly escaped her. She writhed and kicked, squirming like an eel.

'Hold her. Don't let her make a sound,' a man said.

'They wouldn't hear her now, even if she did,' another replied, pulling her back by her hair so violently that she went flying into a tree. The wind was knocked out of her. She glanced up clutching her side and distinguished four men against the moonlight. Three were all wearing Imperial Army uniforms and the fourth was the hooded man who had secured passage on the ferry. Standing to her feet, she drew her katana quickly.

The hooded man laughed. 'Are you that idiotic? Do not kill her.'

Amaya recognised his voice but without a face she could not place it. She heard the tell-tail sound of ringing metal as all four of them drew their katana. Without warning one of them lunged at her, sheathed blade raised. The moonlight glinted from the length of Amaya's katana as she stepped to avoid her assailant. She swept Meiyo up in one clean stroke letting out a shout with the motion. The man grunted in pain and turned to face her, holding his side. She could see dark blood oozing between his fingers. His confusion was clear on his whitening face.

'I told you to watch yourself. She isn't helpless. This is Kazu Takeda's daughter,' the man with the familiar voice said in a harsh whisper. 'The Prophet of Ueten with a strong samurai spirit.'

Amaya braced herself again, concentrating through her panic. Two of the rebel soldiers moved, from either side. She pivoted gracefully as one thrust their katana forward. She tilted her head and thrust her own katana forward at the same instance. His blade glanced from her cheek but hers found its mark in his abdomen. With her other hand, she brought the sheath down upon the other man's head. A horrible crack sounded. However, before she could pull Meiyo from the falling corpse the hooded man dashed forward with surprising speed. He twirled his blade playfully and struck her with the hilt of his katana. She stumbled back, the breath knocked out of her for a second time. The air she tried to inhale stuck in her throat as the hood fell from the man's head, he moved toward her and she mouthed his name incredulously, *Daiki Kimura.*

Her katana protruded from the dead soldier's body a few feet away, and she had dropped her sheath when Daiki struck her.

'Do not challenge me, Amaya.' His angered eyes had traces of a plea in them.

Still struggling to regain her breath Amaya backed into a tree. With no air, her legs felt weak. Daiki was close and Amaya could smell blood on him. She wondered who he had murdered to cause the distraction.

He inched closer until he was arm's length away. Amaya eyed him closely, waiting. When he made to grab her she slid down the trunk and darted away. Rolling across the leafy floor, she collided with the corpse, and wrenched Meiyo free. Staying low she pivoted on her heel, sweeping her other leg in front. She held her blade up, steady and unwavering.

He stared at her, his comely face collapsing into frustration. 'Amaya,' he growled, dashing forward, his shoulders low. Again, Amaya waited, and when Daiki was feet from her, she pushed hard against the ground sending her light frame into the air. She sprang over Daiki's back and brought her blade down with the momentum of her leap. Daiki lifted the scabbard of his katana quickly and deflected what would have been a lethal blow. However, he did not pause. His hand snaked out and gripped her ankle as she descended. Amaya landed heavily but instantly flipped onto her back, a searing pain expanding the length of her right side. She lifted her hand in a whip-like movement, batting Daiki's katana aside. She kicked her foot forward and he slipped over, barely stopping himself from collapsing upon her.

'What are you doing?' Amaya hissed at him, her eyes felt warm and prickly. Daiki stared at her, his mouth trying to form words, but nothing came. Amaya grabbed hold of his cloak and yanked him closer still. 'Why are you doing this?'

'It is my duty. A Prophet cannot be allowed to roam Akegata. It is too dangerous. I will not forsake honour.'

Amaya suddenly understood Kin's apprehension of honour, and the danger it had the potential to pose. She closed her eyes. 'Daiki, you are forsaking honour with each action you take, with each order you follow blindly. The Prophet Ueten is not dangerous not with the nurture of those around. Stop now. Help me.'

For a bizarre moment, Amaya thought he was going to listen to her but then, in one motion, he gripped her neck and pushed himself up from the floor, dragging her with him.

'Come,' Daiki said, to the two wounded men. 'We are already late.'

As they dragged Amaya deeper into the woodland, she heard her name being called out. Frantic voices filled the night as people realised she was missing. She heard Kenta bellowing instructions, his voice desperate. Then she heard Akio's infuriated yell. Tears fell as she tried to scream his name, she kicked and struggled against Daiki and his two men, but they had her in tightening grips. Meiyo and its sheath lay in the clearing beside the rebel soldier she had managed to slay.

Soon the sounds of the camp grew faint and then died completely. Amaya slumped in resignation, her body becoming limp with exhaustion. The men slowed as they approached a small path which cut through the trees. Amaya was thrown into a large palanquin. She looked up at Daiki as the two men tied her hands and feet together.

'They will find me. They will know where I am,' Amaya said, thinking of her Elementals.

'Unlikely. Even if they were to locate you, who's to say you would still be alive?' Daiki stared at Amaya but there was no hint of his usual taunting. His face even seemed a little gaunt, and the turmoil was as stark as Shun's usually was. Again, Amaya thought he was going to let her go but he slammed the palanquin door closed.

Daylight filtered through the slatted bamboo covering on the palanquin window. Clear, unbroken beams of light fell across Amaya's body and face. She squinted as a strand of frigid sunlight stretched over her eyes. Her head pulsed dully with each movement and sound. She moved to a kneeling position and pressed up against the window looking out between the bamboo. An icy vista stretched out before her, sparse and glittering. The Face of Winter always seemed to keep one eye upon the north but as Amaya caught glimpses of the blanched terrain, she could see the full effects of the season. The ice plains stretched out, only stopping when they reached the distant mountain range which rose like uneven fangs into the near-white sky. Black, naked trees sporadically disrupted the view, marking the occasional boundary of land. Amaya found the iridescent chill terrible and enchanting all at once.

Sitting back, Amaya wrapped her arms around herself beneath her cloak and reflected on what had happened. She had never thought that Daiki Kimura was a decent man but since his aid in the Fire Province a hope had bloomed, and that hope was slowly diminishing with each pounding footfall of the men outside leaving only antipathy behind. She mulled over all the events, which had led to her present position. She considered that, perhaps, it really was Daiki who was Rai's accomplice; the second rebel leader. She had seen Daiki in the Fire Province, and now he had followed her from the palace to the camp where he had abducted her. A horrid realisation swept through Amaya, she wondered if had been following her for a long time and she recollected the attack in Rikujou. The Shizukawa shinobi clan would not have known her face, unless someone who was acquainted with her was informing them. Then after the incident at the Kageyama village, on her return from the Fire Province, she had seen Daiki on the road to Chuto and had been arrested immediately on her return. Amaya had a cooling sensation which dampened her quickening thoughts. Shun's camp had been poisoned and Amaya was certain Daiki would not harm his older brother, no matter who gave the order. He could not be the second mastermind, he was only Rai's puppet, like other numerous Court Officials. For the first time, she felt pity for Daiki. Pity that he had been raised to be such a person, for he had not been born with such darkness. The flashes of virtue Daiki had shown were severely overshadowed by the power Rai had over him. Again, Kin's words came to mind *'It must be very difficult to have Rai as a father'*. She shivered slightly in the stifling palanquin as the shriek of a hawk sounded overhead.

The palanquin juddered to a halt around midday, the men carrying it cursed under their breaths and words were exchanged in urgent whispers. Amaya moved to the back, away from the window as the door was opened. A fresh, icy draft replaced the stale air and sunlight streamed in, casting a glaring blanket of light on the interior of the palanquin. It was not as finely decorated like the palanquin of Lady Mari Ito but the black lacquer was unblemished, the gold inlay intact. Amaya had one true glimpse of the ice plains and distant, craggy mountains before the view was obscured. Daiki climbed in next to Amaya and closed the door the with sharp snap. He was extremely close to her in the restricted space. She could feel the heat egressing from his body even through his heavy clothing.

'Not a sound from you.' He held a finger to his mouth. Amaya followed his gaze, a small tanto dagger was resting against her ribs. She faced him fully, but he seemed unable to meet her gaze.

They travelled a few more minutes and then Amaya heard a number of new voices.

'Have you travelled from Chuto or the camp at the

Seishin no Tani? I will not pretend that I'm not surprised to see you here.'

Amaya almost screamed out. The voice belonged to Shun. He was no more than a few feet away, speaking to the imposing Imperial guards on the other side of the palanquin doors. She glanced at Daiki who did not remove his eyes from the direction of his brother's voice. His face was a mask of detachment, but the cracks were visible to Amaya, and through these cracks she could see the taint of shame; a thing she hadn't thought Daiki capable of feeling.

'Good day, General Kimura. Some of us have travelled directly from Chuto but a few from the camp at the Seishin no Tani joined us. The first day of battle was severe but both sides suffered heavy casualties. His Majesty predicts another three days of fighting.'

Amaya heard Shun sigh as his shadow moved in front of the window blocking the strips of sunlight. 'How fairs His Majesty?'

'His Majesty is unharmed and leading the men well. Do you have news, General?'

Amaya bit her lip with the effort of remaining silent. She willed Shun not to speak of anything, she did not want him murdered here on the road.

Shun didn't speak for a moment and Amaya began to wonder if she had spoken aloud. 'The news is for His Majesty's ears only. I will report directly to him. I also received a letter from Lord Katou just before my departure from the Seishin no Tani.'

Amaya was desperate to crash through the palanquin door to Shun. An unbearable need for him, to warn him, had suddenly risen in her chest. She was unsure how many men were there with him and even less sure how many of them were loyal to him. Amaya considered that he may be the only true Imperial soldier out there, and if that were the case Shun would be outnumbered. That single thought held her tongue.

'Who rides in the palanquin?' Shun suddenly asked.

Amaya's eyes stayed on Daiki, whose brow was furrowed so deeply his eyes were in dark shadow and for a moment he looked spectral. Amaya closed her eyes and shouted Shun's name in her head repeatedly.

'The palanquin is occupied currently by the son of a Court Official who resides in the Air Province. We fear he has contracted the illness which has been spreading throughout the region.'

'I see. Have you had news of my brother, Daiki? Is he unharmed?' Shun spoke, concernedly.

'He is currently at the Seishin no Tani, and he remains unharmed, sir.'

Shun paused, and Amaya heard him shift his feet. 'Is there news of Lady Amaya Takeda?'

Amaya opened her eyes wide in the silence of the palanquin and her heart trembled rapidly at Shun's words. His presence offered her comfort, as it had done many months previous when they had travelled together. His reserved nature, so unlike his adoptive father's had intrigued her and, once she had seen past his connection to Rai, it drew her to him.

'Amaya Takeda has been executed for high treason.'

The stillness that followed the guard's statement was heavy, ominous. She could feel Shun's anguish from behind the bamboo slats and when he spoke every word shook with rage. 'Who authorised the execution?'

No body replied, seemingly taken aback by Shun's sudden change in temperament.

'I said who authorised it?' His tone was baneful.

'Your father, sir. Chancellor Rai Kimura. He authorised her execution.'

'On what grounds did he have her executed?' Shun's voice had gone quiet in its rage. Amaya heard the smallest sound of metal as Shun gripped his katana.

'Plotting against Emperor Kenta Yamashima, sir. And forgery in the severest degree.'

'Ridiculous,' Shun bellowed. 'She was working *with*

him. Her heart was pure. Does he know what he has done? Her death means the death of us all.'

Amaya could hear the despair in Shun's animosity. She wanted to yell out and placate him, she couldn't bear to hear the agony. He had never risen his voice the entire time she had known him, instead he always quietly observed others and contemplated their actions. He had always looked at her with unassuming eyes which never judged but only ever held care.

'Please, General. Chancellor Rai must have had his reasons. He could not have ordered an execution without ample evidence and support within the Court.'

'Something is wrong here. I will return immediately.'

Amaya shook her head vigourously as she heard Shun step away from the palanquin. His retreating footfalls caused her panic to peak. The men hoisted the palanquin from the ground and began to walk further into the Air Province, further from Shun. Amaya strained her ears until the sound of Shun and his men vanished and all she could hear was the wind rattling the bamboo covering. The absence of Shun's presence had left a strange feeling in Amaya's stomach, which she could not explain. It felt as if something important had slipped through her fingers, but she was uncertain as to what it was.

She whirled about to face Daiki. 'Your father has turned you into a monster. How could you lie to your brother? I thought you cared for him,' Amaya shouted.

Daiki raised his hand to strike her but steadied himself. 'You know nothing of my relationship with my brother. Or my father.'

'I do not have to know. I can see it in your eyes, Daiki. You cannot deny the care you feel for Shun, yet you continue to obey the monster you call father.'

Daiki did not respond, he simply gazed at Amaya, a miscellany of jealousy, regret and enmity battled in his captivating irises. 'You – ' he didn't continue, but jumped from the palanquin, leaving her to ruminate in the quiet of her own company.

Night took the sky, rendering it a dark starry mass through the bamboo slats. Amaya's unease heightened in the blackness. She felt as if all her senses had become intensified. Every shiver of a lonely tree, every scurry of startled wildlife, every scream of a red-crowned crane reached her clearly. Her stomach was aching from hunger and her mouth was dry. She allowed herself to drift into an uncomfortable, buffeted sleep.

A fitful dream ensnared Amaya's mind. She found herself falling through images similar to the ones she had previously had at the Hidden Mountain Village. She tried to wake but the nightmare had her in its grip. A flood of faces: nameless village people, Imperial soldiers, Court Officials, all embroiled in one massive struggle. Red was the only colour Amaya could see and a deep hate filled her as she struggled against the painful dream. Suddenly, Kenta's face surged forward blood-soaked and inert, behind him was the palace. It was aflame. Black smoke darkened the sun over the capital until it covered everything in its shadow, even Kenta. His face was quickly replaced by the visages of her Elementals, each of them were as marred as Kenta had been. Waking ghosts. Lastly, Akio's face came into focus. Amaya stretched out a hand to touch him, but the smoke snatched him away. She released a strangled scream, reaching for Akio, her heart aching.

The smoke dissipated, leaving her standing solitary in the centre of the Seishin no Tani. The ground was uneven to stand upon but when she looked down, instead of grass she saw red. Red everywhere. The lumps and indistinct shapes formed corpses which lined the Seishin no Tani as far as her eyes could see. Even as she stared around in the noiselessness the corpses began to rise. People with only half a face, men with broken limbs and exposed bone, cracked skulls; the ghosts of war surrounded her. She felt Ueten writhing inside. Her father's decapitation coursed into her mind, strangling the sob before it could reach Amaya's mouth.

She woke to a hand shaking her. Daiki had re-entered the palanquin. 'Amaya. Are you ill?'

The palanquin swayed gently as the sun's glow declared dawn's arrival with a thin euphony of birds overhead. The pain she had felt at Gekai's illusions sparked an old feeling she thought she had discarded. Vengeance settled deep within Amaya as she opened her eyes. All those faces: dead. All the soldiers inanimate, never to hold their families again. 'No, I am jus shaken. You can leave.' She sat up silently, her resolve strong. Daiki slid from the moving palanquin and snapped the door closed behind him and in that instant, her thoughts all led to the murder and destruction of Rai Kimura.

Another day had passed since they had met Shun on the road and they had briefly rested twice. Amaya could only distinguish time by the density of the light which filtered through the window of the palanquin, and the sparse cawing of the birds. Little food had been spared for Amaya and her resentment was slowly transforming into a bubbling loathing. A loathing she no longer cared to inhibit. She shuddered at the position she was in, the shame of it, and chastised herself for allowing things to develop to the state they were in. She pondered over the missing Water Elemental, and her frustration swelled but she was not afraid any longer. Her father would often surface in her thoughts.

'You've surpassed your peers in the bo staff, Amaya. I am so proud,' Kazu Takeda had said, his hands on his hips, his black hair falling from his ponytail and sticking to his forehead.

Amaya looked up at her father. His face was in silhouette because the sun was so bright behind him. 'How do you know? I have never sparred with another besides you.' She gripped the bo staff, waiting for her father's reasoning. Sweat beaded upon her brow and she wiped it away with the back of her arm cuffs.

'I oversee the training of those your age. Boys who are training to become soldiers. The sons of samurai.' Kazu crouched down so that his eyes were level with hers. 'It would be a bit embarrassing if I took you along and you showed them all up.' He laughed and took the bo staff from her with one hand, and with the other scooped her up.

Amaya giggled loudly, pretending to fight against her father's grip but secretly enjoying the playfulness.

'I thought I had given birth to a young lady, and here you are; a beautiful, little samurai.' Megumi had stepped onto the veranda which over looked the garden Amaya and her father were in the centre of, a small Kyo in her arms.

Kazu kept hold of Amaya and walked toward his wife and adopted son. Amaya looked up at her father's face and the smile which devoured it.

'She has all the talent of a young lady and then some, but she carries the Takeda samurai spirit,' Kazu remarked, handing his wife the bo staff and cradling Amaya like a baby, nuzzling his face into her neck and blowing a loud noise.

'Father!' Amaya half laughed half grumbled as she wriggled free of his arms and clambered onto his shoulders like a monkey. Kyo shrieked out in delight, his tiny hands reaching out for his sister. Swinging on her father's neck, Amaya leant out and touched the tip of her forefinger to her brother's.

Her mother chuckled and, leaning forward, kissed her husband delicately. He returned the action. Pulling Megumi and Kyo into a one-armed embrace he reached upward and plucked Amaya from his shoulder easily. Amaya squirmed, her arms and legs kicking but she couldn't stop laughing.

'Our daughter.' Kazu grinned, placing her on the floor and ruffling her hair. Amaya glowered at her parents, but she couldn't hold onto the expression, and a moment later she threw herself at them giggling as much as her baby brother.

The humble memory brought both joy and guilt to Amaya. 'I'm sorry, father, mother. I have let you both down.' She was abruptly presented with a window to Daiki's situation, and she was able to comprehend a little of the reasons behind his actions, comprehend why he was loyal to his own father.

An unexpected sliver of cool air streamed in and enveloped her, it smelt of ice and cold earth. Amaya shuffled to the window and squinted through the covering. The vision before her was difficult to distinguish, the bamboo distorted the landscape, but she was certain that far off in the distance were the deep ice planes which were situated on the eastern side of Shiroshi. Winter lived there, as did one of the Five Masters of Akegata. Amaya's heart raced, if she could only reach her uncle in Shiroshi, she would be protected in the confines of his estate. She pictured his handsome home clearly, but it's exact location in Shiroshi was more difficult to recall. She had not visited the Air Province since Kyo was adopted into the family. Sitting back, she re-tied her hair but still a few strands fell about her face. She crossed her legs and waited, her back straight and her body taut with anticipation.

The day waned into evening before Amaya heard one of the men comment that Shiroshi was ahead. She twitched her head and strained to listen to their plan.

'We will enter Shiroshi and meet him immediately. I do not care how late the hour is,' Daiki said. The men's voices were whispers as they conversed, trying to keep her from hearing them. She caught a word amidst the mutters that stunned her into shock. Gekai. One of the men had said Gekai. The feeling the name incited within Amaya made her nauseated. She struggled to hear more but it was futile, they had fallen quiet again.

Amaya leant back against the palanquin wall, her chest heaving in anxiety. Her resolve was shaking precariously with each step they took to Shiroshi and the success of her pilgrimage seemed to diminish with each stride of the men outside. As they passed through the gates a sudden need to escape her captors at that moment overwhelmed her. She restrained her urge to leap from the palanquin and instead tried to focus her efforts on her other senses. Footfalls of people as they milled the streets; the bartering of late-night shop owners with customers hoping for a fair price at the end of the day; the odd cheer from an izakya; the occasional marching of samurai. There was a hushed hum of life to the city but Amaya couldn't dislodge the tension which clutched at her. The smell of barbecued meat and salmon caused her stomach to twinge and Amaya had deny the wafts of sweet Zenzai soup as the permeated her confine. Slowly, the sound of the main street depleted as the palanquin was taken further into the city. Now Amaya could hear the unmistakable jangle of a priest's holy staff. They were passing by Shiroshi's temple.

The palanquin came to an abrupt halt and Amaya had to catch herself from falling forward. A flurry of voices close by indicated they had reached their destination. There was silence for a few moments and the temptation to dash from the palanquin surfaced again. However, before she had the courage to act on her impulse, a familiar voice broke the silence, and at the same time it broke her heart.

'Where is she?'

She heard her uncle's voice, so like her father's.

'In the palanquin, sir.'

Footsteps followed by the soft sound of a kimono scuffing the floor. The door opened and Amaya was grabbed roughly and yanked into the night. On her knees, she looked up at her uncle whose face was illuminated by a swaying paper lantern. Insubstantial flakes of snow trailed through the oddly silent air. Daiki was standing just behind him, his handsome face in shadow. Again, his eyes avoided hers, but her uncle looked at her directly, his face full of a disdain Amaya had never seen before. Her comprehension was eclipsed by the betrayal, but rather than the tears she expected only more fury came. She rose to her feet slowly. Daiki and the men shifted, poising themselves.

'Uncle,' Amaya said, faintly. He didn't respond but simply continued to observe her, the look of contempt contorting into loathing as his eyes met hers.

'Take her to the cell, I cannot bare the sight of her. She has Kazu's eyes.'

The mention of her father snapped Amaya to her senses. 'What are you doing, uncle?' Her voice was low, but she could not keep the furious tremble from it as her hand twitched forward.

'What am I doing? Something that should have been done years and years ago.'

Amaya shook her head; she was still grappling with her uncle's emergence. The person she had hoped to run to for help stood before her, in the place she had expected to see Rai. A man entered the forecourt and joined Jiro. Amaya could not stop her mouth from opening wide and her chest from growing tight with fear. Serene and impassive, Sen stood beside her uncle, his hands clasped together under long sleeves.

'We meet again, Lady Takeda. How is my brother?' A smile crept up his face.

Amaya faced Jiro. 'What are you doing with this man? You know he is the leader of the Senkaku Nin, uncle.'

'Stop calling me that!' Jiro shouted, suddenly, his face ugly. 'That is a term of affection. I have none for you, so please stop forcing yours on me. I have endured it for years.'

Amaya flinched and took a step back, all similarity to her father had evaporated in that moment. She looked back at Sen, his tattooed head catching the moonlight as he tilted it forward, observing her. Amaya could see a clandestine desire skulking behind his black eyes. *He knows everything. About Ueten and Gekai. All of it.* Amaya could see the truth in his wide pupils.

'Always so concerned, so angry. My group are not involved directly. You have nothing to fear from the Senkaku Nin. Not yet at any rate. I see no need to involve them. They may not feel as curious about you as myself.'

Amaya laughed; she didn't believe Sen's assurance. She turned to her uncle again. 'You are involved with Rai, the man who murdered father,' Amaya's indignation was barely suppressed. 'Do you know that a devastating battle is being fought because of the Chancellor? Do you know what you have done by siding with him and weakening the north?'

'The moment your father assumed the head of the Takeda clan I knew what had to be done. His folly in believing Prophetic stories was dangerous for the Takeda clan.

Before Amaya could respond, Sen turned to Jiro. 'She has been conditioned to believe in false hope. When Rai arrives, we can begin.' He faced Amaya. 'You believe you are the Prophet of Ueten; that you are the first to resurface and the one to help Akegata avoid war? You are just a girl. A dot in the vast history of our culture. You do not have the capacity to speak for Ueten. War will bleed his country of arrogance and ignorance. And you will help us.'

'I will never aid a man like you,' Amaya spat, pulling against her restrainers.

'Daiki, take her to the cells,' Jiro said, turning his back on Amaya.

Without pause Amaya lunged forward, slipping past the men either side of her. As she did so, she wrapped her fingers around one of their katana and pulled it smoothly from the sheath. Spinning the blade in her hand, she careened forward, unable to perceive anything but her uncle. She was dully aware of everyone moving together, but she pirouetted away from their grasping fingers and wielded katana.

She rose her blade in a high arch just as her uncle turned, and brought it down with a savage strength that only rage could induce. It sang as it cut the air. Moments from striking Jiro's head, her blade was brought to a ringing stop.

'Sen.' Amaya's voice rumbled with her ferocity.

He merely looked up through his eyebrows, his placidity gone, his expression serious. His metal-cuffed arm which was raised above his head had been nearly cracked clean through with the strike of her katana. Beyond Sen, Amaya watched as Jiro staggered back, a deep laceration running the length of his face. He clutched his eye which was indistinguishable amidst the blood.

'Take her away before I rip her throat out,' he hissed.

CHAPTER EIGHTEEN

Amaya felt dirt and grit embed itself into her cheek as she was thrown to the floor of the cell, but the sting was forgotten when she lifted her gaze.

'Kyo!' Her brother sat gaunt and pale, his legs crossed. His face had aged with lack of sleep and sunlight. Amaya had no words, instead she rushed at him, enveloping him in an embraced him. She did not unwrap her arms for some time.

He gripped her tightly in return, trembling. 'Amaya.'

'I knew you had not died, Kyo,' Amaya said, finally, leaning back to look at him.

'I cannot believe uncle Jiro has done this. I hoped he would not capture you. I hoped that you would be safe with Akio, Kin and the others,' Kyo said, hoarsely.

'What do you know?' she asked.

'I was captured by Daiki on Rai's orders and brought to the Air Province. That morning, I had discovered documents regarding Jiro and Rai, in Rai's quarters. Letters detailing transactions and meetings which had been privately arranged by both. I could not believe it. Firearms have been stored in Shiroshi and in the Fire Province since before we met the foreigner. Rai, Jiro and Sen have been working together for a long time, Amaya.' Kyo looked down sadly, drawing in a hollow breath. 'Father had trusted Jiro with everything. He knew your identity as the Prophet, the Takeda heritage, the hope Kazu had in you.'

'Jiro has been manipulating us, treating us as family for all these years.'

'Amaya, some of the documents I read detailed Jiro assuming the head of the Takeda clan.'

Sickness rumbled through her stomach. 'He would not. Not his own brother. I mean I *saw* Rai. I saw him murder our father.' Amaya felt light-headed as she recalled her uncle's despair at Kazu's death. He had paid for the funeral, thanked people for their love of Kazu, and had expressed his own so sincerely. He had spent many an hour comforting her, Kyo and Megumi.

'Rai may have swung the katana that killed father, but Jiro and Sen as good as put the blade in his hand. Rai could not have achieved all of this completely alone. He had something to offer Jiro and Jiro had more than enough to offer Rai.'

Her shoulders fell under the weight of the new information. 'The Takeda clan Prophet and my hand in marriage to Daiki.'

'When you did not marry Daiki, Jiro's position became weakened. Perhaps that is when your death became their primary focus. It is all still unclear, half-shrouded in lies and deception.'

The betrayal her father had suffered tore at her; talons of sadness scratching at partially-healed wounds. Had he known about his brother's true nature, is that why he was so detached the last day she saw him alive, or had he discovered something different? Amaya shook her head as if trying to dislodge a stubborn thought. 'It still is not clear to me why Sen has inserted himself into the clan rivalry.'

'That is the terrible truth of it, Amaya,' Kyo whimpered. 'Sen brought Rai and Uncle Jiro together. Sen was the man who sowed the ideas from the outset. His motives are strangely simple: to rid this world of what he perceives to be corruption and injustice brought about by the spirits. He does not believe in the Divine Right to Rule. I do not know where this desire stems from, only Sen would know his own mind, but his goal is clear; to upset the balance and start afresh.'

'So that his ideals become the ideals of Akegata. He seeks to destroy the Yamashima dynasty and halt the arrival of another Divine Heir. It seems he is willing to start a Second Warring States Era to accomplish this end.'

'It is all supposition but, from what I have gleaned of my conversations with him and all that I have discovered, it seems he wants to remake Akegata and open the doors to the world beyond our land.'

Amaya knew she would never have answers to the questions which clamoured for attention. She looked at Kyo, his face bore the evidence of tears and anger. She realised he'd had to bear all of it alone. She embraced him again, letting him lean upon her.

'Amaya, there is something else. The Kageyama have visited Jiro. He invited the Doyen, and all the Doyen of the other shinobi clans.'

Amaya frowned but did not dwell on it; she could not think on something she knew nothing of. Instead, she informed Kyo of what had occurred in his absence. 'The battle at the Seishin no Tani has been fought for four days now.'

'I know,' Kyo said, his voice tired. 'Rai has been visiting often, with new information. The last I heard was that the rebel army were winning. Heavy casualties on both sides but the Firearms are proving superior. There is also going to be an attack on Chuto any day now,' Kyo said.

Amaya buried her face in her hands. 'I thought there would be. It is coming from the Fire Province. Rai has infected all of Akegata with his jealous ambition.'

'He has spread the Imperial Army to the farthest corners of each province and placed its vulnerable heart in the most dangerous battle.'

'When I was last at the camp, Kenta had decided to take some troops back to Chuto to defend its walls.'

'That will not be enough.'

'What do you mean?'

'The rebel army is much larger than we thought. They are using shinobi clans to reinforce their numbers, and attack from the inside. It is why the Kageyama Doyen was here, to form an agreement with the Shizukawa Doyen. There are Kageyama shinobi within the Court and Imperial forces. The army planning to attack Chuto is the same size as the army in the Seishin no Tani. There are not enough Imperial samurai to fight both battles.'

Amaya bit her lip. 'I haven't found my Water Elemental, Kyo.'

Kyo's eyes darkened and he placed a hand on Amaya's. 'You have done everything you can, Amaya.'

'There is still more I can do.'

Kyo narrowed his eyes at the cryptic tone behind her words and made to resist but Rai's voice sounded from nearby.

'She is in here? Good.' The door opened loudly as he stepped across the threshold and into the dim prison. 'How are you finding your visit to Shiroshi, Lady Takeda? Enlightening, I hope.' Rai peered at Amaya and Kyo.

'You cannot think your plans will bear any fruit?' Amaya shouted, her anger towards Rai flaring up.

'They already are, girl. Kenta is dead. The war is as good as over. The Court now answer to me, not some Divine ruler and his Prophet.'

Amaya buried her nails into her palms as she beat back the cry which desperately wanted to be heard. 'You are lying.'

Rai looked at her, suddenly irritated. 'Why would I lie? I have absolutely no reason to lie to you. Not now. The Prophet of Ueten is powerless, a Divine Heir will never assume the throne and Akegata will no longer have need of a useless monarchy compelled by the Way of the Spirits. A military leadership has been sorely needed. Look how easily Firearms entered Akegata.'

'Under your orders!'

Rai grinned, his expression almost pitying. 'The citizens of Akegata will be only too willing to support a defensive military after suffering and witnessing Firearms.' Rai turned slowly away, seemingly satisfied.

Amaya watched him leave, succumbing to the paralysis

his words had left: Kenta was dead. Dead. She clutched her chest, wanting to beat the ache out of her heart. She had failed to help him. His bloodied face in the vision she'd had in the palanquin was painfully prominent. She jumped at Kyo's touch as he held her hand.

'If Kenta really is dead, Amaya, which I do not believe,' he forced himself to say, 'then we have to do everything we can now. Akegata and the spirits are going to need you, the Prophet. The last thing you should do is abandon hope. Keep your resolve, Amaya, and forget your vengeance.'

The dullness lifted slightly but she did not tell Kyo of the vision. She wanted Kyo to believe the worst had not yet happened; she wanted him to believe that Rai was lying. Amaya closed her eyes and tried to feel Ueten, tried to garner a direction she should take, but only mute grief swaddled her. She didn't comprehend the Way of the Spirits in that moment and it terrified her.

Dawn arrived and passed. The sun streamed into the cell from the large gap around the sliding door, bringing the scent of the frozen new year. She and Kyo had fallen asleep against each other. The worst for them both was the death of their father and mother. Neither Amaya nor Kyo wanted to envision their uncle involved in such crimes. Amaya's thoughts were disturbed by the screech of a hawk close by the compound, overhead. She turned to Kyo, but he was already watching the doorway.

'Amaya, we have to escape this prison and return to the capital. I cannot linger, my mind will shatter with this fear.'

'Rai wants to torture our minds, Kyo. We will not be kept in here forever and when they retrieve us, I vow to return us to our home.'

Amaya shivered as the sun slowly dimmed. When twilight came, it was gone in the blink of an eye and night stole any comfort the sun gave. Amaya's frustration had manifested into a physical pain. Her stomach contracted every time she thought of the battle in the Seishin no Tani and the immanent attack on Chuto and the citizens who were oblivious to the death which approached them. She slaved to prevent thoughts of Kenta entering her mind for fear of an uncontrollable panic. The last of the Yamashima could not perish. The exhaustion from this struggle allowed Amaya only moments of disturbed sleep. The more she was trapped, the more she felt drained as if an external source was sapping her of her energy.

It was deep into the night when Amaya was startled awake. She had felt Ueten flutter and was immediately alert. Her spirit's increasing movements had become a distant feeling, but it made Amaya realise how much she truly felt the presence of her Elementals and how their separation affected her. She stirred Kyo awake.

'What is it, Amaya?' her brother asked rising into a crouch.

'I think Kin is here. Tomio and Rin as well.'

Kyo jumped to his feet and ran to the bars to stand beside Amaya. He opened his mouth to yell out, but Amaya held a finger to her lips.

'We do not want to draw attention to their presence.'

'They don't know that Jiro is involved. They will openly approach him. Rai is here also. And Sen. It is hazardous for them.'

Before she could decide on the best action, there was movement outside of the prison and the door slid open. The moon was clear, and a man's silhouette was inky against it. He strode to their hold and paused. It was Daiki who stood before them, Amaya recognised his lithe figure. Daiki proceeded to unlock the iron door and reach a hand into the hold. He hauled Kyo violently from beside Amaya.

'Wait!' she screamed out, grasping at Kyo's arm. 'What are you doing? Where are you taking him?'

'Amaya,' Daiki said, imploringly.

'Please,' Amaya begged, reaching her hand to him

through the bars and gripping the sleeve of his black kimono. 'He is my brother.'

Daiki remained silent; his eyes unusually solemn.

'How can you accept your father after this?' Amaya blurted. 'Can you not see what he is? You are better than this. You proved so when you helped me in the Fire Province. You have never been truly committed to your father's ideals.'

'You know nothing of me, Amaya. Nothing. How could you? You have been the focus of my father for as long as I have been alive. I will have him acknowledge me. I am a good and dutiful son.' Daiki's disquiet was clear in his tone. 'Do not ask me to help you, Amaya.'

He pushed the cage door closed before Amaya could answer. The force of his push sent Amaya reeling backward. Her foot caught in her cloak and she felt herself topple. The clanging of the cage was all she heard as her head hit the floor with a heavy crunch.

Amaya's mouth was dry, and her head panged with pain when she moved. Sitting up, she crawled to the iron bars and glanced around looking for Kyo before recalling Daiki's arrival. She touched the back of her head and found that a lump had formed but no blood. Ignoring the pain, she watched the door as the day sent its light through the crack. Her terror for Kyo accompanied her despair for Kenta as the hush outside pressed upon her. The sensation Ueten had momentarily sent through her was almost undetectable and Amaya began to think she had imagined the presence of the Elementals in her desire to escape.

Amaya remained seated until evening arrived. She glanced at the door to the outside every time she heard movement or a noise. On one of these occasions, her barred cell caught her eye. She gasped and stood, rushing forward. It was not secured. She studied the lock, unable to believe what she was seeing. She contemplated if Daiki's mistake was indeed a mistake. The lock was protruding but the door was not in place for it to reach the hole. She pushed it lightly and dashed forward. Approaching the second door, she took a moment to listen before sliding it open and stepping out into the fading day.

The memory of her uncle's house was bleak and distant. She tried to remember prominent landmarks and areas that were familiar on the holy estate. A light caught her eye as she silently paced down the veranda which fringed the main house. She took a few steps back until the light came back into view, striped by the nearby cluster of bamboo. Amaya discerned that it came from the small shrine her uncle had had built on the estate. It hadn't been completed the last time she had visited. She navigated the Zen garden of the New Faith, the gravel crunching slightly underfoot. Amaya missed the sound of water that was present in her own garden. The dry representation of the ocean lacked something for Amaya; this garden had no sense of sound, no music to accompany the living art of the plants. She reached the mound of purposefully and meticulously placed rocks. Where rocks appeared to be running, there were rocks chasing. A falling rock was always helped by a supporting rock. Grateful to leave the grit which gave her away with every step, she crossed the small area of grass and slipped between the bamboo, never removing her eyes from the soft glow.

Amaya slithered between the bamboo until she reached the last narrow trunk. The paper-panelled windows softened the glow of the braziers and lamps which illuminated the resplendent shrine. As Amaya studied the building, she thought it resembled the temple in Rikujou but much smaller.

She approached the nearest window but could not even see shadows within the room. Quietly, she moved to the entrance; the sliding door was open slightly, exposing the length of the heidan. Pillars extended before her, supporting a glorious wooden ceiling. Carvings covered every area above, whilst divine screens and ink paintings embellished the walls. Amaya studied the images and, at first, she did not understand what she was observing, but quickly the story unfolding on the walls became clear to her: the history of Lord Genichiro Minamori as the Prophet of Ueten. Golden strokes and purple flourishes depicted his ascension as the Prophet and his marriage to Empress Mimiko. Illustrations of Lord Minamori travelling the streets of Akegata, gracing each place with the presence of the Prophet, brightening the stretches of canvas even after centuries of degradation. Ueten's light shimmered in blue, green and yellow streaks across the rivers and mountains, bringing hope, abundance and life. A once-pristine white accented with purple and green showed the birth of a child; glowing and sacred. Amaya looked more closely at the image, brushing her fingertip over the child, its light and the striking shadow it cast. In the dimly lit hall of the shrine, the child seemed to emit a brightness of its own; this infant was the most vivid thing upon the entire frieze. The true Divine Heir.

Amaya traced her hand over the jubilant faces of the parents, Empress Mimiko and Lord Minamori, and felt her eyes widen and her heart open to the pure joy in the expressions captured by the artist. Yet, as Amaya's eyes continued to travel over the images, swirls of dark flecked with deep scarlet imbued the work; a foreboding presence seemed to have possessed the artist's brush. Black blurs began to encroach the margins of each panel, consuming the colour and light within each. The expressions of all characters grew darker and full of menace. The silhouette of two graves drowning in water consumed an entire panel of the wall-painting. Hovering above were hundreds of moths filling the sky and consuming the sun and moon. Amaya paused, staring at the rendering, unsure of the meaning behind it; the graves had no names.

From this juncture, the imagery became so chaotic and shadowy that Amaya could hardly see the contours of any subject. One still picture, thinly outlined in silver and white, seemed to almost protrude from the wall as if the painter did not want a soul to miss it: the corpse of the heavenly child lay atop a mound of samurai carcasses; each displaying the Imperial Crest. The child's shadow atop a mound mask-wearing shinobi. Amaya frowned in bemusement. Behind this death-strewn scene, were ghostly phantoms with red eyes and red katana. Black moths danced in the painted smoke and filled the mural. *A coup?* Amaya pondered as unexpected tears fell for the murdered child.

She was frightened to follow the images now; she knew it would end with the beginning of the First Warring States Era, and now she finally understood why. The tale came to a violent and sanguine close with Lord Minamori emerging as the Prophet of Gekai. His blackened footsteps spanned the entire map and were marked by the mutilated bodies of his foes; the sky was ablaze with blood and arrows; rivers ran in claret streaks; vegetation and animals withered and died; and, in his hands, he clutched three hearts. Each were a different hue: red, green and white. The ancient mural was damaged, the final panel marred by fire. The only clear form which Amaya could distinguish was the solitary, beautiful, melancholy eye of Empress Mimiko painted with care and attention. It stared out from the scarred wall beseechingly and Amaya wished she knew what the last large panel depicted. What Empress Mimiko had tried to say with that glance.

Amaya scrutinised the scorched image for a moment longer and then turned away, her chest tight with the insight and dread the visual tale had inspired. Lord Minamori's violent rampage had begun the day his first-born child, the Divine Heir, was murdered. The scroll had spoken of his sister being the one to eventually stop him, and Amaya considered how terrible a toll that expectation would have taken on the sister; to have to slay a brother whom you would feel such pity for. Amaya considered how much of the story was still suspended in mystery, hidden behind the veils of centuries past. How much of the Way of the Spirits had been distorted through the lens of mortals. Beneath Amaya's feet, the floor was smooth and unblemished. She squinted to the distant haiden, where the Spirits were housed. Incense clouded the air and swirled above the candles, a dancing haze playing with the heat. Her eyes were drawn from the visible fumes back to the shrine. People had moved in front of it.

A man was bent over at the foot of the shrine and a low muttering reached Amaya's ears. The prayer was unfamiliar to her, but she recognised the voice: it belonged to Sen. Amaya was without a weapon, but she could see that Sen was also unarmed. Assaying the approach to the man in front, she considered how close she would be able to creep. Her fingers itched as she envisioned wrapping them around his throat and ending his recalcitrant campaign, ending his life.

Her legs tensed but, before she could proceed, a pair of hands gripped her arms tightly. She swallowed back a yell as she looked up. Akio stood before her. Without pausing for speech, he pulled her close until his arms wrapped about her fully. One hand cupped the back of her head whilst he buried his nose into her hair and breathed deeply. Amaya felt her body quiver as her relief mingled with the very recent dread. His hand was warm as it found hers and led her away from the shrine. Akio glanced at the mural and his countenance was blighted with fear.

'How did you know to come here, Akio?' Amaya asked, as they entered the bamboo, lifting her free hand to his face. Her thumb traced his lips and cheekbone, before her fingers brushed through his hair.

'Kin, Tomio, Rin and I arrived here late yesterday. The timing of our arrival was guided by the Spirits We witnessed Kyo being dragged from the cell by Daiki Kimura. We had originally come to speak with Jiro, but it seems all is not as it should be.'

'Jiro has been alongside Rai and Sen from the beginning. Since before my father's death.'

Akio's silence implied he understood the weight of what Amaya had told him.

'We need to find Kin and the others. There is something unsettling. This shrine is dedicated to Lord Genichiro Minamori and Gekai. Akio, I do not know how Ueten can aid us here. Not when I do not have the support of all Elementals.'

Akio unclenched her hand and, at once, Amaya wanted to grasp it again. The protection she felt when his hand clutched hers instilled conviction within her. It was only when she looked down that she saw the object Akio was handing her.

'My katana. Thank you, Akio,' Amaya said. She lifted her face, rising on her toes and placed a kiss on Akio's cheek. Amaya drew in a breath as a horrifying memory overshadowed their moment, 'Akio, is it true that Kenta is dead?'

Akio stiffened, his expression startled. 'I have not heard from him since he departed for Chuto. He wanted to come to you Amaya. I have never seen him so wretched than when he had to leave in the opposite direction.'

'Rai told me he was dead, killed on the road to Chuto,' Amaya fumbled her words as her voice rose in panic.

Akio gazed at her, unable to keep the anxiety from his own face. 'I do not believe he is dead.'

'A husband and wife enjoying a stolen moment in the shadows.'

Amaya turned quickly as Akio stood in front of her, pushing her behind him, his hand reaching for his katana. Jiro stood before them, his expression placid.

'Do not draw your blade or raise your bow, Lord Izumi. I know of your incredible skill, but I will not hesitate to bring the wrath of both Kageyama and Shizukawa shinobi down upon you both. Follow me.' Jiro's voice was cold and authoritative as he motioned for them to move. When they didn't, Amaya saw the very shadows close in around them.

Akio clicked his tongue in anger at the shinobi who surrounded them.

'Where is Rin?' Amaya looked at Akio, but it was one of the shadows that spoke in response.

'My traitor daughter will be with your other friends in

the shrine. Corralled like cattle.'

'Why are you siding with these men?' Amaya said, into the blackness.

'Because my people cannot live in such an insipid country of hollow peace nor can we live on the whim of a Feudal Lord or the Spirits which seem to only favour the priviladed. The Kageyama know nothing except conflict, take that from us and what is left? All I have seen in this recent peace is laziness, idleness and dishonour blossom in the hearts of Akegatans. War reminds people what it is to be alive and to be grateful. It encourages strength with the people in a way peae cannot. Conflict creates balance with peace; without it how can any appreciate genuine serenity when it comes.'

'What a pathetic, misguided philosophy,' Amaya said, quietly. Before she could elaborate, two of the shadows swooped down and pulled them to the shrine.

Amaya approached the alter where Sen and Rai were waiting. She was so entirely focused on Rai that she did not see her friends to the side, flanked by Kageyama shadows. Rin made a movement which drew Amaya's attention. The young shinobi's face was impassive, but Amaya could sense her anguish as she looked around, assessing the area, counting the numbers. Next to her was Tomio, and they were clutching each other's hands. His expression was clear, fearful and wary. Kin appeared calm, his eyes never once leaving his brother, Sen. However, the Air Elemental's expression was difficult to look at, and it made Amaya shudder. She wanted to reach out to him and offer comfort, but she was shoved forward into place. Kyo came into view now, he was standing beside an opposite pillar, watching her anxiously. Amaya nodded to him, offering a smile as she was put near to Sen. Akio was still close, standing beside her. When the Kageyama made to stand between them he growled in a low voice, 'do not try to separate us. I will not keep my katana sheathed and, I promise you, many will die.'

Rai smiled widely. 'It seems we are all assembled. No

easy task. I thought you would fail to gather all of your Elementals in time, Amaya.'

She glared at Rai, barely containing her fury. He continued, returning her stare with his own contemptuous one. 'But it seems, unfortunately, you have not acquired all of them. A failure even at the end.' He shook his head deliberately, before a large grin consumed his features. 'Fortune does, finally, favour me. I know who your Water Elemental is and have done since before your father's demise.'

Amaya did not move or utter a response. She was preoccupied with steadying her breath and pushing her anger away.

'Your father deduced it amongst other things. In fact, he discovered it the very same day I killed him. I was grateful for his devotion to the Prophet of Ueten and his wholehearted belief that his own daughter had become embroiled in this legend of the Old Faith. But,' Rai said lifting a finger into the air, 'it is to Sen and your uncle that we owe our gratitude.' Rai waved a hand about casually. 'Together, we uncovered the truth behind the history of the First Warring States Era and the *single* prophet, not two, at its core. Jiro and Kazu discovered the Ancient Scriptures but each hoped for a different outcome. It is why Jiro then came to me.'

Amaya hissed, 'if you are so familiar with the story, you know the danger posed by bringing us all together. Why not kill me now? Why have you not killed me sooner if I pose such a danger to you?'

Rai ignored her. 'Can you still not see the reasons? I think it is clear, the evidence is here in this shrine and throughout Akegata. Our patience has proved fruitful and now you have done what we hoped you would, Amaya. I thank you for collecting each individual threat to our goal. It would have been much harder to achieve if we were forced to seek out the Elementals ourselves. What makes you strong also makes you weak. This is something your father understood but you never have.'

As Rai finished his sentence, Jiro stepped into the soft light. 'Ueten and Gekai are only as strong as the Prophet. Since the day I had my brother murdered, we have encouraged you to nurture hate and vengeance; shaping the spirits you share a connection with.'

Kin made a small, angered noise. 'It was never truly a secret, was it?' His anger shook his words. 'Ueten and Gekai are two sides of the same stone, Amaya. Both reside within you and balance will always be a struggle. The true purpose that the Elementals have is to protect the Prophet from herself so that she does not solely become the shadow in place of the light but instead holds harmony between the two and produces a Divine Heir. Do you understand my words?'

Akio reached out and gripped her hand, his warmth spreading from her fingers, up her arm and filling her body. 'This changes nothing. You are Amaya Izumi, of the Takeda clan. Loving wife to me; devoted sister to Kyo; and a seeker of justice and peace for the people of Akegata with the voice of the spirits behind you.'

Jiro looked disdainful as he spoke. 'My brother knew from the moment you were born, Amaya. He knew as well as I did that the birthmark on your shoulder was a symbol of the heritage in your blood; that you were the Prophet, perhaps even the bearer of the Divine Heir. However, which spirit held dominion was yet undetermined; that would not reveal itself until you were much older. As you grew, your temperament developed. You were this unparalleled child with an uncanny nature; people flocked to you. Kazu knew that you were undoubtedly becoming the Prophet of Ueten. So, he kept you from prying eyes and corrupting forces. He was fearful of the history of Lord Minamori and sought to conceal your identity entirely. Kazu told no one. He deflected questions, dismissing them and stating you had not inherited the Takeda clan's divine blood. But I, a priest of the Old Faith and keeper of the secrets of that ancient tale, knew of your affiliation. I was not satisfied with the sparse details we possessed and so I travelled. You have seen the painting here. Why do you think I came to the Air Province? To protect this shrine and the knowledge it holds.'

'And you murdered him for it!' Amaya snarled. 'His only flaw was trusting his brother.'

'We did not agree on how to approach this unique blessing. I wanted to declare you and raise the Takeda up into the halls of the Prophets. A Prophet would be cause for such celebration. You would ascend the throne and marry the next Emperor. Your children may even inherit Amaterasu's favour, the Divine Right to Rule as Divine Heirs. Not for the reasons you think, however. In the public eye, you would be far more vulnerable, easily accessed. However, your father dismissed my hopes. He was prepared to sacrifice the clan to keep your secret safe. He was wary of the story, which only a fragment of had been uncovered, and refused to expose you any further to long-dormant hostile forces. Alone, I could not succeed. My brother was brimming with skills worthy of the title Master of the Sky Province, innovator of the Seishin no Ken technique, the inheritor of the Takeda clan's samurai spirit and father to the Prophet. I was a simple priest with a wealth of knowledge. Knowledge does not have the same bite as a blade but I wielded it with as much deadly force.'

'Your ambition was selfish and dangerous, Uncle.' Kyo muttered from his silent shadow. 'It was never your choice. It was never father's choice. It was Amaya's choice and father wanted to allow her that dignity.'

'There is nothing dignified in neglecting your destiny and abandoning a nation to darkness and infirmity. Yet, there is far less dignity in presuming a divine right over all. This is why I began to consider myself an Enlightened One.'

Beside Amaya, Akio twitched at Jiro's words but he did not voice what recognition had occurred to him.

'You should have been stopped then. Father would have prevented you from pursuing your goals.'

'Indeed, I could not stop him as one person. Yet when he

made an enemy of Rai, I took the opportunity. Our goals had become aligned. The only deviation was that the Kimura clan be the ones to succeed the throne alongside the Takeda for they too shared the Minamori bloodline. The chance of producing a Divine Heir with a Kimura child was equally as high as if you had wed into the Yamashima clan. That would be when we would truly strike at the spirits who have controlled us all this time.'

'Massacring the Yamashima, your rulers by Divine Right, and destroying the stability they had crafted and maintained to achieve this.' Akio did not care to hold his tongue any longer. 'You are ignorant to what is before you, captivated by your own benighted words to the detriment of us all. Sen has truly ensnared you both with his whispers.'

Amaya followed Kin's gaze. Sen's expression bore only amusement as he watched the back and forth. Frowning, she looked at those around her, but ringing questions still went unanswered in her mind: why was she not dead? Why had hey not killed her? Why speak at such length of all this now? Why the theatrics?

Jiro ignored Akio's statement. 'Your father desperately tried to protect you, to keep your mark hidden. We wanted to bring the Prophet into the public eye, like the days before the First Warring States Era.'

'It was to control and abuse the Prophet's power and favour with the spirits,' Kin hissed. 'Kazu was right to keep her hidden. You planned the downfall of the Way of the Spirits.'

Jiro faced him. 'The lesser of the Sanjo brothers. Simply, you are wrong. You have much to learn and your impudence frustrates me. Your brother and I shared many ideals. Our desires were straightforward: to expose Amaya to Akegata. To reveal how little the spirits had control over us; that they shouldn't have influence over us. Sen had posited the danger presented by Amaya and potential Divine Heirs. His translation of the panels in the shrine were far darker, more accurate, than my own. Amaya could unleash Gekai as her ancestor had done, for no one is free from corruption. Not a soul.'

Kin laughed, his eyes moving to his brother. 'I pity you both. Fear and greed and selfishness; very perfunctory ambitions. You do not understand the divination, even now? Amaterasu could not be clearer. In bestowing both light and darkness within her Prophet, she is teaching us the most valuable lesson: acceptance, perseverance, and expression. This will bring about the balance, Ueten's light alongside Gekai's darkness and a Divine Heir to show what can become of achieving such balance.'

'Brother, there is still much you have not discovered on your travels. Your ideals are impracticable. There is no place for a Prophet or a Divine Heir in a world of equality and acceptance. I am disappointed but not surprised by your callowness. It was the same as our father's, as Kazu Takeda's. I too was the same until I garned edification. Akegata must start again if it is ever to be truly free.' Sen dismissed Kin's words.

Before Kin could respond, Jiro continued. 'Kazu's trust in his own brother never wavered but he could not see through his arrogance and popularity that those who despised him were plotting his downfall.' Jiro finished.

'My father had only honour and a deep love for you. This arrogance you accuse him of is a projection of your own jealousy,' Amaya growled, her loose hair flying about her face. 'I would rather the clan become extinct than be used by you in such a way.'

'Amaya, do not allow them to anger you,' Kin interjected, quietly.

'I am afraid her hate is too deep rooted now,' Sen said, his tone calm. He looked at Amaya thirstily, his tattooed head catching the candles' glow. 'It is a hate which has been nurtured for years and years.' He smirked. 'By no one other than herself. A hateful adult has come from a hateful child. Amaterasu's light, Ueten, abandoned her years ago.'

Tomio suddenly burst into speech. 'You cannot take Akegata in one night. There will be an uprising. Too many good people remain in the world, including Amaya. The Way of the Spirits bolster us all. The Ito Merchants Guild is a formidable foe, pair them with the remainder of the Imperial army and Censorate, and your goal is even further from your reach. We will not allow your corruption to spread.' The Earth Elemental's body was shaking, not from fear but out of contempt. Rin gripped his hand, holding him back from rushing into death.

Daiki, who had remained half in shadow to the side, fidgeted. Tomio noticed the movement but as his eyes fell on the man who had befriended him, only disappointment showed. Daiki took small step forward, but Rai laughed a response.

'I have not been idle, as those of this slothful Court and country have been. I had many laws passed. I have been the Chancellor for half my life, to Emperor Kado Yamashima and his late son, Kenta. There were only so many decrees Kazu could deny. So busy concealing and protecting his daughter, he neglected his official duty. I was not so inclined. I am the Minister of War and my son is the General, the Imperial Army and the Court answer to me. As for the Ito Merchants Guild, they will not lift a finger unless there is profit for them. The shinobi,' Rai shrugged his broad shoulders, 'are in full support of our actions. They believe as I, Sen and Jiro do, in spiritual absolution.'

Amaya felt her fury swell despite herself. She watched as Kin struggled to remain calm. The tension coming from Rin was palpable as she gazed at her old comrades, and Kyo had grown silent, his eyes in shadow. As she turned her head to Akio, the door to the shrine opened. Air which smelt of ice streamed down the length of the pillared room, causing the incense to flurry and swirl and many of the lanterns were snuffed out.

Shun was striding towards them, his eyes roving as he surveyed the scene before him. Amaya felt hope swell like an incoming tide as she observed him. Daiki twitched, his face turning from Tomio to his brother. Shun glanced at him curiously, his eyes searching, before he faced his father. His gloved hand rested on the hilt of his katana.

'Shun, my son, I am glad you have arrived. We are all here to celebrate the coming of a new rule. With your arrival we are now complete. You will be the first to help me.'

Shun's eyes narrowed. 'I do not know the intricacies of your dealings, father, but after my correspondence with Hiroshi Katou, I have been forced to acknowledge your part in the civil war. I could no longer ignore it or make excuses. The one behind Princess Kimi's death, Emperor Kado's death, Kazu and Megumi Takeda's death and many others, was you.' As Shun spoke the truth aloud, his face fell, unmasking the pain he felt at his father's betrayal. 'Now I have finally been informed that Hiroshi has been murdered, there is no doubt at all in my mind.' Shun's eyes flickered to Amaya's uncle and the ferocity in his black irises gleamed. Amaya could feel his abhorrence. 'Your brother was a far superior man in every regard. I will not let you harm his daughter any more than you have done. She will decide her own fate and I pledge my katana to her.'

Rai's shock and sadness seemed false. 'It is regretful that you will not follow me. I had hoped that you would remain loyal, but it seems that Kazu and his brat have influenced you.' Rai looked at Amaya. 'But you will help me regardless of consent.' And, without moving his gaze, Rai made the smallest of gestures to an unseen person. At the same time Akio and Kyo made a rapid movement. For a fleeting glance, Amaya saw the same enlightenment blossom upon both their faces.

A shadow lunged forward and gripped Akio's arm, preventing him from running any further. Akio turned, thrusting his fist into his restrainer's abdomen, sending him flying back into the pillar they had been standing beside. He turned, but Kyo had nimbly avoided his captors and was now running at Shun. The smell of gunpowder stung Amaya's nose. There was violent flicker and an angry hiss. The loud crack of a Firearm shattered the ominous quiet. Amaya instinctively threw her hands over her ears, and at the same moment, warm flecks sprayed her face. Sound became muffled and she removed her hands to touch the liquid on her face. Blood was smeared across her fingertips and she could taste it in her mouth.

For an instant Amaya could not move. Her throat had constricted, stifling her voice. Her lungs felt tight as she staggered forward. Blood covered the hard wooden floor and was continuing to spread around Kyo and Shun in a puddle of scarlet. She fell to her knees besides the two. Shun was cradling Kyo in his shaking arms and his face mirrored Amaya's. Shock and desolation muted all else. The wound in Kyo's chest was deep, a hole of darkest red from which blood slowly ebbed. Amaya placed her hand on her brother's brow. His body shuddered as he choked on words, incapable of forming them through the blood which spluttered from his mouth. Then, before Amaya could regain her own voice to speak to him, something vanished from the depths of his irises, leaving them barren and hollow.

Amaya drew in a quaking breath as the sounds around her began to merge together. It was too loud, too intrusive, she couldn't distinguish the yells. Ueten stirred uncomfortably within her as her anger surged forward. A fresh, white enmity which Amaya welcomed. Gekai. In one sweeping gaze, she took in the horror on everyone's faces. All eyes were upon Kyo's body. Akio called out but Amaya barely heard.

'You knew Shun was the last one. You knew when you adopted him,' Akio yelled across the shrine, dismayed tears mingling with the blood upon his cheeks.

Amaya lifted her head to face Rai, and she was glad to see him falter under her stare.

'Yes, I knew that Shun was the Water Elemental. It seems Kyo was no fool; he was so close to discovering the fact I had him removed from the palace.' Rai motioned to the hidden soldier with the Firearm.

'I will stop you.' Amaya moved forward, drawing her

katana, Meiyo. As she did so, several things happened at once. She flew toward Rai ignoring the shadows which swooped down upon her. Rin leapt from her place, slipping from the hands of her captors with unnerving ease. She pulled concealed weapons from beneath her clothing. The clash of metal did not distract Amaya as Rin defended her against those she had once lived alongside, those she had called family. Instead, Amaya continued, Rai smiling as she approached. The only voice Amaya heard was Akio's as he called her name. Then she heard him grunt in anger as he was forced to draw his blade. The distance between Rai and herself was shortening.

Amaya was thrown back abruptly. Sen had come forward. His palm had collided with her chest in such a way that Amaya's breath ceased, returning only in fleeting, short bursts. She fell to one knee and watched him clasp his hands together, his fingers forming an odd series of symbols. And for the first time Amaya witnessed the secret art of the shinobi hand seals. A sliver of fear wormed into her rage.

'No!' It was Kin's yell which reached her as he darted into view. He spun his holy staff about and brought his free hand up to his chest, his fingers also forming a series of symbols. Sen's pleasure shifted, for a moment, to surprise, before it became a snarl. Kin advanced on his brother with the swiftness of a hawk, his staff a haze in its speed. He brought it down and broke Sen's mantra. But Kin did not hesitate, he spun the length of metal swinging it into Sen's ribs. Sen snapped his hand down and gripped the staff with a grunt of annoyance and, in the same interval, slid a tanto dagger from beneath his sleeve. Kin was not idle; he pushed down upon his own weapon launching himself away from Sen's whip-like strike.

Amaya did not linger to witness more. Instead, she jumped to her feet, the ache in her chest from Sen's blow growing but her unwavering hatred and grief carried her forward as her gaze found Rai. She heard Kin clash again and again with Sen behind her, but she did not stop. She stretched her arm high above her head, her katana clutched tightly in position. A memory of her father performing this technique swept through Amaya's muddled thoughts as she brought the blade down swiftly, but her katana was met with another, and again she was hindered. Jiro had come forward, shielding Rai. She pushed against her uncle's blade, but his strength was greater than hers. His bandaged face was difficult to interpret, but his exposed eye bulged with malice. It was then that a movement behind him drew her attention.

Daiki had slid effortlessly behind his father, his features knotted into madness as he raised his own katana. Amaya looked past Jiro the moment Daiki looked past his father. He raised his blade.

A small grin shivered over Rai's lips, before he twisted at the waist and reached his hand back over his shoulder. His fingers found Daiki's throat, and Amaya could only watch as Rai began to choke the very life out of his own son. Daiki lifted his katana, his eyes squinting with the effort, as his face turned redder and redder. In a last effort, he clutched his blade like a spear and launched it.

It was not Rai who fell, but Jiro. Daiki's blade burst through the front of her uncle's white kimono and the immediate flourish of red patterned the silk like a budding camellia. Jiro's katana clattered to the floor, and a moment later he fell too. His visible eye was dark. There was nothing of her father in him now. Amaya looked to the man who had aided her; Daiki had saved her rather than himself. He was unable to raise his blade against his father. Rai had not lost his smile and he maintained his stare: unblinking, apathetic. Daiki was still in his grasp, inert.

Amaya's frustration broke and her shriek was echoed throughout the shrine. Sen watched on laughing. 'You are making this far too effortless, Amaya,' he said, blood glistening from deep cuts to his face and neck.

Rai threw Daiki's limp figure to the floor and faced her again. It seemed as if he were attempting to breathe her in. 'Yes, Amaya. Good. Bring your hatred to my feet. Show us all the true nature of your beloved spirits.'

Kin's warning rang in her head and she stopped for a moment, trying to tame her frenzied feelings. Akio's hand found hers, and a comforting elation sparked inside her. She gripped his hand so tightly that her fingers tingled. The ugliness struggled within her but Akio's free hand cupped Amaya's face, drawing her eyes to his. Amaya could see him willing her to turn away, to change her direction. He pressed his forehead to hers, their lips coming together.

'I will die ending this, Akio. I will not become the Prophet of Gekai; that is my worst fear,' Amaya said, and she was awed that not a whisper of trepidation could be heard in her tone.

'You are not Gekai yet, Amaya. You are able to bring these men to justice without hate and anger. You only need a little time.' Akio's expression puzzled Amaya. She couldn't understand what hidden words were trapped in his dark eyes. He clutched her hand even tighter; the warmth of his feelings streamed up her arm and filled her. She heard Rai bellow out in frustration and lift his kunai dagger. As if his mirror, she raised her free hand with a purpose which felt foreign to her. Her katana was raised and gripped with purpose as Rai careened into her and Akio.

The moment she touched Rai, Amaya felt her strength rise through her hand, like a bright snake. There was a lull in the atmosphere and the very air seemed to ripple out from Amaya's touch. She and Akio were sent sprawling across the shrine. Rai staggered away, unable to draw another breath, his empty hands clutching at his chest.

Akio's hand was in hers, but she did not want to release it. Shun was already moving toward her. Tomio was helping Rin to her feet, Kin holding himself upright. Amaya tugged her stare from Rai and she saw Kyo's still form across the heidan, resting against a pillar as if asleep. The Kageyama were gone, and so was Sen. Amaya shifted into a kneeling position, gripping Akio's hand for support. His fingers did not return the movement.

'Amaya, do not look,' Shun blurted, as he hurried forward. Suddenly fearful, she turned to Akio. The dark metal of her own katana protruded at a downward angle from Akio's heart. In his other hand, he gripped Rai's dagger by the blade, preventing it from reaching its mark. She leant closer, pressing her ear against Akio's chest. The lifeless silence was so absolute that Amaya could not move. She jumped as Shun touched her back, trying to pull her up. Frantically, she searched Akio's face for a flicker of movement, a twitch of vitality, a trace of his humour. His eyes were staring, the ghost of his last thoughts diminishing within them. Amaya watched her own frenzied reflection whilst Akio's beautiful face seemed absurdly content.

His hand still emitted a fading warmth. She didn't realise she was crying until the vision of Akio's inanimate face was obscured by the tears which tumbled, fighting the next to fall. Shun and the others circled around but they seemed distant to Amaya as she refused to accept the truth which was spread on the floor in front of her.

'I should have died killing Rai,' she said, finally, her voice hollow.

It was Kin's soft tone that she heard. 'Akio chose to take that burden from you rather than for you to become the Prophet of Gekai, consumed by hate and vengeance.'

All at once, Amaya comprehended the strange look in Akio's eyes, moments before she and Rai collided. A aberrant anger seeped into her, converging with the grief and misery. With an effort so great, she released Akio's hand, and knew instantly that the torment would remain for the rest of her life.

Amaya looked up at the gasping Rai and rose to her feet, feeling oddly light. With tenderness, she pulled her katana free and took a trembling step forward.

'Amaya,' Kin whispered and there was warning in his tone. She did not care to heed it, her head was too full of Kyo, her father and mother. Akio. Her feet knew where to take her and soon her entire vision and mind converged on Rai.

'Amaya!' Kin yelled at her. 'Think!'

She was vaguely aware of others shouting but they seemed at a distance, in some place she wanted to go but would not be able to just yet. And in that odd silence of her mind she raised her katana.

'Death and loss are not what makes you the Prophet of Gekai. Acting upon them with rage is what will corrupt you,' Kin spoke solidly. 'It is that which my brother sought from you. Do not give that to him, Amaya. Do not allow him to take Akio and Kyo's deaths and use them for his own selfish ambition. Your journey now is a far greater, more challenging one.'

Amaya moved no further; she was stuck in a bizarre internal impasse as she vacillated above Rai's flinching frame. Then Shun was taking her blade, and Kin was embracing her, his words washing over her like a gentle stream. Yet the comfort they brought could not penetrate the shell she could already feel stretching and hardening around her soul. She knew what she had almost done and was petrified she would not be able to stem the urge should it reappear.

Amaya swallowed the sob which had formed and turned away from Rai, gingerly steading herself against Kin and Shun. A misplaced threat of sleep descended, and so she allowed Shun to lift her. She glanced once more at Akio's peaceful face before she closed her eyes.

CHAPTER NINETEEN

Amaya stood on the red, wooden bridge which stretched over the pond in the palace gardens. The sound of the water consoled her, so that thoughts of the events which had occurred in Shiroshi two months previously were bearable. Winter's Face was slowly turning to make way for the Face of Spring; the entire land seemed as though it were weeping. She gazed at the palace for a while, her eyes roaming its black and white facade. As she watched the Imperial guards change at the nearest gate, her thoughts travelled to Shun. She had seen him several times, and with each visit he brought her distracting news and comforting company. Once, he had arrived with Tomio and Rin, who were working with the Ito Merchants' Guild. Rin's discomfort of the Kageyama clan's involvement was still apparent in her eyes, but Tomio seemed to be helping the shinobi manage the dispiritedness. Only yesterday, Amaya had received word from Rin that the she intended to reclaim her clan by first seeking out a man who had once been her father's second-in-command: Oda.

Daiki and Kin had vanished together but Amaya knew that Kin had gone in search of his brother, Sen. Daiki wanted to aid Kin in his search, for he held Sen responsible for everything which had come to pass. She wished Daiki would return for she had much to say to him. Much to thank him for. He needed her forgiveness and she needed his. Her connection to Kin remained the strongest of all the Elementals, and at times she could sense his moods. She had grown accustomed to the strange feelings and hoped that he too could sense her thoughts.

The entrance to the Archives was just in sight. She had a fleeting impression of Akio sitting behind his desk, surrounded by scrolls of which he knew every detail. A fabricated memory of her father detailing to him his concerns; Akio penning her their first of many letters; the day they had met in person; the day Akio realised his love for her. The urge to visit the Archives had not abated regardless of the knowledge that she would find his seat empty.

Taking her eyes from the palace she traced the verandah of the outbuildings. People were busy rebuilding everything which had been destroyed; recovering from the battle was exhausting the capital. The rebel troops had not managed their full assault on city. The successful defence of Chuto against all likelihood, would be detailed in the history of the Yamashima Dynasty along with the Northern Revolt. However, the devastation from the main conflict was widespread. Paperwork, investigations and Firearms were all that Amaya heard of when she happened to be near a conversation. This was a welcome distraction in the face of the alternative. A gnawing sensation had not abated since that night and Amaya could not construe whether it was simple anger or Gekai which plagued her sleep. She understood one thing: she would never be the Prophet to bring balance between the two opposing spirits within, the injuries Rai had inflicted upon her spirit had left deep scars which forever impacted Ueten's hopeful light. She would always feel more affinity to Gekai and this was a fact she could never divulge nor allow freedom. There were a myriad reasons to reject becoming the Prophet of Gekai, but her brother and Akio's sacrifices were iron vices around Gekai's ankles and wrists. This solitary thought steeled her against any lingering animosity she harboured in her heart. Returning her absent stare to the pool surrounding her, she admired the water feature which was reflected faultlessly in its still surface. The early-spring sun glinted red and white from a Koi carp swimming beneath.

'There you are.' A familiar and welcome voice came

from behind.

Amaya felt a genuine smile wake her tired face as she turned. 'Kenta. How are you?' The revelation that Kenta had not been killed had helped Amaya retain her will and sanity. It had been one of Rai's lies to provoke Gekai within her. The happiness which Kenta's presence had brought was invaluable. He was the first person she had seen when she awoke after Shiroshi and had barely left his side since. She had no desire to leave him. They had supported each other in a way most could not; each a balm for the other's wound. Their mutual love for Akio toughened their conviction to strive forward and rebuild Akegata together.

He stepped beside her and surveyed the vista before him. 'I am muddling through.' He looked at her pointedly. 'Things are still unsettled but I will ensure all is right for the people of Akegata. The Way of the Spirits still pervades us all. There is comfort in that.'

Amaya sighed. 'There are few things left which are important to me. I intend to cherish them and carry them into a new, peaceful country.' Amaya smiled at Kenta. She placed a hand on her belly and felt the swell of life within her. Kenta placed his hand over hers, tenderness etched into his expression as he stared at the glow she felt in her cheeks.

'Would you allow me to help, Amaya? Akio was my best friend and brother. I treasure and revere you above all else. Your child will need a father alongside his mother to ensure he is protected and cared for. Allow me to adopt the child of my most beloved peers and keep him, and you, under my protection.'

Amaya turned to face the Emperor, his eyes serious, his manner as kind as Amaya remembered it when they had first met in front of the Archives. 'You are the only one Akio would entrust such a task to,' Amaya said.

'I will never be Akio, nor do I intend to replace him, but I will love his child and you wholly in his stead.'

'I know you will, and I thank you for it.' Amaya felt the

exchange of a deep-seated understanding between herself and Kenta, their friendship deepening. She rested her head on his shoulder.

'These next years will be some of the most difficult. The battle was the beginning, the prelude to the war.'

Amaya nodded, thinking of Sen. 'I fear the same.'

Printed in Great Britain
by Amazon